A Brief History of Living Forever

Also by Jaroslav Kalfař

Spaceman of Bohemia

A Brief History of Living Forever

JAROSLAV KALFAŘ

sceptre

First published in Great Britain in 2023 by Sceptre
An imprint of Hodder & Stoughton
An Hachette UK company

1

A CIP catalogue record for this title is available from the British Library

Hardback ISBN 9781529368789
Trade Paperback ISBN 9781529368796
eBook ISBN 9781529368802

Printed and bound in Great Britain by Clays Ltd, Elcograf S.p.A.

Hodder & Stoughton policy is to use papers that are natural, renewable and recyclable products and made from wood grown in sustainable forests. The logging and manufacturing processes are expected to conform to the environmental regulations of the country of origin.

Hodder & Stoughton Ltd
Carmelite House
50 Victoria Embankment
London EC4Y 0DZ

www.sceptrebooks.co.uk

For my mother, Marie

In an ever-changing, incomprehensible world the masses had reached the point where they would, at the same time, believe everything and nothing, think that everything was possible and that nothing was true.

—*Hannah Arendt*

THE YEAR IS 2029

O
N A COLD morning in late November, I arrived at my physician's office to discuss the results of my annual health exam. From the grim tone of the nurse who'd booked my visit and the dreams of abyss haunting me as of late, I knew to expect bad news, that the time had come at last to face the perilous consequences of my long years on Earth.

I came in early, hoping that old Dr. Škvoreček might see me before my appointment time so as not to risk being late for work. Alas, the room was already filled with a dozen patients, chattering about their aches and pains. *Can u com in now??* my shift manager inquired in a text message as the nurse led me into the examination room one hour later. With no sense of urgency, Dr. Škvoreček poured me a cup of tea, leaned back in his chair, and revealed that an illness had taken root in my body. I was likely to die within a year, give or take a month. The doctor showered me with helpful leaflets on grief and offered to speak with my family to ease my burdens. A great poet of the macabre, Dr. Škvoreček described all the ways in which my body would devour itself—crumbling bones, renal failure, death by brain bleed or fungal infection—and I nodded with appreciation for his honesty as I watched the clock mark the beginning of my work hours.

Only as the doctor launched into a digression about the latest immortality research coming from America—as if suggesting I might be saved by some last-minute God pill—did I reclaim my time, thanking him for a life of service. Rumor had it that my workplace was planning to replace its employees with robots, I explained, and I'd vowed to become the perfect worker to show that I could compete with any machine. I took a polite sip of lukewarm tea, stuffed the leaflets into my purse, and rushed out of the office. The findings of my illness had come from tests mandated by insurance, invasive examinations I would've otherwise skipped. I felt no pain, no new sensations in my body aside from the mild nosebleeds. The abstract diagnosis of death lacked any physical urgency. My need for a paycheck, on the other hand, was concrete and immediate.

As I rushed out of the waiting room, the encouraging farewell of Dr. Škvoreček followed me out to the street: "Don't trouble yourself, Ms. Slavíková! You've lived a beautiful life."

MY NAME IS Adéla Slavíková. Join me on this usual path to work during the final winter of my mortal toil! An early, weeklong blizzard had taken our county hostage with a barrage of snow and hail, shutting down morning commutes, derailing trains, chilling the bones of the children and the old. I warmed my hands inside the pockets of my coat as I hastily shuffled my feet along the black slush covering the pavement of Louny, the northern Bohemian town to which I commuted for work.

My employer was Kaufland, a blockbuster chain of German hypermarkets. I had been a cashier for six years, hating the work but feeling content in knowing I could support myself, pay the bills, enjoy a few basic comforts until age left me dependent on retirement checks issued by a government grudgeful toward its "unproductive" senior populace. As with most jobs that require a name tag, mine also required a suspension of dignity. Shopping had become a religious experience in our country. Families would plan their weekends around trips to the hypermarkets, study the discount circulars for sales and coupons the same way scholars examine pillars of literature. I'd become a priestess of the hypermarket, a representative of the gods of consumption; when I dared to reject an expired coupon or declare items out of stock, my customers threatened me with lawsuits, violence, complete destruction of every facet of my "meaningless existence." They felt that I stood between them and the deities in charge of their fates, deities that promised a life of ever-expanding abundance and convenience. If only the cashier did what she was told, eternal happiness would be possible for all.

I arrived at Kaufland and headed toward the locker room to put on my shirt and name tag. I stopped as I passed the checkout lines. My usual cash register, lucky number 12, had been transformed. All the old registers save two had been replaced overnight by tall thick slopes that resembled miniaturized airport towers, connected by running belts. Register 12 greeted the long line of customers with a voice provided by a world-famous footballer as the tower's blinking red eye scanned the merchandise with a single flash of its lasers. Robotic claws inside the machine bagged the groceries. The footballer thanked the customers for their loyalty and wished them a productive day. The red eye didn't expect them to gaze back, express gratitude. Its claws were at no risk of developing rheumatism or carpal tunnel.

Witnessing the machine's work sickened me far more than the blood-and-guts diagnosis from Dr. Škvoreček. I counted as the next customer interacted with the machine. Twelve seconds, and the transaction was over. Such a pace was impossible to compete with. I continued into the locker room, unsure of what to do next. Marek, the manager, was already waiting to call me into his office. He closed the door, took a profound sip from his BELIEVE IN MAGIC coffee mug, and said I was fired. My job at register 12 had been taken by Register 12. Marek offered a small severance and a Kaufland fridge magnet as a token of appreciation for my years of service. Automation was the key to prosperity in our troubled Europe, he insisted with a bravado that suggested Kaufland's prosperity should be the foremost moral concern of the century.

I had lived long enough not to take this dismissal personally, and yet I struggled to breathe. The shock was far worse than the mild inconvenience I'd felt at the doctor's office. Marek offered me a glass of water, and I told him this was rather unfortunate timing, as I'd just received news of a terminal illness from my physician. Marek said he was very sorry to hear it, but putting the burden of my illness on him was emotional manipulation, gaslighting. His grandfather had passed away recently, and my talk of death renewed Marek's traumas. Visibly shaken by the duress I had put him under, Marek quietly walked me out of the building and pressed into my hands a single piece of paper outlining my severance. Breathing the fresh air, I tried to convince myself this was for the best. Had it not been for Register 12's coup, I would've spent my final days on Earth arguing over the price of ham.

Even the news of my impending death didn't free me from the banality of schedules. I was trapped in Louny for the rest of the afternoon, as the train to my village of Hluboká didn't come again until the evening. I wasn't in the mood to waste money on a cab. Despite my shock, or maybe because of it, I decided to take advantage of my newfound freedom, to do something responsible citizens oughtn't ever do: wander aimlessly. The end is coming; away with routines!

I headed to the winter market at the town center, the one place that was sure to bring me comfort. When I entered, it was teeming with Christmas shoppers browsing the goods, admiring the Christmas tree adorned with silver chains and blue lights. The smell of pine and hot rum made me salivate. The vendors offered ornaments, garlands, Advent calendars. I bought a cup of grog in which to dip my gingerbread, shaped like the star of Bethlehem. I had been raised without religion, but the kitsch of its symbols always appealed to me, especially in biscuit form.

I walked up to a water tank filled with carp whose heads and tails smacked at the surface and splashed at the laughing children. As steam rose from the water, I realized that next winter, these attractions would still be here—the same children, the same parents, the same one-eyed man pouring grog with unwashed hands—and yet I would be gone, and none of these strangers would know. They wouldn't even miss me. I shook my head. Vanity. I wanted my death to mean something to everyone, to be mourned by the whole world at once, even as I found breaking-news stories about famous deaths absurd, puzzled by the authority of those who decided which deaths were a matter of public interest.

I scouted the water tanks for the carp specimen that looked the spunkiest. Some customers had the fish killed with a hammer to the head, while others took their catch alive to keep in the bathtub until Christmas Day. I hadn't eaten the traditional Christmas carp, fried in beer batter and served with potato salad, since I was twelve years old. Back then, I'd named our Christmas fish Gandalf, for its wise eyes and unusually thick barbels, shaped like a wizard's beard. But my father drank too much rum as he prepared to fillet Gandalf for dinner, and the killing turned into a two-hour ordeal as he chased the half-dead fish slipping and sliding all over the kitchen, its guts pouring from the knife wound in its side. I refused to have any part in my father's barbarity and locked myself in my room.

The children around the tank seemed to have no such memories. They squealed and poked at the glittering fish scales. Policemen in balaclavas shouted at the children to settle down as they patrolled the market with semiautomatic rifles in hand. Above the market, a soft hum and blinking lights announced the hovering of surveillance drones. The terror level was set to red, permanently, with all Christmas markets in the country designated "soft targets." The Russian regime had been recruiting the surviving mercenaries of its old wars to launch lone-wolf attacks on European cities. Unofficially, of course.

I was still learning not to panic at such changes, as I had never gotten used to how quickly the world progressed and regressed. In my lifetime I'd seen the resurgence of Russian aggression threatening my continent, an internet-fueled resurrection of global fascism, and the American Reclamation, each upheaval a catalyst for extremism. I'd contributed my years of caring and biting my fingernails and it would now be someone else's turn to worry about the whims of geopolitics. I tried to focus on the things that were simple, lasting—the smell of grog, the sweet spice of gingerbread, the Czech holiday traditions that endured through the centuries.

I asked the fishmonger to choose the carp that splashed the most, fought the hardest against its fate. The man raised his hammer and I said *no,* I wanted the fish alive. He put the carp inside a webbed bag and handed it over. The fish flapped its tail inside the bag, smacked at my thigh. I turned to leave and whispered a bittersweet goodbye to the market. I began to plead with myself. Perhaps this wouldn't be my last time here, despite my diagnosis. Dr. Škvoreček was seventy-six years old and refused to retire, he was becoming forgetful, and all of this could be a big misunderstanding. I tried to soothe the carp with pats on its flapping fins as I headed back to the train station to seek a bit of quiet. I waited for the train home, keeping my new friend alive by giving it baths in the station's lavatory sink.

Shortly after sunset I returned to our house in Hluboká, the ancestral home built by my great-grandfather, sitting atop a hill that cut away from the main road where most of the other village properties stood. The walls had begun to split apart due to the brutal winters, most of the grass covering the front yard had been dead for years, the garden in which my father used to grow cucumbers and strawberries was now a battleground for weeds and moles. My son, Roman, hoped to restore the house someday, make it look new and formidable for the next generation. Though I doubted this would ever happen, given his past struggles, I was happy nonetheless that my child still believed in our family's future.

I stepped into the dark, quiet hallway. My mother, Babi, was already asleep in her room. Roman was on his way to Austria, delivering goods in a refrigerated truck. The real implications of the day's events began to sink in. Without work, I would no longer be able to contribute to the household. Roman and Babi would cover our bills with their wages and retirement checks, respectively, but with little to spare. I had officially become a burden to my family.

But the matter of finances wasn't nearly as dire as the immediate question of how to share the news of my illness. Should I break my family's hearts over dinner, with food half chewed in their mouths? Should I give them the leaflets from my purse, repeat the platitudes from my doctor? *My dearest, my beloved, my fortuitous act of living has come to its end.*

I stepped into my bedroom to change before putting the carp in the bathtub. The dark blue carpet that had been in my room since I was a child gave way like quicksand and let out a wet belch. I looked back into my bedroom for the source of a low-pitched whistle and found the radiator pipe leaking water in a steady stream. Every part of the room had been flooded in my absence.

I removed my shoes, walked to the radiator, and cut off the water supply. Still in my work clothes, I went into my bathroom to fill the tub and release the carp. At first the fish made no motion except for the pucker of its lips. But soon the carp rejoiced at the influx of life and began to swim back and forth, exploring its new home. I was glad to have a confidant sharing in this crisis with me. Within seconds the fish would forget any trauma it had undergone. As far as it was concerned, it had lived its entire life happily in this very bathtub. The blessings of beastly amnesia — though sometimes I wondered whether the memory of animals was the memory of nature, without limits, seeing and knowing all, in ways humans could never understand.

I stripped off my work clothes, relieved this was the last time I'd have to wear a uniform, and wrapped myself in layers of robes as the broken radiator hissed with a mischievous glee. The cold crept around my toes. This bedroom had been mine since I was a child. When I was young, I never expected I would be the kind of person to return to her parents' house well into old age. I had been eager to explore the world, to run far from the place of my birth. But the Prague apartment where I'd raised Roman had become unaffordable decades ago, as city rents skyrocketed and the job market for people (women in particular) over the age of forty-five vanished. The country's retirement system was mostly bankrupt, and I was told not to count on retirement checks to keep me afloat. The prime minister summarized the sentiment of the nation's economy when he called upon the unemployed senior populace to fill the shortage of cashiers in small-town grocery stores. I answered the prime minister's call, and through the years I taught myself to accept that within a world so competitive, so hostile, I oughtn't feel ashamed for honest work and for sharing a home with my family. I had lived a minimalist, stoic life to rid myself of the pressure of expectation and material pleasures. But it seemed that no matter how small I made myself, there was still so much more our world could take away.

From the stash underneath my bed, I recovered a box of wine. I sat on my toilet and reached into the tub to touch the carp's scales. I opened the box and drank directly out of the container. Rage. I hadn't felt it in a long time. To be a stoic was to control one's perceptions, and rage was the abdication of such control. Babi snored in the next room, and I wished I could ask her if she'd ever felt this brand of humiliation, which seemed to me a distinct feature of our time. My mother, who was a hundred and nine years old, had lived through every major event of the previous century following the Great War. A life of torrents and broken ideals, a country invaded and occupied and resold, its people laughing through the pain. And yet, having seen the many forms of terror that people unleashed on one another, she slept through the night unbothered. I had not inherited her good humor.

But sleep wasn't what I needed anyway, as there was much to do. As soon as I'd received my diagnosis from the good doctor, I knew that I could no longer hide from the looming absence in my life. A mission I had put off for decades, a haunting from the past. Now I had no excuses left, nor could I tell myself I still had plenty of time, maybe I'd get to it next year…the final months of my life offered one last chance to travel to America and find my lost daughter.

* * *

ALTHOUGH I HAD surrendered Tereza to her adoptive family when she was but seven hours old, I'd kept close track of her since her high-school years, when her adoptive mother sent me links to her social media not long before she died. A concealed folder on my laptop became the chronicle of Tereza's life. Hiding behind anonymous accounts, I had read through her early LiveJournal posts to learn about her teenage years. I downloaded the photos from her lectures at industry conferences, embraced the novelty of Facebook to cull pictures from her birthday parties. I learned to master the emerging technologies, to use search engines and social media, only so I could watch my lost daughter from afar.

Her Czech forename was the only thing I was able to give her; her parents graciously agreed to honor my wish that she keep it. Each time I typed the name into the search engine, I felt closer to her, as if that single act of naming had bound us forever. Tereza had gone on to work as a bioengineer for the VITA corporation, in pursuit of the company's promise to prolong human life, cure entropic diseases, and, someday, make our species immortal. This sounded like a fairy tale—what kind of a maniac would want to live forever?—but as long as my daughter was happy and well paid in the booming permanence sector, I was content.

Knowing that Tereza was living a successful life and needed nothing from me soothed my yearning to know her. But whenever the night was particularly quiet and I had drunk too much wine, I fantasized about taking one last trip to the United States to reveal myself after a lifetime of absence. The idea of being absolved of my guilt was intoxicating, but the fantasy was never enough to overcome my fear of Tereza's reaction. Perhaps she hated her anonymous birth mother, perhaps she thought I had given her up lightheartedly, out of selfishness. Staying away from Tereza meant I didn't have to find out. But my visit with Dr. Škvoreček suggested I had to act immediately, against my fears, or abandon the idea of knowing Tereza for good. Her adoptive parents had passed away before she started college, and with me gone, she would soon become a true orphan.

Of course, following the Great Reclamation of the United States, the mission of finding my daughter would be even more difficult. During the American election in 2024, all but a few holdouts in the Republican Party had abandoned the tainted GOP to form a new political behemoth: the party of Reclamation. On the night of the successful coup, the new Reclamationist leader of the Senate—with the support of the first Reclamation president, a man responsible for the pandemic deaths of tens of thousands of his own citizens as the former governor of Florida—dedicated this revolution of conservatism to the brave patriots who had stormed the Capitol in January of 2021. Using the voting laws they themselves had passed in recent years, state officials of the old Republican Party certified the election results, thus granting instant legitimacy to an authoritarian takeover that had conjured its own legal standing in the country's system.

Thousands of lawsuits were filed as every democratic watchdog in the world mobilized, as Europe and the United Nations threatened the United States with sanctions, as the police brutalized protesters in every major U.S. city from coast to coast. But this upheaval produced no change in the Reclamation Party's hold on power. Nobody knew how to protect the archaic Constitution against sophisticated twenty-first-century deception. The country's Supreme Court had long ago shown a disinclination to protect its country's democracy, and its refusal to accept cases challenging the Reclamation was perfectly in line with its dismantling of abortion rights. Many people in the world had held a kind of reverence for the American brand of democracy, but now we saw that even the most celebrated systems on the planet were make-believe, a reflection of a consensus that no longer held. Russia's medieval atrocities in Ukraine had destroyed the last hopes for stability anywhere, along with our collective belief in fairness, compromise, and the meaning of old alliances. During its first two years in power, the Reclamation Party was normalized by nativist Americans drunk on vengeance, and it went on to cement its power with narrow wins in the 2026 midterm elections and with the reelection of the Reclamationist incumbent president in 2028.

The first piece of the new government's legislation had been the Reclamation Act, which closed the country's borders to immigrants, refugees, asylum seekers, and visitors, with the exception of tourists from a small number of allied countries. *America can't abide the influence of foreign agents on our native soil,* proclaimed the Reclamation government on its YouTube channel. *The time of the unscrupulous alien seeking our charity has come to an end.* Though the measure was initially billed as temporary, it proved so popular with supporters that it became the permanent law of the land.

The looming disasters of America turned into a full-blown manic depression, unpredictable and volatile. Though my country had a limited visa agreement with the U.S. (our presidents were old business partners), based on the horror stories, I worried about how I'd be received in the Reclaimed America. I worried about the reaction to my accent, I worried about the militias, deputized by the government's Homeland Deportation Force to patrol the streets for stray foreigners. I worried about disappearing, about ending up in a small room with no windows. I worried about finding myself in one of America's growing work camps, spending my final days sewing cop uniforms. Finding my daughter would've been far easier if she'd lived in a stabler corner of the world.

Yet the impending finality of my existence seemed to diminish these dangers. On this cold night of a broken radiator, a happily splashing carp, and a jarring removal from the job market, the idea of finding my daughter ceased to be a capricious daydream and became an immediate obsession. I felt detached from all our antiquated ideas of personal responsibility. Or, to speak in clearer terms, I no longer gave a fuck. I felt free to do anything I liked, no longer beholden to the monthly process of paying bills, shopping the grocery sales, doing it all over again the following week, the routine of paycheck-to-paycheck that kept the kingdom of humans running in an orderly manner and discouraged us from delusions of grandeur.

Yes, I could do it. All of this courage, to resolve the unresolved, excavated itself after decades of fear. As I opened my second box of wine, my head began to ache, my vision became blurry, I no longer felt cold. I retrieved my laptop from the bedside table, returned to the toilet, and began to browse flights to New York. I felt heat in my chest, acid reflux announcing I was officially drunk.

"Do yourself a favor: Live fast, die young," I slurred to the carp, and laughed so hard I slid off the toilet.

As I collected myself, the fish in the bathtub began to glow. Its scales turned the color of melting gold. The fish pursed its lips and started speaking in a deep, human voice. "Find your daughter, go, go now," the carp said. "Idiot. Your destiny awaits in the New World."

"A prophecy!" I screamed back at the carp, attempting to take it in my hands. But the slippery fish swam jovially to the opposite side of the tub. "Tell me what to do," I said. "Tell me!"

But the carp refused to speak again; its scales ceased to glow. I poked at it, begged for more wisdom, but the carp simply watched me with its beady eyes, the frowning curve of its mouth opening and closing to breathe. Was the creature mocking me? Suddenly, I felt awfully alone, craved to get into bed with Babi like I did so many decades ago when I was a girl and the Russians had invaded our country and I dreamed only of tanks and strange men who spoke to me with smoke coming from their mouths. I left the carp and crawled to bed on my own, disappointed, exhausted from the day of terrible news. I ignored my chattering teeth and fell asleep, the second box of wine resting half empty in my hand.

In the morning I awoke to heavy footsteps announcing my son's return from work. The slamming of the refrigerator door, the long pour of milk.

I dragged myself up from bed and splashed my face with water. The carp rested quietly in the tub, expressing no judgment about the previous night. I thanked the fish for understanding and went to greet my son. I tried my hardest to tell him the news of my diagnosis, to force out the words *I'm dying, I'm sorry*—but I couldn't. Instead, I told Roman about the broken radiator.

He cursed quietly, asked if I was okay, why I had slept in the cold instead of taking the living-room couch.

I'd needed the comfort of my own bed, I said, because I'd been unceremoniously sacked. Roman put his hand on my shoulder, and I took advantage of this rare moment of tenderness. Without delay I told him I wanted to use my early retirement to go to America to find Tereza and convince her to come back and meet her family. It was to be my final journey across the ocean.

Roman drank his milk with great deliberation, taking the news in. My son was short and stout, his face marked by age though he was yet in his thirties, the kind of entropy accelerated by anger and disappointment. He moved slowly, he spoke slowly too, with ominous pauses between his words like craters on a battlefield, another salvo coming soon. He always knew better than I did. I expected harsh words about the dangers of Reclaimed America, his usual lecture about the safety of home. A plea to let old ghosts rest, our lives were difficult enough, the same arguments he raised whenever I spoke about Tereza. He'd considered his sister a distant threat, a destabilizing force that would destroy our family's peace.

Instead, he put an arm around my shoulders. He sat down with me and booked the embassy appointment on his laptop within minutes. I was shocked at my son's sudden flexibility to let me go overseas without protest. But as we read through the booklet of rules for embassy visitors, I realized why he seemed unbothered. He didn't believe the Americans would allow me into the Reclaimed country at all. He viewed my trip as a harmless fantasy borne from an agestruck mind.

* * *

UNDETERRED, I WAITED for the appointment, and over the weeks I began to feel the changes in my body, the aches and fatigue, strange bruises, more severe nosebleeds. Babi and I spent our last Christmas together without Roman, eating the prophetic carp and potato salad. Some might judge me for eating the fish that had given me courage to find my daughter, but in fact, I was obligated to consume the carp for good luck. Roman had taken a Christmas delivery route for extra pay, though I suspected he also preferred the quiet cabin of his truck to being shut in with us.

Several weeks later, I took the train to my interview session at the American embassy in Prague. The officers collected my biometrics, ran a full background check, and had their own doctor examine me. The exam seemed designed to be as invasive as possible while identifying no actual health problems, as the issue of my deadly illness didn't come up. I was asked to release my phone records, e-mail communications, social media passwords, and bank statements to the American government.

I sleepwalked through this long session of information gathering, weakened with influenza because I'd been staying in my cold room despite Roman's pleas for me to take his bed. He'd given me a small heater, which I secretly turned off so as not to raise our electric bill. I felt obligated to save every halíř I could. To cover the visa fee and airplane ticket, I'd had to sacrifice all of my severance pay. I struggled to keep faith, to resist the possibility that I'd wasted the last of my money on a trip that would never happen.

After the interview, I spent a month waiting in a resigned haze, taking walks around Hluboká to memorize every part of my birth village, as if I could carry these images into the afterlife, footage on a loop. Every day I felt older, more burdened, every day I lost hope that I could reach Tereza in time. I avoided phone calls from Dr. Škvoreček offering a consultation on my pain-management options. My bones ached, and I dreamed of worms burrowing their way through my marrow, eating what remained of it. February brought even more winter storms, freezing the roads and cutting villages off from train and car travel, making the season even lonelier. In Louny, a man walked into Kaufland and shot five customers and two of my former colleagues before giving himself up to the police.

On the day of this tragedy, unprecedented in the history of our country, I received a decision from the embassy. As always, America surprised me. It granted a "monitored ten-day" visa. The letter explained that upon my arrival at JFK Airport, an immigration officer would attach a tracker to my wrist to transmit my whereabouts and biometrics to the Homeland Deportation Force. Any attempts to remove the device would trigger an immediate manhunt, with the full force of federal and local authorities descending upon my alien presence. This solution accommodated the limitations imposed by the Reclamation while allowing America to hold on to some tourist revenue. White European visitors welcome; surveilled.

Babi and I watched the Kaufland gunman on television, a seventeen-year-old incel in sweatpants and a Donald Duck T-shirt, handcuffed and surrounded by police; according to his manifesto, he'd been admiring the actions of his American counterparts since he was twelve. Babi asked whether I was sure I wanted to leave the comforts of our village. No one could blame me for staying on familiar ground in a world gone mad. I had to go, I insisted, even the carp in the bathtub had told me so. Besides, there was no such thing as a safe refuge, not even the hypermarket in a small Bohemian town.

Seeing my resolve, Babi pulled an envelope filled with dollar bills from her apron pocket. She was able to produce money whenever needed, one of her many superpowers. I'd always guessed that the dressers and wardrobes in the house were padded with cash Babi had squirreled away over the years. I understood this hoarding when my father died twelve years ago, and we became aware of the debts he had accrued at various drinking establishments. Babi was able to pay off all of it from her savings. In a lifetime spent with a man unable to hold on to a penny, she had learned to compensate.

As she gave me the envelope, Babi told me she always knew I would someday look for Tereza. I kissed her right cheek and promised she would know her granddaughter, even if I had to die trying.

Roman arrived home later that afternoon, immediately shell-shocked by the embassy's unlikely decision to admit an old foreign woman into the Reclaimed territories. "Congrats" was all he had to say as he withdrew into his room.

A week later, when a cab arrived to take me to the airport, Roman had already snuck out of the house without a word of goodbye, gone to deliver a truckload of canned pâté to Poland.

BY THE DAY of my departure, I'd become even more ill with a cough and chest pains and an occasional fever, symptoms I blamed on the broken radiator. I tested negative for all COVID mutations, and I wasn't about to let a little cold keep me from taking my chance. I boarded the plane owned by an ultra-budget airline. The plane fit twelve passengers per row, offered no in-flight entertainment or cushioning on the seats. Each passenger was limited to one cup of water. To get into the toilet, I had to pay a cash fee to the flight attendant. But I was too sick to rage at the indignities of travel. I covered my face with a jacket and slept through the nonstop flight.

On arrival, exhausted from the journey, I used some of Babi's cash to splurge on a cab to my dusty Manhattan hotel in the Flatiron District. I'd visited New York only once before, in my twenties, when I lived in Florida for some years, during what felt like an entirely different life. Back then New York was a city fighting madly to stay alive, the evidence of which was in its decay. The neon signs had been rigged haphazardly atop crooked buildings that seemed to have no business standing tall. I'd seen whole city blocks turned into dance parties, an improvised boy band serenading a subway car, a crowd of vigilantes descending on a thief who had stolen from a beloved local grocer. As a young person, I idolized the spontaneity, the chaos. Now, Manhattan seemed anxious and sterile. Pale. The ground under my feet suspiciously clean. The New Yorker stride of bulldozer swagger had turned into a timid saunter of people looking at their feet, as if the whole city had suffered a shared tragedy that bent the invincible spirit I'd once witnessed.

I had expected to be overwhelmed with emotion to find myself in America once again, to relive the memories of youthful wonder, the excitement of a nomadic life. Perhaps I was too ill or too preoccupied as I watched my cabdriver dodge one traffic accident after another, but I felt nothing but irritation, a desire for the comforts of home. Anyway, why should New York owe me anything? It had lived through its own share of tragedies. While I was painting a nostalgic portrait of the city in my mind, it had seen more death than I could ever imagine.

Before my arrival at the hotel, I called Babi and Roman. My son said he was too tired to speak to me. My mother begged me to watch out for guns. "Look for bulges behind the belt," she advised.

The hotel receptionist, an unkempt, sweating man in his thirties, demanded to see my visa as soon as I gave my name. He asked questions about why I had traveled into the country, inquired about my religion, and pushed for my opinion on the omnivaccines.

On his hand I spotted the tattoo of a DNA strand wrapped around a mattock. The identifying mark of a devoted Reclamationist. Blood and soil. The man's eyes betrayed a hunger in the way they darted across my body, and he grew coiled and focused like a predator beginning his stalk. I was sure he'd call the HDF to verify my immigration status as soon as I left, hoping he might be a hero who'd caught a foreign socialist instigator or welfare thief. Seeing I had only silence to offer, the man surrendered the room key, and I rushed toward the elevator.

I hooked the chain on my room's door, trying to shake off these unsettling moments. I unpacked my small suitcase and washed the distress of the flight from my skin. Aches pulsed through my muscles and bones. Blaming the discomfort on jet lag, I decided to get in bed right away, leaving the terrifying business of finding Tereza for the following day.

I spent the night in and out of consciousness and awoke with a fever. New York came to life outside the miniature window of the bathroom as I puked. Already the glamour of the place was pushing me to resubmit myself to the American ideal: *Stand here, ye who are worthy, and look over one of civilization's greatest cities. Go shopping, eat oysters, catch a show.* My lungs burned; my delirium turned me sluggish, at odds with the pull of the cosmopolitan. I poured a triple dose of Advil drops under my tongue, put on a dress I hadn't worn since my son's university graduation, and left the room. As if in reward, I was greeted by a pleasant young woman at the front desk.

I had chosen the hotel because it was the only affordable option within walking distance of Tereza's workplace. Fifteen blocks. I set my foot on the icy sidewalks and made my way across the city. Veteran New Yorkers exhaled their frustrated sighs when they got stuck behind me. This fact of the city appeared unchanged—it reviled anyone who dared slow it down. No patience for aged bones, and yet aged bones I had, and no other option than to share the sidewalk. Whatever else changed, the city still favored the young.

At last I stood in front of an eighty-story skyscraper belonging to the VITA corporation. It wasn't built for the likes of me. No, it was designed for the sexy people of the future, people who would never age thanks to vegetable juicing, people who craved disruption and fought a sense of impending doom with manic productivity. There were no signs or logos on the building, no distinguishing features to offer a clue to its identity. Everyone already knew whom it belonged to. I walked through the glass door and found myself in a minimalist lobby made of sleek obsidian stone.

The man behind the reception desk beckoned me forward. "Positive tidings," he said. "What is your purpose today?"

For a moment I got lost staring at the small round device installed just below the man's ear, where his jawline met his neck. A hWisper. The device unsettled me whenever I saw it. It had been invented a couple of years earlier by the very people working in this building, the first successful attempt at linking the human brain directly to a computer. The machine functioned via two chips, one implanted in the person's brain and one in the hand, through which the hWisperers (as adopters were called) could browse an interface of apps as if the software lived inside their own heads, all controlled by the mere motion of their fingers. This experimental technology was far beyond my desire to accept or understand, a sentiment I shared with most of the world's population. But despite the widespread pushback, the device was gaining apostles among the younger generations. I had seen it only once in the Czech Republic, but here in New York, I'd already encountered several pedestrians who had converted to the hWisper lifestyle.

"I'm here for Tereza Holm," I said to the receptionist, exhilarated that my English, which I hadn't practiced in some years, was still passable.

He maintained eye contact with me as he browsed the hWisper calendar in his mind. "She doesn't have scheduled visitors. Who may I say brings chill vibes?"

"I'm her mother. In a way."

The person Tereza knew as her mother had been dead for some time, a fact that the young man was perhaps aware of. He raised an eyebrow, his positive vibrations ceasing to flow; clearly, I'd worn out my welcome already.

"It's complicated, but she'll want to see me," I said. *I hope.*

The man asked me to wait outside.

Standing in front of the entrance once again, I rubbed my cold hands together and squinted through the tinted glass of the sliding doors. Twenty minutes later, the wall behind the receptionist opened, revealing a secret portal. A woman's silhouette stepped into the lobby.

It occurred to me that Tereza might think I wanted something from her, money or love. I imagined her slapping me across the face, unleashing her rage on the mother she'd never known, the one who'd abandoned her at birth. There was still time to run. Fifteen blocks and I could be back at the hotel, door locked. Tereza would never know I had really been here. Some idiot playing a prank on her, that's all.

The glass doors opened.

Out walked my daughter. I managed to stay upright just long enough to recognize her. Numb and light-headed, I took a step forward, opened my mouth without knowing how to greet her. It felt like I stood there for centuries, one foot forward, mouth agape and soundless. My knees weakened and my vision turned black as my body found a way to unfreeze itself...

Only when I felt the pressure of concrete on my back did I realize that I was no longer looking at Tereza's face but at the sky. Clear and easy, going about its business above the skyscrapers.

She leaned over me. Green eyes, unmistakably hers, identical to mine. Red hair cut midlength, similar to the haircut Babi had when she taught children in our village. I reached up and touched her face. I'd seen it in the pictures, but here it was truly unbelievable just how much we looked alike. A spherical bump on the tip of her nose, long neck, ears just slightly too small for her head. She was the revenant of my youth.

Tereza spoke her first words. "It's you." She knew right away. Most parents don't have to wait decades to witness their child speak for the first time, but my joy was undiminished. She saw herself in me. She knew why I'd come.

TEREZA PULLED ME to my feet as passersby paused to gawk at the reunion. I didn't know what to say after my botched greeting. I whispered the word *mother,* suddenly uncertain whether Tereza had really made the connection. My daughter put her arms around me. She trembled in the cold as I did my best to maintain the stoic gaze that had so often accompanied the most significant moments of my life. When your heart is pulverized into powder, pretend you saw it coming. Control your perceptions. Direct your actions accordingly. I wished for life to stop so that this moment wouldn't be diluted by any other experience to come, so that I would have no chance of saying something to make her recoil, losing her once again.

After exchanging a few awkward words about the hostile weather, we made our way to a bar overlooking the East River. Tereza insisted she could take the day off without issue, she was her own boss. I hoped that facing each other in a small space would force us to break through the daunting pauses, the stiff, polite rhythm of strangers. Make us honest. The first twenty minutes were strained. I felt like setting my forehead on the table and weeping, terrified that my feeling ill would spoil the moment.

Tereza's voice shook when she asked her first, formal questions, as if she were speaking to an intimidating teacher. She asked how I'd found her. I told her that her adoptive mother had contacted me before she passed away and sent links to Tereza's social media so that I could someday reveal myself, should I find the courage. But shame had prevented me from taking this opportunity until now. I told Tereza I was sorry, that I didn't know how to behave, felt unworthy of her company.

She stood and walked to the bar. My nausea struck again. Already my daughter was done with our meeting and was settling our tab to end the misery.

When she returned, I whispered that I understood, that it was wonderful just to spend these twenty minutes with her.

"No," she said, "you don't understand." The bartender came over and placed a couple of drinks on the table. "Martinis, double vodka, dirty through and through," Tereza said. "A tonic for the nerves."

As we emptied our glasses, I told my daughter about the supernatural occurrence that had confirmed I should seek her out despite my fears: the carp in the bathtub speaking to me like a creature from old folktales. I didn't plan on revealing the true reason for the timing of my visit, not anytime soon. "I don't want you to think I came here because I want something from you," I said.

"Why not?" Tereza replied. "I want something from you. Family. To make my world bigger. Isn't that what people do for each other?"

"I don't deserve it."

"Nonsense. You've done nothing wrong. You found the perfect family for me. I couldn't have asked for better."

"When your new parents came to get you at the hospital, I nearly attacked them. I changed my mind a million times. They must have been remarkable, to raise a daughter like you. Working in the Division of Permanence...I've never known anyone so accomplished."

Tereza grew quiet as she tore her napkin into ever smaller strips. "I haven't accomplished much. Not yet."

"I've read the articles. They said you might cure cancer. Alzheimer's."

"Let's just say that my employers' main interest is in...more disruptive models of longevity science. Brain mapping. Cryonics."

"Brain mapping?" I said. "What in the world?"

"Yes! They will put your mind in a bottle, like a genie. Scan your brain to capture your personality, your memory, your very essence, whatever that is."

"And then?"

"Mind upload. Maybe they will transfer your personhood into some indestructible body. Or the cloud."

"I suppose it would be nice to be invisible sometimes. Just a soul. Can they put me in a dog's body? I would quite enjoy that," I said, delighted by Tereza's laughter. It didn't last long.

"I want to eradicate the disease of aging," she said, solemn again. "The pains of a failing body, to make the twilight years pain-free. But my bosses, my colleagues—they want to turn leaders of industry into cyborgs. To upload people's souls as software. It's not quite what I had in mind," Tereza said and drank down the rest of her cocktail in a single gulp. "But I shouldn't complain. They pay me a small fortune. I run my own lab." She nodded at the bartender and spun her finger in the air.

I didn't know what to say. When I watched her from afar in You-Tube videos and read newspaper profiles about her, my daughter seemed to have everything a person could want. What advice could I possibly give? I had nothing to show for a lifetime of labor. Nothing beyond a meager pension looted by decades of government mismanagement. A life lived paycheck to paycheck, never a chance to save or build.

"You're young," I said, and immediately regretted using this tired platitude. "What I mean is, you have the run of the world, don't you? You can always go work somewhere else, do what you want."

"Every permanence company is like this now," Tereza said as the bartender delivered our next round of cocktails. "The new futurists have taken over. They think the body is a hindrance, an obsolete bit of nostalgia for romantics. Like books."

Clearly, I couldn't help this brilliant child, as I didn't know anything about her problems. She probably thought me stupid, naive, a relic with no place in her world. I folded my hands in my lap and scrambled for a new subject, anything to show my daughter that I was an interesting person and could have value to her.

"I like your necklace," Tereza said after a while.

I touched the golden beetle on the chain around my neck. An antique by now, and a reminder of a world that would never be again. "I wore it when I met your father," I said.

"Really? Is he alive?" Tereza said, hope flooding her voice.

"I'm so sorry," I told her, "he died some time ago. We hadn't spoken for decades, but he tracked me down and sent me a letter from his deathbed. I'm afraid we were hopeless together. A couple of dreamers." It was Michael, I said, who had sold me on America, on the life you could live if you had money. "Soon we became reminders of each other's failures. I don't mean to sound negative. I loved him. But I had to leave America, and the only way to do that was to forget him. Sometimes you have to do that to survive. Forget people entirely."

I hated that Tereza had to find out about her biological father's death in this way. The parents who'd raised her—a Danish couple, academics who'd moved to America soon after they adopted Tereza—had passed away before she went to college. She seemed to have no luck at all when it came to family.

"Is that why you...gave me away?" Tereza said. "To survive?"

It was the question I was most prepared for, yet it still caught me off guard. "I've been having nightmares about you asking," I said. "But you say it without any malice. I don't deserve it."

"Having a child—I can't even imagine it. There's no reason for malice."

"I was on the run," I said. "Between countries. I had nothing to give. Along came a perfect couple who looked at you like you were the answer to all of their questions. It's complicated, but I will tell you every bit of it."

"I want to hear it," Tereza said, "but later. Today we're going to behave like an ordinary family. I want to welcome you, a mother visiting her daughter in the big city. Because this should be a celebration. We've been talking about painful things since we sat down. Let's take it easy for a while."

"A celebration," I agreed.

Tereza paid the bartender with a corporate credit card seemingly made of gold as I rose and headed to the bathroom again. My eyes were red, I couldn't stop sweating although the bar was cold. I looked far better than I felt, and I intended to keep it that way, preserve this perfect day. I put six Advil drops under my tongue, washed the sweat off my forehead, and took a deep breath. There was no room for fatigue, for mistakes. This day had to be perfect.

WHEN I CAME out, Tereza suggested we stumble to the Museum of Modern Art, one of the city's most beloved tourist clichés. We locked arms and walked west, doing our best to avoid a march of protesters extending all the way from the UN building to Rockefeller Center as drones buzzed overhead, scanning the crowds. The band around my wrist vibrated, a verification of my legal status in the country.

I asked Tereza about the protest. Americans were angry at the UN for failing to address the Reclamation Act during the recent General Assembly meeting, she explained. Refusing to impose sanctions on the United States for its antidemocratic agenda and crimes against humanity. Why wouldn't the world come to their aid? An old feeling for me, the citizen of a small, often forgotten nation.

Having passed through this scar across America's iconic city — the march of people terrified of an unstoppable plunge toward the collapse of their homeland — we arrived at the museum. As we toured its floors, I forgot the circumstances of our lives, the strangeness of me walking around with a daughter who hadn't known me just hours earlier. It was as if the two of us had been visiting this museum for years, as if it was our tradition to come for special occasions. I hesitated to speak. Our newfound confidence seemed fragile, breakable with a single word. I followed Tereza, listened to her talk about Frida Kahlo and Nadia Ayari, the field trip she had taken here when she was in high school, the classmate she'd kissed in front of *Water Lilies* when the group left them behind. I tried my best not to stare at her too much, utterly taken by every story she offered.

At last, we made our way to the museum's most popular floor, which hosted a famous attraction painted by a Dutch recluse. We stood at the back of a massive crowd as a family of three posed for a photo with the painting, surveilled carefully by a gaggle of guards. The painting wasn't protected; it simply hung exposed like all of the other pieces, easy prey for vandals looking to make their online fame. I was shocked that MoMA hadn't made better arrangements after the series of assaults on works of art around the world committed by a faction of TikTokers who assumed, correctly, that the destruction of famous works would bring viral fame and fortune.

I scanned the crowd for any possible assailants. A little boy who had just taken the photo with his parents suddenly broke left and ran up to the painting. With his sticky fingers, which just reached the village of Saint-Rémy, the boy began to tap the canvas, as if to see whether the painting had a touchscreen. Luckily, the painting had a protective cover after all. The horrified father pulled his son away before the guards could reach him, but the Public Shaming Alarm had already been activated.

A life-size hologram of Vincent van Gogh appeared next to the family. The maestro was dressed in a blue coat and a white shirt buttoned all the way to the neck. He had the same severe cheekbones and focused blue eyes from his self-portraits, although the features seemed a bit cartoonish, not particularly realistic, probably because the museum wanted to avoid customers thinking that the Dutchman's resurrection was real. The cartoon van Gogh opened his mouth and berated the family in Dutch, exclaiming to the skies and waving his fist at the little boy, whose snot and tears dripped onto the floor as his parents dragged him out of the room, mouthing apologies.

Van Gogh turned to the rest of us with a mad look in his eye and spoke in perfect English: "Under the Emergency Art Terrorism Act of 2025, damage to protected works in New York is punishable by three years in state prison." Whereupon he bowed and vanished.

I wasn't impressed by the spectacle—something about the holographic van Gogh invading a space where people came to admire classics reminded me of the robotic Register 12 at Kaufland. What indignity it brought to the deceased artist, this digital caricature, a Disneyfied attraction. I imagined living this kind of afterlife, a holographic version of myself dancing atop the casket at my funeral, performing karaoke hits, making crude jokes about my guests, haunting our house Wi-Fi in Hluboká. In that moment, I couldn't yet imagine how likely it was that digital ghosts would soon roam the earth. I shook my head and asked Tereza if we could move on to my favorite analog activity—more drinking.

We ordered blue cheese martinis at the MoMA bar and tried our best impressions of the hologram's absurd Dutch accent. Despite Tereza's good mood, I felt anxious, as I wasn't sure what to do next. When the museum announced its closing hour and the winter sun began to set outside, I feared that the day might be over, that Tereza would return to her life, leaving me shut up in my hotel room, passing time until I could see her again. Who was I to demand more from my daughter after she'd been so generous? And yet I couldn't accept the thought of letting her go.

"Would you like to see my apartment?" Tereza asked.

Was she humoring me, sensing my dread? "I've already taken up so much of your day," I said. "Are you sure?"

"This is *our* day. I should say that my apartment is more of a storage room. I've barely been there since I re-signed the lease—I live at the office—so I can't vouch for the smell, but I keep all my childhood things there. Things I want to show you."

"Yearbooks? I have always thought about how much I'd love to see your yearbooks."

"Yes. I have everything. I'm a bit of a hoarder—greeting cards and baby teeth and Polaroids and movie tickets—and now I know why I've kept it all. For you."

At my behest, we took the subway instead of a cab, to accommodate my nostalgia for old New York. Neither of us was aware just how dangerous the underground had become. My daughter and I ventured into the unknowable depths of Manhattan, headed for South Slope. By then, I was sure that this time with Tereza was easily the most important day of my life.

We boarded the R train and claimed two free seats next to a rolling pool of unidentifiable brown liquid. Tereza seemed nervous, clutching at the strap of her bag. It had been years, she admitted, since she'd had any use for the subway, as her VITA private chauffeur took care of all her transportation needs. She'd forgotten that the subway tunnels were a different dimension, one in which humans were unwelcome visitors with no guarantee of comfort or safety.

"Let's make this quick," she whispered as we rode, a New Yorker's prayer.

As if her wish had violated some law of the underground, the train came to a halt between stations, so suddenly that a woman sitting a few rows away dropped her container of hot and sour soup. The black liquid and chunks of chilies spilled over the feet of her indifferent neighbors.

"Good news, passengers," announced an obscenely cheerful voice from the intercom. "Today our trains are running with a brief delay of forty minutes. We'll move as soon as traffic clears. Please sit back, relax, and enjoy the Soothe Protocol, brought to you by Procter and Gamble: Keeping you sanitized no matter your destination."

I looked out the windows of the train at the gritty tunnel walls surrounding us. Was this a joke? The train dimmed and all around us the soft glow of blue light emanated from the ceiling and beneath the advertisement frames. I could no longer see the stains on the floor, the duct tape sealing cracks in the seats, the mice excrement, only the soft blue light that reminded me of hotel lobbies. The stereo speakers inside the train played a gentle tune, a bit of piano, a pinch of saxophone, the croon of a bar lounge on a slow weekday evening. As the grand finale, the emitters underneath our seats released aerosol sanitizer, scented with lavender to mask the stink of spilled soup and crotch sweat. I inhaled deeply. As we waited, an advertisement broadcast from the speakers let us know that the scent was available for purchase in the form of candle, spray, or toilet freshener on the MTA website. Tereza said she'd read about the Soothe Protocol when it was first introduced, a response to the countless subway brawls that broke out due to passenger frustration.

"Do you like to travel?" I asked Tereza in an attempt to normalize our circumstances.

"I don't get to do much of it. The world, well, we can't travel as freely as we used to. I did go to a conference in Croatia last year, during the red tide. I watched the tourists evacuate in droves while the army tried to clear millions of dead fish from the beaches. Hospitals filled with people who'd swum in the algae or breathed in the spores. It put me off travel for a while."

"So you do travel to Europe. Close to us," I observed clumsily.

"I'd love to visit you soon," Tereza said. "Don't be afraid to ask."

"You have a brother and a grandmother, and they would love to meet you. Our village is small, I doubt it'll impress you, but the house belongs to you as much as it does to us."

"You don't have to ask me twice. My mother...my other mother? Sorry. When I was little, she showed me pictures of where I came from. Maybe I'll go with you now. America feels less and less like home."

The train doors jerked open, and four men carrying automatic rifles, accompanied by a German shepherd, entered our car. Their faces were concealed with black masks printed with white skulls. The passengers removed wallets from their pockets and held up their citizen IDs as one of the men flicked his fingers to verify their identities en masse in his hWisper database. Tereza's company, VITA, held a lucrative government contract that equipped all federal law enforcement with enhanced devices. The man set his eyes on me as the K9 sniffed at the bags and feet of the travelers. He approached me, and I stared at the letters sewn into his bulletproof vest in golden thread: HOMELAND DEPORTATION FORCE. I didn't know what was expected. He looked at me and inhaled deeply.

"Your tracker," Tereza whispered.

I held out my shaking hand and waited for the man to find my identity in the depths of his brain-computer synergy.

"What are you doing here?" the man asked without making eye contact.

"Visit?" I whispered.

"No English?" the man said as he gestured to his comrades.

The four of them surrounded us, and the people sitting nearby moved to the opposite side of the train. The dog had strained the limit of its leash and began to lick the spilled soup.

"Sorry, sorry," I said. "I meant I'm here visiting my daughter."

"Her papers are in order, Agent," Tereza said. "Is there a problem? I could call my bosses, the founders of VITA, to clear this up."

The man ignored her. "You're this feminazi's mother?" he asked me and nodded toward Tereza.

I knew this man. I had been surveilled, hunted, arrested, and detained by his kind during my country's darkest days. The enforcement of the Reclamation had become one of America's largest industries, and many collaborating citizens found employment as agents of the Homeland Deportation Force, overseeing immigrant work camps, pursuing fugitives, or laboring within the massive bureaucracy of surveillance and public relations to ensure the patriotic wheels turned smoothly. Much like the secret police of Czechoslovakia, the specter of my youth. This man had found his life's calling, his greatest pleasure and joy, within the unlimited mandate of the HDF mission. Authoritarian revolutions offered lucrative opportunities for the natural-born cop. The most important requirement of the job was his passion to dominate.

I said nothing to the man. Silence was the only safe option. I was to show fear and submission, an easy task, seeing that the muzzle of his rifle rested about forty centimeters from my face. Give him the high he craved, reassure him he could do anything he wanted to us. He needed to know we were entirely at the mercy of his benevolence.

Tereza seemed to understand too. The moment passed. The man's face eased up; he saw we would offer no resistance. He was at once fulfilled and disappointed.

"Make sure you don't miss your boat home," he told me. "There are no sanctuaries left."

The men and their dog passed into the next train car. I breathed and counted to myself, determined not to let Tereza see me tremble. At last the fake scent of the Soothe Protocol weakened and gave way to the raw smells of the underground. The music ceased to play, and the train jerked forward, causing pieces of tofu from the hot and sour soup to slip and slide down the aisle. A couple of children stood up and began to kick them around like a football. The passengers resumed eating, reading, watching videos on their devices. It seemed we would all continue on as if nothing extraordinary had just occurred.

Tereza attempted to return to our conversation, but I struggled to speak, to focus. Had the men facing us made another choice—arbitrarily, instinctively, based on nothing but their need to harm, to dominate—they could've hauled me off to one of their facilities, they could've disappeared me until the machine of the Reclamation decided my fate. What would it be like not to have even this minimal protection of my visa, to live in a constant state of being hunted by the HDF? I had no doubt that if I weren't a white European woman, I would've been treated with far greater suspicion, perhaps arrested regardless of any paperwork. I hadn't felt this kind of terror since the days of my youth, when my country had lived through its own nightmares, and the matter of disappearing at the whim of state agents was an accepted fact of daily life.

TWENTY MINUTES LATER, we arrived at the Prospect Avenue station and walked up to Tereza's apartment, a minimalist two-bedroom filled with boxes and unwrapped designer furniture. It was part of a condo high-rise, mostly unoccupied, and on our walk from the subway I had noticed many more luxury buildings sitting empty. Why would the city allow the construction of these towers for ghosts? Perhaps they, too, were made for the hypothetical sexy people of the future: they were aspirational apartments for the coming generations of young professionals. Surely the tens of thousands of unhoused people in the city understood the importance of aspiration while my daughter used the warm, luxurious apartment as a storage closet.

We picked through relics and photos Tereza had saved and I pressed her for the stories that accompanied the mementos and pictures, all while we drank too much wine to suppress the lingering tremors from our subway experience. I told her about the history of our small village, showed her photos of the Hluboká house. I mentioned her brother's struggles, though briefly, as I didn't want to scare her off. We took a couple of trips to buy more wine from a store around the corner ("Just buy the damn crate," suggested the clerk amiably). Twice I was overcome with the fever plaguing me, sweating, unable to breathe, and in these moments I retreated to the bathroom to collect myself, determined to keep the truth of my condition from my daughter. I splashed water onto my face again, took more Advil drops, an overdose.

When Tereza asked whether I was all right, I blamed the alcohol. But my unyielding fever combined with the wine and the image of armed men interrogating me led me to a place that was dark and restless. I had entered my daughter's life under false pretenses. Already our relationship was based on a lie. Suddenly I felt I needed to confess. I will never know whether the impulse was based on selfishness—a need for someone to feel sorry for me—or an attempt to honor our new relationship by being vulnerable, by sharing the secret that only Dr. Škvoreček, Marek of Kaufland, the golden carp, and I knew.

"I have something to tell you," I said in slurred English.

"Wine confessions are dangerous," Tereza said.

"It's so late. I'm sorry. I feel I can't lie to you, keep the pretense up. I just, I haven't said it out loud."

"You're freaking me out," Tereza said.

"I'm sorry, I said too much too quickly. Forget me. Show me more pictures." I looked frantically around the room, searching in desperation for a new topic of conversation. There was nothing to hold on to. I noticed a miniature crack on the wall. "Better get that fixed soon," I said as I nodded toward it. "It'll grow on you—suddenly a crack turns into a gap, and it'll get drafty in here, or you'll get bugs."

Tereza set the boxes of nostalgia aside and crossed her arms. For the first time, I saw her outside the polite, welcoming demeanor she had shown me since my arrival. This small moment of honesty confirmed that we were family. I knew I had to finish the act of drunken idiocy I'd started.

"Some weeks before I came to find you," I said, "my doctor gave me news. A diagnosis. I didn't plan on telling you, it's not your problem."

"What is it?"

"I have a year left on this earth. Maybe less. That's about it."

In horror, I watched my hand tremble as it held the empty wineglass. Generations of women in my family have practiced superhuman calm in times of tragedy, they've lived through the famines and the wars of kings, through the old fascists and the new without so much as a sniff. Were they right in their defiance or was I justified in my honest expression of fear? How could a person face death calmly when she had so much to lose?

My daughter reached for me. She played with my beetle necklace. This was it, I had lost her. In the long minutes of silence between us, I was too scared to speak.

"I wanted us to meet while I still had time," I said after a while. "I understand if this is too much for you."

"This is it," Tereza whispered. "I've been waiting for it."

"What is it?"

"Never mind." She stood and helped me to my feet. She had to make a phone call right away, she said. It was important. Life or death. She would explain in the morning.

It took everything in me not to panic at this jarring change in my daughter's voice. Our night was over, just like that. I was sure I had pushed her away. What had I been thinking? To come into her life and introduce more grief, to oppress her with my problems. Yes, I had to leave immediately. I collected my belongings and stumbled to the door as Tereza ordered a cab for me with her hWisper. I tried to make my goodbye brief, as I could tell she was distraught, distracted. And yet, as I put my foot out the door, she called me her mother and told me she loved me.

"I promise I'll take care of everything," she said. "Just wait until the morning. Don't worry. Don't look at me that way, everything is fine. More than fine, you'll see."

She simply wanted to get rid of me, was giving me this story of an important phone call to ease the parting. I made my peace with it. We held each other, swayed in our inebriated unrest, until the cabbie outside began to punch his horn. I slipped into the taxi, drunk and red-eyed, and asked the driver to turn up the music loud enough to make it hard to think.

Back in the unfamiliar bed of my hotel room, too weak to change from the clothes I'd worn all day, I rested as the fatal fever overtook me, bearing me first to deranged dreams and then to the place I speak from now. I kept my hands close to my face, inhaled the scent of my daughter's hair. I shouldn't have told her about my diagnosis, but the morning would offer a blank slate. After a night's rest, I would beg Tereza to forgive my upsetting announcement. I did my best to forget the panic, the change I had caused in my daughter, her sudden urgency to get me out of her apartment. There was still time to make it right, to start over with her. I continued to soothe myself with these hopes until my body no longer belonged to me.

In the last moments of my life, between the haze of sleep and the afterlife, I hallucinated that my daughter appeared, sitting on the edge of my bed. She whispered comforting words and ran ice cubes along my cheeks and forehead. Was she really there, had she tracked me down at the hotel because she couldn't stand to be apart? I wanted to tell her my stories, too, before it was too late. I began to tell her about my childhood in a small village of few prospects, my escape into the big city and a community of outlaws. The stories she needed to hear, the only thing of value I could pass on to her, tales of her family and how she had come to be in the world. As the cramps sent my body into convulsions, I tried to crawl from bed to reach the phone, but I was unable to move. Yes, best to accept the end with dignity. I stared at the peeling paint on the room's ceiling, at a baby roach making its way in and out of the cracks, the last view I would enjoy during my mortal reign. I turned back to the apparition of my daughter and whispered, the words blending with the silence of the night...I whispered to her about my young life amid the ruins of a failing state.

THE YEAR IS 1978

THE LIVING ROOM of the Playwright's country house was hazy with cigarette smoke and ash escaping the furnace. Thousands of typed pages occupied the wooden floor. Seven of my colleagues and I sat in the narrow spaces between the stacks, typewriters in our laps, copying page after page to add to the disorganized piles of dangerous literature. Every hour or so, my ink-stained hands trembled so intensely I had to pause, drink down the champagne in my cup, and smoke a few cigarettes to ease the jitters.

As I took a drag on my Startka and blew out the smoke, I began to read again through the debut issue of our group's illegal literary review, *Ark,* representing a year's worth of intellectual contraband: poems and essays and novel excerpts from writers banned by the Communist regime. For twelve months we had crossed Prague through dark alleyways to make sure we weren't followed, met with authors and their allies to obtain copies of their works unseen. We had checked our telephones and light switches daily for bugs, engaged foreign agents, and established our smuggling routes. We had made it to this climactic night without being arrested, a feat that was at once exhilarating and suspicious.

In 1977, hundreds of civic signatories—some of the most significant Czechoslovakian activists and artists among them—signed Charter 77, a document declaring that the Communist government had failed to follow the human-rights provisions determined by the constitution and the Helsinki Accords. Following the government's harsh response and persecution of the signatories, we decided to do our part in chipping away at the regime by forming the samizdat Ark Assembly. The cultural climate of my country had reached a critical point—after decades of masterful censorship, the government had managed to discourage the average citizen from expressions of intellectual curiosity. Staying safe in the country meant staying away from political opinion and the public sphere. Interestingly, our country's Communism led to the rise of rabid individualism: *Look out for yourself, ignore injustice, and you shall remain free.* The efforts of the samizdat network were meant to break through this cultural stalemate. To remind us all of our collective consciousness, to assert that whatever was possible in art—rebellion, revolution, a reawakening of the mind—was also possible in life.

We had gathered works from the foremost enemies of the state, some of them exiled from the country or sitting in prison. In the house of the Playwright we prepared our thirty-page publication for distribution, hoping that our commitment to its content would make up for the poor production values, the pages bound together with crooked staples and stained with ink. I wished we could present the powerful texts aimed at the regime's inhumanity in a more appealing form, but we didn't have the luxury of aesthetics. On our typewriters we produced one copy after another until we reached five hundred issues, ready to be delivered to our friends.

The government made great work of turning society against its dissidents: *Look at these drunken sexual deviants disturbing the peace while you try to do your jobs and raise your families.* I tried not to think about the substantial files the secret police kept on my activities, friends, family. My social circle was closed, as any new people I might befriend would also be watched by the regime—or, worse, they could be spies. With my name carved on the jobs blacklist, I could never decide to pivot to a new career and a "normal," state-sanctioned life. I lived for this uncertainty. My activities against the government weren't a flight of fancy, some fickle rebellion. I was fighting for it all, revolution or death.

I set the magazine down and breathed. I knew there would never again be a moment like this in my life. Most likely we were all going to prison. The feeling of invincibility inside this country house was pure delusion, and yet, despite the dangers, I was happy to be there with my only true friends, high on the prospect of fighting back against the oppressor. My coconspirators looked magnificent, ruddy-cheeked and buzzed, kissing one another on the head and neck, belching from the seemingly bottomless champagne at our disposal, editing one another's paragraphs with admiration and a loud mockery of missed errors. I wished I had a camera to capture it, but the dissidents had a rule against creating photographic evidence. Besides, there had been three secret-police officers stationed across the road from the house for hours, attempting to photograph us through the newspaper-covered windows.

Ondráš fell into my lap and buried his face in my neck. He wore a brown sweater I'd given him for his birthday, snug on his slim body. His breath was sour from the coffee he never quit drinking. We had met years ago at an absurdist stage production. I had just run away from home in pursuit of an acting career. My father and I had reached an impasse over his plans to marry me off to the village priest and my plans to move to the city and live like a heathen. We fought about everything—the way I spent my time, the clothes I wore to the pub, the food I didn't like to eat. One fateful night, I suggested I might try to become a vegan. In response, my father forced on me a piece of bread slathered with lard. I tossed it in the garbage. He took my refusal to eat animals as an assault on his lifelong values and threw his piece of larded bread at my face, declaring I was under house arrest until my eighteenth birthday.

I ran away from home the next day, slept on the couches of friends who had escaped the village before me, applied to acting conservatories while I waited tables and looked for an apartment. But I was rejected from schools because my parents weren't members of the party. My server's wages were just enough to cover the rent for an attic apartment on top of a cobbler's shop. The fleas wouldn't let me sleep, and I spent my nights making plans. Everywhere I went, I encountered glue traps set to slow me down, and my rage at the regime reached its peak in those days of my early adulthood. Tired of the poor wages and the harassment from drunken bureaucrats dining at the bistro, I quit waiting tables and began serving drinks at private parties organized by bohemians, hippies, beatniks, all those living outside the arbitrary moral code of the *Homo sovieticus*. Baby steps into dissent.

At a party organized by a theater group, I met thespians who offered to bring me into their world, much needed patronage. I began to spend all my free time with the group led by the Playwright, and their friendship became too intriguing to pass up. On the day of my eighteenth birthday, I attended the premiere of the Playwright's latest protest piece, and I noticed the man pretending he wasn't looking at me. Ondráš.

Despite the brutal effects of the Prague Winter, during which the government had backtracked from attempts to relax the country's authoritarian laws and begun to terrorize its citizens even more, in those days I remained a committed socialist. I believed in socialism with a human face, the concept introduced by Alexander Dubček, which aimed to retain socialism while eliminating the totalitarian aspects of Communist rule and democratizing the country. A direct challenge to the establishment in Moscow. Freed from the crushing influence of imperialist Russia, a true Marxist Czechoslovakia, led by the workers, could become the leader of the worldwide labor uprising. So went the thinking. However, Ondráš believed that the country could thrive only if the selfish interests of the people were an equal part of the process, that a regulated market in the hands of private ownership was integral to preserving the destiny of socialist nations. He wanted to avoid the bad press that came with food shortages and mismanagement of the planned economy.

We argued loudly during every date until we got tired and took each other's clothes off. In the end, we were more united than our fights suggested—we were both young and wanted more of a say in what our world should look like.

Now, in the Playwright's country house, Ondráš refilled my champagne mug and walked to the window facing the road. He peeled off a corner of the newspaper, revealing the vehicles parked across the street, three men in parkas with cameras around their necks.

"No reinforcements yet," Ondráš announced.

"If you keep looking, they'll take your picture," someone called out.

"I'll be the face of the resistance," Ondráš said.

"If you're the face of us, we're doomed," I said.

Ondráš's cheeks turned dark red. Sometimes he was still just a boy.

At last the typing in the room stopped, and we arranged the freshly stapled issues into neat piles sorted by destination. Most of the copies were headed to the godfathers and godmothers of the samizdat network, to be passed along their routes. We planned to leave more copies around university campuses, cultural centers, and movie theaters to reach the wider public. Finally, international agents would smuggle *Ark* beyond the border so that Czech émigrés and interested foreigners could witness the literature produced by a country fighting for its sanity.

Before we arrived at the Playwright's house, Ondráš had taken me to lunch at the Golden Tiger pub and asked me to marry him. I found the idea of marriage idiotic and tempting at the same time. My mother had married my father because he'd inherited a wealth of potato fields, and throwing away such prospects in a struggling post-war country was foolish. What kind of life did Babi forfeit because of this forced pragmatism? But the concept of marriage had grown on me as I watched the dissident couples in our circle, how they upheld each other intellectually and spiritually, fought for common ideas, even allowed themselves the freedom of sleeping with others. The country in crisis was an aphrodisiac. I was in love, and my friends swore that marriage made dissidents bulletproof. I told Ondráš he'd have my answer after *Ark* was out in the world, after our mission was complete. It seemed irresponsible to commit two life-changing acts in such quick succession.

The sorted packages of *Ark* now took up nearly half the room. We began stuffing them into our bags. I disposed of the empty bottles of champagne and checked our field equipment—cigarettes, flasks, IDs, car keys. We looked at the maps one last time, confirmed the diversion plan. The secret-police vehicles were sure to follow us. The fact that they hadn't yet struck meant only that they hadn't figured out the nature of our contraband, and their bosses had ordered them to practice restraint. The government's handling of Charter 77 had caused civilian unrest, and the *fízláci* decided to switch their tools of reproach from hammer to scalpel. They waited and watched, and our hope was that they'd keep their distance a while longer as we slipped into the long night. Drop the packages before they could catch up.

Our parting silence, after a day of cheer and determination, felt startling and grim. We shook hands, we hugged, kissed, and filed out of the house. The policemen exchanged words on their radios. Glared at us and the bags in our hands without any attempt to keep their directive of secrecy. Ondráš and I got in the back seat of the Moravian Poet's Trabant, the duffel bags filled with *Arks* at our feet, while the Poet and the Playwright sat in the front. The Poet started the engine.

We followed the Škoda carrying the second half of our group, a polyamorous trio of actors and our precious literary critic, Hajzl. It was after midnight, the streetlamps had been turned off, and the road was barely visible under the starless sky. Occasionally I dared to look over my shoulder at the cop vehicle following us. We left the village limits, no longer subject to the strict speed limit, and suddenly the engine strained and growled and the Trabant jerked forward at full speed as the Moravian Poet pushed the pedal to the mat.

The road cut through endless wheat fields, with sharp turns that made for a nauseating ride. The Poet jerked the wheel so quickly, we veered off the road and onto the grass, giving the policemen a chance to catch up. The Poet steered us back onto the road and we swerved left to right. I bit my tongue and tasted blood. The drivers behind us realized we didn't plan on slowing down, and with the squeal of a siren, their presence became startlingly public. The Škoda in front of us disappeared into the darkness. At least this part of the plan was working—our vehicle kept the cops occupied while our colleagues vanished on the country roads.

We entered another village and circled the statue of a forgotten saint. Two yellow vehicles of Public Security appeared like hideous fireflies; the screech of their sirens joined in with the pursuers'. They blocked our path, and the Poet screamed as he slammed on the breaks.

"Looks like we're done," said the Playwright.

"That was like a Bond movie," Ondráš said.

I was disappointed he'd say something so superficial in a moment like this. I asked if we should set fire to the magazines.

"Don't!" the Poet shouted. "We'll choke in here."

Unable to see through the blinding flashes of police lights, I lit another cigarette, some relief before I was captured. If they wanted me, they'd have to carry my deadweight. Cold air penetrated the car and extinguished my smoke. The Playwright was pulled from his seat like a rag doll. A boot crushed his cheek against the ground while someone snapped cuffs around his wrists.

I didn't have enough time to worry about what came next before some malevolent force gripped my legs and shoulders and I too felt the asphalt beneath my back. I tried to breathe in and grabbed at the uniforms of the men surrounding me. They turned me onto my stomach and pressed my face into the asphalt. The knee eased off my back after my hands were cuffed, then the cops raised me up. Ondráš and the Playwright were leaning against one of the firefly cars, trying to catch their breath, but I couldn't see our Moravian Poet. I looked inside the vehicle. He was still in the driver's seat, both of his hands firmly on the steering wheel, his teeth bared like a beast's.

"Good luck, dipshits," I told the cops, and the man holding my wrists slapped me across the head.

Two policemen approached, one from each side, and tried to tear the Poet's hands from the wheel. He screamed again, a bloodcurdling sound somewhere between a howl and a warlord's battle cry. The men backed away.

"Let's break his arms," one said.

"He can't show up for interrogation with shattered bones," said the other. "These are politicals. They need to look good for pictures."

"What, then? Tickle him? Sing him a lullaby?"

I relaxed every muscle in my body to force the men to strain as they dragged me to the car. I wanted to be a burden to the end, like the Moravian Poet. In my interrogation, I wouldn't talk; in court, I would laugh at the judge, declare that I didn't recognize the legal authority of a criminal state; in jail, I wouldn't eat. The men placed me inside the firefly vehicle with Ondráš. I looked at him, but he didn't look back. He stared out the window as if he were simply a tourist enjoying the Bohemian scenery. Was it indifference I saw? Impossible. The edge of his eyebrow twitched. Why wasn't he joining us in fighting to the end?

The men who'd captured us sat in the front seats and discussed the previous night's football match. "It pains me just how fucked you are," the driver said casually, "going to jail because of poetry."

I asked Ondráš if he was hurt, but he wouldn't talk. We rode through the sleeping villages, the bigger towns slowly coming alive as the bakers and grocers prepared for the day's work, the roads lined by trees with their crowns stripped bare. The small embers of the cops' cigarettes drew shapes in the car's darkness. The smoke burned my eyes.

"Looks like your boyfriend might not be so brave," the driver said. "So scared he's gone mute." He turned the radio on to a collaborator pop star singing a love ballad to the nation.

I placed my head on the seat, focused on steady breathing. Ondráš's expression worried me. Could he turn on us? Maybe he was embarrassed that the police had subdued him in front of me. No, this would pass. We'd get through the interrogations and do our time.

Continue to live free and young. But these thoughts didn't offer the usual comfort. For the first time I considered the possibility that I had bitten off more than I could stomach. The swift cold violence of the police together with Ondráš's silence unnerved me. Cop cars, it seemed, were designed to make ideals shrivel in the back seat.

We reached the bright lights of Prague, but the policemen parked in one of the darkest streets in the city, in front of a former factory repurposed to host jail cells and interrogation offices. The men led me to a separate entryway as I called out after Ondráš one last time. I told him we had nothing to fear, though I didn't believe a word of it. He didn't look at me before I was forced alone into a hallway that smelled of sour and sick.

My captors led me into the basement cells, removed my hand-cuffs, and pushed me behind a green metal door. There was a cot attached to a wall, a bucket, and a gray blanket with red stains on it. In the corner a mouse decomposed inside a glue trap. I sat on the cot, put my hands on my knees, and closed my eyes. Deep breaths. Soon they would claim me for interrogation. I'd never been questioned before, but I'd heard plenty from more experienced friends. The inter-rogators preferred to torture the men physically and the women psychologically.

There was no reason to keep me here; I'd committed no real viola-tions of the law, no treason. But in the offices above me, some of the most skilled liars in the world were dreaming up the narrative for my heinous thought-crimes. I breathed. I recalled my dream life that would follow the country's liberation: An Old Town apartment with a desk in the middle of the living room, two typewriters set up facing each other. Ondráš and I could write there all day, read to each other in the bathtub at night.

I woke up not knowing what time it was, my wrist numb because I'd used it as a pillow.

The cell door was open and a guard was saying, "Slavíková, free to leave." Just like that.

The guard led me by the elbow into a room with windows where he returned my bag and wallet, now emptied of the *Ark* envelopes and all my cash. He ignored my questions about the fate of my friends and let me out through the same door by which I had arrived.

I stood in the middle of a sunlit street as schoolchildren with backpacks passed me carelessly, as seniors rushed to the store for breakfast milk. With its gray, unkempt walls and the many blacked-out windows, the building behind me was meant to be inconspicuous at first glance but to serve as a petrifying omen. A warning to the nation. Something as ordinary as a rubber factory could be transformed into the most brutal tool of the regime.

I began to walk home, feeling perversely insulted. The cops hadn't asked for my signature upon departure, meaning that my arrest was not on the official record. They hadn't bothered asking a single question. Was it a ploy? Was I to be followed, lead them to the rest of my coconspirators, the samizdat sponsors?

I had to face the more probable reason: I wasn't important. I wasn't a significant threat, they craved bigger fish than a young woman no one had ever heard of. Despite risking everything just like my colleagues, I was an unimportant link in the chain of dissent. It made me sick. Did I want to be more important and spend years in prison? Perhaps. Perhaps I wanted to be one of the famous martyrs I spent my evenings reading about. I can only present my youth as a defense for this folly, the fetishization of dissident misery.

Once I was safely behind the door of my apartment, I ran a bath. Submerged in the water cleansing me of the filthy prison cell, I lit a smoke. Thankfully, I didn't own a radio, which allowed for some moments of silence and comfort, the world on my terms without the intrusive thoughts of strangers. I brushed my teeth twice and dressed. Inhaled the fresh breeze coming through the open window. A much better start to my day than the fecal stench of an unwashed jail cot. I left and walked to the house of the Moravian Poet's girlfriend, who hadn't been with us that night due to illness, to make phone calls.

* * *

WITHIN TWO DAYS, we knew that our colleagues from the second car had been arrested too. Every issue of *Ark* had been confiscated and burned, all our efforts turned to ash. The Playwright and the Moravian Poet, already known and admired among Czechs, were to be put on trial as our ringleaders. The rest of us were unknown to the public and thus unworthy of the expense of publicized prosecution. To my horror, there was no news of Ondráš. I couldn't sleep, lived only on coffee. I pictured Ondráš's ravaged body in jail, how he shivered as he starved, the threats to his family shouted at him in a room without windows.

Every day I rang Ondráš's doorbell to see if he had been released. No answer. Weeks into my struggle to learn my lover's fate, I picked up a newspaper and found a page-long letter of apology to the nation. A strong condemnation of the group who'd produced literary propaganda on behalf of Western agents. The letter's author regretted his misguided attack on the republic, explained that he'd been seduced by a group of perverted heathens bent on disassembling the social contract and ushering in a new era of foreign-sponsored anarchy. Under the letter appeared a familiar signature and finally a name that I read over and over—Ondráš Louka. Former editor of the propagandist magazine *Ark*.

I hurled the newspaper into the street, where its pages separated from one another among the slow-moving cars. A uniformed policeman approached and asked why I felt the need to loiter. I walked away lest I throw him into the street too. Ordinarily I walked the city feeling affection for its citizens. My political efforts were not undertaken to carve out some glory for myself (though I couldn't deny my addiction to adrenaline) but to remove the constraints on our collective lives, the specter of the police state that starved our minds with fear. I felt compelled to love my neighbor, even the informer. But on that day I could only conjure hatred and mistrust for humankind, for the coward dormant in all of us, the milksop poltergeist that awoke within the people you thought you loved and turned them into the enemy's megaphone.

I jumped onto the busy tram and elbowed my way through the crowd. At Ondráš's street, I got out and waited in front of the entrance to his building until a neighbor walked out and let me in. I went up to the third floor. Seeing his name on the door to his apartment made me sick. I knocked with my knuckles, then my fists. I pulled off my shoe and beat it on the door until neighbors began to gather on the stairwell. Finally, Ondráš emerged.

"Let me in," I said.

"I can't be around you," he said. "It's part of the deal. They're watching me." I pushed against him, but he wouldn't budge, his body blocking the doorway. "I can no longer congregate with—"

"The heathens? The perverts?"

He reached his hand out to me and I batted it away with the shoe.

"Fine," he said. "Come inside."

"I don't want to."

"What do you want, then?"

"For you to be someone else."

He shrugged like a little boy caught stealing from the pantry. "I can't throw my life away over some short stories," he said. "In a month people will forget about me and I can go back to living a normal life. They'll let me keep my job. That's worth a bit of shame."

"A normal life. You goddamn idiot. No one is alive in this place."

"Don't be a child. We'll have more chances to change the world down the road."

"I suppose I should've taken your religion of self-interest more seriously," I said with a laugh.

"We are born alone," he said.

I scoffed and turned around, slipped my torn shoe back onto my foot, and walked downstairs. I would never see Ondráš again. I turned his words over in my head. Perhaps he was right. We are born alone. We are knowable only to ourselves. Each friendship, each love, is an act of resistance against this truth. I'd lost my new family as quickly as I had found it. The only protection against such loss is detachment.

I ADOPTED THE DEFEATED, individualistic mood of my countrymen. Walked around in a haze, head down, refused to speak lest a pair of informer ears were listening nearby. I drank an abundance of rum from morning to night and ceased to read the smuggled books the Poet's girlfriend offered me. I stopped going to the dissident parties, annoyed with the married men's double meanings, the ways in which they leered now that I was unattached. Sex seemed inconvenient. Food tasted like paper. What's a revolution without gasoline? We glorify the strength of ideas, but in fact, ideas are as fleeting as a flash of lust. Ondráš had preached liberty or death for years until he faced a bit of danger and retracted everything. How could anyone else be trusted not to do the same? Soon I realized I wasn't much better than him. Revolutionary thought is kept alive within the individual only through the shared faith of others. Ondráš capitulated because his tormentors made him feel alone. I capitulated because Ondráš made me feel the same.

As I distanced myself from the dissidents, I lost access to the resources they shared. The only work I could find was cleaning at a hospital outside Prague. I left the apartment above the cobbler's shop and moved into a cheap studio I shared with a coworker. My new flatmate and I also shared a passion for escape through alcohol, each enabling the other to consume crippling quantities of vodka daily without fear of judgment. The world was ending, and it seemed reasonable to have a bit of fun, if you could call it that, on our way out.

During this hazy period, I also reconnected with my parents. One day, I simply boarded a train to Hluboká and appeared on their doorstep. My mother embraced me unconditionally and began to plan a party to make up for all of my birthdays we'd failed to celebrate. My father and I returned to the relationship we'd always had, polite and cold, until Babi was able to defuse the hostile tension between us. Neither my father nor I ever acknowledged my absence and what had caused it. Though everything else in my life had gone wrong, at least I had the comfort of my mother, the safe refuge of our family home.

Although I visited my parents occasionally, mostly I stayed in Prague. Toward the end of the summer of 1981, more than two years into this mind-numbing existence, I was in my flat alone, getting buzzed before my shift, when I saw a pool of water traveling from our toilet to the living room. I ran to the neighbors to use their phone. About an hour later, two men arrived, one of them tall and strong, a basketball player and a former engineering student who'd gotten kicked out of university and assigned to plumbing after his father refused to join the party. We exchanged phone numbers.

I found comfort and adventure in Jirka's bed, though it was only physical, as I didn't care for his mockery of books and intellectualism in general. "Who's gonna save the country, Adi? The *smart people*?" Soon I found out he was quite resourceful in the outside world. He'd been part of an international smuggling network for years, a part-time job to help him save money to emigrate. Jeans, Belgian chocolate, Western electronics were his bread and butter. Jirka's education, though interrupted, helped him figure out new ways to install secret compartments in vehicles and airplanes. When he'd heard enough pillow talk about my disillusionment with love and humanity, he proposed a solution: A brand-new life. Jirka offered to get me to America to earn the all-powerful dollar. To smuggle me through Yugoslavia and into Italy, through the Iron Curtain and into the West, where I could travel freely. Maybe I'd meet some rich American to marry, he joked. Fuck love and fuck socialism with a human face. Get paid.

My answer could only be yes. Just like that. I had nothing holding me home. Not even the pleas of my mother, who begged me to return to the village and make peace with my father, could change my mind.

I was to find my luck across the Atlantic. My nights with Jirka changed. The plan brought us closer; we were no longer just casual lovers. He improved my English, repeating phrases into the early hours of the morning: "Keep cool, baby. Can I use your restroom? Take me to the hospital." He brought me textbooks and tapes. With every new word I learned, my decision to leap into the unknown became more real.

So much has happened since then. I can barely remember the thrill of the dissidents smoking and laughing at nothing as they typed up their pages, I can barely feel the burn of hatred for Ondráš's betrayal. The Playwright Who Became Prisoner, our fearless leader, was killed in prison, became the Playwright Who Was Martyred. The Moravian Poet found great fortune and success as a professor in Canada. I don't know what happened to the rest of them.

What I do remember are my hopes for the future, how much I demanded of life back then. How could I have strayed so far from these endless ambitions, the sacrifices I made to fulfill them? I asked the apparition of my daughter at the edge of my bed, I reached for her, I begged her for answers and for comfort...

THE YEAR IS 2030

I WOKE UP AND I was no longer myself. The weight of my body was gone; the world offered no scents, no touch. I couldn't feel air passing through my lungs. I had died in a blackout, a complete paralysis, one moment I was begging my daughter for a glass of water and the next I'd become...this. There were no tunnels, no lights, no angels acting as brokers for the journey. It seemed necessary to ask questions, to look for a source of authority regarding my new state of being: What happens next?

My body was gone from the bed, and a piece of police tape blocked the room's entrance. The city lights seeped through the shades. The sheets had been stripped off and would no doubt merely be washed of corpse germs before they were offered to another guest. I felt a strong need to find out where my body had been taken. It seemed unthinkable I could live outside of it. Even in a bodiless form, my consciousness had to be tied to flesh, the flesh I had spent my life feeding, watering. Was I expected to abandon it immediately in search of some untethered ethereal existence?

Simply by wishing to do so, I appeared in the lobby, where the receptionist who had harassed me two days earlier was weeping, a bit too loudly. Was it for me? I spoke to him and received no reply. I tried to ring the reception bell and failed. How could I find out what steps to take next? Perhaps I had to resolve an issue from my past life. I couldn't think of any. I wished to traverse the streets, hoping that time would bring clarity.

It was not yet dawn. In front of the hotel, I tried to touch the people headed early to their jobs — MTA workers, porters, cooks. I shadowed one of them to his small diner for no particular reason, watched him unlock the rolling gate as he sang under his breath. I heard crunching noises coming from the alley next to the restaurant, and I followed them. A pair of yellow eyes looked up at me, followed by white gnashing teeth. A runty dog broke her fast by licking a pile of bones next to a garbage can. I recalled a brief affair with reincarnation from my youth and jokingly asked the dog for permission to live inside her body so I could find my daughter and hope she might recognize me, bring me home. But the lost terrier crunching on bones was merely that, an escaped pet turned scavenger, not a vessel for roaming spirits. She finished her breakfast, unbothered, then looked up at me once again, wagged her tail, and skittered off in pursuit of other bounties.

What else could I do? My desire to understand this world of the dead was undercut by unbearable longing to be near my people again: to be with Tereza, with Roman, with Babi. When I succumbed to the feeling, I appeared in Tereza's Brooklyn apartment a moment later, after a second-long blackout accompanied by a high-pitched whistle. I dreaded my daughter awakening to learn that the mother she'd just gained was gone again, permanently.

But she was already awake or perhaps hadn't gone to sleep at all. I found her sorting through her yearbooks, wrapping them all in brown paper, putting them in a box, writing *Mom* on the package. I reached for her, tried to speak with her, attempted to knock over the piles of storage boxes, anything to alert her to my presence. It was no use. She called a cab with her hWisper and set VITA headquarters as her destination.

Something changed. It was the feeling of invitation, an open door. I accepted. I found myself inside the hWisper's experimental interface: a simple map of pathways leading toward different apps and data folders against the backdrop of gray space, something like the sky of an ugly '90s video game. The app icons stood still, waiting to be touched, like interactive billboards. While hWisperers used their hand chips to navigate these paths, I traveled on them as if walking down the street.

I stood in place, thoroughly shocked by this new realm, for what felt like hours, though only minutes passed, as I saw on the giant sleek clock hanging in the ether—6:30 a.m., it announced. I walked toward the Uber icon and, once I'd reached it, saw a bird's-eye satellite view of Tereza's car fighting through the Brooklyn streets to reach her. I left the app and returned to the main pathway. In the distance I saw the data I really wanted to reach: Messaging. E-mails. Journal entries. Photos and videos. Access to my daughter's most private information, correspondence, memories, feelings, insights. If I'd had a mouth, I would've salivated. For someone who had gotten to know her child through online snooping, this was a dream. I would never again get to ask my daughter a question. Was it so unreasonable to proceed with this horrific violation of privacy, to invade her online realm of information? Well, I *was* dead. Did such moral quandaries even apply to me? Soon Tereza would try to call me, try to reach me at the hotel, and she'd learn of my fate. I didn't want to see it. I wanted to get lost in this place, to hide from her impending heartbreak. I headed directly for the icon labeled JOURNAL and began reading the recent chapters, concerned with Tereza's pursuit of immortality.

TEREZA HOLM—or, if you'd like my preferred version, Tereza Slavíková—had been named by *Science* magazine as one of the foremost experts in the booming field of longevity science. Since before she'd attended university, she had focused on the study of telomeres: the DNA caps that protect human chromosomes from fraying, ensuring healthy cell reproduction. Youth. But every time a cell divides, the telomere caps on its chromosomes shrink. Eventually, the telomeres become so short that the chromosomes can no longer replicate. This leads to the death of the cell. Entropy. To stir things up, the body also produces telomerase, an enzyme that repairs the deteriorated telomeres and can reverse the effects of aging in our cells. At the German Longevity Institute in Berlin, where Tereza became a postdoctoral researcher in 2020 after earning her PhD in Aachen, her team studied the effects of telomere manipulation. The process could also accelerate one's demise, as the overproduction of telomerase and the lengthening of telomeres could lead to cancer. So the key to the God pill—and to glory—was manipulating telomerase without killing the patient.

A breakthrough came when Tereza's team applied cryoelectronic microscopy to map out the structure of telomerase, something they hoped might lead to drug treatments. Their analysis wasn't complete enough to offer a full-blown solution to aging illnesses, but it was the beginning. The telomere obsession began to infect mainstream culture. Influencers traveled to countries in Eastern Europe and South America to inject themselves with unapproved telomerase cocktails. Streaming live. A clever pharma campaign popularized testing kits that allowed customers to measure their own telomere length, the twenty-first-century version of a psychic palm reading.

Tereza didn't mind these dangerous gimmicks, as they increased awareness and funding for her project. The computer-predicted scenarios were for naught until she could experiment on human subjects. Her team lobbied the German authorities to allow testing on people; due to the risks, their request was rejected without a hearing. Meanwhile, across the ocean, the founders of VITA unveiled their new Division of Permanence; they came to Germany to recruit Tereza just as she became disillusioned with the regulatory obstacles in her path. In the United States, there were no such hurdles. Though she wasn't fond of VITA, due to its strained relationship with ethics, she knew that the bottomless pockets of her would-be employers could usher in the beginning of a longevity revolution.

The aspiring saviors of humanity and leaders of VITA Inc. were Steven & Mark, twin brothers so famous that they stopped using their last names. They were the sons of a deceased billionaire who had grown them in a laboratory from the frozen-sperm cocktail of important men, fine-tuning their DNA for greatness. They were futurist gurus, self-prophesized prophets, like many of the "visionaries" occupying their Golden State valley. The brothers had broken out by developing the omnivaccine to eradicate the mutating virus that had plagued the world for half a decade, endearing themselves to governments and expanding their wealth to unimaginable heights. They used this capital for their dream project: hWisper, the first device to connect directly to human neural pathways. Many people rejected the device made by engineers of the omnivaccine, as this combination led to elaborate conspiracy theories about VITA attempting to control the minds of their customers. While building their hWisper cellular-network towers to penetrate every millimeter of the planet, from the oceans to the exosphere, the company bullied local landowners and bribed U.S. congressmen to skip major steps of the regulatory process. While testing on animals, they subjected their specimens to prolonged torture that shocked even the staunchest meat lovers. Following these scandals, large portions of the public began to despise the company, yet its stock soared, as its acolytes believed that VITA was the key to a transhumanist utopia.

Tereza first met Steven & Mark in a Berlin club as she drunkenly climbed an antique elephant statue in the lobby. The club was where she'd spent most of her free time after losing the love of her life, Rita. The boy billionaires looked more like tourist dads than a couple of geniuses, sporting their signature bicycle shorts, I ♥ BERLIN T-shirts, patchy facial hair, and the newest experimental hWisper units, barely visible under their ears. Steven & Mark asked Tereza to climb down from the marble elephant, invited her to the champagne lounge, and pitched her the offer of a lifetime.

They were immortalists, they explained, and their ultimate vision of the future was one wherein human existence could be fully digitized. But the wunderkinds didn't like to take chances, and they had to consider the possibility that ridding ourselves of our biological forms was impossible. Perhaps the path to eternity lay within one of the other theories the longevity field offered. To be safe, VITA had hired experts from every branch of longevity to form the Division of Permanence: cryonicists, or sleeping beauties; those who wanted to merge machine and flesh, known as the Borgs; the singularitarians, who believed the mind to be transferrable into 0s and 1s, digitized souls; and Tereza's people, the meat grinders, who believed the key to longevity rested solely in the body.

Steven & Mark revealed that Tereza was the first meat grinder they'd made an offer to, as the other branches of the field were more groundbreaking. What they meant was *sexier*. The dull science of the telomere was far less exciting than the promise of replacing patients' bad knees with robotic parts or keeping them asleep until they awoke in a beautiful future without death or pain. But this didn't mean that their respect and need for Tereza's work was diminished. She could hire dozens of assistants to staff a billion-dollar research lab inside a Manhattan skyscraper. She would receive a bottomless expense account. A transparent process in the selection of human subjects. There would be no time pressure, no one looking over her shoulder asking, "Are we immortal yet?"

Tereza did her best to mask her disdain for VITA's reputation as she considered the offer. With the backing of an unstoppable multinational tech behemoth, she could do things her colleagues at the German Longevity Institute only dreamed of. The ends justified the grimy means. Just as she had feared, Tereza had no choice but to say yes.

She immediately fell in love with the VITA facilities. She commanded an entire floor dedicated to the research of telomerase and had two dozen assistants ready to do her bidding. The facilities offered several bedroom pods with floating beds and rain showers, as the company expected the employees would become residents of the building, living for nothing but research. Tereza rented a lavish place in South Slope, Brooklyn, but after she spent a night sleeping in the pod thirty feet away from her laboratory, she knew the apartment was for storage only.

At first, she was relieved to return to New York from Berlin. Over the past few years, Europeans had become hostile toward Americans, owing to America's withdrawal from its international commitments, the brutal chaos of Reclamation, and the U.S. refugees fleeing to the Old Continent. The hostility had worn her down, as she couldn't so much as attend a party without someone holding her accountable for America's sins. The political situation at home had nothing to do with her. She was Switzerland, an apolitical healer who cared only for a world full of sick, dying people. It wasn't her job to force them to get along or to fix the corrupt logic behind their voting patterns. It was her job to make them healthier, improve their quality of life, eliminate pain. She'd watched her adoptive mother's slow death, torture by radiation. She'd seen the brilliant, warm, determined woman who'd raised her lose herself in unimaginable pain. This was more important than political parties. The pure intent of her life's mission, she believed, made her justifiably apolitical.

Supported by her fawning assistants, Tereza achieved her first breakthrough in the initial year of her tenure at the Division of Permanence. With the help of VITA's microscopic nanobots, she built on her old work at the German institute and discovered a previously unknown subunit of the enzyme's structure. If properly manipulated, the subunit could enable the researchers to lengthen or shorten the telomere at will. Thousands of computer simulations attempting to manipulate this subunit began to yield results for potential drug therapies. Perhaps the most exciting news was that this model could be applied to curing cancer. Telomerase enabled the growth of active cancer cells; halting and reversing its activity might lead to remission. At the behest of her employers, Tereza gave a widely publicized TEDx Talk in Croatia, presenting the theoretical possibilities of her research and earning international recognition for VITA's efforts.

Tereza wasn't interested in basking in her fame. Every day after her eighteen- to twenty-hour shift in the laboratory ended, she crashed in the sleeping pod she had claimed as her own. She breathed conditioned air and ate whatever the VITA cafeteria had to offer: bison steaks and juice made from grass. When the mood struck, she had affairs with carefully selected coworkers from other floors, women with similar positions of power and casual mind-sets. Tereza sought these connections to remind herself of human touch, of the unmeasurable bond between members of our species, of the humanity she was working to prolong. She feared becoming too clinical, too disconnected from the world outside VITA. But unless the singularitarians could resurrect her former love Rita in their brave new world of code, she had no use for deeper relationships.

IN THE SECOND half of 2029, six months before my arrival, Tereza's team devised a series of serum therapies based on the new simulations just as VITA's army of lawyers quietly secured regulatory approval for human testing. Within weeks, VITA recruited its first subjects, people who would live in the building and undergo trials after they signed agreements that made their bodies the property of the company. Tereza's first patient was Lydia, with whom she felt an immediate kinship. Lydia was an eighty-five-year-old woman from South Dakota, a former language-arts teacher who'd defeated cancer twice before. No family, no wealth, nothing to lose, as Lydia liked to say with a wink. Just a few short months after Lydia started telo-therapy, her symptoms receded, the cancerous mass in her liver shriveled and disappeared, and she went into remission. On the morning she declared Lydia cancer-free, Tereza took a rare walk outside the building and grinned at the people on the street, the people she believed she'd just saved from a cruel fate. Though it was far too early to tell whether the treatment was definitively safe or whether Lydia's remission was a coincidence, Tereza believed she'd just unlocked the next step in human development. When she returned to the lab, she and her assistants unpacked boxes of vodka, danced with Lydia around the laboratory (her rheumatic pains were gone), and settled on the idea that all of them ought to get tattoos of the telomere.

a single circular desk. In the middle of the desk sat VITA's personal receptionist, a camera that captured and evaluated newcomers. Tereza stood patiently as her body was scanned for weapons and bombs, after which the wall behind reception opened, revealing Steven & Mark's suite.

She had seen the office many times, yet her outrage over its excess of kitsch never dulled. The ceiling was painted with angels and devils in the baroque tradition, its style clashing with the modern minimalist furniture, the life-size statues of Lady Gaga and John Wayne, a massive wood carving of an Atari 64 covering one of the walls, Warhol's *Tunafish Disaster* covering another. There were no desks, no computers, no staples of a classic American office. Instead, there were half a dozen couches, beanbags, and yoga mats distributed indiscriminately around the room. Two sensory-deprivation chambers were embedded in the wall. From these chambers, Steven & Mark emerged, dressed in matching silver robes.

"Tereza. Our favorite child," Mark said, though Tereza was fifteen years older than he was.

"We thought we might see you," Steven said as the brothers sat down on a couch.

"Your spies told you," Tereza said.

"Your mother arrived at the port of John Fitzgerald Kennedy two days ago," Mark said. "Yesterday, you forfeited your work responsibilities to spend the afternoon with her. As Karlo from the lobby deduced from your mother's pale skin, shortness of breath, and enlarged lymph nodes, she had received a grim diagnosis before her arrival, a diagnosis we've confirmed with her village doctor's records. You are dressed in business casual, a rare respite from your uniform of T-shirt and lab coat. You are here to see us at the crack of dawn when you'd rather be anywhere else." As he finished, Mark spread some type of green slime on his forearms and face, then handed the unlabeled bottle to his brother.

"Wonderful," Tereza said. "I can skip to the point."

"You always say the right things," Steven said as he slathered the slime on his neck.

"I'm glad you think so," Tereza said. "My birth mother traveled all this way just to find me. She's the only family I have left. I would never suggest you owe me anything. But my mother is in pain. I can't reconcile knowing what we can do in this building with losing another person close to me."

"As they say, a question unstated is a question unanswered," Steven said, his upper body covered in the restorative green goo. From a compartment somewhere in the depths of the couch cushion, he pulled out a box of Muscle Milk, pierced it with a straw, and began to suckle.

"I don't know why I'm dancing around it," Tereza said. "My mother needs our treatment. I'm asking you to do this as a personal favor. I will work off the costs, but I know this really isn't about money. It's about how much you value me, whether I'm worth keeping. My mother's life is the new condition of my employment."

Steven finished his milk and tossed the empty box out the window overlooking Manhattan. He tapped the air with his fingers, performing an unknown search on his hWisper. "Your mother is a very interesting person," he said. "She was a dissident in her country. She tried to conquer the American dream, like, *old school*. She even made a movie!"

Tereza blinked at the last piece of information. So many things she didn't know.

"For months, you've been meaning to ask us a different question," Mark said. "You wonder why we've kept the news about Lydia from the public. Why didn't you ask?"

"You handle business. I handle the research. If you don't think we can go public yet, I agree," Tereza lied. "Sooner or later, what we do here will change the world. For now, let it change my life. Give me more time with the mother I met yesterday. It goes without saying I'll be in your debt."

"Debt!" Mark said. "People embrace it so easily."

"We've never been in debt," Steven said.

"We haven't," Mark agreed. "And we aren't in yours, Tereza. What you've achieved, well, we paid you, we gave you the tools. Like you said, we owe you a big, magnificent nothing. We want there to be no mistake."

"Of course not," Tereza said through clenched teeth.

"We are going to say yes," Mark said. "Because you are our friend. Because an inventor ought to benefit from her own enterprise. I believe it's not in violation of VITA's interests to let you save your mother."

"No violations here," Steven said, checking the length of his fingernails.

"Oh. Okay. Thanks," Tereza said and braced herself for the conditions of her bargain.

"Of course, this kind of favor dissolves our professional relationship," Mark said. "It makes us close. It makes us family. Right?" He turned to Steven.

"Yes, family is forever," Steven said.

"We're drafting two contracts," Mark said. "One is for you, a lifetime commitment to VITA. You will never be able to work elsewhere. That's a commitment fit for family."

Tereza closed her eyes as the men studied her closely. I knew she'd hoped that VITA was only a beginning, that someday she would start her own foundation, rid herself of the associations with VITA's backroom deals and ethical flexibility. She wanted to get away from all this money, the people and the commitments it brought. Still, could a lifetime contract ever be literal? Corporations rise and crash, their leaders fall out of favor and disappear in the sewage line of history. Once VITA began manufacturing cell-repair robots, uploading human minds to the cloud, an old-fashioned meat grinder like her would be of no further use. But even if it was for life, the contract was a sacrifice she was willing to make. For me.

"Second," Steven said, "your mother will, of course, have to sign the usual contract for experimental subjects. After the treatment, her cellular makeup will become the property of VITA. She will be subject to tests, follow-ups, she will have to live on VITA property in accordance with our corporate security measures. Are you clear on what that means?"

Tereza knew. Like Lydia, I could be taken away anytime. Once I signed myself over to the program, I would give up my human rights. I would become the proprietary material of VITA, much like the furniture decorating this office. I felt extraordinary guilt. All this negotiation, my daughter putting herself in the debt of these men, and for a woman already dead, though Tereza didn't know it yet.

"Do you have other conditions?" Tereza asked.

"You can bring her for orientation as soon as she's ready," Mark said.

The men stood up, each raising his right hand toward Tereza. She shook Mark's hand. He wouldn't let go. Steven grabbed her left hand, and the men pulled her into a close embrace.

"Today, we allow you to touch eternity," Mark whispered.

"You asked the gods for a favor," Steven said. "Now you live among them."

Tereza pulled back, freed her hands. There was still time to change her mind. She nodded, managed a half smile in place of gratitude, and ran out of the office and toward the elevator, heaving to stave off an impending panic attack. Back in her pod, she closed the shades and locked the door. She dialed my number on her hWisper.

There was no reply. She tried four more times before conceding that I couldn't be raised, likely submerged in a sleep I refused to interrupt for the glow of an old-fashioned smartphone, the kind of sleep unfamiliar to overachievers. My daughter stared at the wall, turned the TV on simply to hear the voices of other human beings. She was too considerate to wake me up early and tell me she'd used her multibillion-dollar secret and committed herself to serfdom to save me. Instead, she waited patiently for me to return her call.

Having come to this impasse—Tereza waiting for me to call back, my inability to speak from this afterlife—I observed my daughter as she watched a morning show, with some disgust. The hosts were introducing an editor from a brand-new publishing house promising to revolutionize the field of literature by creating custom books for each reader. Through a detailed app questionnaire, the publisher would amass data about the reader's preferences: favorite genre, questions of politics and identity, capacity for empathy, most beloved foods and musicians. The publisher's algorithm would then spin these preferences into the perfectly tailored story containing all of the reader's favorite things, quality-checked and *humanized* by a team of writers. The publisher promised a future in which a book would never offend its reader, never explore ideas that the reader found boring or difficult, turning reading into pure pleasure. VITA was one of the venture's main funders.

I couldn't watch. I wondered whether I could return to the crude network of pathways and icons living inside of Tereza's hWisper, and again I transferred into the device by a simple wish. Submerged in this digital summary of my daughter's life, I felt like I was really with her again, drinking wine on her apartment floor. Just talking. Talking... why hadn't I thought of it sooner? I rushed toward the Notepad icon located at the near end of the hWisper interface and found myself staring at a massive blank page looming over me like an alien monolith. The cursor blinked ominously as I focused on moving it, on wishing for letters to appear, to create a note in Tereza's phone. Reaching out from the afterlife through software. What would I say? *It is your mother, speaking from the land of the dead. Hello.* But nothing happened, nothing at all. The cursor continued to blink, and I decided it was a stupid idea. Even if it could work, it was too jarring, no way to announce one's own passing. Tereza would likely think some hacker was harassing her. Deflated, a bit frustrated by my daughter continuing to idle on the bed, I returned to her journals. Past the adult dilemmas of immortality and directly to her earlier entries on LiveJournal, beginning in 2001. My daughter's childhood, followed by her college years.

AFTER HER ADOPTIVE parents brought her from Denmark to her new home in America, Tereza grew up in Westchester County. She went on weekend hikes with her mother and took weekend trips to the city with her father to see plays and eat Reuben sandwiches. Her parents had enough money to provide her with the stability that was becoming increasingly rare in America but not enough money to teach her shortcuts when it came to conscience. They embraced the American sense of possibility but maintained a European sense of community, a debt toward one another, and they always insisted that when permitted by time and finances, a family meal around the table trumped fast food in front of a glowing television.

Things became more difficult, less safe, after Tereza turned fifteen. Her father passed away from a hereditary heart condition. A short while later, her mother was diagnosed with ovarian cancer, the early threats of which had led to her seeking out a child to adopt. She died a few days after Tereza received her acceptance letter from MIT.

Tereza began the long journey of her education only four months after her adoptive mother's death. On move-in day at her dorms, she watched the parents of classmates help carry their lamps, boxes, and oversize comforters to their rooms as she dragged her own things from the taxi, and she made a silent promise to her new peers: *I won't envy you. I'll become better than you.* Though she hoped to make friends, to create alliances with future colleagues, she couldn't help but feel bitter toward everyone around her not engulfed in backbreaking grief, the wide-eyed children from rich, complete families, eager to begin their lives. Of course, she shared some privilege with them — because of insurance payouts and an inheritance from her mother, Tereza wouldn't have to worry about money for the next decade of her life.

Despite the internal rift with her fellow pupils, Tereza made the effort to belong. During her first week at MIT, she decided to join the Longevity Club to discuss the pressing questions of mortality with like-minded people. She walked up to the reading room on the second floor of the Hayden Library, where the club was supposed to meet. What she found—a bag of potato chips spilled across the floor, showing the imprint of the shoe sole that had stomped them into a mash of crumbs; spilled cola spreading all over the conference table, seeping into pages ripped out of a textbook—seemed more like the aftermath of a music festival than an assembly of bio-nerds. A student was trying to clean it all up on her own, sopping up the spilled drink with toilet paper. She jumped when she saw Tereza watching her, nearly threw the soaked toilet paper at her.

Rita. She loomed over that room, that six-foot-two darling, her back hunched over, Tereza wrote in her journal. *Immediately I wanted to know what it would be like to stand on my toes and try to reach up to kiss her. She looked clean-cut, a blouse tucked into dress pants, but there was that big tattoo of a crow's skeleton on her neck. Fuck. I don't know why I didn't run out of that room. I'm so glad I didn't. "You gonna help or what?" she asked and tossed me that roll of toilet paper.*

In my daughter's own words, this is how she met the love of her youth.

It turned out that the club had been dissolved during its first meeting. The singularitarians, a group that included Rita, had gotten into a vicious fight with the meat grinders. To get rid of the body and upload the mind, the meat grinders had asserted, was the end of the human experience. To allows our brains to be scanned and uploaded into an e–stream of consciousness, our bodies destroyed in the process, would turn the act of living into a mere simulation, a reiteration of previous experiences remixed by code. There would be no such thing as making a true new memory via the senses, no true freedom or experience. What the singularitarians wanted to do to our species was monstrous.

As Tereza began to pick up the potato chips with toilet paper wrapped around her hand, she took deep breaths to keep her voice steady as she asked Rita what'd happened next. She was so happy to have this excuse to keep talking, ecstatic that Rita asked her to help. She was already growing nervous about what might happen when the room was cleaned up and she'd be out of reasons to stay.

It had all gone to hell, Rita continued. With the students' passions inflamed, the club's introductory session had turned into a free-for-all of grievances. The meat grinders had asserted that the pursuit of immortality out of the body was a vanity project taken seriously only by the gods and goddesses of privilege, who couldn't accept the idea of their money and power dissipating into nothingness in the face of disease and old age. Rita had argued that motivations were unimportant, because regardless of what started the movements and funded the research, be it selfishness and greed or altruistic virtue, the goal was the same. The science-fiction future would benefit the rich and poor alike. The world without the body was more equal.

Already people were yelling over each other when a sleeping beauty who was also a member of the Democratic Socialist Party knocked over a bottle of cola with his gesturing hands. What kind of an idiot talks about equality, he asked, if access to any of this technology was dependent on one's wealth? He insisted that any mode of longevity should be subsidized by the government, giving equal access to all. Until such a day arrived, we ought to put the dead into cryonic sleep, especially the workers, so they could wake up in a world of collective ownership where the advances in medicine and longevity would be provided to them at no cost. A cyborg scoffed at the idea of collective anything and argued for a subscription strategy, like Social Security—start paying in as a child, receive the God pill in retirement. This debate over cost led to an outburst of rage from the son of a Santander executive, who couldn't believe his colleagues expected companies to invest billions in longevity research and then hand their product to the poor and the needy for free. He slapped the Lay's bag out of the socialist's hand and stomped over it as he left the room, murmuring about the intrinsic fairness of markets. The socialist took out his economics textbook, tore out the pages on Keynesian theory, and slammed them down on the table. "This school is just a factory for neo-libs," he concluded as he left the room too. He was followed by the remaining members of the club except for Rita, who, as the president, was obliged to leave the room unsullied for the next group.

She and Tereza finished cleaning now and the dreaded moment of parting arrived. Tereza desperately sought the courage to ask Rita to lunch. Why did it seem so difficult? It was Rita's height, she thought; it was like hitting on a beautiful, wise Ent. Impossible to feel casual. But unlike the real Ents, Rita had no fear of being hasty. She told Tereza her schedule had suddenly cleared for the next ninety minutes. And a new sushi place had just opened up across from the campus.

As they slurped their miso soup from small ceramic bowls, Tereza got past that initial rush of "seeing a very hot person" and grew slightly more suspicious of Rita and their impromptu date. Rita was a singularitarian, and Tereza was a dedicated meat grinder. Had she been at the club's meeting, she would've been Rita's enemy. She would never want to live without her body, despite its flaws and indignities, all the times it had betrayed her in important moments, its mysterious aches. All the perceived deficiencies were worth it. The body wasn't a prison, it was life itself.

Perhaps Tereza thought this way because she was healthy. She understood that had her body been a great source of chronic pain or social scorn, she might feel more conflicted, might consider a world without bodies more egalitarian. Perhaps this viewpoint was ableist too? Nonetheless, she enjoyed the experience of living a life with the body as its facilitator. My daughter was no Luddite, she believed in technology and its place in the future of humans, but she doubted that a life simulated—as a line of code uploaded to a server farm—could possibly replicate the joys of living in the flesh, its chaos. The machine brain is the very opposite of chaos. It could only ever be a cheap imitation, a lie.

She did her best to avoid the discussion that ruined Rita's day, but they returned to it anyway when Tereza asked her new friend about her family. Rita was the daughter of an Exxon executive whom she saw only once a year for the holidays. She had been diagnosed with lupus when she was fifteen. Immediately, Tereza understood why Rita had chosen her specific philosophy of permanence. She lived with frequent flare-ups, pain that disrupted her studies, her life, a chronic illness that forced a brilliant, strong person to miss tests, skip classes, and limit her social life. She'd missed a whole semester of high school, bedridden with arthritis aches and infected kidneys. It was clear why Rita didn't trust the body and would've preferred a life outside of it.

"Let me guess," Rita said after Tereza revealed that her father had been a history professor and her mother a publisher of nonfiction. "You grew up with humanists. So you're definitely a meat grinder. A romantic."

"Does that mean we can't be friends?" Tereza said, encouraged by a few cups of sake.

"Oh, I plan to be a very special friend of yours," Rita said, needing no encouragement at all.

I read over these lines of my daughter's journal again and again. I wished I could've known her then, to receive Tereza's call after this first date, to hear the hope in her voice that could be sparked only by early stages of love.

Rita was living in an off-campus apartment paid for by her father, so she walked Tereza back to her dorm. They strolled across the campus lawns as the sun began to set and students rushed to their social gatherings, the most important part of their college lives. Tereza remarked that Rita still looked sad after the club's first-day fiasco—did she feel cheered up at all?

"What gets me fucked up," Rita said, "is that some of those people will be our future colleagues. It'll be up to us to make decisions about the future of humanity. But we can't stand to be in the same room with them for more than five minutes."

"It's a good thing," Tereza said. "We'll be solving the same problems from different perspectives. One of us is bound to win. And until you do upload yourself to the cloud...there are some benefits to be found in the flesh."

Rita smiled as my daughter quickly pecked a kiss on the side of her lips. My daughter turned away and strode toward the dorm entrance, trying her best not to faint as she fumbled in her pockets for the key card. She made it inside without looking back once, though she knew the whole time Rita was looking at her. Rita who was "absolute fucking magic." Rita who wanted to live inside the computer.

DURING THE FOLLOWING months, Tereza slept in Rita's apartment on most nights. Rita burned like a furnace, and with freezing hands and feet Tereza clung to her all night, absorbing the heat. Some mornings she woke up thinking that such nights might not be possible in a transhumanist future, where bodies were discarded, where the whistle of teakettles and the scent of morning skin—saliva and sweat and lotion and soap—would become artificial pieces of code freewheeling in virtual nothingness. She slept next to a person who believed that such reenactment was just as valuable, worthwhile, that one's virtual self could love as easily and fully as its biological counterpart. On some nights, Tereza imagined she would really have to make the impossible choice, decades in the future, to remain in her body and leave Rita or join her in the world of singularity.

They didn't speak of such things at home. When together, Tereza and Rita spoke of biochemistry tests, where they might travel during the next summer break. Following the election of Obama, both of them believed that America was on a course toward a massive public investment in health care and science, ushering in the era of disease-free longevity for all, including, perhaps, the cure for Rita's lupus (and thus, Tereza hoped, a cure for her singularitarian philosophy). There seemed no reason to lose optimism, as the prophets of the early twenty-first century suggested we were on a steady path toward a perfect society. Through the spread of American capitalism and democracy, the world would become fair and balanced and prosperous. What could go wrong?

According to Tereza, these four years were the most hopeful time she'd ever known. Her life with Rita soothed some of the grief over the loss of her parents, their weekend adventures provided respite from all-nighters at the library and brutal exams most students were meant to fail. But as is usually the case, her hope wasn't meant to last. The lovers had planned to attend graduate school in London, but while Rita was accepted into Imperial College's biomedical-engineering program, Tereza didn't have the benefit of a powerful father and didn't make the cut. She was left with her second choice, Aachen University in Germany. The two of them had the rational talk, the adult talk, that it was foolish to attempt a long-distance relationship at their age. It was better to remain great friends than to become embittered, to inevitably betray each other in a year or two.

But their rational fatalism soon turned to anger and accusations to make the end easier. Rita complained that Tereza didn't respect how much pain she suffered during her brutal lupus flare-ups, the effort it took her just to get out of bed. A person as healthy as Tereza could never understand. For her part, Tereza lied about feeling smothered. (On occasion, she did feel suddenly annoyed with everything Rita did, and even her face, her lips, her eyes, her voice all became murderously irksome, but these moments passed quickly, as if Tereza had been briefly possessed by a demon.) They parted after an explosive fight that lasted for a week and moved to their respective new cities across the ocean.

The parting didn't last. They kept in touch, exchanged long e-mails about their new European surroundings. Tereza told stories of Berat, the professor in charge of her lab. Every day he injected himself with a cocktail of hormones designed to rejuvenate the heart and lungs. He'd been undergoing this self-inflicted therapy for two years, and his impressive vital signs and lab values spoke for themselves. His testosterone levels were extraordinarily high for a man his age, he maintained low blood pressure and cholesterol, his eyesight had improved, his irritable bowel disease and insomnia had been eradicated. Small cuts and bruises healed with unusual speed; his blood tests showed accelerated regeneration of the liver. The sedentary, aging academic with a drinking problem became a climber of mountains, a runner of marathons, a powerlifting competitor. He was a walking caffeine pill; he didn't enter rooms, he burst into them. His thirst for life was both obnoxious and infectious. Tereza saw Berat as a sign, a reaffirmation of her mission to bring this kind of rejuvenation to as many people as she could. They became great friends — Tereza even tutored Berat's daughter, Greta, an aspiring cryonicist.

Unfortunately, Berat also became a warning. Eager to heal the tibia he'd fractured during a climb, he decided to increase the dose of his own serum. He was found in his apartment by Greta after he hadn't shown up for work. His heart had ruptured, exploded inside his chest, leaving him dead on his bathroom floor. The grief over Berat's passing moved Tereza to call Rita again. She confessed she couldn't live without her. She admitted that nothing made sense since their parting.

"I've been waiting for you, stupid," Rita replied.

For the next three years, Tereza and Rita took turns visiting each other every two weeks. They went to dinners in London and Cologne and helped decorate each other's flats. Some weekends they spent in bed and nowhere else. The idea of a shared future was unspoken but acknowledged by the effort they made despite the distance. Tereza was excited by the prospect of everyday life with Rita, the shared sweet potato waffles and unreasonable amounts of black tea. It all seemed simple, like happiness was just a matter of routine, like everyone could feel this way if only they committed to it. Unlike in their undergraduate years, they weren't counting on getting research positions in the same city after graduate school. They knew life might split them apart again in the name of their promising careers, but they were going to push through it. Tereza and Rita were the heralds of permanence, and their first successful invention of *forever* would be their relationship.

The announcement of Rita's death came to Tereza from her parents in the form of a brusque e-mail they composed during their flight to London. As Tereza packed up her graduate dorm to spend the summer break in London, Rita traveled to Cumbria for a weekend of hiking with mutual friends. The hike turned into a two-day party in the mountains, lasting well into the working hours of Monday morning. Running on fumes, Rita decided to drive from the camp near Helvellyn to the village of Grasmere to sleep off the remnants of tequila in a hotel bed before returning home to prepare for Tereza's arrival. As she approached the village, she swerved her car off the road and into a small lake. The authorities didn't know the reason for her accident — perhaps a stray dog on the road had caused her exhausted mind to panic and turn the wheel too quickly. The lake was really a miniature pond, barely deep enough to submerge the vehicle. Rita hit her head on the steering wheel and remained unconscious as water filled the car. She drowned before a villager spotted her and called the authorities.

Tereza visited Grasmere two weeks after Rita's funeral. She stripped off her clothes and entered the lake on the village outskirts, the lake that had murdered her lover. The water came up to her shoulders. If Rita had been able to stand up, if she could've lifted her head a few inches, the accident would've been nothing but a notable life lesson. Tereza shivered in the lake as a family walking their dog called out from the shore. Was it this family's dog that had caused the accident? All Rita had needed to survive was four inches of space above her head. She could breathe, await the rescuers, her rich father would buy her another car.

Tereza went limp as she felt a villager's hands on her. A woman was dragging her onto land as her husband and their son and dog watched. The family put a jacket around her shoulders. Where were these saviors as Rita suffocated in their stupid village? They rubbed the blanket around my daughter's arms and tried to put her clothes back on. She lay on the grass. If her mind was merely a line of code traveling the circuits of a server farm, all could be erased. Grief would be incomprehensible, an ancient language with no Rosetta stone to crack it. Unnecessary. So many things would become unnecessary.

Tereza regained consciousness at the county hospital. The police wanted to interview her to determine whether she was a danger to herself. If life was a line of code traveling the memory of a server farm, she told them, pain wouldn't matter. Wasn't that the true goal? A world wholly internalized, confined to artificial consciousness and information? For centuries we had built a civilization in which the body was worshipped, the body was enslaved, the body was privatized, everything was focused on the body, nutrition and health and the cultural movements and luxuries of the modern era all tailored to shelter the body, a devastated environment to satiate the body, but the endgame was not the body, the endgame was the eradication of the body, a reset button, and by the time Tereza explained all this to the policemen, they knew they'd have to hold her for observation, just to be sure...

I COULDN'T TAKE IT. I closed out of the journal entries and ejected myself from the hWisper, returned to my daughter's pod bedroom. So much suffering for her to handle on her own, with no one to lean on. All this time I was just across the ocean, her mother, stalking her online persona, too scared to reach out. All the possibilities of what I could've been to her... wasted. It was too much.

After Rita's death, the work had become the only thing that mattered to Tereza. She had finished graduate school, accepted a position at the German Longevity Institute in Berlin. She frequented burlesque bars and bordellos until the saviors from VITA appeared and took advantage of her confused moral compass, the fact that she had ceased to care about anything but her personal war against death. If I had been in her life, perhaps... but no. I had no right to think this way.

As if she felt my frustration, Tereza huffed and looked at the clock. Ten a.m. She couldn't wait anymore. "Do Czech people sleep through their mornings?" she whispered under her breath as she got up. She needed me to know I was saved, right away. She ran into the shower, sniffed at the various clothing collected under her bed to find a shirt, and ordered her hWisper to find the shortest route to my hotel.

I felt overwhelmed with panic, a strange sensation without a body—no increased heartbeat, no stomachache, only a pure state of anxiety without physical symptoms. I decided I couldn't watch my daughter's manic preparations, her joy at the news she thought she was about to deliver. I recoiled, I tried as hard as I could to disappear, to pass into another world, to trigger the next step in my afterlife. I shouldn't be forced to watch all this! Death was supposed to bring peace.

I didn't want to return to Tereza's hWisper, as I didn't need to further explore the record of her devastating losses. A new sensation emerged, an offer, a possibility. The sound of a car engine straining through the Dinaric Alps, the crashing of waves against the shores of Florida... I allowed myself to travel in time. To turn away from my daughter reacting to the news of my death. To never know what my child's face looked like when she learned I'd left her again, this time for good. Suddenly, my afterlife offered a return to the adventures of my youth, the safe embrace of nostalgia. Perhaps it was finally happening. I was passing through the gates leading to eternity, and in this new world I was to relive the most exciting moments of my life over and over. I submitted to this pull, feeling bliss for the first time since my death.

In a moment like this, who could refuse?

THE YEAR IS 1982

A T FIRST, I didn't take the prospect of immigrating to the United States seriously. It seemed unlikely that the Czechoslovakian government would allow a known dissident to leave. But having a new aspiration felt better than drinking to pass time, planning my days around trips to the *večerka* for more liquor. Following Jirka's instructions, I filed for permission to travel to Yugoslavia, claiming that the Adriatic salt water was necessary to alleviate my allergies. I obtained the required letter of commitment from the bank to exchange my crowns for dinars. The supervisor from my cleaning job vouched for my good standing at work (being a drunk himself, he paid no mind to my occasional stumbling and the vodka in my thermos). The bureaucrats verified that I had no unpaid debt to the state.

I cared little about these successes, as I knew that the final step, a review of my criminal history, would disqualify me for the trip. My name appearing on the roster of dissidents would put an end to the insane endeavor of emigration. I expected the cops might even pick me up again, just to see what I'd been up to. But my record came back clean. My arrest was not on file, and I remembered that I had not been asked to sign anything on my release from my brief hours in the prison cell. Perhaps there was no record. Or perhaps it was stashed in some confidential dossier the secret police kept for future leverage. Or maybe the bureaucrats and the shadow cops simply didn't mind me going, good riddance to the enemy of the proletariat. An amicable breakup between tyrant and captive.

Whatever the reason, I received my dinars and my permission to travel within six months, against all odds. Jirka had to go through the same approval process, but his basketball games with party functionaries granted him nearly unlimited favors. Many of the functionaries used his smuggling skills for their own side businesses.

With our path cleared, I gained a new sense of hope. I felt like I wanted to take up more space in the world. Take it all for myself, as others did. The dollar was strong and the West was decadent and I wanted in on it. I was no longer a village girl looking for an acting career or a fair world for all. I wanted to become the consumerist piggy my good neighbors warned me about, live in the Yankee luxury that was unrivaled in history.

I traveled to Hluboká for a weekend to say goodbye to my parents. I spent Saturday with them as if nothing were amiss, an attempt to enjoy their company without conflict and sorrow, and announced the news of my pending adventure on Sunday morning. I convinced them that I'd obtained permission to fly to America directly; they had no idea I was facing the risks of the smuggling routes. In response, my father put on his rubber boots and went outside to complain about me to the chickens, his favorite confidants. They'd already heard many tales of the daughter who'd broken her father's heart. As she was inclined to do in such situations, Babi produced a hidden treasure, the golden-beetle necklace that used to belong to my great-grandmother. It would bring me luck in America; Babi emphasized that it was also made of pure gold, and I could sell it in case of an emergency. Without meaning to, I promised my mother I would come back in six months, and we both wept through the lie as we held each other and waited for Jirka to pick me up.

This was my first trip outside the country, but I wasn't meant to see any of Yugoslavia's famous beaches. Jirka drove me straight through Slovakia and Hungary, each checkpoint along the way manned by police officers who scrutinized our documents and searched the car, eager to send us back for the smallest reason. Later that afternoon we reached an auto garage in a small Slovenian mountain village, our parting scene.

Jirka introduced me to my new handler, a quiet young man with odd patches of hair growing underneath his nose. Then he kissed me goodbye. "Don't be humble," he advised. "American men like to offer things. Take whatever they'll give but never let them make you feel like you owe them."

"We are born alone," I said, parroting Ondráš's farewell words. Jirka rolled his window up and set out on his return journey.

I crawled into the trunk of a champagne-colored Žigulík where I was to remain as my Yugoslavian contact drove me through the Dinaric Alps to Italy. I drank my allotted two bottles of water right away. It was unusually warm for August and the heat in the trunk was so unbearable I believed I'd suffocate, but I didn't make a sound. That night, after we'd crossed the Italian border, the smuggler released me from my prison to sleep under the open sky inside a cheap sleeping bag.

I forced myself to keep my eyes open, having not an ounce of trust for my guide. He had been paid already, and whatever happened to me on our travels wasn't likely to have consequences for him. But the intensity of his snores turned into a lullaby, and I too passed out. Eventually I awoke to the smell of coffee and eggs he'd cooked on a camping stove. The smuggler exchanged the tags on his vehicle, and we continued on to Milan, where the man provided an envelope of fake documents for Western travel and wished me luck in broken Czech.

I washed up and changed out of my sweat-soaked clothes in the airport bathroom. I flew to London, then from London to New York, and from New York to Florida. Whenever I took my seat on a plane, I passed out immediately as the passengers watched me, whispered about me, about the painful beet-red sunburn on my face, the armpit sweat inked into my clothes. I looked like a feral animal. I didn't give a shit. These Westerners, upset over the lack of ginger ale on the flight, knew nothing.

At last I touched down at Tampa International Airport. I took a taxi to Hotel Goliath, a pale, ugly skyscraper erected in the midst of white sand on the beaches of South Sarasota. Every building on the coast as far as I could see looked the same. The shimmering waters of the Gulf of Mexico met the bright sun that turned the sky aflame, a shock to the retinas.

Florida seemed to hate color. The sun washed the hue out of every surface and turned it into a dull pastel as if eliminating its own competition: *Only I am deemed worthy to shine. The rest of the world can look like a garment washed a few too many times.* The humans living under the sun's reign weren't allowed to exist with their eyes fully open. They squinted or hid behind sunglasses, a permanent state of flawed vision that defined the Sunshine State. I rolled my suitcase to the hotel's employee entrance, located right next to numerous dumpsters. In an office that doubled as an overflow pantry for canned tomatoes, I met Leszek, the Polish man who ran the operation. He had no scruples about describing what went on at the hotel. He brought in Eastern Europeans on tourist and asylum visas and employed us illegally as cleaners and kitchen staff. This ensured massive savings on taxes and labor costs while helping the refugees keep a low profile. Leszek explained with a laugh that American immigration wasn't too concerned with hunting "white illegals." We were tolerated.

He was a man in dire need of an ass-kicking, but I couldn't be the one to do it. I had entered the country on a fake passport and family visa, pretending to be Adina Kowalczyk, Leszek's visiting sister. Czech, Pole, Hungarian—to the Border Patrol it made little difference. We were from *over there,* the places frozen in time by the Cold War. I considered Leszek's scheme to be morally acceptable. I was to clean hotel rooms and in exchange I'd get cash under the table every two weeks. I'd receive no benefits for my labor, had no safety net, and thus I felt no guilt about not paying taxes. There seemed to be no victims in this little scam of ours.

During the first week of my new life, I asked my favorite coworker and roommate, Ljuba, to take a photo of me standing on the hotel balcony during sunset. I leaned back with my elbows on the railing and bent my knee, a pose I'd seen on the covers of magazines. When I received my first wages, I had the disposable camera developed at a drugstore, and I sent the photo to my mother as proof of success. I was going to do well here. I just knew it.

TWO YEARS BEFORE my arrival, Ronald Reagan had been elected president of the United States. As I learned from the old newspapers I read to practice my English, Reagan's presidency was the *end of the country's Carter malaise*. In Carter's America, people used to wait in line for gasoline, and back then our Czechoslovakian state media gleefully mocked the imperialist leader's impotence. Now, I learned, Reagan was guiding the country into a new age of economic utopia, mostly by borrowing money. This seemed like a great idea—could I also become a millionaire simply by borrowing a million dollars? I developed no opinion of the new president based on his promises. I wouldn't allow the newspapers to tug at my old political inclinations. The Americans could vote as they wanted. I was here for money, not civics.

On my first day of cleaning, I found a pair of shit-stained underwear placed on the dining table next to crushed potato chips and a pair of muddy shoes. I was startled by the rudeness of this filth, the fact that a human being would unabashedly leave such a mess for others to pick up, a confirmation that I was in a new culture. With plastic gloves I stripped the bedsheets stained with liquids and replaced them with fresh bleached linens that seemed too clean for any guest to deserve. I peeled used condoms off the side of the toilet bowl, flushed excrement and bloody tampons and puke, and scrubbed the toilets with my trusty brush. Dirty work, but it wasn't hard to find a rhythm.

At night, I would return to the low-income housing two miles from the hotel. Leszek rented a two-bedroom apartment that I shared with five other cleaners. The place was a shithole, with its leaking air conditioner, the brown carpet that smelled like wet underwear, the roaches the size of mice flying about like helicopters with failed rotors, knocking into us as we chased them. Yet we made it into a home. I walked from work along the road as strange men catcalled from their cars. Once, a truck pulled up and two men were about to drag me inside, but an old couple and their two mastiffs stopped to help. The couple seemed angry when I said I didn't want to go to the police. Instead I began to carry a pocketknife. I hadn't come to America to be raped or killed.

AFTER MY FIRST two months on the job, I felt I'd saved enough to reward myself with a bicycle. This added expediency to my days, and in expediency I found freedom. I worked morning shifts and returned home at four o'clock. As Ljuba and I had taken a liking to each other from the beginning, we shared a bedroom, each of us decorating a wall with photos of family and our villages, like students in a dorm. Another couple of friends took the second bedroom, while our youngest roommates slept in the living room. Ljuba and I rested together in the late afternoons, told each other stories and blew smoke out of the window covered with a filthy, torn mesh screen, caught the spiders and roaches trying to get inside with our fingers and squashed them.

After our afternoon snoozers, Ljuba and I would go to the beach. At night, it was no longer pale and dull. The lights of the hotels shone like torches and reflected on the sand, a golden sea; fires burned, music played, the ocean was dangerous and intoxicating as it rolled back and forth in the moonlight. I was wary of the ocean — I'd never seen anything so infinite and unknowable.

Ljuba charmed the rich men who walked around the beach hiding their bellies in white linen shirts unbuttoned at the top. She got them to buy us drinks and give us cigarettes and cocaine. Those nights I could shed the humiliations I suffered during the day, I stopped feeling like my hands were permanently soiled. I paid minimal attention to the men, who spoke of Reagan and the ways in which he would help their business interests. To avoid discourse, I claimed to speak no English. After all, I wasn't here for conversation, for flirtation. I didn't want to make friends. I was here to numb myself before the next day's shift.

Though I had decided to become apolitical, it frightened me that the freedom of capital could turn people into soft-bellied fools. They believed their fortunes were a result of the special work only they could do, that they existed in a more exceptional way than others. Their money was role-play, divorced completely from the reality of labor, of raw resources, production. As I continued to learn during these parties, most of the wealthy men didn't make anything. They had taken the money of their fathers and invested it and made even more. And when "more" didn't satisfy their needs, they used their money as collateral to borrow even more money, so much money that they owed more than they'd actually had to begin with. These lives of luxury, all based on fictions. The difference between rich and poor was made up of chance and a thousand lies. I couldn't quite decide if I wanted to become one of them or poison their drinks and send them all to hell.

Every two weeks, I received letters from my parents. The envelopes were cut open and stamped to confirm they had been inspected by the Czechoslovakian government. My parents wrote of the harvests, the dogs, the preparations for winter. I felt homesick only when I read the letters; there was no time for it otherwise.

The letters I wrote to my parents were always about my activities, never about my feelings. I didn't have the heart to tell them I'd lost my idealism, that I was no longer concerned about Marxist revolutions and the fate of the world; I was barely concerned for my own future. I mistook indifference for independence. I realize now that I was asleep, relaxed and numb. I planned to stay in the shithole apartment until I had too much money to keep safely in cash. No need to make plans until then. Laissez-faire. Let the future come to you. Would I return home, stay in Florida, or take off to another place, Canada or Argentina? Having no plan made me feel like anything was possible. I couldn't share these thoughts with concerned parents across the ocean.

NEARLY A YEAR into my American life, on a day off, I took a morning stroll along the beach. The beginning of June had brought severe tropical storms that turned the fine sand into cake batter, keeping the beaches empty. I'd pulled a poncho over my tank top and shorts, but the plastic steamed my skin and I had to rip it off to scoop the sweat from my armpits. The rain thickened and a strand of lightning vanished in the sea. I had been working more shifts to keep up with the height of tourist season, and these moments of free time were precious. At night I dreamed of nothing but work. I was grateful for this small break, as the cool rainwater washed the sweat from my skin.

I thought I might be the only one out in the storm until I spotted a silhouette of some hunchback, a man hiding underneath a see-through poncho. He held a film camera, turning the lever as he pointed it at the unsettled waves and lightning. I observed him for a while until he looked in my direction and took a few steps back. He put the camera in his bag as if I might rush to rob him.

"Scared me," I heard through the noise of the rain.

"Sorry!" I shouted.

"Just getting some bee footage," he said.

"There are no bees on this beach," I said, confused.

"No, it's . . . for background. I'm making a movie."

"Okay. Good luck." Suddenly the man who was taking footage of the stormy beach didn't seem mysterious or fascinating anymore. I turned to leave.

"What are you doing here?" he asked.

"Walking," I said.

"What for?"

"Just walking. You don't just walk?"

"I like your necklace," the man said and introduced himself as Michael.

I don't know what made me invite him to have coffee in the hotel bar, especially after such a boring line. (*I like your necklace? Really?*) I wasn't interested in him at first, though it helped that he was attractive—no one can tell me this doesn't make a difference. It seemed mad to go to the beach and stand by the water just to film something as ordinary as a storm. Maybe it was his madness I liked. Maybe my weakness for dissident artists had traveled with me to America, though this boy was no dissident and the scope of his artistry was yet to be seen. Either way, by the time we were dry, Michael had written down the number for the landline in my apartment. When he called the same night, he first had to speak to three of my roommates, who mocked him in their respective languages. If he withstood their torture, he'd be allowed to speak with me. "Ring of fire," they told him. "You have to *earn it,* Florida man."

But Michael wasn't the only man I was talking to. After a year of silence, I received a letter from Jirka. It had been sent from West Germany, and thus it hadn't gone through the hands of Czech government censors. Jirka told me he couldn't stop thinking about me, that he wanted to maintain our friendship across the ocean. Would I be willing to exchange letters, to keep him informed of my adventures in America? Happy to hear from him, I replied with a letter twice as long, detailing all of my exploits so far. I sent him postcards from the places I frequented: Siesta Key, Saint Armands, Anna Maria Island. *Greetings from Manatee County!* the card beckoned, and I adorned it with a drawing of a manatee holding a sickle in one flipper, a hammer in the other, a personal touch I thought Jirka might appreciate. It became a correspondence we maintained for the rest of my time in America.

ON SLEEPLESS NIGHTS, Ljuba and I often discussed people's immediate assumptions about the two of us. Some imagined we came from hamlets without electricity, where donkeys carried wheat from house to house and women in traditional skirts baked bread for the men who worked in the fields. At night, we entertained ourselves by candlelight with homemade violins and danced the Cossack and whittled figurines for our pagan gods. "Wonderful," people would exclaim when they found out we'd come from behind the Iron Curtain to America, as if it meant we had traded primitive tyranny for enlightened liberty. I felt that with their assured exclamation of *Wonderful!*, the assumption that by reaching America, we'd found the sweet life of unbearable lightness, they were taking ownership of us. The men in white suits felt like they'd directly contributed to our salvation.

This gave them a great sense of entitlement. *Wonderful!* They behaved as if I owed them thanks, as if by merely paying their taxes, they had saved my life. Some felt entitled to more. They asked me to marry them in a drunken slur, tried to follow me into hotel rooms as I worked. They were shocked, even outraged by my lack of compliance when I ignored them or cursed at them in Czech or picked ice out of my glass and threw it at them. On a particularly troublesome night, the heir to a ketchup fortune dialed the INS tip line right in front of me and reported the hotel as a harbor for illegal immigrants. Ljuba and I decided it was no longer safe to attend the parties of the rich.

A few days later, I agreed to have dinner with Michael. I had made him wait a full three weeks after he'd asked me out during our first phone call, but he didn't seem to mind at all. During our early dates, he asked about my homeland, its history, the first American man to do so. He understood I could be attracted to the allure of his country and yet remain suspicious, a harsh critic of my new home. Any country should appreciate its immigrants as objective observers—the immigrant views a country without the hue of nostalgia, the childhood indoctrination that establishes that our country must be good because it produced us, and we are good. But the criticism of governance, of systems, of cultural values is a necessary catalyst for progress, not a personal insult. A few times I grew frustrated at trying to express complicated ideas in my very flawed English, but Michael never interrupted me, never corrected me, never tried to fill in the words. Today I view this as basic decency, but back then, it seemed miraculous enough to make me want to see him again.

I didn't realize how lonely I had been until I began to spend my nights at his apartment. Until his hands caressed my hip bones and we slept entangled despite the stifling heat. Being with another person wasn't unlike being in one's own invented country. We made up our own language and our own customs and names and local foods, and these secrets served as accelerants for romantic free fall. Always I fell for the dreamers, except this one felt *safe*. He told me he loved me one month after our first date, and I waited to say it back. Waited four months to see if my hesitance might discourage him, wound his ego, make him angry. But he stayed, he waited, without pressure, until I could no longer deny myself.

In simple terms, I fell in love despite my best efforts. The cash I'd hidden in the hair-coloring box and under my mattress no longer felt like an end in itself. I allowed myself brief visions of the future, possibilities that went beyond the numb hustle. I saw fragments of the woman sipping champagne with other dissidents in the Playwright's house, the woman I'd been before my arrest and Ondráš's betrayal. I was doomed. These small reminders of who I used to be felt an awful lot like hope, and for such a crime, the punishment could be severe.

INDEED, PUNISHMENT WAS imminent. On a Monday morning in February, INS agents acting on the old tip from the ketchup magnate arrived at Hotel Goliath in full tactical gear, semiautomatic weapons in hand. They rounded up the managers along with Leszek, Ljuba, and six other coworkers from housekeeping and the kitchens, then they zip-tied their wrists and placed them in a van and drove them out of my life.

I received the news from Alenka, another roommate of mine who had watched the whole scene from the parking lot because she'd arrived late for her shift. She and I were the last survivors in the apartment, picked by fortune simply because our work schedule had misaligned with the raid. We packed immediately, wished each other luck, and left the apartment as it was, filled with the other women's belongings. Despite the panic of being hunted, expecting the agents would snatch me from the parking lot before I could escape, I felt sorrow at leaving the only refuge I had.

Michael picked me up in his red Buick and took me to his apartment. I locked myself in the bathroom and wept for Ljuba, who would be held in jail along with the others for an undetermined amount of time before deportation. Leszek had described the options to us during orientation. In case of capture, we could plead for amnesty, thanks to the policies of the Reagan administration. We should speak of the danger awaiting us in our authoritarian home countries; we should bad-mouth the Russians, insult the Soviet Union, flatter the American sensibility, anything to provoke the smallest bit of compassion. I knew this wasn't going to work. Every successful INS raid was heavily publicized, and the story of undocumented Eastern Europeans moving around America during the second wave of the Cold War could only end in mass deportation.

As I tried to shake off my despair, I came out into Michael's living room, furnished only with a couch and a television and unruly piles of VHS tapes. He sat on his couch and fiddled with a small black box. I swallowed. My throat and eyes and ears burned. The skin underneath my eyes itched. I tried to tell myself it was all bound to happen, that I'd known from the beginning this was temporary, and it wasn't for nothing that I had saved up three thousand dollars, the result of my awful diet of bananas and tuna fish, of riding my bicycle instead of paying for the bus, of letting others pay for my alcohol and cigarettes. This money meant independence. In a way, I had fulfilled my mission.

Here was Michael, a waiter at the Ritz by day but a filmmaker by heart, running around town, filming storms crashing in the midst of the sea. I tried to gauge how easy it would be to leave him behind should I decide it was time to go home. I feared it would not be as easy as I'd hoped, even though it was only eight months ago that he'd been a complete stranger. The bastardy of love.

"Did I ever tell you I met Reagan?" Michael said, eyes still on the box.

"The president?"

"Well, we didn't really meet, but I *saw* him," Michael said. He had seen Reagan when he was still known as an actor and a governor at a dinner benefit organized by movie studios. Michael had been working catering gigs to rent equipment for his graduate thesis, the kind of routine Scorsese rip-off most men wrote in film school. In the middle of the event, Reagan stood up and walked to the bathroom, and he touched Michael on the shoulder as he passed. Their eyes met, Reagan flashed his famous smile, all teeth, as he swaggered by like some cowboy diplomat, and this brief contact reminded Michael of his deceased father. Michael understood immediately that Ronald Reagan had a message for him, only for him: *Hear you're a good kid and you want to be in the movies. Push for it. No one is coming to save you. Don't count on others to offer a hand. Make your way. I'll see you at the top. Son.*

I didn't ask Michael whether he'd considered the possibility that Reagan had touched him by accident and meant to say nothing at all except *Let me lean on you, waiter, as I make my way to the shitter.* This is the difference between the New World and the Old.

"Whatever you think of him, Reagan made it far with that philosophy," Michael said. "America is for the bold." He paused, as if realizing how he must sound to me. "I know you want to go home. You must feel unsafe here, exposed in ways I can't comprehend."

I didn't pay much attention to him as he spoke. I feared I already knew where the speech was headed, and I felt the need to keep an eye on the front door, expecting any minute that the *Mayflower* police would burst through and take me to a shared cell with Ljuba.

"I love you, Adéla," he said and quickly added, "I want us to be practical. I would've waited much longer to ask, since I don't even know if you want this. But if we go to city hall tomorrow, we can apply for your green card and take it from there."

He opened the box. I had never been particularly fond of diamonds, and thus the small jewel set in an old silver ring—a family heirloom—didn't make much of an impression. But the words did, despite the fact that due to my illegal entry into the country using someone else's identity, legal marriage wasn't possible for me. Michael didn't know this yet. But the sentiment felt good on the day I'd lost the few certainties I had in America.

"You want to marry me and wipe my sins clean," I said.

Michael flinched but I didn't have the energy to apologize. His timing seemed at once opportunistic and kind. I explained that I had entered the country using a fake identity—though he knew me by my real name, Adéla, the name on my passport was Adina, I said. We couldn't even file paperwork to get married at city hall without the authorities catching on. It wasn't that my answer was no, rather that our marriage could only ever be unofficial, between us, an agreement underscored by ceremony. Why do it at all?

Michael took this news in. "Okay," he said, his eyes bright with a new idea. "Then let's make it simple." He held the ring box toward me and swore he would do anything to keep the INS agents away. He would support me if I couldn't find another job that paid under the table, hire a lawyer to see if there was a way to alter my status. If the worst happened and I was deported, he would come with me. I wouldn't have to feel alone ever again. We were going to build our own private empire, and we didn't need official papers to do it.

I didn't answer the roundabout proposal in words. I never said yes. I straddled him and kissed him and with that I decided, on a whim, to stay in America indefinitely. It wasn't a leap of faith but a plea to fate: *Please don't chew me up too badly when this backfires.* Michael offered me a way to anchor myself, to replace the friends I'd lost to deportation proceedings in a single day, to provide the sense of family I missed.

After the proposal, he took me to Red Lobster to celebrate, and I gnawed on dry biscuits and tried my best not to retch at the heinous smell of crab Alfredo permeating the restaurant while I thought of the sweet scents of a Hluboká pub, the spilled beer and pickled wurst and the endless fog of cigarette smoke. I decided it was time to exorcise my attachment to these memories of home. I'd come too far to trap myself in homesickness, to suddenly idolize the country I had been so eager to leave not long ago. With a single gesture, Michael had opened a new future for us. Now it was time for me to take the lead.

THE YEAR IS 2030

AWAY WITH YOU, frivolous memory! I rushed to return from my private limbo, burdened by the guilt of having left Tereza behind. How much time had I lost? I came back just as she was leaving her pod to head to my hotel. As she opened her door, she ran into a messenger dressed in a devil's costume, a red satin jumpsuit complete with horns and a tail. He held out a stack of papers: Tereza's new lifelong contract and the admission forms for my telomere treatment.

It was an absurd and sinister flourish from Steven & Mark. Normally, Tereza would seal her new commitment with a biometric signature, as hand-signing of carbon documents had gone out of fashion. Yet VITA had sent their own private devil to let Tereza know what was expected of her. She had now become part of the inner family, and ever greater moral flexibility would be required. Her obligation and loyalty were to VITA only.

"I haven't owned a pen in years," Tereza said to the messenger.

He offered a golden pen engraved with the VITA logo.

Tereza signed the contract without hesitation—why pretend she might change her mind?—and retained the admission forms for my review. Then she ran to the elevators. Coworkers bade her good morning. She seemed to have a hard time remembering their names.

She rushed out of the lobby and into the cool, crisp New York day. She squinted at the sudden sunshine following a rain shower. New Yorkers surrounded her, their eyes sunk deeply in their skulls, in the sleepless hustle of their lives, stepping hungrily into the streets to run any errand that would give them a reason to be outside after the long winter. The elderly pushed carts from grocery stores, the young carried bags bursting with fast fashion, parents reminded their children, many born in quarantine, that a vast world existed outside the confines of their apartments. Tereza had told me she forgot sometimes how comfortable and natural human contact was, that most people moved in public spaces every day and were used to these crowds, whereas she had exiled herself to her workplace, a privilege and a curse, something in between. Now that she had a family again, the possibilities of her life had expanded, seemingly without limit.

She took a cab to my hotel. In the lobby, she smiled manically at the receptionist, red-eyed and slumped in a chair behind the front desk. He reeked of gin. Tereza inquired about a Ms. Slavíková, staying in room 306. We had reasons to celebrate.

"Three oh six," the receptionist recited, his bloated eyes glistening. He laughed and took a sip from his coffee cup. "I'm sorry, it's not funny. It's just that this isn't even my real job. I'm a podcaster. I'm not supposed to be involved—"

"I'm sorry," Tereza said, "I don't know what you're talking about. I just want to see my mother."

"There was an incident," the man said. "The lady from three oh six, she…but maybe it's not your mother. Maybe it's a mix-up, the wrong room number."

"Incident," Tereza said.

"She died in the night," the man said. "Natural causes. The Reclamation police came, and some dudes in rubber suits, and they wheeled in a big box, like a coffin with computers attached to it. They took her. I knew she was an illegal, I knew it, foreigners come to this country to die just to take advantage of our free cremation services."

Tereza winced at the mention of men in rubber suits. A coffin with computers.

Why couldn't I remember what they'd done to my body?

Tereza turned away from the desk, walked to the emergency stairwell, and ran up to the third floor. She studied the door to room 306. It was closed and locked, a piece of police tape stretched across the frame. Tereza knocked. No answer. She knocked again. She beat on the door, kicked, until people from the neighboring rooms came out to stare at her. My daughter searched their faces. None of them were me.

She ran out of the hotel, onto the street, and wandered without direction. Was life anything but a series of losses? One big grief parade?

"Mom," she said to no one.

"Fuck off," said the man attempting to pass her on the sidewalk.

She looked to him for explanation. The man hastened his pace.

Tereza stood in the middle of the sidewalk, forcing the current of pedestrians to divide around her, like a boulder in a stream. She heard the whirring of a machine above her head and looked up to see the glimmer of a drone. In the street the roar of an engine announced a white Humvee with a water cannon, tearing along as taxis pulled out of the way. The Homeland Deportation Force had proudly named these vehicles "dogcatchers." During the first wave of deportations, the vehicles had dominated the evening news as they rammed into crowds of people trying to protect their neighbors from the HDF, as the water cannons indiscriminately drenched passersby with scorching water between salvos of tear gas. In those days, the New York skyline had been infected with hundreds of blinking drones, carefully scanning, analyzing, and recording the names and alien numbers of noncitizens as they were captured. All this while Tereza slept in her pod on the fifty-first floor, unaffected, until now.

The crowds around her dispersed, citizens and noncitizens alike quickly withdrew into stores and shadows, the man selling vaporizers and e-currency harvesters began to pack up his merchandise. Tereza faced the vehicle as it pulled up next to her. The drone descended a few feet from her head and scanned her while the water-cannon nozzle took aim at her face. Tereza was recognized as a citizen and the crablike drone played a brief rendition of "The Stars and Stripes Forever" from its speakers. The Humvee pulled away.

"The Reclamation police." Tereza whispered the words of the receptionist. If the HDF had taken me, they would know where to find me. She followed the Humvee for several blocks, screaming, "Where are you keeping her?" as her jog turned into a sprint.

The siren drowned her out and the vehicle shot forward through red lights. Tereza lost its trail by the time she reached the Brooklyn Bridge. She took a moment to catch her breath and tapped on her wrist to activate her hWisper. She located the Reclamation Bureau in Manhattan, near City Hall.

Tereza ran. The pedestrians and the roaming vehicles and the concrete paths and the blue skyline and the stale shop awnings all blurred into a sludge of surreal vastness, a world with too many moving pieces. She bumped into strangers who cursed at the back of her head as she flashed past. Finally, she stood in front of the gates of the Reclamation Bureau, an annex that had been built between the CIS district office and the IRS offices in the early days of the Reclamation regime.

As she approached, the massive glass sliding doors opened, and an ice-cold breeze washed over her body. I wondered whether Tereza had ever thought she'd have to enter this building. No one wanted to reclaim anything from her, exile her from the soil under her feet, dictate her movements around the world. This monster of white marble was meant to decide the fates of others.

Inside, she encountered a vacant lobby and a white wall covered with small screens. In the early Reclamation days, when the Bureau buildings were notoriously overcrowded, the media televised helicopter views of Reclamation victims forming lines around the block: The families of those who'd been disappeared from the street by the government's kidnapping squads. The immigrants who'd come to beg for their lives before they were disappeared too. American citizens who'd been wrongly served with deportation notices. To curb the chaos, Reclamation agents began sweeping the lines at the Bureau for deportees, taking the crowds away by busloads. They would separate and interrogate family members, keeping them locked in basement cells for days. Eventually these methods discouraged everyone from seeking the Bureau's services, resulting in clean lobbies scrubbed of human suffering.

Tereza tapped on one of the screens, let it scan her fingerprint and retina. The machine asserted that Tereza had no open cases with the Bureau. Was she here on behalf of someone else? "Adéla Slavíková," Tereza said. "Biological mother." A grainy photograph of my face taken at the airport appeared on the screen next to the word DECEASED in red. Tereza bent over and breathed through the nausea. The hotel receptionist wasn't mistaken. I had died in the night, alone, far from home.

Tereza straightened her back and shook her head. She couldn't afford to lose control, not until she'd handled the logistics of grief. Forms to be filled out, policies to follow to rescue me from state custody. There was no time to fall apart until my body was back with family. I knew that after Rita's passing, Tereza hadn't had to deal with the international bureaucracy surrounding her death, a mercy that wasn't afforded to my daughter now. She swallowed sobs and screams. In less than a day our meeting had reinjected her life with hope, with love, beyond the clinical walls of the VITA labs, the lonely nature of ambition. A new path built and destroyed all at once. Who could stand tall as a witness to such cosmic cruelty?

Tereza proceeded deeper into the lobby, a hall of marble, and followed the blue lines drawn on the floor that led to five teller windows made of reinforced glass. The lonely echo of each step caused her to flinch as she approached the only window that wasn't shuttered with a LUNCH BREAK sign.

Behind the thick glass sat a young woman applying paint to a miniature Orc figurine, paying no mind to the newcomer. The woman wore a T-shirt bearing the HDF logo and the phrase HI, MY NAME IS LORI.

Tereza knocked on the thick glass, but Lori made no acknowledgment of her presence. Tereza waited awhile, studied the window for some kind of bell or buzzer. She knocked again and again. After a few minutes, the woman raised her eyes from the figurine and pressed the intercom button.

"Case number," the woman said.

"I'm not sure. My mother, I'm told she died last night. I don't know where to go."

"And the case number is?"

"I don't have it. Her name is Adéla Slavíková, on a leisure visa from the Czech Republic. She died last night, that's what they said, I...I just need to know where to collect the body."

"Collect?" the woman said with exasperation, admiring the robust gray Orc standing proudly on her desk.

"I can't tell if you're talking to me or your goblin," Tereza said.

The clerk looked up at the ceiling and tapped her fingers in the air. "It's called a Greenskin, actually. Slavíková, you said? Found her. Died of natural causes, it seems. No foul play, she's already been processed."

"What does that mean?"

With a great sigh, the clerk stood up from her chair, stretched her spine, and disappeared behind a door leading into the mysterious hallways of the Bureau. In ten minutes she returned with a piece of paper.

"Here you go," the clerk said, sliding the paper through a small opening in the glass.

Tereza picked it up. In two terse paragraphs, the document stated that the location of my remains was presently unknown, due to the high volume of cases in New York. It advised Tereza to access the provided link and register her inquiry. The Bureau would launch an investigation and let her know about the status of my body within six months.

"Excuse me?" Tereza said.

"Yes?" the clerk replied, seemingly surprised Tereza was still there.

Tereza stared at her, then let out a loud, hideous cackle. A tear rolled down my daughter's chin. "You fucking *lost* her?"

"The logistics are complicated," the woman said. "With the current death rates in the city, authorities have to prioritize taking care of the remains of citizens."

"That's…how do you lose a human body? I have to bring her back to her family."

"I thought you were her family."

"I need to talk to your supervisor. Shit, I'm going to speak to the president and take this to the pope. You kidnapped her body. No one gave you permission."

"The process is standard for any illegal body found on American soil. The government provides this service at great expense. Mistakes can happen when the system is overwhelmed, as you can imagine."

"Illegal? I just told you she came on a visa. She had eight days left."

"Death voids any paperwork issued to aliens. The moment she died, her visa status was forfeited. Reclamation amendment section two. Your mother broke the law."

"By *dying?*"

"I'm not a lawyer, I'm a customer-experience specialist." The clerk carefully pushed the drying Orc figurine aside, then leaned forward on her elbows. She gazed at Tereza through the thick glass, which made her head look absurdly small. "I understand you're in shock. But the government took care of all costs for processing your mother's remains—that's good news, right? It's always nice to save a buck. They'll find her for you. Just hang on a month or two."

"I want you to know I'm going to tell the world about this."

"It's important to speak your truth," the woman said. "I believe that! And really, you have my sympathies. Now, the average Reclamation Bureau appointment is supposed to take two minutes. You've been here for nearly fourteen minutes. If we keep this up for much longer, I'll get a talking-to from my supervisor."

"All of this makes sense to you? What you do here?"

The customer-experience specialist named Lori crossed her arms and leaned away from her desk. She was done humoring her guest.

"This job has health insurance. I have Crohn's disease. That makes sense. Is there anything else I can help you with?"

"You...fucker," Tereza whispered.

Lori reached for the shutter above the window and pulled it down. LUNCH BREAK, the sign announced.

Tereza looked around the lobby, hearing the echo of her own breathing.

"Please make your way outside, citizen," declared the voice of Lori from the speakers.

So I was truly dead. I admit that until that moment, part of me had still hoped for some kind of reversal, to find out that my ghostly form was a temporary misunderstanding and I would soon take up residence in my flesh again. I felt indescribable grief. The vessel that had carried me all of my life—the body, a wondrous source of joy and deepest frustration—was irreversibly gone. Tereza shuffled through the lobby and back outside, weeping quietly; the strangers surrounding her paid no mind. She crumpled the page with the Bureau's instructions and shoved it in her pocket.

TEREZA STOOD IN front of the Bureau. Lost. She had no friends to call, no one who could share her pain or offer advice. Odd as it was, her family of strangers—a brother and a grandmother—were the only people in the world who had a reason to understand her loss. It had become her responsibility to inform them of my death. With her hWisper, she registered her inquiry about my remains on the Bureau's website and threw the instructions in the garbage.

For the first time I wondered: How could I perceive Tereza's thoughts and feelings so easily? Her facial expressions, her posture, the way she walked, every motion and lack thereof were clues. As if the afterlife had provided some kind of analytical software allowing me to unpack the mind of my progeny. Or perhaps I was simply imposing my own meaning on Tereza's actions, a kind of wishful thinking that there was still a way for us to communicate.

After a while, she called a cab through her hWisper, entering the address of her Brooklyn apartment. She couldn't face her coworkers, not in these vulnerable moments. When she arrived home, Tereza armed herself with a bottle of gin and found the website of the Czech consulate. Though the Czech bureaucracy was slow to accept American refugees and asylum seekers fleeing conflict and extreme climate events, Tereza, like all wealthy Americans, could obtain a visa within hours. She filled out her application and went to bed, where she wept as she tortured herself with the photos we had taken together during our day in Manhattan until she fell asleep, spooning the nearly emptied bottle.

She woke up to the gentle buzzing of her hWisper, texts and video messages from Steven & Mark, inquiring after her whereabouts. She ignored them. The new contract she'd signed that morning banned her from traveling outside New York City without VITA's approval, which meant that the contract she'd entered into to save my life legally barred her from connecting with the rest of her family. It didn't matter that VITA wasn't able to hold up their end of the contract—Tereza's new terms of employment were contingent on the company's "best-faith effort" to treat my illness, and even the greatest of faiths couldn't treat the ailments of the dead. Not yet, anyway.

She didn't care one bit. As soon as her visa approval arrived via e-mail, she found a red-eye flight to Prague leaving LaGuardia that evening and packed a small suitcase. Within the hour, she was in a cab heading to the airport.

The plane sat on the tarmac for three hours before takeoff, a standard occurrence at New York airports, as vermin and garbage plagued the runways. The crumbling infrastructure was not among the city's priorities after the federal government cut off financial assistance to the state. Tereza looked out the window at the stray dogs and raccoons digging through the tarmac trash around the plane's wheels, the TSA employees attempting to chase them off. Another delay was caused by a fistfight in the economy section, separated from Tereza's first-class cabin by the same steel doors that protected the cockpit. I passed through the door a few times to observe the flight attendants tasering the pugilists into submission, to watch the cheering passengers record the violence on their phones in hopes of reaching viral fame by sharing the very worst of humanity. I disliked these titillated onlookers far more than the men who fought.

As Tereza waited in her seat, her hWisper received a message marked *urgent* from an unknown sender. After she opened it, she gripped the arm of the woman sitting next to her and nearly spilled the tea on her tray.

"Need a Xanax?" the neighbor asked.

I reentered my daughter's device to see the source of her reaction. In the midst of the drab interface appeared a GIF of my face. A photo I had never seen. The contours of my likeness seemed unnatural, as if they had been animated. A dark blue hue cast ominous shadows along my features. As the GIF moved on its tireless loops, the shadows moved across my skin, and the irises of my eyes turned red, as if contaminated by some internal fungus. The image was interrupted by letters that concealed most of my face. *Have you misplaced your mother?* the text inquired.

What was this? Some prank from the Reclamation Bureau? Internet trolls targeting Tereza for reasons I couldn't begin to imagine?

Tereza quickly moved to delete the file, then changed her mind and concealed it inside a password-protected folder. She jumped up and rushed to the restroom, where she took an Ambien and changed into sweatpants. Looking at herself in the mirror, she took out a pair of tweezers and brushed aside the hair covering the hWisper chip under her ear. She gripped the device with the tweezers and took a deep breath. I was alarmed—I'd seen diagrams of the device in magazines, the ultrathin wires connected to the brain stem. This didn't seem safe, not at all. But I wasn't surprised she wanted to separate herself from the hideous image someone had sent her. With a shaking hand, Tereza began to tug at the device gently. She screamed out in pain and dropped the tweezers in the sink, her hWisper undisturbed. Grimly she gathered her things and returned to her seat.

For the duration of her flight, Tereza kept ordering more gin until she fell into a drunken slumber, sweating, uneasy, her lips trembling with words as she argued with someone in her dreams. Underneath the clouds outside her window, the empty vastness of the atmosphere joined the black surface of the sea, as if there were no difference between sky and earth. It resembled an idea of the afterlife, a long image of nothing, an absence, a primeval lake of oil and tar absorbing our consciousness. Suddenly I was glad that my afterlife didn't resemble the abyss, that death wasn't the nothingness I'd expected. Instead, I was able to witness my daughter's first flight to the country in which she was born. I spent the flight observing the first-class passengers picking at their teeth, binging on complimentary vodka, stripping their feet of ripe socks. Air travel was much easier to bear without a nose.

Lulled into a temporary state of calm now that my daughter had made it through the news of my death, I humored myself with memories of the early summers I'd spent with Tereza's father, the madness of ambition, the manic pursuit of upward mobility. Living American. As I watched my daughter sleep, my ethereal form disappeared again within the life-size images, an in-flight movie of my greatest strivings and failures. I was seduced by yet another calling of memory.

THE YEAR IS 1984

FOUR MONTHS AFTER Michael's proposal and my decision to stay in America, we moved from his apartment into the guesthouse of a wealthy couple he'd met during his job at the Ritz. Michael told the Fairchilds that his "wife" desperately needed a job that paid under the table, and they graciously offered to let us move in and pay me a minuscule wage for keeping their six bedrooms tidy. Michael presented the option as a new start for us, and again I felt the need to remain agreeable, to repay him for convincing me I shouldn't give up and leave the country. I was so determined that I even allowed him to call me his wife, as he insisted it made us look more sympathetic and serious and open to opportunity. This was the beginning of our shared fate, and the guesthouse of the rich already sounded like a major upgrade after Michael's small, scarcely furnished bachelor apartment. To celebrate this "step forward," as Michael called it, he took me for a weekend trip to New York to see *Dreamgirls* on Broadway and meet some of his filmmaker friends who had gone to the city after graduate school.

We moved to the guesthouse after we returned. It was a gray box more reminiscent of a trailer than a house, surrounded by unkempt palm trees that at least deflected attention from the dirty smudges on the facade and the spider infestation, the thick webs and long hairy legs that crept from every crevice. Inside were a small kitchen, a living room, and a bedroom, all with a fresh coat of asylum-white paint. The palm trees separated our property from the main estate, where a massive fountain gushing water onto a mosaic pathway of stone reminded me of a postcard I'd once seen on Babi's night table. The path led to the castle-door entryway of the four-story mansion itself, along with its two garages. On my first day, during the orientation,

Mrs. Fairchild asked me to enter the house through the small sliding door next to the pool, saying the main entrance was for official guests only.

In the morning, Michael went to work, and I enjoyed the silence of our new home. It'd been a while since I'd had a place of my own. It was hopelessly ugly, but it was mine, decorated with photos of my old friends, my parents, the small tokens I'd collected since I'd arrived in the country. For breakfast I made turkey sandwiches, tall and sloppy, stacked so high I hurt my jaw eating them, standing in the kitchen with melted cheese and ketchup dripping onto the floor. After breakfast I killed the spiders who dared peek from their hiding places and vacuumed their intricate webs. I made my way across the lawn, entered the mansion through the entrance for the help, and picked up my cleaning supplies, which shared a closet with Mr. Fairchild's golf clubs.

Almost every night I'd find Mr. Fairchild's bedsheets stained with urine or feces from midnight accidents. The second Mrs. Fairchild, thirty years her husband's junior, slept in a separate bedroom and never entered his bedroom, and thus any damage was left for my eyes only. I was instructed to carry the reminder of her husband's indignity out of the house and dress the bed with brand-new sheets. Dozens of freshly purchased sheet sets waited in the closet. I wasn't to bring up a word of the accidents to Mrs. Fairchild, who was busy waiting for her well-earned inheritance. But the fortune she anticipated would come from Mr. Fairchild's position as the CEO, now emeritus, of a health-insurance company, a career that gave him access to some of the finest health care in the world. Despite his increased decrepitude, Mr. Fairchild had been kept alive by his many nutritionists, cardiologists, geriatricians, and physical therapists for far longer than Mrs. Fairchild expected. As her husband spent his days alternating between doctor visits and drinking gin and tonics at the country club, she packed her own life with hobbies—tennis, book clubs, trips to New York—to fill the empty hours of anticipating her husband's passing, the path to freedom. I have to wonder what Mrs. Fairchild would have thought of VITA's pursuit of the God pill, the promise to shield Mr. Fairchild from death indefinitely.

I kept my contemplations of the couple's tragedies to myself and went about my work. In their attempts to avoid each other, the Fairchilds spent scarcely any time in the house, making my job easy. The kitchen was used only once or twice a month for parties, and the catering people always cleaned up. The spare bedrooms were unused. My work was confined mostly to disposing of Mr. Fairchild's bed dressing and making the common areas look like the house was occupied by a loving family. I vacuumed and swept and mopped, and I watched too many hours of television. I became addicted to *Bewitched* and *I Dream of Jeannie* and *Dallas* as ways to sharpen my English; each time an unknown phrase was uttered, I studied Mr. Fairchild's dictionaries for context. Initially, I found the American accent perfectly ridiculous, the rolled *r*'s and prolonged *l*'s, as if everyone carried hot potatoes in their mouths. But as my attachment to the Czech language faded, refreshed only through monthly phone calls to my parents, American English started to feel true. I caught myself chewing the hot potato without thinking. I had nightmares of being the last native speaker of my language, of dying and taking the mysteries of Czech with me. In the afterlife, every Czech who ever lived gathered to curse my name: *Murderer. She killed our language.* What if, someday, I learned to speak English better than Czech? I couldn't bear the shame, and yet I practiced the foolish words of the characters on the screen: *Try to understand, Darrin, you're only a mortal. No offense.*

At night, Michael did his writing as I drank wine and smoked on the porch. Our relationship was comfortable and safe and often unsatisfying. There was nothing revolutionary here. Michael was beautiful and optimistic in that American way. He truly believed that happiness was a human right, whereas any Czech could tell you that happiness was a glitch, a rare alignment of chaos, like a bird that sings beautifully before roosting on electric wires. He even went down on me unconditionally and without fail, yet I knew that someday I might become fatigued. In a life that was just comfortable enough, in the shadow of this beautiful empty mansion, ours was an uneasy alliance that wasn't based on love as much as on circumstances and immigration law. There was no plan, only Michael's twelve-hour shifts at the restaurant in the Ritz, his hair smelling of hollandaise, the promise that laboring without complaint would lead to some prosperous future.

Two years passed in this new life, this endless routine. As I began another week of keeping up a house that wasn't mine, I ironed Mr. Fairchild's shirts and stared through the sliding glass doors that served as my servant's entrance toward the pool that nobody used (Mr. Fairchild and his first wife, long dead, had built the pool for their future children who never came, and the new, younger Mrs. Fairchild had entered the scene when it was too late to procreate). Yet the pool-cleaning company came every week to collect drowned spiders and leaves, to keep the water pure. Staring at its surface, I had a vision of my own children. Two of them, a boy who looked like me and a girl who looked like Michael, swimming in the pool, a pool that didn't belong to me and thus didn't belong to them. They played and screeched and laughed until Mrs. Fairchild came outside to tell them the noise was upsetting her husband, that they should be good children and return home. My children left the pool that didn't belong to them and came back to the house that didn't belong to them. They slept in the bedroom while Michael and I, loveless and sexless, slept on a pullout couch. All of us cramped in the servants' quarters, waiting for something better. The idea of this future terrified me.

I returned to reality as I smelled the burning fabric of Mr. Fairchild's shirt. Snapping out of the daydream, I carried the shirt to the neighbors' garbage can. I left work early without sweeping or mopping, and I biked to a phone booth, used a calling card to dial my mother's number, and asked her to send as many books as she could put together, along with my old journals. I wanted to remember who I had been before America, before my arrest by the secret police and the depression that had sparked my indifference. The time had come for me to remember the woman who stared her father down after he threw a massive slice of larded bread at her face. I had laughed then, laughed to make him feel like a fool, watched him storm out of the room as I decided to leave his house, to break free. No one would slow me down; not even my own father had the right. I missed the zeal of my rebellion, the optimism and the thrill as I held a mug of champagne and the pages of *Ark* with my blackened fingers. I knew I couldn't let myself get stuck in the world of the Fairchilds. Michael was passive about the way forward. He was content making good money at the Ritz and writing screenplays no one would ever see. I needed to push for both of us.

Ecstatically, my mother pledged to send as many books as she could fit inside a box. "You sound like yourself again, Adélko," she remarked, "but why is your accent so strange?"

WHEN SCIENTISTS DISCOVERED the fossil of *Andrias scheuchzeri*, extinct cousin to the giant salamander, at first they believed the remains belonged to a human who had drowned in the biblical deluge. This case of mistaken identity inspired one Karel Čapek, Babi's favorite writer and in turn a favorite of my own, to write his most beloved novel, *War with the Newts*.

Čapek remains one of the most significant voices in Czech literature, and copies of his books are likely to be found in most households, having survived literary cleansings by the German protectorate. Babi's copy of *Newts* was a gray hardback featuring a carving of the salamander fossil on the cover, and as a child I played with its yellowed pages before I could understand the words. I finally read the book by the riverside when I was ten years old, mesmerized. It was my first true literary love, the first time I felt genuine compassion and understanding for people (and salamanders!) who'd emerged from a writer's imagination. Beyond the confines of my reality, my village, my family, unlimited worlds and stories awaited. *Newts* had made me crave the life of an adventurer.

The same copy of *Newts* I had fallen in love with as a child arrived carefully wrapped in newspaper in a package from my mother. A couple of books had been stolen by government inspectors, but for whatever arbitrary reasons devised by the censors, Čapek came unharmed. I decided to cut my workweek from six days to three, cleaning the Fairchilds' house every other day, since it seemed impossible they'd ever know the difference as long as I kept up with Mr. Fairchild's accidents. I spent my unauthorized days off sitting on a blanket on the great lawn, reading. The cynical state in which I'd arrived in America had nearly dissipated; the reminder of this literature that had shaped me hastened the process. What good was the dollar when I'd lost all sense of my own identity, of what defined my personhood beyond the list of daily tasks prescribed by my employer? The book in my hand made me feel again like a person with memory, senses, dignity. More than just a human version of a toilet scrubber here to sell my labor until I perished.

In Čapek's most famous work, salamanders first emerge as creatures with an extraordinary affinity for learning, exploited by the world's capitalists as pearl hunters and underwater laborers. Due to their incredible adaptability, the salamanders soon build a powerful civilization of their own, challenging the human reign on earth. I felt a kinship with the creatures. Within the capitalist hierarchy, I lived at the bottom. I was without capital, without land, I couldn't be promoted as my own supervisor, the Supreme Cleaner of the Fairchild household. Trapped in this power dynamic, reinforced by my employers doubling as my landlords, I had no choice but to turn against them. I received the same low pay whether I cleaned the house six times a week or two. Why not dedicate the shortest amount of time to a task that was useless to me and assign the rest of my time to personal improvement? Having no personal stake in the cleanliness of a stranger's house, I couldn't be expected to spend most of my life pursuing it. Capitalism claims that self-interest is at the center of human prosperity, and yet, if people were truly encouraged to look out only for themselves, the global economic order would collapse.

I devoured the book like I hadn't read it before. Eager to finish, I extended the reading of the last chapter into my evening sit-down with Michael. As he watched me read, my love encouraged me to retell the entire plot of the book. He seemed fascinated with the novel's scope, the dynamic cast of characters from all corners of the newt world, the global condemnation of warmongering and fascism and materialism. His childlike interest, his immediate passion for a treasured work, stirred up feelings that could only be love.

The next day, Michael came home from his job a bit later than usual, carrying something wrapped in a brown paper bag. He revealed a copy of *Newts* in English translation with a colorful cover that resembled a B movie poster portraying an ugly yet noble salamander emerging from water, looking out over the towering buildings of human creation. Michael began to read it immediately.

As we crawled into bed underneath the mosquito net that protected us from cockroaches, he continued to read. I rubbed my naked inner thigh on his leg, hips, and stomach; our discussion of *Newts* reignited desires that had been dead for some months. But it took me ripping the book out of his hands to get his attention. Even when I straddled and kissed him as we both exhaled heavily in the rare cool night, I could tell his mind was off in this new world occupied by salamanders. I felt closer to Michael than ever before. For the first time in a while, I was satiated and slept through the night.

In the morning, I made a thoroughly insane proposition. As the gatekeeper of our future, I had decided it was time to be bold. We were going to make a low-budget independent film based on Čapek's work, with Michael behind the camera and me as the star. In a country that valued overnight success much more than a lifetime of work, our dreams would be realized at once. The shock and awe of success. Our time had come.

OFTEN I'VE COME dangerously close to confusing my afterlife for reality. I forget that I'm a spirit gone from the world and start to believe I've returned to the days of that *Newt* dream, with my life still ahead of me. It seems the ideal picture of what happens after death: by choice, we can relive our fondest memories, an unstoppable loop of nostalgia. Perhaps utopia isn't a kind of shared future but rather individuals submerged within their own versions of the past, confined to the moments they felt safe, loved, full of expectation. I would love nothing more than to return to the days of creative obsession, my mind consumed by the singular project, the singular story only I could tell. It was more satisfying than any romantic affair or friendship. More satisfying than motherhood.

During Tereza's flight I'd once again fallen for this allure of memory. I had no concept of time without a body—how long had I diverted my attention from her airplane? Was the fistfight in the economy section resolved? With difficulty I forced myself to forget about the newts, about Michael. I left the beaches of my youth and returned to my daughter, expecting to find her strapped into her first-class seat in anticipation of arriving in the motherland.

THE YEAR IS 2030

NSTEAD, I APPEARED next to the wreckage of a rental car crashed into a tree, smoke rising from the hood, broken glass scattered along the pavement. Tereza sat in the driver's seat, slumped over the wheel, her eyes closed and covered in blood. Was she breathing? I studied her face in horror, wishing I had lips to scream, to call for help. There was nothing I could do but stare and wait, experiencing the strangest sensation of terror as a purely intellectual exercise. My heart wasn't pounding, I had no lips with which to pray or hands that could tremble at the shock.

Where were we, and when? I seemed to have no sense of time. That human instinct that made the limbs heavy with late hours and the mood improved just before noon had been taken from me. My travels in memory kept me from the present for a few minutes or several hours, without distinction.

I recognized the crash site as the Hluboká memorial, our village's only landmark. Tereza was a mere five minutes' walk from the house of her family. While I was dreaming of my *Newts* summer, she had landed in her birth country. Here she was, so close to meeting her brother and grandmother, so close to delivering the news of my passing. I waited and waited, but my daughter didn't move. What if ... was it possible she could join me in this afterlife? I looked for a sign of her presence here, some ghostly form. Did I wish for her to be dead so that I would no longer be alone? Thankfully, a question I didn't have to answer. Tereza gasped and pulled her forehead off the steering wheel. The blood in her eyes dripped onto her lap. She cursed at the bright morning sun burning her face, checked her extremities and torso for puncture wounds, her cheeks for bits of lodged glass. A gash extended along her forehead, her only wound, not deep enough to require care beyond bandaging.

A quiet but persistent squeal rang from the dashboard computer, overpowering the sound of the steam escaping the radiator, of the tree branches scraping against the car. Tereza kicked the door open, rolled out onto the gravel road, and crawled to the grass. With a flick of her thumb, she reset her hWisper to see if it had survived impact. The VITA boot screen welcomed her, and while still on the ground, she pulled up the map and saw that her destination was just down the main road, over one more slump and one more hill. She laughed and wiped her eyes.

For a moment she sat in the grass to let her shaken bones settle again. She looked at the curve in the road that had led her astray. The object that had distracted her resembled a tombstone, a slab of rock rising from the dirt. Far behind the stone, beneath a wall of shrubbery, there used to be a four-story dormitory, built in the 1960s to house workers from the mines, now a ruin overgrown with weeds.

Tereza stood up and, with a new limp, walked toward the stone. She read the five names carved into it. Two of them she recognized as Anglican, most likely American; the third name was written in an alphabet she didn't recognize, and the last two seemed of Middle Eastern origin. The Hluboká memorial, the only thing that made our village remarkable and yet a source of great shame. The dedication on the memorial, written in Czech, eluded Tereza's understanding, and she had better things to do than ask her hWisper for a translation.

She removed her suitcase from the car's undamaged trunk, took a step, then two, and passed the sign announcing the village limits, marked by a row of barren plum trees on each side. She limped her way to the first building she encountered, which turned out to be an empty pub. The bartender showed no surprise at Tereza's bleeding forehead or her American English. She merely offered to sell her a bottle of peroxide and some bandages, at a tourist markup. The clock above the bar showed it was nearly noon.

After Tereza sat down at one of the tables and dressed the wound, her hWisper informed her she'd received a greeting card from an unknown sender. She opened the file. The card was a snapshot of Anna Maria Island photographed from above. I'd been to the island many times during my Florida years. As the sea surrounding the island swayed in the image, glittering letters appeared: *Greetings from Manatee County!*

Suddenly, the letters vanished. In their place, my photo appeared. It had been taken five years ago, the same picture from the passport I had used to enter New York. The photo flashed a few times before the greeting-card text materialized once again. Tereza dropped the bottle of peroxide onto the floor. She opened the digital card. *Find her,* the message inside commanded. No signature. She watched the card to see if it might change again. She splashed her face with cold water from a glass the bartender had left on the table.

Tereza opened the card again. And again. My photo blinked at her. It was a clear provocation. She was finally pulled from her hWisper when the bartender asked if she was in the village to visit the refugee memorial.

Tereza said she knew nothing about it.

She noticed the bartender's wrist, which bore the tattoo of a DNA strand encircling a mattock. I could see the shock in my daughter's eyes. Reclamationists here? Yes, here. My daughter had no idea just how quickly her country's sinister influence had expanded into the world.

The bartender noticed my daughter's gaze and pulled her sleeve down to her palm.

Tereza, unable to contain her curiosity, asked about the purpose of the memorial.

"Five foreigners were killed," the bartender murmured almost under her breath as she triple-checked the spotless glass she was polishing.

"When?" Tereza said.

"I'm not the tour guide, look it up," the bartender said, then poured herself a shot of fernet and retreated into the kitchen.

I'd hoped that my daughter's desire to reach her family would overpower the urge to read about the events that had cast shame upon our village. I was wrong. She began scrolling through the endless news coverage of the time, the essays and academic studies that had made us the center of the nation's attention three years earlier, when America's Reclamation movement infiltrated our country and initiated the Summer of Madness.

What is there to say? After Russia's barbaric invasion of Ukraine in 2022, my country and its neighbors had to face not only the prospect of a new world order—including the possibility of our own future wars with Russia, given its gluttonous desire to unite all Slavs under its neofascist grip—but also a reckoning with our own immigration policies. During the Syrian refugee crisis, Czechs had followed the shameful example of Poland and Hungary in denying our obligations toward the globe's vulnerable peoples, accepting only a very small quota of refugees onto our soil. When Facebook prophets spoke of Muslim invaders overrunning our country, enough of my countrymen possessed the right combination of media illiteracy and bigotry to accept imaginary threats as truth. We hid from our responsibility to the refugees of war and helped very few.

How differently we Czechs felt about the people of Ukraine, who looked so much like us: Slavic cheeks and blue eyes! Immediately we were willing to accept as many refugees as our infrastructure could handle. The assertion that this double standard was based on our shameless Islamophobia was completely true and only a fool would have denied it. It was also based on proximity and history—in the past, the Russian imperials had invaded us, threatened us, felt entitled to what was ours. The grudge against the Rus flows in the blood, the same blood that boils when the Rus threaten and slaughter another Slav. The complex issues of geopolitics reduced to basic tribalism, as ever. And yet I can't deny that I felt it too, that fire in the chest. I wanted to pound Putin's head with my own fists.

But almost as quickly as they arrived, the Ukrainian people began to return home to resist and repel the oppressor. Our government was left with the reckoning of its own hypocrisy, the outcry of activists and human rights organizations over its immediate agreement to accept many European white refugees a few years after it had denied the Syrians, the Iraqis, the Yemenis fleeing similar horrors.

This signaled our nation's brief awakening. To put a bandage over its failures in the previous refugee crisis, parliament significantly raised the refugee quota for the country and established an independent watchdog council to probe the fairness in our migrant-acceptance process, to root out racism and xenophobia. Furthermore, the government established a revitalization program for our "dying villages," villages like Hluboká. Most of our young people had fled to the cities, and the old, loyal residents, like Babi and me, were hardly able to keep our villages afloat, much less create economic or cultural opportunities that would lure new residents and uplift our population.

It seemed obvious that the people displaced from their homes across the world, by war or climate catastrophe or economic devastation, could inject new life into the flagging Czech countryside. By matching migrant applicants' skills and demographics with the needs of any particular area, villagers could open new businesses, reopen factories, watch children once again fill the streets, and feel realistic in the hope they might want to stay and take over their parents' trade, crop fields, or well-paid spots at the factory.

Thanks to the impressive application from the town's mayor, Hluboká was accepted as one of the pilot villages for the program. A bus carrying twenty refugees arrived from Prague. Among our new neighbors were Americans fleeing climate devastation and their fears that a civil war would soon break out in their country; Syrians, Afghans, and Yemenis seeking new places to settle far away from the traumas they'd left behind; and a dissident Russian journalist and his family who faced immediate execution if they ever returned home.

A construction company had renovated the long-abandoned dormitory built for the coal miners in the 1960s to serve as a temporary home for the newcomers, with the hope that they might soon be interested in purchasing and renovating some of the village's vacant houses with the help of government loans. We welcomed our new neighbors with a countywide festival of food and beer, carousels and swan-boat rides for the kids. Not everyone had been eager to welcome the new villagers, but most of us were genuinely excited to make them feel like part of our community. I was hopeful that, with its new residents, my dying village might once again flourish.

But the Czech Reclamationists had another plan. Inspired by their American counterparts, members of our own nativist movement gained traction precisely because of the government's sudden willingness to admit past mistakes and open the country to immigration. As the new families settled across the countryside, the Czech Reclamationists moved their focus away from the loud protests in Prague and concentrated on infiltrating the villages, recruiting local residents to harass their neighbors, staging intimidation protests in front of refugee houses, and making fake videos of the newcomers attacking innocent white Czechs in the streets. Extremists flowed into Hluboká, and there was nothing I could do but impotently stand by and ask the cops why they weren't intervening.

Finally, as the county approved the first round of loans that would enable our new families to move from the dormitory into houses in the village, the Summer of Madness reached its peak. In five different villages, Reclamationists gathered under cover of darkness with firebombs. In Hluboká, four men were seen throwing Molotov cocktails at the dorms while the one county-hired bodyguard fled the scene. Six residents of the dorm were absent that night. Nine got out with severe injuries. Five people, including two children, died in the fire. People were killed in other villages and in coordinated attacks on migrants living in cities, and the body count of that infamous night rose to thirty-two.

I will never forget the night of the fire. Standing in front of the dormitory, only a few steps away from where Tereza later crashed her vehicle, Babi and me holding each other up as the county firemen carried out bodies wrapped in bedsheets, the survivors looking at us with unanswerable questions as they withstood hostile interrogations from the first policemen on the scene. The early consensus, it seemed, was that the refugees must have done this to themselves. Meanwhile, my son sat at home with a burn wound on his chest and knowledge of events he would never share with the police.

Seventy percent of refugees living in the Czech Republic left the country within the next six months to seek better fortunes elsewhere. The government abandoned its ambitions to rejuvenate our villages, and the watchdog council for fairness in processing was disbanded. The Reclamationists across the nation celebrated their victory quietly, humbly; the official leaders of the movement distanced themselves from the "disgusting extremists" who were behind the firebombings. At the same time, the movement continued to encourage the online conspiracies claiming that the refugees had attacked themselves in an effort to make their plight in the country seem more desperate and to squeeze the government for more benefits. Many believe the lie to this day. Babi and I attended the quiet ceremony as the memorial to the Hluboká five was unveiled by our mayor. The hope of our new neighbors—all of us united in the remaking of our future—was as dead and cold as the slab of commemorative rock that would go unseen by most people in my country.

The bartender returned, and Tereza paused her reading about the Summer of Madness to study her host. "I like your tat," she said, clearly to provoke.

"Yes. Anything else?"

"Do a lot of people come through to see the memorial?"

"Some. You know. People who are into that sort of thing."

"And you are . . . not into it," Tereza pushed.

"Look, congratulations, you saw my tattoo. I'm in the movement, but I'm not an animal. Even kids were murdered here. It's evil."

Pretending to be done with the subject, Tereza ordered a shot of bourbon, a peace offering. I wished desperately I could join her. She knocked back the shot, stood up, and slammed down a five-hundred-crown tip. "For your kindness," she said. "You know, you might feel it has nothing to do with you, but that tattoo, the belief behind it, binds you directly to the men who started the fire."

The bartender scoffed and rearranged the prepackaged sandwiches in the refrigerator. Tereza turned to leave.

"Europe should remain Europe." The bartender spoke to Tereza's back. "It's reasonable that the people of Hluboká want to hold on to the ways they live. When was the last time you opened your home to a stranger?"

"Most of us," Tereza said, "will be uprooted from our homes in the next thirty years. Borders collapsed by oceans and fires and droughts. I hope someone takes us in and gives us a hot meal when our place in the world is gone."

As TEREZA EXITED the pub an hour later, dark clouds overtook the skyline and raindrops tapped on the roof and windows of the car she had crashed a mere hundred meters away. She called the car-rental company and reported the crash as she walked down the main road.

On the northern and southern ends of the village, Tereza saw silhouettes of the coal power plants that had been built in the country when I was a girl. Babi had protested when the construction began, declaring that the devil himself was putting down roots and would soon spread soot and sulfur in our skies. With the plants came jobs, and Hluboká's population of one hundred fifty doubled with the developments. New houses expanded the village beyond our main street, while pollution became a permanent part of the horizon, just as Babi had predicted. The temporary economic renaissance brought on by the plants came with poisoned water, infertile soil, respiratory infections plaguing the lungs of Hluboká's children. Through the decades, the new and old families left Hluboká to escape this decline and build new lives across the country and Europe. The ones who stayed contracted lung diseases and cancers that killed them or plagued them well into old age. It wasn't out of the question that these power plants were responsible for my illness too.

Tereza walked down the main road and turned onto the dirt path leading up a hill to the house of her ancestry. She passed the pitiless, unkempt piece of land where apple trees crowded by the dozens no longer bore fruit, thirsting for care that no one had provided since my father's passing. The once-tall fence demarcating our property now sagged into the softening earth, and the cracks in the foundation awaited Roman's promised repairs. The chimney that had once let out the fury of flames that kept us warm through the cruelest of winters now threatened to keel over and take a bite out of the roof.

Tereza rang the bell at the gate, massaging the whiplash injury in her neck, sighing at the pain. She was waiting on the doorstep of strangers, subject to their whims, arriving as the abandoned child, a messenger to bring her unknown family the worst news they could ever receive. She waited. Soon, footsteps shuffled toward the gate and a key was turned in the lock.

Tereza attempted to introduce herself to Babi, who couldn't understand English but waved her in nonetheless, recognizing my likeness immediately in her granddaughter. Babi pointed to Tereza's bandage.

"I'm okay," my daughter said, her voice breaking.

Babi wiped water from her cheek, knowing from the fact that I wasn't accompanying Tereza that something awful must have happened.

She pulled Tereza through the front yard and into the house. Here my daughter saw her half brother for the first time. Roman stood over the television, watching a tense football match. He turned to face the newcomer and stumbled backward. We weren't used to unknown visitors, but he knew who she was within seconds. She looked so much like me, though nothing like him—the only thing my children shared in their appearance was the bump at the tip of the nose. Their fathers had been so different in body and in spirit.

"My name is Tereza Holm," my daughter said. "I'm your sister."

"Well, I guess I knew that Mother would bring you here, but not this soon," Roman said in English. It had been his favorite subject since middle school. He looked behind Tereza. He walked past her, searching the hallway. Searching for me.

"I have something to tell . . ." Tereza said, trailing off.

Gripping her handkerchief, Babi gestured for her to sit down. "Offer your sister tea and biscuits," she said to Roman.

Tereza refused the offer, an affront to her hosts, but she wanted to get the words out before she lost her courage. They sat in the living room, Babi in her reading chair, Roman on the couch, while Tereza, unknowingly, sat in the green recliner that had belonged to me. How to tell these strangers who shared her blood that a person they loved had gone from the world. That it had happened anonymously, in a hostile land. That my body had been handled by indifferent strangers, without love, without respect.

She chose the scientist's path. She stated the facts as she knew them, without embellishment. I had come to meet her in New York, and we'd spent a miraculous day together. I had died in the night, in my hotel room, for reasons unknown. Strangers had come and taken my body away.

Babi didn't have to wait for Roman to translate the news into Czech for her. Often she knew things before they were said. She wiped a tear from the corner of her eye. "Já to věděla," she told Roman. "Podruhé se mi nevrátí." *I knew. She wouldn't return to me the second time.*

"What the hell happened?" Roman growled at his sister.

"I think she was sick," Tereza said. "A fever she tried to hide. I don't know. We spent the day together, I put her in a taxi, and I didn't hear from her again."

"I knew it. I knew they'd kill her. To the Americans, we are all enemies. Well, why did you come all the way here? Surely this could've been done over the phone." Roman scratched frantically at his earlobe.

"I don't think anyone killed her," Tereza said. "She looked so ill. I should've insisted she see a doctor, but I worried maybe she looked like that because she was tired, and I was afraid to spoil our time together."

I could tell she longed to be vulnerable, to bare herself to these strangers as if they were indeed family. But the hatred in Roman's eyes and his volatile gesturing didn't allow for any kind of intimacy. She couldn't afford to show weakness in front of a man she didn't know or trust.

Roman wasn't particularly imposing, a man of average height with small shoulders, but my son made up for this lack of threatening physical attributes by being loud and hostile. "I knew this would happen," he said. "I told her, America's no place to be. Unforgiving. No reasonable person goes there. Well, then. We Czechs don't delude ourselves. We accept the death of our elders as a necessity. Have they already shipped her remains?"

Something seemed off about my son, more so than usual. As if he wasn't completely surprised by the news of my demise. I confess I wanted to see his grief nakedly on display.

"There has been a bit of a . . . complication," Tereza said.

"What's that?"

"The remains. Well, she was taken by the Reclamation Bureau, but apparently they've lost her. For now. And we will find her, of course, I just . . . I wasn't sure what to do first."

Roman stared at her for what felt like hours. Babi's head turned between her grandchildren, back and forth, trying to read them. Roman translated for her. She sat back in the chair and closed her eyes.

"My mother is dead," Roman said to Tereza, "because of you. And you couldn't be bothered to bring her back? We don't need condolences from a stranger. We need to bury her."

"It's really my fault," Tereza said.

"Yes," Roman agreed.

They sat in silence. Babi placed her hands on her cheeks and rubbed up and down, repeating my name in whisper. "When she was born, she was the fattest little newt," Babi said in Czech, "stubborn and strong and hungry. She tried to get away from us as soon as she could crawl. Adéla the adventurer. Roman, you will be nice to your sister, you will show respect, or I'll poison your food. Do it for your mother."

Without a word, Roman jumped to his feet and walked outside.

Babi smiled apologetically at Tereza. I wondered whether she could ever learn the language well enough to have a word with her grandmother without relying on Roman.

From the pocket in her sweatpants, Babi pulled out a tangerine. She stared at the fruit as the seconds passed. "Já zapomněla jak to voloupat," she said. She had forgotten how to peel it.

Tereza didn't understand the words, yet she took the tangerine from Babi's lap and dug her fingernails into the skin. She divided the flesh into two halves and handed them over to Babi.

As she chewed, Babi stood up and put her hands on Tereza's shoulders, squeezed to measure her granddaughter's strength, then moved her hands to Tereza's face, as if the feel of her granddaughter's cheekbones would reveal whether she was honest. Satisfied at her findings, Babi smiled a toothless smile. "Yes, it's you," she said. "I've wished to meet you for a long time. You are wanted here, Terezko."

Though she understood nothing else, Tereza felt warmth spread around her head and neck as her grandmother pronounced her name.

"Time to reheat some bramboračka," Babi said, wiping her nose with her handkerchief. One of the foundations of Babi's life philosophy was that good soup was the most powerful deterrent for sorrow. She tied an apron around her waist, pulled Tereza up by the hand, and pointed outside, shooing her away.

The language of the world's grandchildren is universal. Whatever Grandmother says, you do it. My daughter walked out to the yard to face her brother. The worst was over. The moment she'd dreaded had passed, and her family hadn't thrown her out of the house, they hadn't immediately disowned her as the cause of my doom. I knew it was a release, to share the pain of losing me with those who cared. Now she could try to know them, to see whether she'd find a way to attach herself to this new family permanently. Just like we talked about.

Inhaling the smell of marjoram and garlic coming from the kitchen window (Babi liked to cook with windows open regardless of the season, as she found kitchens stifling), Tereza realized she hadn't eaten since her arrival in the country. For that matter, when was the last time she had eaten a homecooked meal, not one made at the VITA cafeteria or served by a Manhattan restaurant? She leaned against the shed in the front yard and watched her brother split wood. What would it have been like to grow up in this house, this village, which must've been picturesque back in the day, surrounded by trees and rivers and Bohemian hills?

"Seems like a good way to warm yourself up," Tereza said to her brother, rubbing her hands together.

Roman sniffed in response, placed a wedge inside a small crack in the log he was splitting. He hit the wedge with a hammer. The wood cracked in half, and the echo of the strike resonated through the air. My children stood together in the front yard of my birth house in the same frozen mud I'd once roamed clad in a diaper, chasing chickens. The sandbox my father had built for me was emptied of sand and filled with dirt for Babi's cucumber seeds.

"You're not much of a conversationalist," Tereza said.

Roman glanced at her. He wasn't used to comments about his temperament; my mother and I had stopped correcting his behavior years ago. It was a waste of time. "You have my grandmother's hospitality," he said. "As for me, I have nothing to say to you."

"I'm your sister."

"Yes, the famous, brilliant, long-lost sister. Our mother died as soon as she met you."

"You're in pain. I get it. Me too, if you can believe that. But you can't possibly think it was my fault."

Roman set a thinner round on the chopping block, picked up the ax, and took an unnecessarily wide swing, causing the slat that split off to fly away into the distance. A splinter struck his right eye. He dropped the ax, bent over, spat into his palm, and began to rub his eye.

"I know she really wanted us to meet," Tereza said.

"You knew her for a day," Roman said. "You have no clue what she wanted. You're welcome to stay here until your flight back, but I don't want to talk about this anymore. I need to focus. Since you didn't bring her body back, it's up to me to find out what your crazy country did to her."

Tereza sat on a log and drew shapes in the dirt with the tip of her shoe. A horde of chickens clucked around her, most of them picking through the scraps on the compost pile. They knew well enough to stay away from Roman and his long ax swings, but they were curious about this newcomer, pecking at her laces.

"We will find her together," Tereza said.

Roman's eye was red, tears sliding down his right cheek. He wiped the splinter on his pants and stared up at the sky. He seemed far less petulant when in pain. His left eye began to water too, and he swallowed a sob, clearing his throat to cover it up. "She's there all alone," he said. "What if they put her in some potter's field? Or, worse, use her body for evil things?"

"It's not productive to think that way," Tereza said, wincing at the suggestion. "Roman. Did I pronounce it right? You're not alone in this. I'm going to file petitions, lawsuits, write to every media outlet I can think of. We'll bring her home."

"You think they give a shit about lawsuits? This is what your country does to foreigners. We're not special. My mother should've stayed put, with her tribe."

My daughter dug her fingernails into her thighs. I figured she was used to walking away from conversations like this, paying no heed to this kind of pettiness. But she had to tolerate Roman, at least for now. For me. "I understand. We will come up with a plan we both like. But the costs of recovering her, and the funeral, let me at least—"

"We don't need your money. Besides, who knows if we'll ever find her? She could already be corrupted."

"What do you mean?"

"Never mind. We don't need your help."

Babi called from the window, announcing dinner was ready. With obvious relief, Tereza returned to the house, washed her hands, and joined Babi in the kitchen. A massive pot of bramboračka that could easily feed an army brigade rested on the table, filled to the brim, accompanied by a bottle of Maggi sauce, a basket of cut rye bread, and a pile of four bowls. Tereza checked her hWisper to see what bramboračka was, whether there were any tricks to eating it according to tradition.

As she sat at the table with her grandmother, Tereza did her best to hide her professional curiosity about Babi, to avoid studying her. At one hundred and nine years old, Babi would make a worthy test subject in Tereza's longevity work. Around the age of one hundred, Babi had seemed to stop aging altogether. Aside from a tricky knee and some kyphosis of the spine that rendered her hardly bigger than a child, she had a clean bill of health—no signs of dementia or Alzheimer's, no signs of advancing entropy. She was still filled with ceaseless energy as she puttered around the house that was clearly her kingdom, her face marked with smile and forehead wrinkles. She would've been the perfect person to represent VITA, to make longevity appear beautiful and serene rather than a torturous extension of life's tedium and aches. But VITA was not welcome at this table, and Babi was more than a guinea pig of permanence.

"We're glad to have you here," Babi said in Czech. "You have your mother's kindness and resolve, and those are the things that matter."

Tereza nodded, hoping the words were favorable. Roman was washing up and unable to translate.

He entered reluctantly, his hands red after the scrubbing, his wounded eye half shut. He poured two glasses of beer and a water for himself. Tereza began to salivate at the thought of the hair of the dog. She was still feeling the gin hangover, or maybe it was a mild concussion from the accident; either way, the golden nectar promised relief and, perhaps, less tension in the room, which had been darkened by Roman's temper and Tereza's guilt.

"Who else is joining us?" Tereza asked Roman, looking at the fourth bowl.

"An offering, for those we lost," he replied with irritation.

I only wished I could take my seat at the table and accept the offering, dine with my family. I couldn't feel hunger, yet I had a burning appetite.

Babi gestured for Tereza to fill her bowl first. Tereza stirred the soup, and massive cubes of potatoes, carrots, and mushrooms floated to the top. Her hand shook slightly with hunger, but she maintained decorum, ladled slowly so she wouldn't spill on the table. She took two pumps of Maggi seasoning and a slice of bread, which she dipped in the thick broth, following the instructions she'd read online.

"Please tell our grandmother this is one of the best meals I've ever had," she said.

"Nonsense," Roman said. "I'm sure you've had much better food." But he mumbled the translated compliment nonetheless.

"Thank you! We have a fly," Babi announced as the intruder made itself known, buzzing above the window plants. Babi shot upward as if this were of the gravest concern to humanity. She liquidated the insect with a swift backhand strike of the flyswatter, letting out a powerful groan reminiscent of professional tennis players, then plucked the fly carcass from the flyswatter and appraised it. Her skin was so thin, I worried it might tear.

"She said we have a fly," Roman translated.

"Not anymore. Does she have questions for me?" Tereza said.

"She doesn't really ask questions. She's practical about these things, unsentimental."

"I guess you're practical too?"

"I have plenty of questions. Mother mentioned you had some glamorous job, but I never asked what it was."

Tereza waited a beat to reply. She had told me she often claimed to be a real estate agent, as that job description required no follow-up. But I think she felt obligated to show good faith with her family. Even though Roman was a difficult man, she had come here to know him, and she wanted him to know her. Besides, wouldn't a confession feel good? She had run away from New York, from her responsibilities. She was unmoored, afraid of VITA's wrath. It had to be lonely, keeping such fears to herself. "I work for a company in the permanence sector," she said. "VITA. You may've seen us on TV."

"You work for them? The immortality people?" Roman's voice rose an octave as he momentarily forgot to act with disdain.

"You could say that."

"You'll make us live forever, hmm?" Roman's iciness returned. "Your company is what's wrong with the world. Enslaving us with the hWisper."

"What about you?" Tereza said, ignoring the slight. "I heard that you drive a truck."

"Someone has to keep the wheels turning while others pursue eternity. But I have a degree in economics. Hence my English."

My children continued eating as Babi filled their bowls again to the brim. She told Roman she was fatigued and was going to let them talk for a while. She sat in a reading chair facing them and opened a book. Occasionally she looked up to ensure her grandchildren were eating at an acceptable pace.

"I don't want to push things," Tereza said as she chewed. "But I'm ready to go home right now and return only when I've found the remains. You can come with me if you want, I can try to sponsor your visa. Or not."

"I would like to enjoy my meal," Roman said. But as he slurped another spoonful, the smartphone in his pocket chirped. He checked the message and closed it before I could see it; I found I could not enter my son's phone in the same way I'd penetrated Tereza's hWisper. The blood drained from his face. He cleared his throat loudly and threw the phone across the living room; it landed on the couch.

"Who was that?" Babi said from her chair.

Roman growled and filled his mouth aggressively with soup, the thick brown liquid running down his chin. "Isn't it ironic?" he asked his sister. I could tell he was at the edge of a tantrum from the drops of sweat forming around his neck. When he was a child, I called them his anger beads. "You work at the Division of Permanence to extend people's lives. But as soon as you met our mother, she died! So in a way, you shortened her life instead of extending it. Am I right?" He laughed without meaning it.

"It's not really irony. More of a coincidence," Tereza said quietly.

"Aha. Well, now your country has my mother," Roman said. "And they can use her for their experiments. That's what you do with foreigners, right? You steal their bodies. Fill them with chemicals and machines so they can serve you. Is that what you've done to our mother? Don't you think I know that your company works with the government to enslave us all?"

"I see. You're a red-pill guy." Indeed, my son had been red-pilled long ago. The term had gained different meanings throughout the years—in this instance, Roman was referring to the theory that VITA and the U.S. government worked together to raise an army of reanimated soldiers to fight a war against China.

"I merely like to read and think for myself," Roman said. He dropped his spoon with a clatter into his empty bowl.

"I don't want to be insensitive," Tereza said. "I think that perhaps here in the village, you've become a bit isolated from the world. And it's made it easier for you to believe certain things."

"Oh, sister, you speak beautifully! I wish Babi could understand this. You call us stupid shitkickers, and you do it like a poet. Here, let me translate for her!"

Tereza set down her spoon and cleared her throat. I watched my children with disbelief. When had my son become the kind of person to buy into tales about armies of the undead attacking Asia? He'd sworn off politics after his regrettable involvement in the Summer of Madness, promising Babi and me that he would never again be a part of any movement, become involved in conspiracy theories, or revisit his old insurrectionist forums. I had convinced myself that that brief part of his life was over. Perhaps my death was dragging him back to his old ways, or perhaps his promises were lies I had been foolish enough to believe.

"To answer your question," Tereza said, "no, I have not stolen our mother's body to launch an attack on China. Have you told our grandmother about your . . . theories?"

Babi, who had begun to doze in her chair despite the intense conversation, dropped her book on the floor.

"Forget it," Roman said. "Here, just have more soup." He picked up the ladle and poured the bramboračka into Tereza's bowl, more and more, filling it to the brim, until it nearly spilled over the edges and onto the table. Tereza pushed his hand away.

"I'm finished, thank you," she said.

"Right!" Roman shouted. He dropped the ladle back into the soup pot. He jumped to his feet and grabbed the pot from the table.

Tereza picked up her spoon and held it tightly, ready to jab him if necessary. I hadn't seen Roman like this in a long time. Was grief driving him to such beastly behavior?

"Our soup is not good enough for the American sister!" he shouted. "Only the best for her." He turned away and bounded to the kitchen sink.

Babi woke up, gasping at the commotion. Before Tereza could react, Roman began to pour all of the soup into the sink. He turned the faucet on and watched the muddy mixture of bramboračka and water circle the drain. Finally, Tereza brought herself to her feet, unsure of what to do.

Somehow Babi was faster. She appeared at the sink and began to beat Roman over the head and neck with the flyswatter, screaming and cursing, "Ty dobytku, ty parchante, nech toho!" *Animal, bastard, leave it alone!*

As her brother's neck reddened from the lashes, Tereza didn't know whether to restrain him or Babi. Finally, Roman dropped the emptied pot into the sink, returned to his chair, and exhaled heavily, ruddy-cheeked, his eyes bulging. Babi stared at the remnants of her labors disappearing down the drain.

Tereza stood behind her, unsure of her place in this scene. "You need to take a walk before I call the..." She paused. Most likely she wanted to say *police,* but no crimes had been committed here, except for assault by flyswatter. Hers was a very American reaction, one that assumed the police ought to be involved at the slightest suggestion of conflict or wasted soup. I was glad that my daughter had stopped herself, as cops would only bring more chaos.

"You're a stranger in a strange land, Terezo," Roman said. "Don't think our family is your business." He stood, drank down a glass of water, and walked toward the hallway. "You should say goodbye to Babi and leave tonight," he said. "Forget us. Forget any of this ever happened. I need to make a plan. I'm going to find my mother and bring her home. And then we can forget about the stain you've left on our lives. We can try to forget that she left us to find you, and you didn't protect her, you didn't keep her safe in that place you call a country. Please go back to your life. There is so little happiness to go around. We have none to give you." He walked outside and through the front gate.

Babi and Tereza watched him until he vanished in the distance on the main road, heading in the direction of the pub. In my purgatory, I was helpless. The chaos of my death had torn through my family and left it fractured. Had I driven my son mad? Could my mother survive the grief, living with Roman on her own? All I could do was observe.

Babi dabbed at her nostrils with her handkerchief. Tereza took her grandmother by the hand and led her to the couch, sat her down, and placed a blanket over her legs. Babi stared at the wall, exhausted and confused. In the fridge, Tereza found a bottle of milk and poured a tall glass. When she brought it back to the couch, Babi pointed at the kitchen cabinet, where Tereza found a bottle of cognac, which she poured into the milk. Babi drank it down. She lifted her hand up with her pointer and middle fingers turned downward, then wagged the fingers back and forth. A walk? Tereza nodded.

They walked out of the house in the middle of the sunset and headed west, in the opposite direction of the pub and memorial where Tereza had entered the village. The path led to the untamed ends of Hluboká, where no houses had been built. In this wilderness of long grassy fields and used condoms left behind by frolicking youths, they approached Snake Hill. From the time I was little, all the children of Hluboká had been told to stay away from the hill during the warm months. It was littered with dozens of snake holes, though I'd never actually seen a snake emerge. Growing up, I often thought that the presence of snakes was a collective fantasy cooked up by our parents to prevent teens from coming to these parts to fool around. During winter, however, Snake Hill was considered not only safe but a paradise for all, and the entire village gathered here for sledding. Some even attempted to ski and snowboard. Babi told Tereza all about it while my daughter nodded along as if she understood the strange language of her ancestors. I knew that her hWisper had a live-translation function that could allow her to communicate with Babi, but I suspected she didn't want to involve technology in what was an intimate moment, a human moment. She was seeing the places that had shaped me. They walked to the stretch of road where I first learned to ride a bicycle and to the old pig farm, long abandoned, where Babi used to take me when the farming collectives still existed and the villagers toiled together to grow their shared stock. I used to scratch the pigs behind the ears and gave each one a name.

Two hours passed. By the time they returned to the house, it had long been dark, and their spirits were lifted considerably. In front of the gate, they encountered a young woman dressed in a tailored suit. She had come to oversee the pickup of the rental wreckage Tereza had left by the memorial. It seemed Tereza had already forgotten about it. The woman was rather upset, but as she prepared to call the police, Tereza offered to pay the cost of a new vehicle, to avoid entanglements with the authorities. She transferred the money immediately and the insurance woman left, satisfied. What was it like to wave problems away so easily with the right number?

Inside, Tereza found that Roman had returned and was sitting on the living-room couch, scrolling on his laptop. He reeked of rum, though he didn't seem drunk. I envied him. I had no way of numbing myself, of tricking a body I no longer possessed into a chemically induced state of indifference.

"Had a nice stroll?" he said.

"Dude, give it a rest," Tereza said, exchanging a look with Babi.

Her grandmother kissed her cheek and announced it was past eight o'clock and thus past her bedtime. She said something to Roman before vanishing inside her bedroom with her trusty book.

"She says you should wake her if I bother you," Roman said. "She'll give me another whipping."

"That's a tempting offer," Tereza said. "It was fun to watch."

Her brother said nothing else and turned back to his computer. Tereza took this idle moment to scan through the thousands of new e-mails and messages in her hWisper. VITA had bombarded her with texts and calls she had so far ignored. I was beginning to wish that she would simply book a return flight to New York, go back to her work, and forget about chasing my remains. Stay in touch with her grandmother but continue to live as she had before I'd changed her world with my visit. But it seemed that her obsession with the fate of the telomere had become a distant problem for characters from science-fiction novels. My daughter was too much like me: She couldn't back away from a challenge. She wouldn't stop until she found out what had happened to me in America.

Finally, Roman set the laptop aside and asked her to join him on the couch. Again, he seemed more like himself, the more reasonable man I had gotten to know over the past few years. Perhaps it was the rum.

"If I went too far," he said, "I'm sorry. Sometimes I don't really understand the things I do."

"We can chalk it up to the shock of grief," Tereza said. "Start over."

Almost too benevolent, I thought. Did her brother deserve it?

"It has been a long day," Roman said. "Thing is, I'm not sure how to say this, but I wasn't surprised that she's dead. In a way, I already knew."

Tereza crossed her legs, inadvertently putting more space between her and Roman. "It's instinct," she said. "I've felt it before. Knowing something awful has happened."

"No, it's...fuck it. You already think I'm a lunatic. What's the point?"

She leaned in and sought his eyes with hers. My son rarely returned someone's gaze.

"I've been receiving strange messages," he said. "I thought they were pranks at first, but how? I don't know who could've sent them."

My daughter raised her shoulders, straightened her spine, lifted her head. Alert. "What kinds of messages?" she said.

Roman pulled out his phone and scrolled. "This is the one I got earlier today."

The drawn image on the screen was me. A black-and-white sketch of my likeness. My eyes were closed, my hair was gone, and on my bald head, the sender of the sketch had drawn a series of thick lines. Were they scars?

Underneath the image appeared these words: *I'm waiting*.

Roman tinkered with his phone again. He played a long audio file. It was a series of tapping sounds, nothing else.

"It's Morse code," Roman said. "I got it yesterday. It spells out *Don't let them steal me away* in English."

Tereza was silent.

"Do you think your government sent these?" Roman said. "To mess with me?"

"I'm sorry to say it," Tereza said, "but my government doesn't know or care about you."

"Maybe some hacker."

Tereza activated her hWisper. With a few flicks of her fingers, she sent two files to Roman's phone and instructed him to look.

Roman stared at the GIF that Tereza had received before her flight: My likeness soaked in dark blue shadows, my eyes black. Letters appeared and concealed my face: *Have you misplaced your mother?* Then he looked at the second file. *Greetings from Manatee County!* My passport photo flashed over the beaches of Anna Maria. "Someone is fucking with us?" he said.

"Logic concurs," Tereza said. "But I can't imagine to what end. My days keep getting stranger. Like a constant dream state."

"I've been having these dreams for a while," Roman said. "Of the army of the undead raised by the Americans to colonize the world. Of scientists like you cutting people open to harvest their brains and turn them into computers. A way of breeding machines with humans. Did you know that the Russians tried to reanimate animals by sewing human heads onto their bodies? This feels like one of those dreams."

Ranting seemed to comfort him, and he continued, asserting that the Reclamation Bureau had been stealing the bodies of immigrants for years. No one knew what happened to them. Rumors spread of black sites in warehouses in the southern part of Florida, where devastating tsunamis had driven out the population, leaving large gaps of unoccupied territory. Away from the prying eyes of its citizens, the government conducted sinister experiments on the bodies of non-Americans. As a former member of the Czech Reclamation movement, Roman was no friend to immigrants—everyone ought to stay with their own, he claimed, make a life in the place where they were born—but in his opinion, not even those who didn't belong deserved to be used as pawns in America's conspiracy to take over the world.

I too had heard of the strange Reclamation facilities rumored to hold stockpiles of dead bodies for experimentation. When the story became a viral phenomenon, official sources raced to declare that the rumors were false, the surveillance photos and videos of warehouses manipulated. The deepfake experts—Twitter, TikTok, the Department of Justice, all of the most respected institutions in charge of facts—maintained that the rumors were propaganda planted by foreign interventionists to further divide the American people. In the world's leading Christian nation, the Reclamation government insisted, the dead were still buried in cemeteries.

Tereza stared into the darkness of the living room, offering an occasional polite "Hmm" to her brother's rambling. "I don't know about you," she interrupted when she finally ran out of patience, "but I won't move on from this until we've found her."

"I will never move on," Roman said.

"Come back with me," she said. What followed was a long silence. I had feared that their talk was leading toward this mad conclusion. "I have some contacts. I'll fight to get you a visa. We'll track our mother down."

"America," Roman said, then bit his lip. "It's the last place I want to go."

"For her," Tereza said.

"For her." Roman slowly nodded. "We will tell Babi tomorrow."

I felt great distress at the prospect of Roman traveling to America.

Between his politics and his temper, it was a risk to bring him to a place filled with such violent tensions. It was best for him to remain hidden away in a village where people had known about his quirks since he was a child, where the worst his personality could bring about was a bar fight, not a hail of bullets from a semiautomatic rifle. Finding out what had happened to my body wasn't worth it.

But the tentative agreement seemed to soothe my children. Tereza turned away from Roman and retreated into her hWisper, where she began to read about the elaborate conspiracies that informed his thinking. Her brother, meanwhile, kept dozing off, his head bumping gently against the wall as he fought sleep. In this silence, I pictured the fictional warehouse in Florida's swamps, slabs of concrete walls sheltering a rabid horde of the undead, myself included, waiting to be airlifted and dropped onto Chinese battlefields. Ridiculous.

Tereza had begun to fall asleep too, despite Roman's exasperating snores, the workingman's slumber. I settled in to observe my children in their peaceful state. But in the darkness of the living room, something changed. Amid Roman's snores, I heard voices resonate from within the plane of my afterlife. At times they sounded like me, though more guttural, skewed by white noise and echoes:

"Adéla."

"The obstacles are made of mist."

"Built to be torn down."

"Impose your will."

Or was this the voice of the magical carp speaking to me from my bathtub? Or perhaps the croaking call of a heron? I had a vision of the bird dipping its feet into the shallow waters of the shore next to those concrete walls I'd imagined. Hadn't the heron gone extinct?

In this vision, the hum of a generator cuts through the bird's call. I am inside a large building, and the skin I no longer possess is cold. At my feet are a thousand faces, but I cannot stop to look closely. I am inside some kind of glass box and I cannot move. My world is made of gray walls, icicles hanging from the ceiling, ugly fluorescent lighting, and a pair of generators taking up most of the space, roaring to keep these horrors alive.

This is my true afterlife. I know it.

Now I am outside the glass box. I can see inside. I see my face, robbed of life. I am frozen in time with an expression of oblivion. My eyes are fully open, bulging, but my lips are sealed shut and blue. A red mark blossoms across my face, like the roots of a tree, as if some disease has set my veins on fire. My hair has been shorn, my bald head scarred with crusty, stapled cuts flecked with white powder—bone shavings stuck to my flesh. They opened me up so quickly, so eagerly, and didn't even bother to clean up afterward.

I ran down the empty, ugly paths of Tereza's hWisper interface. A safe place—or safer. How had I gotten here? Why? Around me the icons of modern life loomed: Contacts; 834 New Messages. Was there music playing? A massive hourglass materialized above me. Syncing. A software update was delayed until the device could be restarted. The hourglass sand poured down toward my face and I leaped forward and crashed into the icon shaped like a massive microphone. The image of my scarred head appeared before me over and over, like a replay. Why couldn't I see anything else? I screamed again, into my oblivion: *Save me. Save me. Save me.*

I returned to the living room of my family house. My children were still asleep.

Within seconds Tereza awoke with a gasp. She reached out to Roman in the darkness, startling him awake. "Did you hear that?" she asked.

"There's mice in the attic," he said.

"No. The voice. I think it's her." Tereza squinted into the corners of the room, as if I might simply be standing there, waiting to be noticed. Finding nothing, she flicked her thumb, and the absent look in her eye suggested she had reentered her hWisper. I followed. Above the network of her interface paths floated the massive icon of a new video file: Unnamed.mp4. It blinked and began to play.

First, I heard my voice. A distorted, scratchy echo that sounded as though it were coming from a great distance, as if I were trying to speak while someone choked me. But it was unmistakable. Two words recorded in my own voice: "Save me." The video was merely a grainy screenshot of collapsed trees with the moon looming above, accompanied by the songs of cicadas. A warehouse made of concrete interrupted the swamplands, the harsh lights on its roof cutting through the darkness around the building. A few men dressed in Homeland Deportation Force uniforms stood around the perimeter. "Save me," repeated the recording as a series of numbers appeared over the image. They looked like GPS coordinates. Then letters appeared—*Bring a casket!*—before the video cut off. Tereza restarted the file, which blinked and played again. Again. And again. "Save me."

I returned from her hWisper to the living room as Roman opened his computer. The unnamed file landed on his desktop as Tereza stared at him intensely. He clicked on it, and the sound of my plea filled the living room. Hastily my son turned down the sound to avoid waking his grandmother.

"Tell me that's not her," Tereza said.

"What? No. Mother had a news-announcer voice. A lot of people sound like her."

"I heard it in my sleep. When I woke up just now, the file was waiting in my hWisper. It just appeared."

Roman played the file a few more times. "Maybe it sounds like her because I want it to," he said. "Someone is messing with us. Just another prank."

"You're so rational all of a sudden."

"Just go to bed already," Roman said. He placed his laptop on the floor and leaned his head back against the wall. He closed his eyes, but I could tell he was wide awake, unsettled by what he'd just seen.

My daughter, too, was fully awake. Tereza flooded her cranium with the sound of my voice a hundred times over. *Save me.* What did the appeal have to do with the other cryptic messages she'd received?

Had it really come from me? Could I communicate with my daughter after all? I tried but could do nothing to reach her now. In the depths of her hWisper, I was still powerless, merely an observer. I wished to narrate an entire book for her, to explain everything. To apologize for my jarring visit and sudden demise, for upending her life this way. But it seemed that all I could give my daughter was a disturbing sound-bite. In the moonglow seeping through the shades, her face hardened in anticipation of the troubles ahead.

She searched online for the coordinates in the video and pulled up a satellite view of ravaged Manatee County. The images showed abandoned flooded territories except in the exact spot marked by the coordinates, where a massive black square concealed the area. Even close up, the website map yielded no results at all. Next, Tereza searched for *Manatee County black sites*. Strangely, not a single result appeared here either.

Listening to my plea on loop, she reached a decision and woke her brother with a jab to the ribs. "We have to get her."

"I know that," he said. "I'm not sure how, but the voice is hers."

"Something's fucked up here."

"Always," he said.

"Do you believe in ghosts? Hauntings?"

"She raised me to be an atheist. Thank God. When the body goes, it leaves nothing behind. It's simpler that way."

"Did she ever tell you what her wishes were? Where she wanted to rest?"

"Hluboká," Roman said without hesitation. He leaned closer to his sister. "The family plot. Each of us has a rectangle of dirt already measured and marked. It used to creep me out until I found out that Mother was comforted by it. She knew that in due time, all of us would be in the same place. Close by. She thought our tombstones and the bones underneath might outlast civilization."

"I've always found preparations for death . . . alienating. I refuse to do it."

"I know she'd want us to add a plot for you. But the cemetery is all booked up—"

"My employers own my remains," Tereza said. "I prefer not to think of what they'll do with me. We have to bring her home, Roman. Are you up to it?"

"I am," Roman said. "I feel the pull."

In whispers, they theorized about how to reach the coordinates in the strange message. They knew that the abandoned territory of Florida—the same area, strangely enough, where I'd spent many years of my youth—was nearly impossible to access by conventional means. The land had been seized by the Reclamation government, and trespassing carried a long prison sentence. There were stories, Roman told Tereza, of people venturing to these lands to look for the bodies of their deceased loved ones, but the stories vanished almost as soon as they appeared on the internet.

The last means of accessing the land was via the freighter shipping routes, which formed the remnants of trade between the two continents. Freighters traveled legally to Miami and Jacksonville, on the east side of the state, but enterprising captains looking to make extra money risked the trip up the western coast to pick up American refugees seeking Europe's shores. With the resources of the Coast Guard already stretched thin, patrolling the abandoned territories was not a priority. The few outlaw survivalists who remained in Florida's forgotten territories served as reliable guides through the wilderness. Roman knew of these smuggling routes thanks to his job driving freight to Bremerhaven, Germany, where the captain of a ship called *Markyta* was rumored to provide such services for the right price. Roman revealed to Tereza that he'd been approached by the captain to help smuggle the refugees farther into Europe in the back of his truck, though he had refused.

If Tereza could pay for their passage, Roman said, he would take care of the rest. Since the illegal passage by freighter didn't require dealing with the Reclamation authorities, Roman argued it was almost easier this way. Instead of begging for a visa that would never be granted to a young Czech male of no means, they could enter America together and investigate my body's disappearance via this more *unofficial* route.

Tereza resisted the idea at first. If they were captured, her brother was likely to lose years of his life in a work camp, the usual punishment for foreigners who violated America's border laws. Tereza would have some chance of escaping punishment due to her job and status, but the Reclamation authorities were unpredictable on such matters.

"Is this crazy?" Tereza said.

No. Yes, I wished to reply. While I had the same doubts and great concern for my children's safety, I couldn't forget those images of my body, the red scar on my face, the box I was trapped in. I had an intense desire to know what had been done to me—to the remains I still felt attached to.

My children continued to speak deep into the night, and with each word, the unlikely trip became more inevitable. In the end they agreed that if Roman could secure passage on the freighter, the effort was worthwhile. The odds of being captured weren't high enough to overwhelm my children's desire to find out what had happened to me, to recover my remains and reunite me with Babi so that I could rest in the village of my birth. The nature of the messages they'd received haunted them—they seemed otherworldly more than a mere prank by an unknown force.

They had to acknowledge that perhaps none of this made any sense, and they were merely acting on survivors' guilt and the depth of their grief. Finally, Tereza expressed what had remained unspoken: "It feels like she's calling us to her." She could sense her brother nodding beside her in the dark. They hadn't moved from the couch in hours. "Two days ago, I would've said it sounds like bullshit. But now..."

Had I really, somehow, dispatched these messages, these calls to rescue me, to my children without knowing it?

The sun came up with them veering between the urge to sleep and the urge to plan. While Babi shuffled out of her room and poured water into the kettle, they shook hands to make their pact official. They would reveal the plan to her later in the morning. Roman sent out messages to his network of truck drivers extending to Bremerhaven to locate the captain who might be willing to smuggle them into the Florida wildlands.

I found it unlikely that my children could enter a country so brutally guarded, much less find my body in a godforsaken swamp—did this warehouse even exist? All night long I wished I could recant my voice reaching out from the afterlife, make them abandon this insane undertaking, leave me where I was, and get on with their lives. Why should we care what happens to the flesh once it's vacant? But I cared. I cared about my disfigured head, the cuts dividing my skull, the hideous scar on my face. What had they done to me? I felt what Tereza felt—a pull. The calling of the strange. In the ghost stories of my youth, spirits were trapped on this earth because of the unsolved mysteries of their bodies. And so perhaps the journey of my children was inevitable. They had to find my physical remains to free me from whatever this liminal prison was, to release me into whatever comes after. Despite my lack of religion, I couldn't accept it was the fate of the dead to roam the world of the living forever alone, unheard, observing joy and tragedy without participating. Such an afterlife was akin to eternal madness. There had to be a way forward, toward a death that held meaning or, better yet, toward a death that would release me from the burden of consciousness.

My children finally retreated to their bedrooms for a few hours' rest just as Babi was beginning her morning. Exhausted from this night of strange visions, I too drifted off in my own way, seeking comfort in the chaos of my youth in Florida. The days ahead, it seemed, were going to be as harrowing as the most uncertain moments of my mortal life.

THE YEAR IS 1987

MICHAEL AND I spent over a year developing the seed of my *Newts* idea into a script, then a better script, then, against all odds, a full-blown production. In October of 1987, as the passing of the tourist season thinned out the herd of visitors on the Siesta Key beaches, we began to shoot our adaptation, titled *The Great Newt War*. Michael had rented a 35 mm Moviecam and decided to act as his own cinematographer, a monumental addition to his directing responsibilities. Five of his film-school friends had joined us to help, in exchange for experience and free food. Then there was my counterpart, the second star of the film: Rostislav, an animatronic salamander puppet who would represent the entirety of the salamander species. Rostislav had been built by Alphonse, a disgraced Hollywood puppeteer with a gambling problem who had come to the Sunshine State seeking opportunities to remake himself. Alphonse constructed Rostislav from an old animatronic skeleton he'd stolen from the Universal lot upon his departure from Los Angeles. Spielberg had managed to make a timeless blockbuster using a beach town and a half-broken animatronic shark — why couldn't we?

My character was Ava Andersson, a rich young widow living by the sea, finding little satisfaction in her money and the lifestyle it affords. She lives in a world on the brink of something new, as the destiny of the salamander species has become interlocked with our own. The newts have been deployed to mine for manganese, iron, copper, and nickel at the bottom of the ocean. They maintain massive fishing farms and build complicated power plants that convert tidal energy into mainland electricity. They are learning human languages, living in underwater settlements along most of the world's major coasts. The salamander has become a part of human economy and culture, yet humans still treat newts as degenerate sea monsters with a knack for underwater engineering. This tension will soon result in a hostile takeover.

I channeled these thoughts as I shot my first scene of the film, walking around the beach near my mansion, lost within the march of modernity.

Ava first encounters Rostislav during her daily walk on the shore in the shadow of a massive rock formation. He is dressed in a white button-down shirt with the sleeves rolled up, his black tie loosely hanging around his neck, as if he's come from a day at the office. Ava has never seen the newts dressed like this before. She knows that because salamanders have no protections under the law, they are shy and cautious toward unknown humans. In her intrigue, she struggles to decide whether she should leave the salamander alone or ask if he needs help.

Before she can decide, the creature approaches her and introduces himself in flawless English. "Greetings, madam, my name is Rostislav Adriatic. Would you like to engage in conversation?"

Recognizing his name as Slavic, Ava asks Rostislav where he's from. Despite having just met her, the newt shares all of his story at once—it seems that he's been waiting for some time to unburden himself. He was born off the coast of Yugoslavia, where he grew up helping fishermen untangle their nets. Eventually, an old professor of linguistics from Charles University came to Yugoslavia to see the ocean, and over long conversations about the beauty of Prague, he and Rostislav became best friends. At the end of his holiday, the professor invited Rostislav to come see the city for himself. He asked his colleagues from the engineering department to build a wheeled water tank in which Rostislav could move around the city. The two friends took long walks together—they saw the castle in which the president lived, they visited cake shops that served rum cake and custard pies, the kind of food a salamander couldn't eat. Regardless, the colors and shapes of the desserts brought Rostislav joy. The professor taught his friend to speak Czech and asked him to stay in the city permanently, to become his assistant, should he be interested in such a position. Rostislav agreed, to the chagrin of the faculty of Charles University. Most of the learned men considered this an inappropriate interspecies friendship that spat in the face of nature or God.

Disillusioned by his countrymen's view of the friendship, the professor decided to accept a visiting position at the brand-new University of Miami, in America. Living a quieter life along the coast, Rostislav and the professor enjoyed the Florida sun, stuffed their bellies with seafood, took daily strolls on the beach, and practiced their English during dinner parties they hosted for students and neighbors. They were inseparable, surprised and delighted by the depth of their love for each other.

Shortly before the end of his visiting tenure, the professor walked out the door to go grocery shopping. He never returned. Rostislav wandered the streets looking for his friend for days. When the university noticed the professor's absence, they filed a police report, naming Rostislav as the likeliest suspect in his disappearance.

Rostislav fled the apartment, leaving behind all the belongings he and the professor had shared, including his water tank. He began sleeping on the beach, torn between retaining his status as a land dweller and obeying his strongest instinct: to leap back into the sea and build a salamander nest in which he could hide from his sorrow. And it was in this state of abandonment, deciding between land and ocean, that he met Ava Andersson, a wealthy widow out for a stroll.

DURING THIS FIRST scene of the shoot, I already felt defeated and frustrated, as it was my job to make Rostislav seem alive despite the grotesque machinery slithering under his polyurethane skin, a seemingly impossible task. The training I'd received under the direction of the theater dissidents in Prague hadn't prepared me to exchange lines with a robot. But as heat fatigue set in early in the afternoon, compounded by the three beers I had drunk in secret during our lunch break, I asked Michael to read Rostislav's lines, and suddenly the newt's eyes projected wisdom, awareness, familiarity. I could believe in Rostislav the newt as long as he spoke with Michael's voice. I could project onto him my own desires and fears and expectations. This is the way in which people—and salamanders—fall in love.

Michael and I agreed from the beginning we didn't want to make a direct adaptation of *War with the Newts*—there was no one to give us, complete amateurs, millions of dollars to make such a film, and our crew's skills were better suited for an intimate drama, not an action epic. The book concerned itself mostly with the epochal events of the salamander uprising, but we wanted to create an alternate storyline that focused on a relationship between members of the different species that would soon be at war. Could they save each other?

But even with our humble approach to the material, we needed a considerable amount of cash. We found our financier in Derek, Michael's best friend since childhood. When the two of them were little, Derek created simple Ponzi schemes to scam kids out of their lunch money, and Michael found the right way to spend it: the boys saw every movie coming out in their local theater and dreamed of making their own. While Derek eventually embraced the obvious path of a stockbroker, Michael skipped meals in film school. Despite the ensuing alienation between them, Derek agreed to finance our film before he finished reading the script, to fulfill the oath he'd made as a boy. He saw Michael and me as a worthy investment. I could see how eager he was to put his name behind some art, to give his obscene wealth meaning. Derek supplied $250,000, which covered equipment, a small wage for the crew, and Alphonse's gambling debt. He signed himself on as a producer with a 60 percent profit share. The money wasn't much to him. It roughly amounted to the tax cuts Derek would take that year thanks to Ronald Reagan. For Michael and me, it was a decade's worth of paychecks.

I considered investing some of the money I'd saved up at the hotel. It would be a gesture, a commitment. I loved the script we'd written, believed firmly in its success. At the same time, I needed to keep an escape fund in case my American life came to a quick end. Some nights I stayed awake with eyes fixed on the door, waiting for the immigration agents to burst through and take me away. I refused Michael's offers to let me drive, as I couldn't risk getting pulled over. At the grocery store I looked over my shoulder for the police or for American informants who might report a suspicious woman with a foreign accent. If I was caught, immediate deportation would be the best-case scenario; indefinite detention was more likely. If it came down to it, Michael could do nothing to save me, despite his promise. No, I couldn't afford to sacrifice a single dollar of my escape fund. If I sensed the smallest threat of being discovered, I would leave the country without looking back.

As I wrestled with paranoia, Michael indulged fully in his Reagan dreams, his Hollywood fantasy. He believed our low-budget film would replicate the success of *Mad Max* and earn millions at the box office despite its camp aesthetic and blockbuster competitors. He thought we would soon live in a mansion on Sunset Boulevard and make Newts into a studio-budget franchise. I knew that relying on becoming wealthy *someday* was a recipe for lifelong unhappiness, the same dissatisfaction that radiated off Americans like heat waves. When I thought of *Newts,* I didn't picture the resulting wealth or fame. I saw a legacy. The film was to become proof that Adéla Slavíková once walked the earth.

Inside her mansion, Ava Andersson shares a bottle of scotch with her dearest companion, Rostislav the newt, as the pair listen to a radio broadcast announcing the war between their species. The state of Louisiana has been violently split from the rest of the Gulf Coast by a powerful weapon the salamanders have constructed. Hundreds of thousands of people drowned before they could escape inland. The same has happened off the coasts of California, Japan, France, and Florida. Having reached the peak of their evolutionary development, the salamanders need to deepen the shores to accommodate their exploding populace. The reign of humanity is over. Newts are soon likely to drown the entire state of Florida, Ava's home included. On the radio, the squeaking voice of Governor Salamander dictates the terms of surrender to the humans of the world, an offer of mercy should the entire race capitulate unconditionally.

To preserve what remains of their civilization, human beings accede to Governor Salamander's demands for increased oceanic expansion. They move farther inland as their homes are destroyed and drowned. Countries that once were landlocked are becoming coastal. This is the sacrifice Governor Salamander demanded for a peaceful protectorate—as long as humans continue to move out of the way of newt expansion, they will be left unharmed, free to tend to their own affairs. The species are to remain in their separate realms of land and ocean.

An alliance of the world's nations are planning to mount a resistance, but so far the inner squabbles and negotiations have left the exposed civilians no choice but to obey their new governor.

"It's humbling," Ava says, "how quickly we've been demoted. Humans won the evolutionary lottery twelve thousand years ago when we discovered farming and herding. Today there's a new victor."

"You blame the rise of the salamander on bad luck," Rostislav says. "But what if we're simply superior? A natural replacement?"

"The ability to destroy a lesser species makes for a narrow definition of superiority."

"Humans have worshipped their own penchant for destruction for thousands of years."

"And today we pay the price."

IN APRIL OF 1988, we reached the final stretch of our *Newts* production schedule. We were underslept, straining the limits of our budget, chronically sunburned, and angry with each other. Our only distractions from the shoot were our day jobs and the depressing guesthouse of the Fairchilds. But there was freedom in our exhaustion—we knew we'd come too far to stop; we were fully submerged, committed, driven by fate. Now I yearn for these days of hunger and mania and hope, which reminded me in many ways of the striving to publish *Ark*. Immersed in the frantic uncertainty of art, the most unlikely undertaking translated into hundreds of meters of celluloid, tangible proof of our presence on earth. Many months of labor and resources spent to produce 110 minutes of storytelling—a mad crusade only a human being could pursue.

Ava swallows the scotch and refills her glass. The salamander sniffs his. All of Ava's family and friends have been killed in the salamander wars, meaning that in many ways, she has already disconnected from the world and won't mourn its fall like the others. She thinks of the future she always imagined for humans, the flying cars and free renewable energy, the distribution models for food and water that were equitable for all. The opportunity to build this utopia for the species has passed. Now there will be no more chances.

"Some say that Governor Salamander is actually human," Rostislav says. *"That he's manipulated salamanders into serving his cause and taking over the earth on his behalf."*

"I wouldn't be surprised," Ava says.

"I won't let them take you, you know," Rostislav says. "To make you a slave or harm you. You're safe, Ava."

"I feel like dancing," Ava says and puts her glass down. "I want to see what it's like out there as the world drowns."

Having grown used to keeping only each other's company every day, Ava and Rostislav have forgotten how they look to the outside world. They fail to consider that their presence together will be a provocation to mourning humans. They drive to a beach on the west coast of Florida, a place still untouched by salamander conquest, unlike the submerged, massacred eastern coast of the state. They don't have to walk long before they spot a bonfire, its flames and smoke shooting high toward the stars. As ever, humans mourn in their own peculiar ways. Dozens of people dance around the fire, scream; they punch each other and they couple up to fuck on the sand among the shattered beer bottles and soggy cigarette spliffs. A party for the end of the world. Dirty, raw, hopeless. Rostislav asks Ava if they can leave. This isn't a safe place. But Ava wants to lose herself in her species' doom too.

MOST OF THESE beach dancers were acquaintances of ours, movie extras whom Michael and I paid in beer and burgers and gas money to get to our location on Lido Beach. We had taught them the salamander dance and asked that they act mad and drunk. Exhausted from the day's shoot, I danced as if the end really were nigh. This night reminded me of the countless thespian afterparties I had attended in Prague. The blazing fire we'd built looked magnificent on celluloid against the backdrop of the setting sun, the darkening sea waves.

We paused to change film, and I threw more wood on the fire as our friends continued to drink and dance, a fictional party turning into a real one. Michael bade us to action again, and the music and the dancers carried on in their mayhem.

Ava loses herself in the dancing crowd, forgetting her newt friend for just a few moments. Rostislav follows her meekly, attempting to get around the human bodies without touching them, terror in his eyes. He asks to leave again, but Ava doesn't hear him. The dancers turn and notice the salamander in their midst and the woman he is speaking to. The sight of an unarmed, vulnerable newt produces a mob rage powerful enough for them to ignore the threats of Governor Salamander. The mob pounces. Ava tries to push them away as they grab at Rostislav. She punches and kicks and curses, pleading for mercy as Rostislav helplessly reaches out for her. The mob knocks Ava to the ground, and the bodies block her view of Rostislav. His small body battered, he drags himself toward the water, then stands up and runs toward his element to save himself. Before leaping into the waves, he hesitates, looking for Ava one last time. In this moment of weakness, the mob seizes him by the arms, and . . .

"Cut!"

A puff of smoke spilled out of Rostislav's eye. His jaw opened and closed erratically, then ceased movement altogether. The extras stepped back from the malfunctioning puppet. Alphonse picked up his robotic child and carried it to the parking lot, away from the water and sand, as if he were a lifeguard. The extras looked on quietly, a few of them returning to the cooler by the bonfire to drink more beer. Michael and I followed Alphonse, and the party continued without us.

Alphonse opened Rostislav's body, looked inside with a flashlight between his teeth, and cursed. "I told you he can't take all this sand and moisture!" he shouted at Michael. With that, Rostislav's creator set to work.

Within the hour, we had our diagnosis. Sand had gotten trapped in the animatronic engine and eroded a few key wires. According to

Alphonse, the fix would add about five thousand dollars to the budget. Michael and I dismissed the crew and extras and drove home.

In between phone calls, Michael told me that he couldn't ask Derek for any more money. He suggested that perhaps the Fairchilds would embrace an investment, but the idea of owing them made me sick. We could take out a loan, I proposed—Reagan's America was supposedly all about the support of small business and individual aspirations—but Michael laughed bitterly and said there was no way a bank would back us based on our income and lack of any property other than his old Buick. As soon as he mentioned the car, I sensed the idea flash through his head, and I warded it off by reminding him the Buick was hardly worth even a few hundred dollars. Besides, we couldn't finish the movie by riding bicycles between locations.

That evening, I gathered the savings I'd accrued during my time in America. I counted. Six thousand dollars. I had managed to double the amount I'd had when I met Michael. I separated out two thousand and put the other four thousand back in the hair-dye box. It would have to suffice to fix our broken newt. I convinced myself that my contribution was not only a physical investment but an act of faith. This was how America worked. You made a bet. Those willing to risk all and work harder and smarter than others would inevitably be rewarded, a manifest destiny. Reagan looked at us with hope and he *meant it*.

I dropped the cash on the living-room table in front of Michael, who was engrossed in reruns of *Hill Street Blues,* beer in left hand, Hot Pocket in right. When depressed, he binged. He looked up at me and he seemed both adorable and foolish with the junk food sagging in his hand, the cheese oozing out onto his thumb. He should've been used to surprises from me by then—after all, I'd brought him the book that had inspired our film and suggested we put all we had into this make-or-break project. Unexpectedly, he pushed for an explanation of the cash, as if aware for the first time that he didn't know everything about me. In response, I returned to our bedroom and locked the door behind me. I took a long shower and sat down with the script to sharpen my dialogue. With every day I spent on the set, my understanding of Ava's character diverged from Michael's original vision, and I was eager to make her wholly my own.

After a while, Michael began knocking on the door, insisting that we weren't wealthy enough to keep individual savings, that we needed to be honest about the total sum of our finances. What did he know about living in a country that you didn't know or trust, about the fear of becoming trapped with no means to flee an unhappy relationship or life, of waking up every morning thinking immigration agents might show up at the doorstep and imprison you, uproot you? I didn't reply. I was entitled to my secrets, to my escape routes. Perhaps I should've tried to explain, but the very idea of it annoyed me too much. Where I came from, people were much less eager to explain themselves all the time.

Over the next few weeks, Michael managed to get the money needed to fix the puppet by pawning our possessions, donating plasma, and participating in clinical trials for drugs that made him puke for months afterward. Alphonse repaired Rostislav's wiring, refined the structure of the facial skeleton, and mended a few tears in the skin. Rostislav looked shiny and new, and I felt a strange affection for my improved onscreen partner, as if the puppet were really a friend recuperating from a dangerous illness. July arrived, the hottest month of the year, and we raced to finish the film.

As the beach mobs drag Rostislav from the waves, they stomp one of their drunken companions into unconsciousness and leave him to drown in the shallow waters of the shore. But when the bobbing corpse is finally noticed, the celebrants forget Rostislav long enough for the newt to slip away and swim along the shore until he discovers a peaceful spot to rest, exhausted, bleeding on the sand. Ava searches for him, walking the shore all night until at last, at sunrise, she finds him. She wraps a blanket around him and carries him back to her mansion to tend to his wounds.

At noon, the police show up at her doorstep with an arrest warrant. Rostislav Adriatic stands accused of drowning a human man, a cold act of murder and a hate crime against the human race. Over one hundred witnesses have attested to seeing the salamander hold the poor boy's head underwater. The police carry off Ava's only friend, still bleeding, as he calls out her name. Then the policemen handcuff Ava and read her rights. The trial will become a condemnation of their interspecies friendship—Rostislav the murderer and Ava his accessory. An unnatural coupling that led the pair to evil acts. By violating Governor Salamander's wish for newts to live separately from humans, Rostislav has put himself entirely at the mercy of human law. He is to receive no intervention from his own kind.

WE DROVE OUR crew to a Presbyterian church that allowed us to turn their house of worship into a house of law in exchange for a charitable donation. We replaced the minister's pulpit with a judge's bench, the choir stand with the jury box, and the white drapes with black curtains bearing the symbol of the United Human States. We filled the church aisles with extras, the same friends who had performed as a crazed mob on the beach.

Ava walks into the courtroom wearing handcuffs, as does Rostislav, his custom restraints made to fit his small hands and massive hind legs. Behind them arrive four judges wearing medallions portraying a human foot marching upon dry land, the symbol of the nations uniting against the newt threat.

THEN ENTERED OUR lawyer, played by Alphonse the puppeteer, who'd had his hair trimmed and his nose hairs plucked for what he hoped would be his big break. He removed a thick notepad from his briefcase. My character's name, Ava, appeared on the top page, handwritten, several times, along with a scribbled recipe for key lime pie.

"Mr. Traeger," the lawyer says, introducing himself, "representation for Mrs. Ava Andersson."

"Where is my friend's representation?" Ava asks.

"As the protection of the law extends to humans only, we were unable to secure counsel for Mr. Rostislav Adriatic," one of the judges replies.

"Reach out to my people," Rostislav says. "Many skilled lawyers live in the ocean."

"As humans were the ones affected by your crime," the judge says, "you will be tried in a human court without any newt interference. Look at the weeping family behind you."

As if to underscore the kitsch of the court's righteousness, the victim's family sits in the first row of the audience section, all rage and tears and balled-up fists.

"I am a newt accused of a crime," Rostislav says. "Hand me over to Governor Salamander for a just process. I do not believe this court can judge me fairly."

"You committed a crime in the realm of men. You will thus be judged as a man."

"The realm of men is no longer, Your Honor," Rostislav says.

At this, the crowd rises, rapturous, shouting and spitting in anger.

"Guilty!" declares the judge as the crowd echoes his declaration. "Guilty! I sentence you to de—"

The doors of the courtroom swing open. In walks a man supporting himself on a cane, a stack of papers in hand. He is accompanied by uniformed men of the United Humans army, who push the crowd back, their rifles raised.

"This trial," the man announces, *"is in direct violation of the Human Salamander Peace Pact. Please dismiss the defendant immediately."* [The man is played by Derek, our financier, who felt his good looks would be wasted if we didn't offer him a cameo in the film.]

"A peace pact?" the judge shouts. *"There is no peace pact!"*

"As of twenty minutes ago there is. The salamander delegation has handed over a list of prisoners who are to be released immediately, and it has been accepted by the president of the human alliance."

"Shame!" the crowd shouts. *"Traitors! Collaborators!"*

The soldiers point their weapons at the crowd to subdue them.

Rostislav looks at Ava and says, "I told you we'd be safe."

In the midst of the chaos, Ava and Rostislav stand together, confident in the righteousness of their cause and their friendship.

IN THIS MOMENT, I truly was Ava Andersson. But it was the second-most-complex scene of the entire film, requiring dozens of takes, and we couldn't sustain the power of the scene for the duration of the shoot. The extras complained of hunger, and some of them had gotten far too drunk to function, proving the foolishness of our alcohol-as-pay efforts. The church was sweltering, as someone had stolen the AC and the fans we'd brought with us were not for the crew but to keep the equipment cool. Morale was at an all-time low.

Even I rebelled and snapped at Michael, asking whether the temperature of the camera was more important than me getting heatstroke.

"Just a while longer," Michael pleaded. "This is the breaking point. This is it. Afterward, we eat. Cold beer?"

The man with the cane orders the court officer to remove Rostislav's handcuffs. The bailiff begins to unlock Ava's too, but the man with the cane says, "Not her."

The crowd is quiet, all eyes on the defendants.

"Pardon?" the judge says.

"Ava Andersson is herewith convicted of treason against the human and newt societies," the man proclaims, "for carrying out espionage on behalf of both sides of the conflict."

The spectators, still frozen in silence, want someone to pay. For everything. But they want this justice carried out against a newt, not one of their own.

Witnessing the concentrated hatred the humans have for him, Rostislav realizes that he will never really be able to trust them. In a single moment, he loses all strength to believe in people. Ava might betray him someday too, might begin to feel revulsion, resentment toward his superior species. He will never be safe in the human world. Only his own kind can save him, just as they are doing now. Survival is imperative.

He steps away from the defendants' bench and follows the man with the cane and his protective detail. He doesn't give Ava a single glance. He offers no words on her behalf. It is a refusal of her life in exchange for his own. The people in the crowd sneer, clenching their fists, but none are willing to risk attacking and getting themselves shot.

Ava stares at Rostislav's back until he leaves the courtroom, but he doesn't dare return her gaze. It doesn't take her long to understand. She is led away quietly, accepting she's become a necessary sacrifice in this war her species is bound to lose. She walks with dignity toward the future that awaits us all.

AFTER THE DRAINING scene at the church, I needed to be alone. I took some cash from the hair-dye box, left Michael at home, threw caution aside and drove our Buick to the Goliath, the hotel where my American life had begun. I slipped past reception and took the elevator to the rooftop bar, where I ordered a shrimp cocktail and a mojito and looked out over the ocean, still enigmatic and ominous to someone who'd grown up landlocked. I imagined all kinds of monsters in its depths, waiting to feast. Had Čapek gotten the same feeling when he traveled to the sea? An uneasiness that helped him capture an existential threat lurking in its unknowns?

We were so close to having a film despite the setbacks—the sun that made each shooting day thrice as difficult, the onlookers who got in the way, the cruel grains of sand penetrating our equipment and our clothes. Every day I scooped it from various crevices, and the sand constantly littered our guesthouse, as if it had escaped from some invisible hourglass.

I convinced myself to book a room at the hotel and spend the night. I took an hour-long bath, wrapped myself in the bathrobe, ordered a couple of burgers and a whiskey, and watched television until I fell asleep. When I awoke in the morning, with crumbs and pieces of meat stuck to my neck, the whiskey glass lay overturned atop a golden stain on the sheets.

By the time I was ready to leave, I was three hours late for my shift at the Fairchild house. I considered leaving a heinous mess in the room—garbage spilling out of the can, piss on the toilet seat, bacon grease on the TV remote and pillows—but I couldn't even role-play a person so self-absorbed, weaponizing my indulgence to punish the hotel's workers for nothing in particular. Best to leave the room as I'd found it. I made the bed, wiped the sink and toilet, stacked my dishes atop each other, and left a tip of one hundred dollars.

When Michael asked me where I'd been, complaining that he'd almost called the police, I told him I'd taken an immigrant's version of a holiday. After he left for work, I grabbed my bathing suit and a book, and I swam in the Fairchilds' pool for the rest of the afternoon. I knew our life at the mercy of the Fairchilds wouldn't last much longer. A voice buried deep within me was encouraging me to accelerate this departure.

THE YEAR IS 2030

LEFT MY YOUNG avatar to plot her future in Florida and returned to my children just as they woke up from their short slumber. Roman had entered the spare bedroom to tell Tereza he had already received replies from his contacts in Bremerhaven. The captain of a ship called *Markyta* was willing to take them to Florida's western coast for two hundred thousand euros. The freighter was to leave Bremerhaven in a day. Tereza agreed to the price. To her, such an amount, while not negligible, was not enough to make her think twice. Roman would drive to the German border that afternoon to meet the middleman and discuss the details.

They emerged from the bedroom to find Babi in the kitchen, eating cake for breakfast and watching the news. Roman explained to her that he and Tereza were going to America for a few weeks so Tereza could use her influence to clear up the confusion surrounding the misplacement of my remains. The journey was safe, and they were certain they would bring me home.

A harmless lie, though I wasn't sure whether Babi believed it. As she processed the news, she looked truly small, exhausted, scraping the frosting off her beloved dessert plate, which she had proudly owned for almost a century. "I no longer understand the future," she said between sips of tea.

Tereza sat quietly with her grandmother until her attention was diverted by the images on the muted television of thousands of bodies tightly packed in the streets of Prague. Given the number of shirtless young men holding cups of beer and sticking their tongues out at the cameras, it appeared at first that this might be some kind of overblown block party. But the digital picket signs above their heads soon made things clear. OUR NATION, NOT YOURS, a slogan declared as it unrolled in glittering letters before exploding into a thousand pixels that formed a new declaration: RECLAIM CZECHIA! NO TO MUSLIM SETTLEMENTS! Tereza unmuted the television. Children sang the nation's anthem as a group of young Czech men proudly displayed forearms sporting fresh tattoos of a DNA molecule wrapped around a mattock. A TV reporter pushed through the crowds and tried to describe "the mood here on Ancestor Day" as some of the protesters catcalled and threatened her, encouraged by their children's laughter.

"What the hell is this?" Tereza asked.

Babi spat into her empty cup and let out several curses. Roman hesitated. Tereza was witnessing a live broadcast of Ancestor Day celebrations. Once a year, Czech Reclamationists gathered in the streets for a public show of strength.

The nativist wing of the Czech citizenry couldn't resist the influence of American Reclamation. If the Americans could reject the idea of a global society, why shouldn't they? Nationalism was an acceptable response not only to immigrants but also to fires, to hurricanes, to droughts and food shortages. Only the nation-state could restore greatness. Somehow?

The movement began in our country as a loose organization of local militias, thugs with knives egging each other on via underground message boards, until it reached the height of its fever during the Summer of Madness. Though the Reclamationists had achieved success in driving a major portion of the country's immigrants farther west, the organized slaughter of refugees on our soil didn't bring the full revolution they had hoped for. They were immediately reviled by most of the country, and the government responded to the events by becoming more benevolent in its immigration policies and by tamping down its rhetoric on the "dangers" of large-scale migration from Asia and Africa. But of the dozens of men physically responsible for the Summer of Madness and the murders in Hluboká and other villages, only six were successfully prosecuted and imprisoned.

As extremists often do, the Reclamationists realized it was time to put away their weapons and advance their cause by donning suits and infiltrating the institutions of government. They entered a coalition with the country's foremost far-right party, the so-called Freedom and Direct Democracy Party, and the new movement began referring to itself as the Ancestor Party. Its leaders felt nothing but contempt and disgust for the criminals who murdered refugees in the Summer of Madness, they claimed, though they were sure that many among the perpetrators were well-meaning (if misguided) citizens who deserved to be treated with compassion and forgiveness.

The movement hoped to claim enough seats in the elections to become a part of the parliament coalition, to spread its influence and normalize its policies. Years after the Summer of Madness, the country began to forget the Reclamationists' sins, and the field was ripe for slightly more civil attempts at seizing control. The Ancestors unleashed a new wave of anti-immigration propagandist attacks against the leading party coalition. Meanwhile, the party's online apostles carefully planted assertions that the Summer of Madness was overblown by the sensationalist media, and as the conspiracy theories grew, some citizens convinced themselves there had been no refugee deaths at all. They believed that the media had plotted with the government to fake the event in order to open the nation's borders to a Muslim invasion. Pillagers of the white Bohemian countryside, impending hordes coming to steal our language, land, and liberty. The fact that the Summer of Madness led to the lowest immigration numbers in decades, stymieing the revitalization that had been under way and causing troubles for our economy and job market, didn't seem to factor into their thinking. To further accelerate its rise to legitimacy, the party declared Ancestor Day a nationalist holiday so that all Reclamationists could march in the streets clothed in the nation's flag, utilize the free media coverage of the events, and normalize the existence of a militant party in the consciousness of a skeptical nation.

America had unleashed this mania, had shown the nativists just how ambitious they could become. On TV, Tereza watched the leader of the Ancestor Party give his speech next to the statue of Holy Roman Emperor Charles IV, voted the most popular figure in Czech history. Filmed and photographed next to this idolized Czech, the party leader gave a speech filled with calls for unity and peace, only to follow them with a denouncement of the liberals' dream of the world's tribes unified in the common cause of human progress. The idea of progress was different for every tribe, the leader asserted, and with the crises facing us, each country was better off facing the challenges individually. Nothing personal. It was simply a sober assessment of human nature. Some of the world's most significant countries—the United States, Russia, France, Iran—had already accepted this truth and begun their transition to deglobalizing. It was the duty of Czech leaders to take us in the same direction.

Tereza asked Roman to turn the TV off. Somberly, my family sat in the quiet living room. I had left them in the midst of this continuous onslaught, the perma-crisis of our new century, to fend not only for themselves but also for me. And in this moment, for the first time, I was glad to be dead, to not be sitting there with them, absorbing the gleeful hatred displayed on their television screen, pondering whether in a decade or two they would be fighting their neighbors to the death over a bottle of water or a can of peaches or the purity of their bloodline. There were no missions left for me. I didn't have to wonder whether I would die painfully as a casualty of war or extreme weather events, whether I'd lose my final remnants of hope in the human experiment before I perished. Such monumental concerns were left for the living.

In this depressed silence the clock struck noon, and Babi began to doze off again. Roman covered her with a blanket and asked Tereza to follow him down the road to the house of Mr. Lavička. Once there, my daughter dodged the pecks of aggressive chickens roaming the artisan's yard. Leaning against the pigsty was the vessel that was to carry me home, a black wooden casket adorned with lines of silver along the edges of the frame.

Mr. Lavička emerged from his house, supporting himself on a trembling cane. His wrist was wrapped in a filthy bloodied rag.

"You okay there, Mr. Lavička?" Roman asked as he shook the man's non-injured hand.

"This is the last casket I'll ever make," Mr. Lavička responded between snorts and coughs. "She took a bite of me. Snagged my hand on the edge."

"A casket?" Tereza said. "We don't know if we'll ever have a body."

"It's easy enough to store on a freighter," Roman said. "If we do find Mother, I'm not going to bring her home in some garbage bag the Americans wrapped her in."

Roman handed over a bundle of cash as Tereza ran her hand across the casket's surface. It had been meant for Mr. Lavička's sister, but she had made a last-minute request for her ashes to be scattered in the river, and thus he had been waiting to refurbish it for someone else.

"This your new girlfriend?" Lavička nodded toward Tereza.

"My third cousin," Roman said. "From America."

Mr. Lavička spat on the ground. "You see those Ancestor maniacs today? Well, I'm sure she's a nice enough person. Coming to the vigil tonight?"

"Oh, sure, sure," Roman lied.

"I hope I'll see your Babi there too. Hell of a woman. Only better with age." Mr. Lavička winked. He shook his cane at Tereza—was this a goodbye or an accusation?—and at a turtle's pace, he made his way inside.

Back in the day, Babi was rumored to have had an affair with the man. Then again, there had been dozens of these rumors, some long after she got married. The curse of being a woman in a small village—never a moment's peace. Another reason I had been so eager to escape when I was young.

My children gripped the casket by the handles and carried it down the main road as neighbors observed them curiously from their windows. I was impressed by the work that had gone into my death vessel, as this was Mr. Lavička's finest creation—he'd made it with love for his family, but I was to benefit. I wished I could tell his children this was enough. If they buried only this beautiful casket, perhaps with a few trinkets of mine, it would do just fine as a ritual of my passing, and they could visit the grave to be with me, speak with me. What did it matter whether my bones also resided in this wooden box?

They rested the casket in the garage. Roman departed to pick up the rental van and meet his contact at the German border. He instructed Tereza to pack and say her goodbyes. This was it. By the evening, they were to embrace the road and make their way to the ship in Bremerhaven, Germany.

Tereza changed her clothes, packed her suitcase, and lay in the dark living room with a faint hope that she might get some sleep, encouraged by Babi's snoozes. But just as she dozed off, she was jarred awake by Babi standing above her, pouring schnapps into shot glasses. Babi slapped the cheeks of her granddaughter as they took one shot after another, sitting on the couch, exclaiming toasts in their respective languages. The moment didn't need translation. Babi had never had a granddaughter; Tereza had never met her Danish grandparents. Despite the circumstances, their bond was sealed.

I hoped they could have a long future of such shared moments, far beyond the uncertain, chaotic days they were living through. Within the two of them lived my past and my future. Where I'd come from and where I was headed. Across the distance of the afterlife, this bond remained strong. Even if their meeting was the only good thing to come from my passing, I was happy. Outside the sun began to set again, the last of the short winter days.

Having boozed herself into stutters and heavy eyelids, Babi held Tereza tightly, kissed her cheeks and forehead and hands. She shuffled to her bedroom in her slippers, got into bed, and applied mint cream to her face. I could swear I smelled the scent of the cream despite the barriers that separated us. My memory of the scent of mint provoked in me unrivaled yearning. As if my mother could sense what I was feeling, she was too restless to sleep. Instead, she reached for a framed photo of the two of us posing in front of Hazmburk Castle. She placed the photo on the pillow next to her and turned off the lights. Tereza stood in the doorway, took one last glance at her newfound grandmother, then shut the door.

ROMAN RETURNED AT eight o'clock and insisted that he and his sister had to leave right away. The freighter was to depart at five in the morning, and missing it would mean delaying their journey by a month. Roman opened the door to Babi's room, hoping she might still be awake for a goodbye, but she had already fallen asleep next to the framed photo. He composed a note promising that Babi would get to bury me in the dirt of my homestead, that they would see each other again soon.

Under cover of darkness, my children loaded Mr. Lavička's fine casket into the rented black van and began their drive north to Bremerhaven. As they passed the village limits, Tereza opened her window for a better look at the scene unfolding in the exact spot where she'd crashed her car. The monument to the Hluboká five was surrounded by dozens of people holding candles and flashlights. One by one, they laid down flowers and Hluboká postcards with messages written in honor of those murdered in our village. We used to hold the vigil on the anniversary of their deaths, but once the Reclamationists declared Ancestor Day a national holiday, the committee for cultural development in our county voted to move it to the same day to counteract the shame the Ancestors brought to us. We'd hoped that the media attention for the vigils would surpass its thirst for broadcasting the salacious, dramatic images of the theatrical Ancestors. We were wrong. I spotted just a single man with media credentials in the crowd my children passed, looking bored, an idle camera in his hands. Old villagers lighting candles to absolve their guilt for what they'd allowed to happen to their neighbors was no match for the spectacle of many thousands of fanatics waving the Czech flag against the photogenic backdrops of Prague.

Tereza observed her brother as they passed the vigil. Not once did he allow his eyes to gaze upon the mourners. Did she remember all the secrets I'd told her about Roman during our only night together in the careless abandon of intoxication?

In less than an hour, my children reached the German border. The pleasant background noise of '90s rock changed to a news segment, a summary of the events of Ancestor Day, asserting that twenty-five thousand Czechs had attended the celebrations around the country, a new record for the movement. After he'd passed the border, Roman turned off the radio, stopped the vehicle, and asked his sister to drive. Disturbed by the images of Ancestor Day and the Hluboká vigil, she gladly accepted the distraction. In the passenger seat, Roman exhaled deeply, crossed his arms, and closed his eyes.

But Tereza refused to let him rest. "Do you ever attend the vigil?" she said.

"I'm not much for public displays of sentiment. It's a wound on our village. People like to poke their finger in it to feel righteous."

"What did *you* think of the new neighbors?"

"I thought they'd be better off with their own tribes. Trust your own. You know how I know I'm right? They're dead."

Tereza glanced at him. "You're saying they got themselves murdered by seeking help?"

"I'd rather not talk about this," Roman said.

"We've danced around it long enough. You're a Reclamationist. Right?"

"What do you want me to say? I used to be in the movement. People do shit."

"That's a sad excuse."

"You'll get no argument from me."

* * *

I WISHED I'D HAD more time to tell Tereza about her brother's troubled past, to warn her. As I watched Roman grow up, every day I'd looked for signs that he might carry the rage gene of his father, whom I'd left when Roman was an infant. I anticipated he might mistreat other children on the playground, disrespect his teachers, or even raise his voice or hands to me. But he was a nice boy, a quiet boy, everyone said so, and with relief I dropped my guard. Roman wasn't yet in his teens when I realized that his silence wasn't simple introversion or shyness. It was fear. As if he still remembered his father screaming as he grew in my body or calling him a devil's child in the cradle, Roman grew up terrified, but he concealed his anxieties, his mistrust of the world. He wouldn't tell me about the bullies who pursued him at school, he refused to explain his bruises, acting casual even as his teachers reported to me that he'd been caught hiding in the bathrooms during recess. With desperation in his voice, my son swore nothing was wrong, and I chose to let him deal with the abuse on his terms. Stupidly I believed that perhaps this was how men discovered their strength, by facing adversity on their own. Soon, in this emotional vacuum, the internet and Roman's friends would teach him to weaponize his self-repression, convince him that people couldn't hurt you if you hurt them first.

He was a good student, a graduate of the economics program at Charles University. But despite good grades, Roman had no luck in the job market. During his interviews, a great anxiety would overcome him, and he would mask his panic with aloofness, sometimes anger. After witnessing his bad temperament, employers were not interested in him. Then a Japanese conglomerate purchased a fish cannery near Louny and began to hire temporary workers from the area, no interview required. Every morning, Roman would line up with other men of the county and hope that he looked strong and reliable enough to be selected.

Thus began the labor of his youth and the late after-work hours at the pub, where he blew off steam and drank away the stink of fish. He would return home to the apartment he lived in with Ilona, his high-school sweetheart, covered with random cuts and bruises. Sometimes he was so drunk that Ilona had to remove his soiled pants and throw them in the wash. She tolerated this behavior for less than two months before throwing him out. Roman returned to us at the Hluboká house, and the lack of a partner and financial obligations further enabled his new lifestyle.

As the leader of his work pack, Roman would find any excuse to start fights, to intimidate Romani and Vietnamese workers drinking at the same pubs. He and his crew followed women on the street. In silence and horror, Babi and I observed his scabbed knuckles; the features of his face that vanished behind the bloat of vodka; the visits from policemen.

During one night of drinking and fighting, Roman was noticed by one of the founders of the Czech Reclamation, Lubor Zoufal, a local boy who would give my son a new manifesto for living. The two became great friends, and together they were determined to advance the cause. Not only had my son been involved in the Czech Reclamation movement; he was one of its founding members, marked proudly with the tattoo of a DNA strand enveloping a mattock just below his shoulder blade.

After Roman became Zoufal's friend, I rarely saw him. He'd come home to sleep off a binge once or twice a week, then ceased to return at all. Babi and I couldn't deny that we got used to the peace of living without him, but it wasn't meant to last. On the night that started the Summer of Madness, Roman showed up on our doorstep at one o'clock in the morning in torn clothes, a nasty burn on his chest. He was feverish and drunk. Babi stripped off his clothes and began to apply a wrap of herbs and ointments to the wound as Roman ranted about all the forces of evil that pursued him. The enemies were closing in, he said, but he wasn't strong enough to fight.

The things men do to feel extraordinary. All the stories of old heroes, warriors, hunters—we retell them with great nostalgia.

Regardless of how we feel about conquest and violence today, we present these tales of history's bloodthirsty killers with affection and glee. They signify greatness. And what of the soft-bellied modern boys living in first-world luxury who have no battles to fight, no cities to conquer, the boys whose perception of the world lies in a hard drive and a Wi-Fi connection? They want to make their own stories. They invent conflict to christen themselves warriors. Bloody hands conceal mediocrity, loud voices mask self-doubt. Roman and his comrades brought their imagined battles to our county. Under Zoufal's command, they assembled at the pub and marched on the dormitory where the Hluboká refugees slept, a mere five-minute walk from our house.

I know only the bits and pieces I forced my son to tell me over the years, and yet a vivid portrayal of the horrors committed that night replays in my mind as if I were there. They were ten strong: Roman, some of his coworkers from the cannery, and members of our county's branch of Reclamation. They brought Coca-Cola bottles filled with gasoline. Matches. Knives and baseball bats and a pistol. Roman and his friends approached the entrance as the security guard hired by the county came to face them, blocking the door. He was a massive man, and he seemed entirely unfazed by the mob, inviting them closer as he folded up his shirtsleeves. Then a firebomb flew over his head, landed on the first-story window of the building. The guard looked at the flames spreading behind him, the glass melting and dripping onto the sidewalk. He ran.

As soon as Roman heard the first bloodcurdling scream come from behind the window, he realized he wasn't the fearless warrior he had imagined himself to be. That was true pain, authentic, it was dying pain, it was the pain of horror, the fear of losing not only the body but also the *self,* the only thing a person could truly own. The scream was the ultimate test of cruelty. Those who could hear it and withstand it, carry on in their intent, would become true soldiers of the Reclamation. The man next to Roman threw another bottle of fire, and a small drop landed on Roman's chest, burning through cloth and skin. My son dropped the gasoline bottle in his hand and tossed his knife into a sewer grate. He ran without looking back down the road to our house, back to the family he'd nearly abandoned.

My mother and I were sitting in the living room watching reruns of *Kommissar Rex* when Roman arrived on our doorstep, drenched in sweat, the hair on his forehead singed, his cheeks black and red. He smelled like a gas tank as he crawled into my lap and wept. I petted his hair and filthy cheeks with an animal's affection, the love that makes you capable of ripping limb from body, love I hadn't felt since he was unable to speak or walk. And yet I felt disgust, pity for this vile creature under my hands, because I knew that despite my lifelong effort to bring into the world a good man, he had done something unforgivable.

He'd come home to stay, Roman swore. He was ready to make amends. But only if we didn't call the cops or ask for any more truths. Only if we'd let him start over, without conditions.

He and I both knew it wasn't possible. Blank slates are a kitsch sold at the dollar store, whereas every act in a human life is added to a tally carved in stone. What we've done cannot be undone. This is true not because of some biblical sense of divine justice, but because of the nature of human memory. We are our own history, we store our past actions within our bodies whether we like it or not.

I pushed Roman for honesty, refusing to let him go unaccountable, hoping the tough love would at last instill in him a sense of responsibility. I followed him around the house as Babi watched us, chewing on her fingernails. He needed to confess only once, I said, to tell us what he'd done, because the truth could never be as bad as what I imagined.

Suddenly he raised his arms and slapped my face, one strike from the left, one from the right. They were weak hits, clumsy, the fumbling of a drunken bar brawler, not a trained fighter. He drew a bit of blood from my nose as I fell back against the wall and prepared to claw his eyes out should he strike again. It was over as quickly as it had begun.

I looked upon him and his reddened hand, he looked upon me and my injured face, and we knew each other, we recognized each other in this moment because we both knew it had been coming for years. Roman fell to his knees; he put his hands around my ankles and begged for forgiveness with spit and snot dripping from his chin. But I knew we had lost each other that night. This moment would define our relationship for the rest of our lives, as Roman would spend his attempting to make up for what he had done to me. But I would never forgive.

We stayed up for hours, waiting for the police to bust down our door and haul Roman away or show his face on the news and declare him one of the nation's most wanted criminals. But the sirens and police lights remained on the opposite side of the village as the firemen fought the flames all night and the police struggled to find eyewitnesses. Eventually, Babi and I walked to the burning dormitory to see if we could help. We watched until morning, when the firemen were able to carry the singed bodies out onto the pavement.

It took two days for Roman's fever to retreat, a few more for him to regain his senses and color. From dawn to dusk I asked my son what had happened that night—about the source of burns on his chest, what he knew about the ruin of a dormitory in our village— and Roman pretended there was nothing to talk about. Our village became the epicenter of international attention. The Czech police and Europol and journalists from across the EU flowed in and out of Hluboká as our neighbors roamed the streets like lost children, looking for an explanation, some understanding of what had occurred in our serene countryside. What could I tell them? I knew my son had been there, though he refused to confess. I stayed inside as the weeks passed and the investigations concluded. Roman's moment of reckoning never arrived, as those Reclamationists who did get arrested refused to rat on their friends. The loyal murderers.

For days I struggled with whether I would provide an alibi for

Roman should he need one. No, I kept telling myself, no way in hell would I help him escape punishment. In the end, the police came to our door only once, asking about Roman's criminal record, investigations of his bar brawls and street assaults. He treated them with cold politeness, answering questions about his predisposition for violence. When the cops turned their attention to me, I swore that Roman had been at home with us on that horrible night, watching reruns of *Kommissar Rex*. Babi followed my lead and confirmed this story, though with obvious distaste. To this day I am disgusted by how fortunate my family was in that moment. Before the Summer of Madness, the police hadn't considered the Reclamationists to be a serious threat; they had kept no database of members or open files on the movement's leaders. Thus Roman's clear connection to that terrible night remained hidden, and the police never returned to our house.

Within months, Roman had sobered up and we began to build new routines based on avoidance and silence. Roman dedicated himself to a new job driving truck routes around Europe, making money for the family. I mostly tolerated him, occasionally showing some small bit of affection, which my son lapped up. But beyond our fragile peace pact, born of familial obligation, there was little else except mistrust and sometimes downright revulsion. I fantasized about banishing him from our house but found myself unable to follow through. Eventually, the chasm between us was normalized.

SELECTIVELY, MY SON told pieces of this story on the way to Bremerhaven. He said nothing of hitting me; apparently, he couldn't bear for Tereza to know. I understood. I hadn't told her either, not only because I didn't want such a story to ruin our first day together but also because I feared she'd judge me for not abandoning Roman, for taking his abuse. In his telling, Roman offered only the bits that made for an easily digestible redemption tale wherein he returned home and was saved by the maternal healing that Babi and I offered. But from

Tereza's steeled expression, the muscles twitching along her jaw, I could tell she saw no redemption here.

"No wonder the vigil makes you squeamish," she said quietly. "You're one of the killers."

"I've never killed anyone," Roman said.

Tereza laughed with such vehemence that her hand slipped on the wheel, and the car briefly veered out of its lane. "Why would anyone believe you? I see now. This working-class-hero thing you have going. An honest job, taking care of your old grandma. Fuck. You're good at hiding."

"I did something I can't take back. I thought I was a real hell-king, born to be bad, you know, until I realized I was just another dipshit who thought the world owed him more than he'd gotten. Do you know how hard that is? To believe fully that there is some greater destiny for you in a war between good and evil and find out you were wrong? That's what my life is now. Acceptance."

"I'm stuck with you for a while," Tereza said. "But I don't believe you. I don't see any humility in you. Seems like you just got better at deflection."

Roman wiped his nose with his forefinger and switched the radio back on, so loud that the seats vibrated. But something had changed. He turned the volume down and spoke softly. "You've known me for a couple days, but I've thought about you all my life. Since Mother told me you existed. I always imagined how much happier she would've been with you as her child. Should've been me, the fuckup, to grow up with strangers."

"She forgave you," Tereza said, "which I take into consideration. But I know a few things about denial, Roman. It will all come bursting out of you. The guy who decided to go to the dorm that night is still here. Hiding."

Roman didn't answer. As my daughter drove along the flawless autobahn, my son closed his eyes and pretended to sleep. Since the night he'd hurt me, Roman had been pursuing the impossible, trying to make up for what had happened between us. He separated himself from his friends, he stopped pursuing women and abandoned the idea of starting his own family, all to take care of Babi and me, his self-assigned punishment. The same idea had brought him on this journey, an insane attempt to rescue my body from the Americans, his final act of love to erase his guilt. I wasn't around to tell him otherwise. I wasn't around to tell him the redemption would never arrive, that even in this afterlife where old slights fade, I still couldn't forgive the pain caused by the boy to whom I'd given life. Tereza was right — Roman had never really faced what he'd done, and his role-play as a much better man couldn't last forever.

I needed to turn away from the sorrow he'd caused me, at least for a while. I let my children continue their drive to Bremerhaven on their own, and I retreated once again into my *Newts* summer, the sweet allure of my and Michael's achievement enveloping my bodiless form like a healing spring. More and more, this intoxicating dive into memory seemed a much better alternative to the pain of the real world, a pain I participated in willingly. Could I, someday, disappear in the sweet supply of nostalgia forever, sever my bond to my kin and the concerns of mortals for good?

THE YEAR IS 1988

A FTER MY IMMIGRANT's holiday at Hotel Goliath, I lived and breathed only for our film. I spent every spare minute rereading the book, tweaking what remained of Michael's script, practicing my diction in front of the mirror. During the days we couldn't shoot because of work, I became easily irritable, impatient with the small, meaningless tasks that make up a life: grocery shopping and cooking, brushing my teeth, chasing the spiders in our house with cans of Raid. Even going to the toilet made me angry. It seemed unfair that I had to waste time on these things while the story haunting my mind was on pause. Art elevates life above these tasks, making the banal all the harder to accept. I wrote letters to my mother expressing these frustrations, and she replied with the soothing wisdom I'd hoped for.

When I have to stop writing poetry to feed the chickens, Babi wrote, *I want to murder the chickens. But when the poetry won't come, when the words elude me and the empty stanza laughs at my foolishness, I'm most grateful for the chickens that need feeding. The small tasks are a respite from what truly matters, and vice versa.*

As my obsession peaked, the crew of *The Great Newt War* gathered in Siesta Key for the last day of the shoot, which would include our most expensive scene. We began with the establishing shot.

Rostislav sits in a living room filled with luxurious antique furniture, holding his scotch and reading a book. He gets up and roams the mansion that was given to him by Governor Salamander in the redistribution of all human property acquired in the war. Years have passed. His clothes have become more elaborate to display his wealth (sleek black tunics embroidered with silver thread). He has learned four languages, though there is no one to speak them with. He employs a staff of humans who tend to his dietary needs, maintain the pH balance in his water tank, and keep dust from his books. The humans also soothe his ache for Ava, a longing that is clear in his walk as his massive hind legs tap and echo in the empty mansion, leaving drops of salt water on the extravagant ivory floors. He never leaves the house, this Newt of Xanadu.

During these days of feeling lost, Rostislav orders a typewriter with enlarged keys to accommodate the large tips of his fingers. He begins a letter to Governor Salamander, introducing himself as a scholar and a student of everything salamanders and humans have in common. "Though we are now able to subject humans to newt rule without any consideration for their lives, should we? Is endless expansion the point of our existence? What if humans and salamanders could live satisfying lives alongside one another, refusing to participate in the hamster wheel of competition among nations? Is the newt a moral creature or a sheer force of nature? Doesn't having the power to destroy all life also mean having the power to preserve and safeguard it? Why mimic the failures of humans so loyally, Great Governor?"

After these musings, Rostislav moves to his main point, a personal plea. During the war, he relates, he fell in love, or friendship, or something in between, with a human woman, and she was set up to take the fall for him. Thereafter she was sent to a human work camp in the Mediterranean, helping local salamander armies manufacture machine and harpoon parts. He begs for Governor Salamander's mercy and asks for Ava's release. "She was a friend to salamanders," he writes. She protected him from a human mob, and he betrayed her, broke his promise to protect her in turn. If Governor Salamander cannot show mercy for an innocent human, perhaps he can do it to unburden the soul of a haunted fellow salamander.

Rostislav sends the letter and continues to roam his halls. He *receives no reply, sends another. And another. Years pass. The coasts of the world give way to newts, and humans migrate farther inland, to mountainous areas of Latin America and Central Europe and the deserts of Africa and the Middle East. The human populations that have not yet been touched by the newt expansion resist the flow of millions of coastal refugees coming to their land. Conflicts arise. Humans wage war against one another even as their species is being replaced by another.*

Rostislav never receives a reply from Governor Salamander. In despair, he stays in his water tank, barely moving, growing fatter. He suffers painful infections on his skin. Some of his servants begin to treat the house as their own and sleep in its many bedrooms, cook lavish meals for themselves, and organize end-of-the-world parties for their friends. Once in a while, salamander enforcers come to take a human servant away to the work camps. Rostislav ignores these disappearances, ignores the pleas from his other staff to protect them. The only human he is concerned about is Ava; his guilt shrinks his world, his body, his intellect.

Rostislav has sent sixteen letters to Governor Salamander by the time the enforcers arrive for him. The butler opens the door and leads a trio of newt soldiers, armed with specially designed rifles, to Rostislav's bedroom.

MICHAEL AND I had spent several sleepless nights planning this scene. We needed three more newts to appear in the film, but of course we had only one Rostislav. In the end, the local high-school theater department saved us, as their musical about the occupation of Earth by lizard people had just finished its run, and the reptile costumes were therefore available. With a few adjustments—newt armor and weapons—we were able to make the soldiers look like a large specimen of salamander. We dressed our PAs in these costumes and asked them to kneel. We'd fix the rest in post. It was hardly the perfect solution, but we hoped the strength of the story would keep audiences from judging the effects harshly.

"Rostislav Adriatic?" asks the newt captain.

Rostislav crawls out of the tank and wraps himself in a dark blue robe. He beams with hope—are these the royal bodyguards accompanying Governor Salamander on a personal visit so that they can discuss Ava's case?

Rostislav tries to excuse himself to get properly dressed but the captain shakes his head. "As of last week," the captain says, "all salamanders who originated in the Adriatic Sea are declared inferior to all other salamanders. You are to be relocated, to serve the salamander cause at work camps."

Rostislav studies the yellow spots on his green and brown skin, a contrast to the dark blue and green spots of the soldiers before him. "Newts are rounding up newts?" he says.

"We can allow you to get dressed, although you will be assigned a standard work uniform once you arrive at your destination."

"This is my house."

"No longer."

"You can't just take salamanders as prisoners. Don't you feel ashamed of this order?"

"Law is law," the captain says.

"And when they outlaw your kind?"

The salamanders chuckle at this, a noise not unlike snakes hissing.

"Salamanders of the Indian Ocean gene are the superior breed," the captain says. "We're the ones who build our Empire of Salamander, Adriatic."

Rostislav looks at his butler as if the man can save him. "This is my house," he repeats.

"You took it from someone and now they'll take it from you, sir," the butler says.

Per law, the newt soldiers make no acknowledgment of the human butler by speech or glance.

"It makes no sense," Rostislav says.

"I find it's best to settle for your place in life," the butler says. "We, your loyal servants, have conspired to murder you in your sleep for years, but we could never quite bring ourselves to do it. Even servitude can become a habit, to my own horror."

"I never realized you were here against your will," Rostislav says. "I am sorry."

The soldiers leave the bedroom, and the butler helps Rostislav dress, the man's eyes lingering on his captor as if he's undecided whether their parting is an opportunity to punch him or embrace him. Rostislav puts on his Sunday suit, bow tie and all, and the butler wishes him luck. Rostislav ambles down the halls that had given him refuge from his grief. He listens for the excited shouts of servants celebrating his demise, popping champagne bottles, so that in this final moment, he can feel himself a villain justly punished, not merely another clueless victim swept up by currents he failed to consider. But the confirmation of his evil doesn't come. He departs the house silent and solemn, never to learn about the fate of its human inhabitants, though he can make a guess.

Slow fade-out...

...and slow fade-in to salamander industrial zones in the Mediterranean [a beach in southwest Florida transformed with a few cheap tricks]. Ava stands inside a factory, a collar on her neck announcing her new name: 2108761. The window in front of her workstation offers a full view of the ominous ocean. She looks at the conveyor belt in front her and checks the quality of harpoon parts manufactured for the salamanders' ongoing war against the shark population. There is a jarring cut to Rostislav, stripped of his clothes, his back hunched, wearing his own collar number: 31087. He is hauling pipes

slung over his shoulder down to the sea so the salamanders can build
a stronger, better infrastructure for their submerged world.

DURING THE LUNCH break, Michael didn't talk much. The rest of us
were ecstatic that the shoot, countless early mornings and hard labor
in addition to our day jobs, was almost over. He felt disappointed by
the limitations of the budget. Ideally, this last scene would have been
an epic panorama of a Mediterranean port with the roofs of massive
towers peaking above the ocean's surface, cargo submarines and
amphibious excavators pushed into the ocean, hammers swung by the
arms of ten thousand newt prisoners. A wonder of industry and effi-
ciency. Above it all would reign the statue of Governor Salamander,
twenty times as tall as Lady Liberty, overlooking the rise of his
civilization.

But the budget didn't allow for such a vision. Michael hoped that
we could still get a large group of extras to fill the beach out with bodies and convey the idea of a lived-in world, but our friends were tired
of getting up early to stand around, and we had no money left to bribe
them with booze.

I didn't mind. Showing the world as bare, empty of other people
and salamanders, underscored the perfect isolation both characters
felt at the end of their journeys. The empty spaces were a powerful
contrast to the vast backdrop of the sea's horizon.

Rostislav marches along the beach to the sound of shouts and
pipes crashing to the ground as exhausted laborers faint in the heat.
He pulls on a rope to the count of one, two . . . and again. His hands
slip and he falls into the sand, and he glances up at the factory on the
northern end of the beach.

Does Rostislav know that the woman he loves works in this exact
factory?

Ava looks out the window of her workstation. Her hands are cut up and bloodied from her job, the foul-smelling oil having congealed around her wounds. Her hair is shaved, all life and defiance vanished from her eyes. All she can see, staring past the Dickensian factory around her, is the ocean, the same ocean she used to adore once upon a time in Florida, before it brought destruction to everyone she knew. She cuts her finger and lets the blood drip onto the floor, fully aware of the punishment she will receive for soiling the factory.

Rostislav trudges up the beach toward the factory, leaving imprints in the sand. Dents appear on his skin where infection was cut out by salamander medics. He drags his heavy hind leg in a limp acquired from a beating for disobedience. The guards pay him no mind; he walks with such purpose that they assume he has been reassigned to the factory. Rostislav doesn't miss his human clothes or his wealth or playacting a scotch drinker. He misses books. He misses the days of learning the history of a new city, strolling around Prague with the professor. He misses the stories of Ava's childhood, the beauty of her youthful discoveries, denied to him because he spent his childhood fighting sharks while hunting for pearls.

Ava wipes the sweat from her forehead. She has tried to drown herself in the ocean countless times. The newts came quickly to save her, every time. They put their hands around her ankles and arms and carried her to shore. Then they beat her and starved her, let her know that peace must be kept and that obedience was essential.

Rostislav appears at her window.

What was. What is.

He sees Ava.

Her reflection merges with his image. She seems to recognize the salamander. What was his name? Rostislav? Perhaps she forgives him and is glad to see him here, at the end of everything. Or perhaps not. Perhaps she simply looks out on the ocean, recounting its betrayals. Or planning a better, quicker way of drowning.

Or perhaps she dreams of those days when she swam as far as she could, until she reached a point of panic. Suddenly aware of the dangers that lurked in the ocean, she would rush back to the beach and run to her parents, who would assure her there was nothing to be afraid of. That the world was connected, and the ocean was the bond. It would never harm her. There was always peace and safety to be found somewhere ashore.

No more.

Fade out . . .

THE YEAR IS 2030

WHEN I RETURNED, my children were safely aboard the freighter *Markyta* as it embarked from the port at Bremerhaven. Tereza stood at the ship's forecastle, under a sky cut with silver in announcement of an impending storm, a terrifying overture from the open seas.

I wished I could share with her what Babi used to say when I couldn't sleep during storms: That ancient Slavs believed all life on earth was subject to the circle. The constant battle was not between good and evil but between neutral elements, a contest between skies and oceans and dirt that ensured the balance of the circle, thereby rendering the earth capable of caring for the life inhabiting it. Babi always encouraged me to play in the rain, swim in wild rivers, face thunder and lightning, so that I would accept nature as the essential part of being and never abandon it for cities of concrete, never alienate myself from the animal yearnings that live in every human. I wanted to tell my daughter not to see the storm as an omen of bad things to come but rather as an encouraging sign that some of the world's forces, the natural ones, functioned to preserve us.

The freighter crawled across the surface of the sea, gaining speed. A rainbow of shipping crates formed a valley through which Roman strolled, an array of containers loaded with sneakers and insulin and smartphone chips on their way to America. My son was crossing the Atlantic for the first time. Behind him, the lights of Bremerhaven faded as the storm unleashed a blinding downpour.

The freighter *Markyta* had been sailing the same route for thirty-five years. Its deck floors were gray and marked with cracks and holes; the painted stripes of red and blue on its hull had faded long ago. Three crew members passed Roman in a rush, advising him to retreat to his cabin and rest until the storm cleared and the view became noteworthy. They spat at their bad luck, beginning the journey with foul weather. Lightning struck the ocean, then retreated as the surface hissed and steamed. Against the pressure of the wind and rain, the salted air burning his nostrils, Roman continued to walk to the front of the deck. He recognized the shadow that stood at the railing. He'd found Tereza, the only other person on the platform, watching the ocean part and reunite again, stronger, more dangerous. She stood with her shoulders raised, neck tall, as if looking for something in the distance. Her clothes, soaked through, resembled frail strips of paper. My daughter looked like a heroine of old legends, a conqueror of worlds about to go to war. She was so much like me, predisposed to leap into the unknown. I knew that Roman was no longer afraid of her. Quite the opposite. She made his grief smaller, easier to bear. He needed her.

She turned toward him. On her face a delighted grin, her soaked hair arranged like plaster around her eyes. "This, brother, is living," she said.

It had felt like that to me too, once. The plunge into the unknown. The need to fidget, the awe of lives yet unlived. We were on our way to America, and I felt much adoration for my children, for the risk they were taking to bring me home. Despite the danger and the infuriating mysteries surrounding my body's vanishing, the long-dormant adventurer in me rejoiced.

Battered by the storm, Roman retreated belowdecks. Tereza remained on the surface for a while longer, her body shivering. Through the barrage of rain, I noticed the point of her focus, a small light, a dot in the distance, flashing on and off. She squinted at it. The light continued to blink, hovering and wavering from side to side as if struggling to stay aloft in the weather.

The light reminded me of something I'd seen in the streets of New York as my daughter roamed the city to find me. One of the many gadgets designed to merge the future with the now. I was nearly certain that the shape in the distance was a VITA drone.

THE SKIES CLEARED on the third day of our voyage. Nevertheless, Roman suffered from seasickness and hid out in his room, where he watched TV and stared sadly at the ineffective sea bands around his wrists. Tereza, intrigued by the novelty of maritime life, attempted to help crew members with various tasks around the freighter, only to be cursed out in a plethora of languages. The captain, a jovial Austrian with an orchid tattooed on his neck, told Tereza that allowing civilians to perform work would hex the ship with a storm that would sink it. She sat on the deck looking out toward the horizon for hours at a time, dictating her thoughts into her hWisper journal. She was waiting for the suspected VITA drone to make another appearance, to confirm her fear: That Steven & Mark had been with her the whole time, watching every step of the journey, but, for whatever reason, had chosen not to interfere. Due to her new contract, she was their property, and yet they hadn't come to repossess her. They'd stopped calling and messaging. Why? She had a premonition that they were closely connected to the mysterious disappearance of my body, to the conspiracies haunting her brother's mind, in ways that would jeopardize all the work she had done for them.

ON THE TENTH day of *Markyta*'s journey, the storms returned and disabled the freighter's generator. Roman emerged from his room and spent hours in the cafeteria, where he ate peanuts and practiced card tricks on a table illuminated by candles he'd found in a closet.

Tereza came upon him there in the middle of the night as she sought any unsecured snacks. Surprisingly, Roman was with another man, a nervous type with a golden tooth. Tereza had seen him before at the captain's dinners. Sergei. He half laughed, half coughed as Roman removed a queen of hearts from behind his ear. "What are you two doing?" she asked.

"Making magic," Roman said, "for my new best friend. The captain taught me." Sergei grinned, charmingly, his golden tooth reflecting the flicker of the candle flames.

"With these?" she said, and extinguished the candles with a single wave of her hand.

"What's your problem?" Roman spoke from the darkness. Sergei flicked his lighter and studied Tereza with some hostility.

"Those are paraffin candles," Tereza said. "They burn benzene and toluene. Chemicals that enter your blood, your liver, your brain."

"Not everyone wants to live forever," Roman said, relighting his candles with Sergei's lighter.

"Been debunked," Sergei said with a thick Germanic accent, his voice hoarse. "The paraffin candle. Doesn't hurt you, not really." Tereza blinked at him a few times and left the room.

She couldn't sleep for the rest of the night. "Why try to keep people alive at all?" she whispered into the darkness of her cabin. They proudly claimed their right to do themselves harm under the guise of freedom until they were on their deathbeds, begging only then to be saved.

WE SPENT THE first two weeks of March crossing the ocean, unbothered by additional storms or other complications, and reached the final stretch of *Markyta*'s journey. The freighter made its scheduled stop to exchange goods in Jacksonville. Roman hid inside a chamber near the ship's engine room, covered in space blankets to evade the port authority's heat-signature scanners, while Tereza presented her documents and claimed to be taking a freighter trip to engage more Instagram followers. In twenty-four hours, the ship departed and continued south along the Florida coast, giving it a wide berth to avoid shore patrols. It passed the great concrete seawalls of Miami and beyond them the shining lights of a city that had survived the state's disasters and kept the southern territory alive.

On a pleasantly cool evening of calm seas, after having rounded the swamped tip of the state and the drowned Key West, we approached the abandoned section of the western coast. To the north, the city lights marked the lands that hadn't yet been drowned and broken, the inland territories that had survived the hurricanes and tsunamis that destroyed the coasts. But much of the southern territory, stretching from Tampa all the way down to Cape Coral, was shrouded in darkness. As if the newts of Čapek's imagination had really claimed the shores as their own.

In reality, the inhabitants of the cities ruined by the shocking tsunamis of 2027 chose to leave instead of rebuilding. They had seen too much suffering and death, as they had been stranded for weeks before the government could rescue them; books about the disaster were filled with unlikely anecdotes of cannibalism and bloody doomsday cults. Most of the survivors were diagnosed with severe cymophobia and now found it impossible to live in a state surrounded by ocean. After the residents' massive flight, the state had given up on rebuilding the territories, focusing its resources on upholding the cities that remained. Only the rare speckle of glittering light betrayed the few survivors in the abandoned lands attempting to live their postapocalyptic lives off the grid, without institutions. A nightmare for most, a dream for a few.

I remembered when I lived along this same coast decades ago, the bonfires burning on the beaches, the skyline illuminated, hotels and condo behemoths all melted into the same golden hue. A city alive... no longer. In the chaos of my afterlife, I didn't have much time to wonder why the site that supposedly held my remains was so close to my first home in America. It was too easy to slip into conspiracy theories—my son's sustenance—to look for some connection between my past and our arrival here now. Something awfully strange and rotten was happening in this forsaken place. I knew I was playing a part. Still, I relied on the living to discover the truth.

My children packed their waterproof backpacks while the captain and a few of his men uncovered the enclosed lifeboat attached to the side of the ship and lowered it by crane to the water. *Markyta* dimmed its lights. The calm ocean was nearly invisible; the lifeboat descending to its surface seemed to be approaching nothingness, or antimatter. I knew that Tereza had felt this way toward all bodies of water ever since Rita's death. But while she thought of the ocean as a kind of hell, Roman seemed almost giddy, a significant change to his usual demeanor. Perhaps there was something liberating in the madness of this mission, a violation of what is considered a "normal life," something that my son hadn't experienced since his days with the Ancestors. Here was the kind of adventure the ancient poets spoke of, a larger-than-life pursuit of the impossible, the unreachable, the punishable.

My children stood by the railing with *Markyta*'s crew as the captain climbed down the ladder to the lifeboat, entered through the hatch, and turned on its lights. Tereza descended, followed by Roman. Once they reached the rocking tail of the lifeboat and crawled inside, the crew lowered their backpacks with a rope.

The enclosed interior of the lifeboat was simple. The captain sat on a comically small chair at the helm. The rest of the vessel consisted of white walls, with a row of bench seating along each wall, safety straps, and, for some reason, a couple of long mirrors. Tereza opened the compartment beneath their bench to reveal ration boxes and inflatable vests.

As Roman and Tereza used the straps to secure themselves to the wall, the captain steered the ship forward to the roar of its engine. The water offered little resistance, and the green line of the Siesta Key shores—now mostly underwater—inched closer on the captain's GPS screen. The captain kept his eyes focused on the darkness ahead to ensure he encountered no surprise obstacles. My children avoided looking at each other. Through the hatch window on the boat's tail, they saw the silhouette of *Markyta* towering behind them, the sea titan making its best attempt at stealth.

Ninety minutes into this silent journey, the captain brought my children ashore. I could still remember the news stories of the state's downfall. First had come the tides of red algae, killing the sea habitat and bringing the corpses of sea life to shore, shutting down tourism for Tampa, St. Petersburg, and Sarasota. Then had come the most devastating wave of tsunamis in American history, leveling entire counties, turning thriving communities into no-man's-lands of rubble and flesh and shell shock. Sarasota County—the county where my children were now coming ashore, just a couple of miles from the sacred places of my youth—had been abandoned. Only a few buildings had survived the disasters, and the streets that had once hosted museums, theaters, retirement homes, and highly regarded art schools had turned into a swamp.

The captain drove the lifeboat as far as the waters reached, to what had once been the marina parking lot. He tied the boat to the marina gate, and he and my children, wearing rubber boots, stepped into the seawater. They turned on their flashlights. Two half-submerged cars in the lot had been crushed by a collapsed palm tree, their paint eaten by the sun and salt water. In the distance, on the other side of the marina, loomed the tower of the Ritz-Carlton hotel. Half the building had been swept into the sea by the tsunami, while the other half held steady, turned into an unofficial lighthouse. A fire burned on the roof, apparently the faint sparkle of light Tereza had spotted from *Markyta*. She could see more fires in the wasteland ahead, along the flat Florida landscape that had been flattened further by the loss of its skyline. Around the flames gathered moving shadows, the only other sign of life.

The captain, followed by my reluctant children, walked toward the distant flames. Roman asked who kept these fires going.

"The shadow citizens," the captain replied, and Tereza scoffed at the theatrics. There were three kinds of people here, the captain explained. First, there were those waiting for ships like *Markyta* so they could pay for passage to a different port and a new chance at life. These desperate souls were the captain's main source of income, filling his retirement fund so that he could give up the seas for an estate in New Zealand. Second, there were the citizens of the ghost city, those who had declared the rubble their home, those who were banished from the fickle, selective privileges of society, the destitute and the homeless, who'd been unwelcome to civilization even before the greatest struggles of our time began. Here, they could live as they wished, without the police to harass them or drag them to prisons or herd them into dangerous shelters. In this no-man's-land they were their own council, the congress of the fallen city. Finally, farther north, lived the third group, members of the Muscogee and Seminole tribes that had been here from the eighteenth century until they were murdered or deported to Oklahoma. Their descendants had returned to the land after the occupiers dispersed, and they lived in a trade alliance with the shadow city.

My children trod carefully around the rotting wooden frames that had once formed houses, the towering piles of broken glass, pieces of furniture, dried palm leaves, the husks of cars stripped of engines and seats and wheels, and so much clothing, fast fashion caked with sand and mud, floating in the small patches of marshland. Whole blocks of former mansions and strip malls had been turned into mud by torrential storms pummeling what was left of the city, by the high tides that reached far inland. Massive swarms of mosquitoes clustered above the swamps. Bins filled with years-old rubbish attracted gangs of fattened raccoons who felt no urgency to scatter as humans crashed their feast. Here, it seemed, nature had begun its own reclamation. How long would it take before the land was scrubbed of this wreckage? The places I loved in my youth were now cursed, forgotten. When I witnessed these disasters on television a few years earlier, I'd felt only the general discomfort of a bystander. Florida had become a place of failed ambitions and unpleasant associations, a place that truly existed only in my flashes of nostalgia. But my attachment to these moments had been resurrected by the memories I saw in my afterlife, and Florida was again a place with real people who had undergone real suffering. The loss I saw around me was nearly unbearable.

As my children approached the glow of the fires—beacons in the dark—a series of whistles carried through the streets. They reached an old USPS office, with a mail truck picked bare resting in front of it. Slowly, with his hands raised, the captain led Roman and Tereza around the corner, where shadows turned into dozens of bodies huddled around a fire. Some held cans of Chef Boyardee; others hung laundry on clotheslines erected between doorways. Children ran and squeaked, chased by tail-wagging dogs with extraordinarily clean, shining fur.

The shadows turned as they noticed the newcomers. One of the men sitting around the fire stood and gestured for them to approach. The concrete here had been cleared of rubble and sand, the windows of the remaining buildings repaired or covered with wooden panels. Aside from the dogs, there was no wildlife. This street almost resembled the city as it used to be.

The man who greeted my children was dressed in light khaki pants and a colorful shirt printed with hibiscus flowers, unbuttoned to his sternum. He had a well-kept beard and wore a flat cap on his bald head. He stretched out his hand to the captain. The two men laughed and embraced.

The bearded man introduced himself as Benjamin. "It's our bread and butter," he said, "guiding the visitors to our treacherous country." They had been building this camp for about a year, he said, ever since the city had been finally and completely abandoned. At first, there were only about a dozen of them, but others arrived in the ensuing months. "Those who want to live out these final days with something resembling true freedom," Benjamin said.

He beckoned them closer to the fire. The apocalypse here seemed to be a party for beach bums, an antithesis to the libertarian *Mad Max* visions of water wars, Darwinian superdomes, and sadistic cruelty. Like Benjamin, the other people around the fire wore loose Banana Republic shirts, they were tan and healthy, they grinned at the newcomers without any sign of suspicion or hostility.

"We didn't bring cash," Roman whispered to the captain as they sat with the group. He eyed the shadow citizens nervously. "What will they want from us?"

"You paid me," the captain said, "and I pay them. There are eighteen people here who no longer wish to stay in America. We have small boats hidden by the marina. They'll follow us to the freighter to find sanctuary in Europe."

Benjamin passed around a bag of tortilla chips and shared the brief history of this new city with a patient smile. The area had been abandoned in cycles, first by the National Guard, then by municipal services and local government, until its remaining business owners and residents saw no reason to stay. The hastiness of the exodus had left an overabundance of comestibles that could keep Benjamin's group alive for years. They drank and ate whatever they felt like, gorging on the processed, nearly unperishable foods manufactured by the twenty-first century. Their numbers grew beyond a hundred. A first child had been born in the camp a couple of weeks before our arrival. They used a communal hWisper embedded in one of the residents to create educational curricula for the children and to keep an eye on the news of the world. The three nurses living in the community provided better health care than most of its members had received back in so-called civilization.

For a half hour, Tereza listened with forbearance to the story of the camp, but at last she interrupted the jovial conversation between Benjamin and the captain to discuss the task ahead. "How does this work?" she asked.

Benjamin took a pull from his flask and rubbed his hands together.

"Of course, business. The children are going to bed now, we can get on the road soon. We have to make sure they're asleep before we depart. The brats like to sneak out of their beds and follow us." From here, he said, it was a two-hour hike north to Manatee County, the Reclamation Bureau territory marked by the coordinates, where some civilization resumed. From there, it would take another hour or two to reach the coordinates. They would have to watch out for HDF patrols. "With me," he said, "you stay invisible. You stay invisible because you're patient and you listen to me. I've guided many people through this land."

"We don't even know what we're looking for," Roman said. "Do you know the place we're headed to?"

"The building marked by your coordinates has been there awhile," Benjamin said. "Last time I went in that direction, the place was abandoned. But things change quickly."

"Do you know what's happening there?" Tereza asked. "Is VITA involved?"

"You mean you don't believe they're creating an undead army to attack China?" Benjamin said. He let out a boisterous giggle at her expression. Then his face turned solemn. "I wish I knew what they were up to. Lots of fancy people come and go from that territory, dressed in suits, chauffeured in massive shining SUVs. Not government people. Corporate. They build structures in the middle of the swamp and fill them with scientists, guards, equipment. Then they bring the bodies in freight trucks and store them inside. Hundreds of corpses come through these parts. Medical trials, maybe; best not to let the imagination go wild. Yeah, I reckon I've seen the VITA logo a lot these past few months."

"Are you sure?" Tereza said. "You've seen this firsthand?" Bodies. She disappeared into her hWisper, where I joined her to see her enter the search keywords *VITA black sites rumors*. A few conspiracy threads claiming that the Reclamation government provided VITA with corpses of foreigners for unknown experiments.

The captain and Benjamin left to pack shovels and mosquito repellent while the people gathered around the fire peeled off to put their children in bed. One of the couples, a pair of men, walked to a convenience store with shuttered windows. Out of curiosity, Tereza abandoned her hWisper to follow them and lingered in the open doorway. Inside, between the bare shelves, a trio of bunk beds sheltered five fidgeting children. The two men sat on a couch placed in the middle of the triangle of beds, and one of them pulled out a paperback torn in half. *Notes from Underground.* He held the two pieces of the book together as he opened it and placed his finger on the chapter heading.

Noticing her in the doorway, the men gestured for Tereza to join them. "Would you like to read this passage?" one of them asked.

"I'm here for something else," she replied with her arms crossed.

"As long as it isn't utopia," the man said with a laugh, raising the halves of his book.

A little girl on the top bunk lifted her head and stared Tereza down with a deadpan expression. "'To rely on man's self-interest for advancement of society,'" she said, tripping over a few of the memorized words, "'is to live in perpetual wilderness. To feel human, man will strike against the status quo, even if the status quo benefits him most.'" The girl broke into giggles as she finished reciting the lesson, and the other children joined in.

For them, there was no such thing as a past or a future; they simply lived from one moment to the next with neither nostalgia nor expectation, these children whose chance at prosperity we'd buried long ago.

"Very good!" said the man with the book.

Tereza left the group without a word.

Her brother sat alone by the fire, picking lint from his pockets and throwing it into the flames. At last, the captain and Benjamin returned with supplies and gestured for Tereza and Roman to come forward.

The captain wished my children good luck, as he had to stay

behind and sleep before heading to *Markyta* at dawn. They were in the hands of the most capable man in this wasteland, he assured them. If there was any chance of finding what they were looking for, it was with Benjamin by their side.

MY CHILDREN SET out on the concrete path ahead, outside the light of the fires, and Benjamin turned a small crank on his lantern to illuminate the way. Within a half hour, the shambles of the razed city turned into marshlands. But Benjamin guided my children around every patch of grass drowned in mud, barely looking at the ground, knowing every inch of safe dirt. After an hour, they'd left behind even the ruins of civilization. Here, nature had reclaimed its own lands entirely. Creatures moved audibly in the darkness beyond the lantern's reach, and my children kept close to their guide, who seemed to have no concerns at all.

"What is that?" Roman asked when yet another shadow passed a few meters ahead of them.

Benjamin opened his backpack and revealed a shining object, his silver pistol. He nodded somberly and suggested they'd be smart to hurry. "Strange new creatures breed here," he said.

At the conclusion of the trio's four-hour journey, my rescuers came upon a shockingly bright clearing seemingly lifted from some twilight zone. They hid behind trees at the edge of the clearing as they observed the swamp. Buzzing security lights illuminated a massive one-story warehouse built on top of a raft the size of a football pitch. The building swayed lightly back and forth in time with the raft, its walls and insides moaning and creaking with each subtle motion. Along the side of the building ran a series of small sheds housing dozens of groaning generators that powered the monstrous houseboat. The walls were sleek and windowless, impenetrable. The building's only entrance, at the front, was guarded by six HDF grunts perhaps thirty meters from where my children hid. The men sat under a small tin roof, playing cards on a picnic table.

"It's really here," Tereza said, her boots sinking into the muck.

"That's a lot of guns," Roman said.

"These people weren't here a month ago," Benjamin said. "I swear, it was abandoned."

"Tereza is important," Roman said. "They won't hurt her."

"They're handing out five-year federal sentences to people who trespass here," Benjamin said. "Just how important are you?"

"I won't risk it," Tereza said. "They'll bury Roman in a work camp."

The three of them sat with their indecision at the edge of the clearing for nearly an hour, bickering about their course of action, waiting for something to change. The guards didn't move from their card game except to urinate over the edge of the raft.

"This is pointless," Tereza said at last as she stood up and took a step forward, into the clearing. "You two stay here. I'll handle this."

Just then, the front door of the building opened and Roman pulled her back by the arm.

A woman dressed in white scrubs appeared in the door. The guards turned their faces toward her. But she looked directly at the spot where my children were hiding and waved with both hands.

The guards stood up and raised their guns in our direction.

"Easy, boys!" the woman shouted. "I see an old friend."

"We have to run," Roman said.

But Tereza had already begun walking toward the building.

"No point in getting shot in the back," said Benjamin. He raised his hands in the air and followed Tereza.

At last, Roman revealed himself too. The three of them gathered at a makeshift bridge between the building and shore as the HDF troops observed them with their guns half raised. But the woman showed no caution. She asked the men to stay behind and walked onto the bridge. I recognized the logo on her shoulder: VITA.

"I thought you took that professorship in Spain," Tereza said to the woman.

"Got tired of drinking wine for breakfast," the woman said. She was actually grinning.

"Roman, Benjamin," Tereza said, "this is Greta, one of the world's most distinguished immortalists. Her father, Berat, was my mentor in Germany. He made my career possible."

"He always said you'd become his boss someday," Greta said.

"If he could see us here, at the end of the world..."

"Tough time getting here?" Greta pointed to the bandage on Tereza's forehead.

"Car accident," Tereza said. "Thought I saw a ghost."

The two women embraced.

"You still look like a kid," Tereza said.

Roman and Benjamin eyed the rifles of the HDF guards. I was as confused as they were.

"I was wondering when you'd get here," Greta said.

"You knew we were coming? Did you send the message?"

"No messages from me," Greta said.

"Does this place belong to...them? Us? I mean, the company?"

"Follow me," Greta said, stepping back toward the building. "I have a gift for you. But your guide stays outside."

Tereza followed Greta to the building. She beckoned for Roman to come too. He did so, keeping his eyes fixed on the guards. Greta held her face steady for the biometric scanner as the doors slid open.

"You dudes got a smoke?" Benjamin asked the puzzled guards right before Tereza and Roman left him and vanished into the building.

The massive space was nearly empty, like a shuttered warehouse. The walls were adorned with blinking servers locked behind metal grates. On the ceiling, a dozen noisy vents exhaled cold air, turning my children's breath into clouds. A panel of monitors showed the feeds of security cameras, one of them aimed at the tree line where my children had been hiding. Along the floor, thousands of wires traveled between the servers and a black sarcophagus placed in the middle of the room. It was surrounded by computers and unidentifiable machines big and small, all of them branded with the VITA logo. Tereza and Roman studied the unusual object.

"Don't worry about the Reclamation grunts," Greta said. "They do whatever I say. But we should talk about *this*."

She approached the sarcophagus as my children stared at it in silence. Tereza walked closer, put her hands on the edge of the vessel, and leaned over the glass cover.

Finally, I saw what she saw.

I saw myself.

Inside the black chamber rested my frozen body, submerged in the blue cryonic fluid. My eyes were wide open, my face calm; I looked as though I were just about to ask someone for a mildly inconvenient favor. Or perhaps I was about to sneeze? Either way, my face betrayed no surprise over my death, no realization of mortality frozen in time. Oddly, I was proud of myself. The state of my flesh, however, inspired a feeling of terror. It was exactly as I had seen it in my strange visions. The skin and bone atop my head was sawed through, the flaps held in place by massive staples. My face was marked with a red scar that extended from my chin to my hairline, as if someone had injected red dye into my veins.

To my great surprise, I was still wearing the dress in which I'd spent my day with Tereza. The golden-beetle necklace still hung around my neck. Was this normal?

Roman and Tereza stood over me quietly, their hands touching the glass that separated us.

"I'm sorry you have to see her like this," Greta said. "The cryonic fluid makes a mess. I don't have the tools here to make her more presentable for you."

More presentable. Would I ever get used to the funny ways in which the living spoke about me?

Tereza recoiled from the sarcophagus while Roman continued to stand perfectly still, observing me.

"Greta," Tereza said.

"Right. Steven & Mark really wished they could be here to explain this. But you know their schedule."

"Greta, I haven't seen you since you struggled with biochem homework. Now you're the assigned chaperone of my mother's stolen corpse. I've never been one for suspense."

Greta tapped her finger in the air to activate her hWisper—apparently a brand-new model, nearly invisible on her neck—and drew a shape with her right hand. The cryonic chamber hissed and began to open. A gray liquid poured over my face and down into the machine's innards. Roman stepped back as my face thawed and reacted to oxygen. Instantly my cheeks sank, my left eyelid drooped closed, my lips turned from blue to a tint of green. The red scar became darker. Tereza ran her fingertips along my forehead. Roman didn't move. His skin turned pale, and he put a hand over his stomach.

Greta seemed to be searching for the words to explain the seemingly unexplainable, the parts of it she knew. I listened as intently as my children. When I died in my sleep in a mediocre hotel room, the tracking band on my wrist sent the news of my demise to the Reclamation authorities. The usual policy was to burn the bodies of dead foreigners immediately, without investigation, just as Tereza learned at the Bureau. But the monitoring of my biometric information no longer fell under Reclamation jurisdiction. By then, Tereza's bosses had already taken an interest in me and requested that the Bureau send my biometric information to them. I was family, and they wanted to keep an eye on me.

Immediately after my death, VITA had dispatched a cryonics team to preserve my body. Tereza knew this was standard policy for the subscribers to VITA's Last Chance insurance program. If a wealthy customer died unexpectedly, he or she was immediately frozen in hopes that future technology would allow for a resurrection. But why would they do this for me? I was nothing to them, and though Tereza was valuable to VITA, the expense of my preservation couldn't possibly be worth it. After all, they already had her signature on the lifetime contract. What was the point?

Greta insisted that Steven & Mark had had every intention of informing Tereza of my death. But as the cryonicists began the process of freezing my body, en route to the VITA labs, they encountered an unprecedented phenomenon. Though I was presumed dead—that is, all of my other organs had positively shut down—exactly 0.4 percent of my brain function remained steady. Before the VITA vehicle carrying me from the Flatiron arrived in Midtown, my body experienced a series of seizures, during which my brain activity spiked to levels even beyond the living, then crashed back down to 0.4 percent. VITA had hoped to present my frozen body to Tereza with hopes for a future revival. But it seemed that within my body, against all previously known physical possibilities, my brain had refused to die. No such seizures had been reported in human history. Instead of presenting my body to Tereza, Steven & Mark had me taken to the black ops laboratories of the VITA building, the same place to which Lydia, the eighty-five-year-old teacher from South Dakota, had been spirited away. They wanted to study me.

Greta wasn't entirely sure what their intentions were, then or now. All she knew was that two days after my body was found, she was transferred from the VITA lab in Atlanta to this swamp facility in Florida, and my body was here when she arrived. She'd been given only the brief explanation she'd just shared, with a personal assurance from Steven & Mark that the preservation of my body might change the future of humanity. They had chosen to keep Tereza in the dark temporarily. They said they couldn't allow Tereza to thwart their research with familial emotion. Once they achieved the results they were after, they were certain that Tereza would approve of their actions.

"You mean she's still alive," Roman interrupted at last. His face had turned a pure alabaster as Greta spoke. "If her brain's alive, she's alive. She needs a hospital, they can—"

"I'm afraid her remaining brain activity ceased five days ago," Greta said. "On my watch. I don't know why. Whatever spark was fueling her, it went out."

According to Greta, VITA had tasked her with watching my body because she was one of their most accomplished cryonicists, though it was clear her personal connection to Tereza wasn't lost on them. As long as any brain activity, no matter how low, continued, her mission was to monitor it and inform them if the seizures resumed. When the brain activity ceased, she was asked to maintain the stability of my cryonic state. Somehow, Steven & Mark knew that my children were already on their way to rescue my body, to bring me home, and they told Greta to expect them.

As Greta took a moment to breathe, Tereza approached her and stood close, betraying a grimace of anger. I thought she might attack Greta any second. "All this time," she said. "Stealing my mother's body. Cutting her open, freezing her, whisking her to Florida to keep her in this shithole. Playing games with us, her family. Do they think I don't have the balls to destroy—"

"I hate it, T. I wanted to call you as soon as I found out. But I guess I also became swept up in it. Your mother is extraordinary, you know. For a while it seemed like she might... resurrect. So I did what I was told."

"You don't know anything else?"

"Nothing for sure. I'm guessing all of this has to do with brain mapping. Mind upload. But they swore they'd tell you everything. They want you to bury your mother and come back to New York. For an important chat. You're an essential part of their plans."

"Why didn't they just send the body to us?"

"When her brain finally died, they were going to send her to you in a jet. But by then you were already on your way here. They thought it was romantic. Sailing across the ocean to save your mother. They didn't want to spoil it."

Roman slammed his fist into the glass cover of the cryonic chamber.

He bent over in pain and rubbed his wrist. My left eyelid opened again; my eye fixed on my son. Roman couldn't look away.

"So who's been fucking with us?" Tereza said. "The messages we received, guiding us here."

"Like I said, I don't know anything about that," Greta said. "I was told you'd be here today to collect her. They kept track of your every step, of course. They told me not to be in the room alone with you, but come on, how long have we known each other? I know you know this isn't my fault. God. The world has just gotten so *weird*. You prepare for it in our line of work, but still you're not ready."

"You can't even tell when you're dreaming," Tereza said.

"They said they wanted you to see this place," Greta said. "It's the seed of things to come. They've leased this ruined land from the government. The HDF helps them patrol it. Keep secrets. They want this whole region to become a VITA republic." Their vision was a network of cities built on technology and community, Greta said. No one hungry, no one unhoused, all working toward a common goal—the success of the corporation. Protected by massive biodomes that would allow the natural habitat to restore itself. And at the center, Greta said, VITA wanted to build a museum to honor Tereza's mother. A tribute to Adéla Slavíková. "Because whatever their plans are now, she is at the center of it all."

"A museum," Roman scoffed. "I've heard enough." He again approached the chamber, which was now entirely drained of the gray liquid. Carefully, my son touched my shoulder, searching for a way to lift me out of the vessel.

"She was just a person," Tereza whispered. "Lovely. Looking for peace. She came searching for me and she ended up in this...horror. It is absolute horror, do you see that, Greta? How could you agree to this?"

Greta looked away in silence. She tapped the air to activate her hWisper. "Come help us," she commanded. Two of the guards entered the building a moment later. They disappeared at the other end of the room and returned with a massive dark blue box just the right length for a human body.

"Can we?" Greta asked.

"Box her up, like a cake?" Tereza said. She nodded, just barely.

The two guards lifted my body out of the sarcophagus, and my arms hung limp, as if in exasperation. Roman jumped forward to hold my right hand up so it wouldn't drag on the ground. An unidentifiable dark green liquid began to pour out of my corpse's ear. I regretted seeing my body without life. It seemed plastic, rigid, alien, as if there hadn't ever been a connection between who I am and the flesh that housed me for a lifetime. Had I already gotten so used to my ethereal form that I viewed the ownership of a body as inconceivable? The guards placed me inside the blue box and closed the lid of this makeshift casket in visible disgust.

"You have refrigeration on the ship?" Greta said.

"Dry ice," Roman replied. He waved the guards away from the box and stood over it.

"I feel like I'm leaving a part of my sanity here," Tereza said. "For good."

"Go home," Greta said. "Forget all this. It's no place to be for those who still have a mind to lose."

"I won't work for these people," Tereza said. "You?"

Greta looked down at her feet. "I'm too curious to stop," she admitted.

Under the watchful eyes of the guards, my children lifted the box holding my body and carried me out. The doors slid closed behind them. The HDF guards who'd remained outside sat at their card table with Benjamin, watching in fascination as he made a queen of hearts disappear behind his ear.

"I presume this is your late mother?" Benjamin said, standing and gesturing toward the box.

Neither Tereza nor Roman answered. Birds chirped in the distance. The early stirrings of dawn reigned blood red over the morning sky. The HDF guards waved goodbye as if parting with old friends, and my children and their guide left, bearing me back toward the coast, to the city of those who remained despite all odds.

As Tereza, Roman, and Benjamin retraced their steps, the beautiful dawn transformed into a torrential storm. The sodden ground beneath their feet grew even softer, and the walk back to the settlement took twice as long, complicated by the weight of my remains. It was almost noon by the time we arrived. The captain and the eighteen new passengers—the fleeing American refugees—awaited us in small fishing boats. Roman and Tereza placed my sagging, ripped casket inside their own lifeboat, and the captain steered us away from land, shouting goodbyes to Benjamin, who had already lit up his weed pipe to relax after the encounter with the HDF.

Half a mile from shore, *Markyta* was ready for our return. Tereza kept looking out the lifeboat window as if expecting that the Coast Guard would foil us at the last minute, reclaim my body, reclaim her, reclaim Roman and place him in a labor camp for the rest of his life. How had she lived in this country all these years?

At last, we reached *Markyta*. My final visit to the United States of America was over. The world I had longed for, the past I had wished so badly to relive, was lost, never to be recovered. Despite the maddening, largely unknown circumstances of my death and afterlife, I tried my best to feel comfort in the reunion of my body with my family, in the depths of their love demonstrated here on these shores, the risk they'd taken to bring me home, to gift me a final act of dignity.

The crewmen lifted the lifeboat up by crane as the refugees abandoned the fishing boats and climbed up the rope ladders hanging over the edge of the freighter. Back on deck, with the help of the captain and the few sailors unburdened by superstition, my children ripped open the wet box that had served as my temporary home. I recoiled at the sight of my shriveled skin, the flesh that had begun to decompose in Florida's humidity. They swiftly transferred me from this paltry vessel of the Reclamation into the beautiful casket crafted by Mr. Lavička of

Hluboká and buttressed me with packets of dry ice. Then my children placed the casket inside refrigerated cargo container C-7815 and surrounded my remains with packages of imitation crab, a deflection for the German customs officers. By the early afternoon we had set our course for Europe. Tereza and Roman dropped the dark blue box that had briefly held me into the sea, leaving it to drown in America's waters.

But America wasn't done doling out surprises just yet. As we embarked from Floridian shores, the captain called my children to the helm. Exhausted and angry at being summoned before they could even shower, Roman and Tereza reluctantly obliged. Staring out the window in silence, the captain handed a pair of binoculars to Tereza and pointed in the direction of a faraway ship. Tereza focused the binoculars. The ship was unmarked, but the captain noted it looked like a large fishing ship. Suddenly, a net filled with a mass of flapping objects was released by a crane and plummeted into the sea. Was it a fishing barge? But why return so many fish to the ocean?

"What is it?" Roman asked, squinting.

The crane lifted another net over the deck of the strange ship, and the objects came into focus at last. The flapping wasn't caused by writhing fish but human limbs jerked about by the unsteady crane. It was a net filled with corpses.

At the bottom of the net hanging from the crane, a series of weights were attached, ensuring that the bodies would not float to the surface before sharks and other sea creatures could gnaw through the net. The crane strained upward with the weight of its cargo, hovered over the sea, and dropped dozens more of America's dead into the ocean's depths.

"Hundreds of bodies come through this place every month," the captain said. "People who aren't known or missed. They keep them in those buildings. Cut them open, probe them, put machines inside them. Some of my people claim they've seen the dead creep on the horizon, almost like they're dancing. But eventually, it seems, they all end up with a sea burial. What's it all for?" The captain spat into his right hand and rubbed his forehead as he prayed in several languages. "Cursed country."

The three of them looked on as first dozens and then hundreds of corpses found a new home in the abyss of the Atlantic. I could watch no longer. I had to flee this place of death and destruction. Desperately I wished to return to the Florida of my youth, with its hostile sun and pastel colors, the exposed frolickers on the beach, young and old, swaying in the water, so filled with life, with hope. The exact opposite of the devilry I had witnessed here. Again I felt the pull of the past, and with my body recovered and my children safely on board, I submitted to its comforts.

THE YEAR IS 1989

MICHAEL AND I held our first showing of *The Great Newt War* at a small theater in Sarasota, a purple building surrounded by ceratiolas. We had rented out the whole building to screen the film for our cast and crew, using the last remnants of the budget to get everyone free soda refills as a final token of gratitude.

We had spent the previous eight months in a limbo of work and editing, driving at night to the postproduction facilities in Bradenton, where, on Derek's dime, we imposed order on the chaos of our footage. Who needed sleep? There never seemed to be enough coverage to make up for scenes that had been ruined, whether by onlookers or the sun or Rostislav's stiff expressions. Halfway through the process, I realized I didn't have the stomach for this part, to see our great efforts in the physical world reduced to flawed images, beats and scenes on celluloid. The reality could never match the film I had already made in my head. I left Michael to finish editing the rest of the film, and thus our private premiere with the cast and crew would be my first time seeing the completed opus.

To offset the nerves, I had accidentally gotten champagne-drunk before the screening. Michael snuck another unopened bottle to our seats. I wore a mint-green dress I had gotten from Macy's. Prom season was upon us, the discounts were deep, and I felt comfortable pulling a little more money from my savings. This was to be a momentous day in my life. We had made something. I had made a movie in America. I'd placed much of what I thought was important about myself in it. Michael wore a three-piece suit he'd obviously owned for too long, with yellow sweat stains showing on the fabric around his armpits and neck. But it was fine. He looked handsome because he looked happy.

My vision blurred as the film started. I was nauseated and desperately thirsty when Ava spoke her lines. I looked amazing, the screen suited me, but it was small consolation when every line spoken in my voice (a voice that seemed to belong to someone else entirely) made me leave permanent fingernail impressions on my velvet seat. I kept blinking to focus, breathed deeply to stop the trembling of my hands and lips, but by the time I was finally calm enough to enjoy myself, the film was over.

We all applauded, though I had no idea whether I had liked the film or hated every moment. We left the theater to indulge in cigarettes, smokers and nonsmokers alike. I held a Marlboro in my shaking hand as Michael kissed me and I kissed him back, if only to distract myself. Around us the voices of friends and extras hummed in semi-whispers, and people came up to us to tell us how impressive it all was, how proud they were to be a part of it. Anxiously we searched the crowd for Derek until he finally emerged from the theater lobby in sunglasses. He embraced Michael and me in an intimate hug. Reeking of whiskey, he told Michael he felt like a proud father. Like he was part of something bigger.

"If I know anything at all about art," Derek said, "this movie is going to change the world as we know it." He kissed my cheek and released me, then dragged Michael away and offered his flask. The two whispered like overeager boys.

I accepted this praise, infected by the enthusiasm of our friends. We had made a movie! Reagan's America was alive. Our overnight Hollywood fame was inevitable and all it had taken was honest American labor. Already I was scheming for my next project. Some years earlier I had read an article about a couple of famous Czech artists planning to make a film about a small village that turns itself into a Kafka theme park. Chaos, tragicomedy, existential roller coasters. The men who had planned it were dead now and someone else needed to make their film. Why not me? I had no shortage of ambition and at my drunkest, I even believed that America would reward my artistic achievement with honorary legal status.

Hitchcock had once said that when he closed his eyes, he could project the entirety of his next film on the backs of his eyelids. Some applauded the master for another profound expression of egoism, while others questioned whether it made sense to make a film the auteur had already seen. What of the surprise of discovery, when the greatest moments in life and art occur? But I wanted to attempt the master's method nonetheless. I closed my eyes and I projected the perfect future. Why not indulge? If a minor Hollywood actor could become president of a nuclear superpower, then a village girl and amateur dissident could become a Hollywood star. It was about movement, about biting off more than you could chew and then chewing until your jaw dropped off.

I drew up the plans in my mind. We would tour the festival circuit and agree to a multimillion-dollar acquisition of our film. Next, Michael and I would leave the Fairchilds without notice. We'd build our own house on the shore. I'd become a runner, sweat on the beach every morning, dip my sore feet in the sand that always stayed cool regardless of the heat, this crystal quartz powder that had traveled down great rivers from the Appalachian Mountains into the Gulf of Mexico and landed on these beaches over billions of years. We would buy Rostislav the puppet from Alphonse and keep him in our living room as a reminder of where we'd started, a conversation piece for the American parties we'd throw for our American friends.

Then, children. Not yet, but soon. We would become people our children could be proud of. We would give them everything money and kindness could buy. I'd bring my parents over for visits. I knew I could never convince them to move to America — they loved their village too much — but they would spend summers here, get to know their son-in-law, their grandchildren. The fresh sea air would relieve aches in their bones and extend their lives. I'd be happy at last in this country that didn't require one to be political, in this country that rewarded generously those who dared to imagine good things for themselves.

My life had never been as clear to me as it was in this moment. I expected everything, riches and happiness, and I was truly convinced that I'd earned it. That I deserved it more than others. That it belonged to me. Because I was brave enough and tenacious enough to take it. If Reagan had been there, I would've kissed him on the mouth. I was with him, and the world was great and America was Great.

I enjoyed the rest of the night, drank to excess, fucked Michael with a hunger I hadn't felt since I had first explored sex with my boyfriend in Hluboká. America was mine. Here, I would live forever, made immortal by my art.

WE SPENT THE next few months submitting the film to festivals across the country. Our inquiries were met with a damning silence. In the end, we were accepted by a single student festival, mostly a showcase of the work made at the local art school Michael had attended. *The Great Newt War* hadn't been made by students and thus didn't fit the festival criteria, but Michael's friendship with the organizers bought us an exception. We should've seen this as a bad sign and a reason to despair, but Michael and I blamed the competitiveness of the industry.

As we awaited the festival, I cleaned the Fairchild place once a week and avoided our landlords at all costs. I stole food from their fridge, cake leftovers and sodas. I was soon to part with my serfdom and felt justified in these small acts of revenge.

We were to attend the film festival premiere in October. I planned to dress down—a pair of jeans, a white shirt, and a leather jacket, the uniform of an actress going casually about her day. Michael was insisting on wearing his three-piece suit again. I thought this might bring bad luck, so the night before the screening, I poked a few small, jagged holes in the jacket and blamed moths for the destruction. The suit could be easily fixed, but there were no fixes for a jinx.

I saw our film for the second time. This time my vision wasn't blurred. Something was off. The images on the screen didn't quite match the effort and emotional investment we had deployed. I figured I was just being overly critical and nervous, but I watched through the film with my jaw clenched, attempting not to squirm and cringe at the occasional chuckles in the auditorium in response to the story's most serious moments. A few of the audience members left the theater halfway through the film. At the end we received no applause.

I sought comfort in Michael, but he had none to offer. Despite his outward professions of confidence in the film, in truth, the many rejections from festivals had taken their toll. He hadn't been his normal, talkative self for weeks. He'd stopped writing and begun to work longer and longer hours at the restaurant. I had attributed this to the stress of expectations about the upcoming screening and left him alone. He had always been the dreamer of our bunch, but now I seemed to carry our collective vision of grandeur on my own.

We walked outside the festival theater unrecognized, ignored. I went to the restroom to scream into my purse. Upon my return, I caught up with Michael speaking to the festival organizer. As soon as he saw me, he said we had to go; he was mute in answer to my questions as we hurried to the car. At home, he shut himself in the bedroom and asked for space.

The morning following the festival, I threw up. Nerves, I would soon learn, weren't the cause.

The review of our film in the local newspaper came out two days later.

Ambition and passion cannot be denied in this strange film, based loosely on a literary work of the famous science-fiction writer and inventor of the word robot, *Karel Čapek. But the inconsistency of its writing and the technical inadequacy of the filmmakers make it an uncomfortable, occasionally laughable, bloated disappointment. The film strives to be at once a thrilling period piece, a dark dystopia, and a philosophical soap opera about the nature of love, but the writing shows that its creators can barely handle a single subject, let alone three. Though there are a few moments that elevate the film, scenes that might even be unforgettable, it is hard to pass over the atrocious performance by the unconvincing, creepy salamander puppet, the uneven, overly theatrical performance by the lead actress, and the sloppy work of the director, who seems to have no natural feeling for the language of visual media. If this were a student film, we would foresee some hope for its makers. But as it has been revealed to us that the film wasn't made by young students, we can only recommend it to those interested in studying absolute failure.*

By NOVEMBER, A month after our film premiered, a change was under way in my home country. On International Students' Day, a week after the Berlin Wall fell, riot police attacked peaceful protesters in Prague, an act of violence that became the inciting incident for the Velvet Revolution. Following a mass uprising of citizens, the one-party Communist rule, which had brutalized Czechoslovakia for more than forty years, collapsed in less than two weeks.

Meanwhile in America, I found myself living in the back seat of our Buick. It occurred to me just how little attention I had paid to the car before it became our home. The seats were plush and reminded me of the underground jazz lounge in Prague where I had once been considered a dissident VIP guest. The ceiling of the Buick had three knife holes in it, courtesy of the previous owner. I slept in the back, and Michael took the reclined driver's seat. When I woke up, the holes were the first thing I saw. I would sit up slowly and massage my neck, then crawl out of the back seat on all fours. As the Buick had only two doors, I had to lean the front seat forward and fall through the small space until my palms touched the concrete and I rolled fully onto the pavement. To avoid the cops, Michael and I squatted in beach parking lots and used the public bathrooms for our morning business. Inside a desolate toilet stall, I'd start my day throwing up, then brush my teeth, wash my armpits, and put on deodorant, half a swipe, to make it last.

How had this state of affairs come to be? Three weeks after our film premiered at the festival, Mrs. Fairchild invited Michael and me in for a talk. Curious about why her house didn't seem quite so sterile and clean anymore, she had installed a few hidden cameras. She'd captured me standing around idly during cleaning hours, taking food from her fridge, and spending much of my time reading, watching television, or taking a dip in the pool. She fired me immediately, and we were given three days to vacate the premises. Without a lease or contract, we had no choice but to comply. Michael begged Mrs. Fairchild to let us leave our furniture behind until we found a new place, but she shrugged and said it wasn't her problem.

"I'm pregnant," I said.

Michael grabbed my wrist. His eyes were wide and instantly red-rimmed and he looked as if the worst tragedy possible had struck him.

"Please," I added.

Faced with the vulnerability of my confession, Mrs. Fairchild agreed to let us leave our things behind for a few weeks. It wasn't the best way to share the news with Michael, I knew. I still had no idea how I felt about it. The timing was devastating. Things were imploding and I felt my old apathy return. Perhaps it was unfair, but I was furious at Michael and his idol Ronald Reagan. Between the two of them, my lover and the president, they had convinced me that the world was ripe for the taking, that with some dreaming and some effort I could be anyone. I had become complicit in a lie. I had abandoned my practicality, my ability to see through kitsch, my refusal to simplify the act of living. And with this newfound idealism, I had once again become trapped and vulnerable to the whims of others.

As we packed our possessions into boxes that had once stored bananas, Michael spoke to me only to discuss the items we needed with us in the car. Some precious jewelry, a pocket radio, clothes and toiletries, and books, though we refused to take any of Čapek's work. Our curse. When we were nearly done, Michael explained that he didn't have the money for an apartment security deposit, and he couldn't afford even a cheap motel until his next paycheck, which was eleven days away. Since he had become a shift manager and lost his daily cash tips, the paycheck was our only hope. Meanwhile, we weren't close enough with our friends to ask for a room in any of their homes. Derek no longer took our calls following the failure of the film, a lost investment that meant nothing to his wealth but much to his ego. I still had the money in my hair-dye box, plenty enough to buy us a motel stay until we figured out the next step, but I no longer thought of Michael and me as partners. We had failed together. We had entered into a delusion together. I had bought into his Hollywood dream, and now my investment was lost. He'd made me believe, and when reality punished us, he had little to give but silence. I didn't reveal my secret cash fund, as I wasn't about to risk being robbed of my escape hatch. Most likely I'd soon have to purchase a plane ticket home.

Michael was angry, of course—I had gotten us kicked out of our guesthouse—but why did it fall on me to scrub shit and piss to keep a roof over us? He was angry because I'd told him about the pregnancy for the first time in front of Mrs. Fairchild, but I had every right to organize my thoughts before I told anyone else. And he was angry because I didn't have much to say about our situation. The blame for our silence fell on both of us.

Four days into our car squatting, I spat toothpaste in the sink of a public restroom and washed my face. Despite the impending winter, the temperatures remained in the mid-eighties, and I found myself in a permanent state of fatigue and migraines after sleeping inside the hot car. Whatever appetite the pregnancy sparked was killed by heat sickness. This was fine, as we couldn't afford much food anyway. We had seven days to go until his paycheck, Michael told me that morning before he walked to work. The Ritz was only half a mile from our squat in the beach lot, and Michael stopped at an air-conditioned Friendly's nearby to wash his armpits and groin and put on his dress shirt and vest in the bathroom. He had to keep up the ruse of being middle class, since visible poverty was against the Ritz employee guidelines.

He left the car with me so I could go to the doctor in case of an emergency, look for jobs, and get the occasional relief of air-conditioning, though we were careful not to overuse it because our gas budget was a small step above nonexistent. But I didn't spend my days looking for jobs; instead, I took this time to make a decision. I had begun this American mission with absolute devotion to myself and myself only. I had accrued money and learned English and lived a life that was enjoyable and my own. Now all of this was gone, save for the bit of money I had left. I parked at a Denny's and drank coffee, and the visions of the future that I had imagined after the film premiere dissolved.

On the eighth day of our vagrancy, three days before Michael would get his paycheck to pay for a Motel 6 at the edge of town, he returned from work in a great mood. It was as if he'd simply decided he wasn't angry with me anymore. He insisted we walk on the beach in the dark, and I went along. He held my hand and I let him.

For the first time since the premiere, Michael spoke about the film. He said that after the review he'd considered tying cinder blocks around his ankles and jumping into the sea. I flinched, ran my fingertips along his neck and kissed his cheek, all the while wondering whether the pondering of suicide was manufactured to blackmail me into some show of emotion. Michael told me that he'd learned a couple of new facts about the world. He realized that he was capable of complete, absolute failure. Few people accept this fact, he said— everyone knows failure to some degree, most of us learn to accept it early on as part of the natural order, but such a complete, massive, all-encompassing feeling of failure was beyond comprehension until experienced. Growing up immersed in films, studying screenplays when other kids were playing outside, Michael had thought that his dedication and passion must inevitably result in genius, which would reveal itself sooner or later. He had felt that success was owed to him simply for making a spirited effort. But clearly this wasn't going to happen. He wasn't strong enough for the devastation that came with thwarted ambition. If he made another film, put another extension of himself out into the world, and failed again, he couldn't keep living. This was how he knew he wasn't made for Hollywood greatness.

Michael also understood that society abhorred those who failed. It was the most natural thing in the world, to fail, and yet seeing people do so disgusted us. It sparked the most extreme reaction possible. We worshipped the statistical minority, those who bit off more than they could chew and succeeded, while we passionately hated those who tried to fulfill their wildest ambitions and failed, which was the far likelier version of life, the truth unembellished. Michael knew this about others because he felt it within himself. His own failure disgusted him. For weeks he had felt he had no right to exist in the world.

He told me he had been dying to know what I'd been thinking, how I was affected, but he wasn't quite sure how to ask.

I remained silent.

Michael was happy to keep talking. He had no idea how much I would have preferred silence, just to enjoy the sound of crashing waves and contemplate whether to stay or run.

He told me that he knew what to do now. We would rent an affordable apartment and have our child. He'd get a second job, start saving up, request a loan from the bank. By the time our child went to preschool, we'd be the owners of a new family restaurant. Tourism in Florida would never dissipate; if anything it would only grow, and tourists had to eat. Betting on the lowest common denominator made humble men rich. His words.

I became angry again. Disappointed. It was the same mantra

repackaged, that old story of rebirth. You must wish hard and work harder. He'd abandoned the vision of endless wealth as a Hollywood magnate to settle for the aspiration of the comfortable middle-class family running a safe business. He'd probably gotten the idea inside the Friendly's bathroom. It was so wholesome and so reasonable that behind Michael's voice, there in the darkness of the beach, I imagined Reagan's floating head delivering the decision. In my situation, living out of a car, knocked up, I wasn't in the mood for more bootstrap slogans designed to artificially uphold the mood of the desperate. And desperate we were, albeit in different ways.

I told Michael it sounded wonderful. A family restaurant to pass on to our children, to give them a good start in life. I pushed him onto the sand and straddled him and took his clothes off, saying my good-byes, though he didn't know it. Afterward, we washed the sand off our bodies in the ocean and returned to the car, and I waited for him to fall asleep, for those peaceful exhales, and I lay with my eyes open, planning my escape for the next day. Michael made no attempt to touch me as he usually did, whispered no sweet nonsense as he fell asleep. Perhaps he felt he'd talked his way out of his failures, and he no longer needed to beg for forgiveness. I know I should've told him there was nothing to forgive. Our failures were shared.

When Michael left for work the next morning, I kissed him and held him for a long time. After he left, I vomited, though not because of my pregnancy. The guilt of freeing myself had made me sick. In a way I could finally understand my old boyfriend Ondráš and how his desire for liberty had trumped his decency. In each person's life, there came a time to cut one's losses and run. The ache of it was like a fever, a flu, the sore limbs and the lethargy. I drove to buy a new suitcase and went to the Fairchilds' guesthouse to pack the clothes I'd left behind. I made a phone call to Jirka, the plumber who had helped bring me to America and with whom I had kept up a periodic correspondence. In the chaos already being wrought by the coming Velvet

Winter, he was turning his thieving and smuggling into a lucrative full-time job. It was strange to hear his voice across this time and distance after so much had happened.

Jirka recognized me right away. "There's a goddamn revolution going on here, if you aren't aware," he said. I could hear the tram bells in the background. The sounds of home.

I acknowledged that I knew and was happy our people were breaking the totalitarian stalemate. I had a few personal problems, I admitted, that prevented me from thinking as deeply about politics as I once had. I'd dedicated my youth to the very ideas that had sparked this revolution and now I felt it had nothing to do with me.

"No, sure, come back," Jirka said. "We'll take care of you. I'm making a fortune selling cigarettes. Revolution is a great time for business."

"You were born for the open market," I said.

"Write down this address," he said.

I drove to a tailor's shop in downtown Tampa and walked to the back room. An old woman with a shaved head was already waiting for me in a den that smelled strongly of mint. I handed her an envelope with fifteen hundred dollars. She sucked on a lozenge as she got to work on my new passport. I was no longer the sister of Leszek the convict but a Czech journalist émigré in Chicago returning to her motherland to observe and record its resurrection. The bald-headed counterfeiter put the proof of my new identity inside a crisp white envelope, and my years in the States were erased. As soon as I crossed the Czechoslovakian border, I could finally resume my official identity of Adéla.

With the fake passport, I drove to a travel agency, where I booked a flight home. I brought Michael's Buick back to the beach parking lot, where he would expect to find it after his shift. On the driver's seat I left a note describing the ways in which I had decided to break his heart. Letting him know I wasn't fit for the capriciousness of American life. How lonely it was to hope for so much and never get it. I assured him that I had loved him, but I had long ago learned to leave things behind. Moreover, it was *okay* to leave things behind. I didn't know if I would keep the child or not, but I knew I didn't want to give birth and forever bind my daughter or son to a land of strangers. I didn't want to have a family with him, I confessed. I needed to escape from the life I'd lived here.

I didn't have to be so honest with Michael, of course. But I wanted to ensure I wouldn't be followed. This way, I could count on his pain and rage to blind him. He'd never want to see me again. I needed to be sure I could disappear successfully, without him launching some misguided search.

From a beach pay phone, I called a cab. The sadness over leaving Michael was overpowered by the prospect of reuniting with my parents in that same living room where I had grown up running laps around my father sitting and reading the newspapers. I hoped desperately it might still smell of my mother's beloved Turkish coffee. I was even willing to eat a thick slice of bread slathered in lard, a peace offering to my father.

I waited inside the Buick, slumped low in the passenger's seat. Since I had left, seven years earlier, my father had gone blind in one eye and fought through surgeries to save his other one. My mother hobbled on a cane while she recovered from a knee replacement. I had sent money to help, but my mother assured me they were saving the cash underneath the mattress in my room to help me reacclimate when I finally wandered back home. I'd always gotten mad at her for saying this, but now I had to be grateful. Had my parents' hair turned white? Had they started to shrink, to lose some of their strength? Did they quietly resent me for not being around to lend a hand?

Here I was, coming back not to help them but to ask for their help, again. To help me return to normalcy, overcome a tragedy of my own making. *Comfort.* There comes a point when a person must stop drawing it from nostalgia and the desire to return to some simpler time. There are no simple times. I was a backward runner, sprinting away from troubled futures and retreating into reassuring pasts. I began to second-guess my decision. The note to Michael lay on the driver's seat like a ticking bomb. The air-freshener tree trembled below the rearview mirror even though there was no movement to cause it. It used to be green but had turned piss yellow, it used to smell of pine but now smelled of the stink it had soaked up inside the car: cigarette smoke and hamburger grease and cologne.

My taxi arrived. In the few brief seconds it took to leave Michael's car, I changed my mind a thousand times, *stay* and *go, stay* and *go*. I knew I would never again inhale his scent, feel him close. Every lovers' parting brings its own unique taste of agony.

I would think of the Buick's scent while reading Michael's letter in the winter of 2021, more than thirty years later. Somehow, he had found my address in Hluboká. From his quarantined hospital bed, ravaged by the virus, he said he had finally forgiven me. My vanishing had led him to leave Florida for Boston, where he married the daughter of a McDonald's franchise owner and became its manager. Eventually he had taken over the franchise, lived a prosperous life, had two sons who'd grown up to be lawyers.

Reagan's dream, just less sexy, he quipped. *I am near death, and I write to you because we share grief. Grief over the life we could've had. I have stayed angry with you for decades, out of reflex, though I can barely remember what you look like, and I have no photographs left to reference. It makes no sense. Whoever you are now, I love you, just as I loved the woman with whom I shared an impossible adventure. My sons are trying to track down our film through archives and dealers of old reels, and I hope that it can be the last thing I watch before the time comes…*

I kept the letter hidden under my mattress. I could never read it again, but I needed to know it was still there. The last, the only piece I had left of Michael. The proof of his forgiveness. The kindest thing anyone had ever done for me.

* * *

THE RED-EYE FLIGHT to Prague was filled with tourists and journalists curious to see how the Continent was faring through its world-altering political changes. At one point, we could see the sunrise on the right side of the plane, and many passengers from the left side got up and leaned over the seats on the right side to look out the window. I imagined the plane becoming unbalanced because of the vacated left side, spiraling out of control and crashing into the ocean, ending once and for all my efforts to find a place and a life. But I arrived safely in Prague, so exhausted and so unsure of what had transpired in the past twenty-four hours that I just stood outside the terminal, waiting. I felt strange at hearing my birth language all around me.

I decided I didn't want to get in touch with my parents yet. Instead, I left the airport in a taxi called for me by the airline clerk ("Where are you visiting from?" she had asked me in English after hearing my Czech) to meet with Jirka, who was operating from a newly opened pawnshop. All was taken care of, he assured me.

I exchanged my dollars for crowns and rented a studio in Háje, on the outskirts of Prague. I bought a pullout couch and a TV. For the first two months I immersed myself in Czech movies and books, old favorites and many of the new works I'd missed. Hearing my native language come out of the magic box felt strange at first, as I'd gotten used to English, with its rolled *r*'s and sharp *s*'s and the *w*'s sounding like the beginning of a wolf's howl. We Czechs seemed to speak with such propriety and grace, it was almost comical.

In the streets, I expected to see the remnants of a revolution—the evidence of battle, battalions of civilian warriors singing of their victories, the facade of the city changing right in front of my eyes. *Something.* But around Háje, this settlement housing mostly working families, not much seemed to have changed. Old men and women strolled with their webbed bags to buy fresh rolls and milk for lunch; children climbed on the barren trees; the statues of two spacemen, the Czech Vladimír Remek and the Russian Aleksei Gubarev, smiled jubilantly with proper Soviet pride, watching over the citizenry and the subway station named in their honor: Kosmonautů. Uncertain about what the fall of Communism meant, people settled for following their routines until the nation could collectively reach some clarity.

I had missed out on the revolution I was once ready to sacrifice my life for. I never saw the armed policemen lining up against the protesters, never witnessed the violence of the front lines and the chain resignations of party functionaries. When I left the country, any hopes for a revolution seemed misplaced. The state had broken me, made me believe that the world would always be divided by this struggle between capitalist West and Communist East, that the nuclear standoff would forever guarantee the stability of the Russian and American empires and that no one else would come to the aid of republics caught in the middle of the cockfight. By the time I died, I would come to know that empires can vanish as quickly as they are built; they can also be recycled, like crumpled plastic bottles.

But it was easy to forget about my remorse over missing the revolution when a new life pushed against my insides. I gladly submitted to cravings and invested my dwindling funds in pickled eggs, mashed potatoes, sauerkraut (which I ate directly from the jar), and, my favorite, French fries smothered in a combination of ketchup and mayonnaise.

The fate of the fetus, I soon learned, would be my decision. The abortion commissions (wherein a group of male functionaries interrogated the mother and pressed her for "legitimate" reasons to abort her pregnancy—humiliation by bureaucracy) had been disbanded. I could abort my pregnancy without judgment from strangers. But faced with the choice, I decided that the option Jirka had proposed seemed the best one. A Danish couple was prepared to take the child as their own in exchange for money, which I needed to survive. The Danes were eager to help our people, the "other" Europeans attempting to free themselves and join the West, and though they initially wanted a child from our orphanages, they felt even more drawn to helping a newborn and her struggling mother. I had no doubt that I wanted to give the child away. Had Jirka not suggested this method of handling things, I would've gotten the abortion soon after I landed. But this way, everyone involved would get what they needed. I wouldn't have to return to my parents penniless.

During those final months before Tereza arrived, I stayed around Háje, going outside only on short walks for groceries and books. I avoided Čapek, but I read everything else I could find from Czech writers, especially poets, their brief vignettes of time and sensation, something I craved. The farthest I ventured outside my apartment was to the hospital for my prenatal appointments.

Occasionally a well-meaning but nosy passerby asked me how many months I had left or whether I was excited to bring a child into the new republic. Once, an old man asked if I realized my duty to the country was to raise a moral, anti-Communist child.

"Were you with the secret police?" I asked him.

The man took a step back, let out a shocked exhale. "I'm no traitor," he said.

"You interrogate women on the street," I said.

He never spoke to me again.

I stayed hidden in my neighborhood on the outskirts of the city because I dreaded running into old Prague friends, especially those who knew my parents. To make Jirka's plan work, I had to stay anonymous until the end. I resolved not to talk to Babi for the remainder of the pregnancy, as I was afraid I might break and reveal that I was back in the country. She would worry, perhaps tell my father, who would mobilize the entire village to find me. For now, I could trust only Jirka and lie low until our plan had come to its conclusion and I'd been paid.

My water broke in the middle of the night. I walked outside the apartment building to call a cab from the pay phone, but the night bus was just passing through. I got on and rode two stations to the hospital. There I declared Jirka the father and asked the nurse to call him. After eight hours—excruciating, searing, exhausting hours—Tereza was born. I held her but refused to look her in the eye, as this seemed to be cruel to both of us. When the doctors and nurses left, Jirka told me that the Holms, the Danish couple adopting her, had already arrived in Prague. They could be at the hospital within the hour. I agreed.

The woman who would become Tereza's mother smelled of lotion and powder. The man had thick hairy forearms, the kind I always associated with fathers. The couple took turns holding Tereza, introducing themselves as if she could understand them, and I was reassured. She could be theirs. As if I had never been here.

They asked how I was feeling, and I told them I was in pain and happy to know them. I asked if they'd mind calling the baby Tereza, my favorite name.

"It's perfect," the mother said.

We left the hospital a couple of days later, and Tereza's new parents put her in a carrier and strapped her into the back seat of their rented car. They were headed to their hotel, accompanied by Jirka, to carry out the rest of the plan and take Tereza out of the country. I didn't say goodbye to any of them. I waved and started walking in the direction of the bus station, but the pain was so severe I had to sit down and let Jirka call me a taxi.

To fill the silence, he assured me that he would take care of the bureaucrats, pay off the right people, get the proper documents so that Tereza could travel back to Copenhagen with her parents and become a Dane. The child would be happy, he promised, and I needed to let myself heal and see my parents.

I didn't want to know how much the Danes had paid Jirka. I took my cut and let him keep the rest. For a moment, I wanted to beg him to come back to the apartment with me, keep me company. I was terrified of being alone. But the baby needed his help, so I waved at him from the cab, mouthed the words *Thank you* a few times.

Decades later, Jirka would go on trial for racketeering and eventually die from testicular cancer while in custody. I would outlast him. Such is fate. As the cab pulled away from the hospital, I suspected that I would never see Jirka again. Within a year of Tereza's adoption, her new mother wrote to tell me that the Holm family had moved from Denmark to the United States for work—it was as if my daughter couldn't avoid the destiny of becoming American.

AFTER GIVING UP Tereza, I needed to celebrate my ability to drink again. Back in my apartment, I began a days-long binge, killing one bottle of gin after another, soaking the couch with it, watching television with the shades drawn, never quite knowing whether it was night or day. Unable to sleep, I entered a state of panicked, immobile stupor. I could hear the neighbors shouting in the apartment above mine, smell the stink of my own unwashed body sticking to the couch cushions, and see the trails of ants making their way to the layers of crumbs on the coffee table, but I possessed no will to participate in my own life.

As I tried to kill myself bit by bit with alcohol, the rest of my body nevertheless continued to improve. My postpartum bladder infection and swollen, clogged milk ducts began to heal, though not as quickly as I'd hoped. My recovery made me guilty about my refusal to engage with the world. I could hear the words of my mother: *You are too young to be sad.* As if anyone in her right mind could believe youth was a deterrent to tragedy.

Wanting to break through the haze, I got up and packed my clothes and a bottle of gin in the same suitcase that had accompanied me to America and back again. I walked outside, surprised to find myself in the middle of a sunny afternoon, and took the subway to the bus station, where I stumbled to the ticket window and asked for a ticket to Hluboká. The man behind the window hesitated, surveilling the state of my being—hair and face unwashed for days, a coat pulled over the sweatpants I'd been sleeping in, eyes red and swollen—but as soon as I produced the wad of cash, he printed my ticket and wished me safe travels.

My hands trembled as I waited at the station. In the bathroom, I drank more gin. I had to keep myself steady for just a while longer. The shakes worsened on the bus, and I drank more, making no attempt to hide it. I felt the direct stares of elderly men, guardians of old-world morals. My seatmate buried her nose in her shoulder and slept leaning against the window, as far away from me as possible.

The same girl woke me up later. I didn't know how or when I had blacked out. One moment I was looking out the window as we left Prague's city limits behind and the next my seatmate was shaking my arm and telling me I had screamed in my sleep. We were driving past the Hluboká cemetery, past the pub, past the house chimneys releasing soot into the sky. I was home.

I kept blacking out for microseconds as I walked down the main street. Then, without knowing how, I found myself on my knees, my suitcase flat on the ground. I got up, walked a few more steps, fell again. By the time I reached the house, my knees were rubbed bloody and there was no more gin and the shakes had returned. I thought this was it, delirium tremens would be the end of me. I wasn't an alcoholic, the hex didn't live in the blood of my kin, and yet I was going to die from the poison right at my family's doorstep. I knocked and knocked again, collapsed against the door. Nobody came; only the cats responded with their muffled meows, and I was sure they were singing me to sleep, the final sleep, until I heard familiar voices speaking my language.

I looked up to see my mother and father standing at the open door, clad in their Sunday best, and I thought, *Have they started going to church? Found religion? Or maybe a wedding? Or is today the anniversary of the founding of the village?* Such mystery, that my parents would be so finely dressed just as I arrived. I considered that perhaps they had the gift of premonition and had dressed up for my funeral, anticipating that their only daughter would return from America in a box. They held me and brought me inside, and the last thing I felt before I blacked out again for the entire day and night was warm water running over my skin.

My mother caressed my hair in the bath as the cats rubbed against her legs and purred. "You're home now," she said. "You're home now and you are never leaving again."

WITHIN A FEW months of returning home, I had healed from my infections and regained my color and, with it, some appetite for living. Every Saturday night I put on a red dress and the perfume my mother had given me and took the bus to a pub dance in the neighboring county. I kept to three drinks, never four, and with closed eyes, I danced and imagined I was back at the beach drinking alcohol bought by rich men I would never have to see again. The village bachelors and widowers watched from their benches, their faces masked by smoke, their eyes swollen and red, engaged in a creepy gaze I never returned. The men waited until they were so drunk that spiderwebs of blue and green veins formed on their noses and only then did they join in on the dance floor. By the time they gathered the courage to add words to their glances, I was heading for the cab that always idled by the pub.

But on a late-fall night that marked the last dance of the season — no one would come out here during winter — the devil emerged, sober, from a cloud of sulfur and interrupted the men's game of quiet stalking. He was lean, meaning he hadn't gotten into the habit of nightly beer drinking, and his face was clean-shaven, suspicious in the village. He had city-boy mannerisms. Yet for a man so obviously out of place, he moved with confidence.

He asked if he could join me in dancing.

I said I danced alone.

That was a relief, he replied, because he didn't know how to dance anyway, and I had spared him the humiliation.

"Happy I could help," I said.

He disappeared back into the cigarette smoke as the other men laughed at him, a pretty boy striking out like the rest of them.

"The devil himself is putting down roots in the county," my mother had once said. In our myths and legends, the devil often chose a pub to solicit his victims. This always made sense to me—if the devil was out hunting for souls, why not first approach the institution for drunkards, where he could easily find at least a few men who would gladly trade their souls for wealth, a younger liver, or a plate of sausages? I watched the newcomer to see if he was whispering in the ears of men, making his offers. But he sipped his whiskey from a shot glass and quietly observed me, the other women who preferred to dance alone, and the few swaying couples in the midst of a mating ritual.

I stayed late that night rather than making my typical escape to the taxi. The drunken men stood up and approached the single women. An old man with sausage breath asked the name of my village. I slipped around him and headed to the bar to join the intriguing stranger.

"Hello again," we said to each other. He asked what I was drinking. I called him the devil, and he told me he was on holiday from signing people up for eternal damnation. His real job, it turned out, was quite the opposite—he worked in insurance. If people were headed for hellfire, at least their families would be provided for.

He knew when to speak and when to be quiet and let the moment carry itself. He smelled of aftershave, which I imagined him rubbing along his jawline before he came here.

I had spent the past few months of my life guarded by my parents, who had policed my drinking and forced me to eat and constantly asked me to sleep more, to relax, to watch some television. Always they had some idea of how I could feel better even though they didn't know what caused my pain. Eventually, I told my mother about Tereza's birth, because I knew she could understand and forgive. But my father could never handle the idea of a granddaughter raised by strangers. To him, family was the only thing worth committing to. An otherwise agnostic man, he considered betraying blood to be the only unforgivable sin.

Living again under my father's oppressive code, I was susceptible to temptation outside the house. I was bound to make a mistake. Indeed, I gave in to the lure of this devilish stranger. We climbed into his car and drove just outside the village, into the pitch-black woods, and I showed him where to put his hands on me as if I were a teenager, sneaking away. It was exhilarating.

For one last time, I entrusted my life to a man. Six months later, I moved into Šimon's house, thirty kilometers south of Hluboká. The sex was the best we'd both had, to the point of becoming toxic. We needed to fuck everywhere, all the time, regardless of whether we liked each other at the moment. I mistook passion for trust. After I told him where to touch me once, he needed no further advice, and those nights before the pregnancy I felt like we were really animals. There was nothing but blood and skin and taste. We stayed wrapped in each other for five, six hours at a time. It's difficult not to mistake such chemistry for a sign that you've found something unbreakable.

I was pregnant again within three months of moving in. Then Šimon's sober cruelty began. He was angry with me for everything. The house was never clean enough, so I handed Šimon a broom and he broke it in half. Daily he complained that I didn't cook his meals, a gift plenty of lesser men received from their girlfriends and wives. I bought a week's worth of canned pork and beans and posted reheating instructions above the stove. Šimon put the cans in a plastic bag and threw them into a lake. He made sarcastic remarks about my pregnancy weight and often stayed out drinking until the morning. I had done it again, trusted someone without proper cause. Despite all my denials, my mother said that I was grieving my lost daughter and that having another child was a way to cope. The father, she insisted, was only an afterthought.

Our child was born — six pounds, three ounces — and during the first few months of Roman's life, things were better at home. Šimon and I ignored each other and focused on the child's needs. Roman didn't cling to his father, though; he was agitated by Šimon's touch.

One night—I can see in retrospect that Šimon was orchestrating the whole thing to smooth his exit—he told me that *I* was the devil. He claimed I was heartless, that I had never felt anything for him, that relationships were a matter of procedure for me. He had been lashing out, he said, because he felt this coldness from me. And from the child, he added. His own son seemed to hate him because he had learned it from his mother. The she-devil and the son-devil, Šimon repeated as he lit a cigarette.

I put Roman in his crib. Then, with punches and kicks, I chased Šimon and his cigarette out of the house. Locked the doors and windows. "No devils here," I told little Roman as I took him with me into the bed and cooed him to sleep. "There are no devils, but there is your father, and I will not let him ruin you."

The next morning, I packed a few things for myself and my son (I had become an expert at emergency packing by then) and took the train back to my parents, convinced this time that the last remnants of trust in romance had been exorcised from my body. I felt good about it. I had put faith in things outside myself and lost my way. Now I would trust only in the things that came from within me—my son, my family, the achievements ahead. There was still so much life ahead of me, so much to see and know.

BUT THAT'S ENOUGH of longing for the naïveté of the past. I will return now to the final voyage of my body, its transatlantic crossing to reach home. I had come alive in a time of despair and rebellion. I had lived well, loved well, betrayed well, failed well. In all my triumphs and in all my faults, no one—not a cosmic force, not a god, not my children saving my remains—could ever accuse me of letting life pass me by, of capitulating, of giving in once I'd been broken. Perhaps America and I had this in common, and for this reason we couldn't resist each other. There is something to be admired about a person or a country of endless beginnings.

Or perhaps what I had in common with America was really the susceptibility to believe in my own exceptionalism. Perhaps we enabled each other. Perhaps my retelling of this story enables us even more. The difference is, I'm dead. My actions no longer have any bearing on the world. I am unable to face consequences, and I do not have to worry about survival. America does not share this good fortune. At least for a little while longer, America will remain alive, victim to every one of its carefully crafted stories and delusions. It will continue to spread its influence in the world, along with the other countries still playing at empire, and bring us to the edge of extinction.

It is a fool's errand, to feel an indestructible kinship with a country that doesn't want you. But as it turns out, even well into my death, I remain a fool.

MEANWHILE, ON *MARKYTA*...

I REJOINED MY CHILDREN aboard the freighter *Markyta* as the ship moved sluggishly toward the relative safety of Germany's shores through the endless expanse of the Atlantic Ocean. It seemed like we were the only ship left on these waters; I spent hours on the deck looking for the shadow or lights of another vessel but observed only the flashes of rolling waves and, once, I thought, a whale's fluke. After the excitement of the escape, the first eight days of the journey passed slowly. My children mostly kept to themselves in their rooms, emerging only to check on the state of my body in the shipping crate and to collect their meals from the kitchen. Roman had been indulging in his world of conspiracies on Reddit, connecting with others who had experienced the disappearance of a loved one at the hands of the American Reclamation. At night my son stared out of the small circular window of his cabin. He had ceased to sleep almost completely. He visited my crate three or four times a day and whispered to my casket. Apologized for failing to protect me. For allowing the Americans to have me. For letting me die away from home. Never again would he allow strangers to desecrate my remains, he swore.

My daughter spent her days obsessively calling her coworkers, attempting to glean more information about VITA's black ops, searching for the reasons that had led to the bizarre theft of my body. But her colleagues were well versed in the company's NDAs, revealing nothing in their small talk. I had expected that Steven & Mark would reach out to her, as Greta suggested they would, but the silence between the visionaries and their scientist continued while Tereza considered her options—whistleblowing, lawsuits. But in her journal, she also recorded her inevitable curiosity. What had VITA discovered after snatching her mother? I didn't blame her, as I wondered the same thing. Why did they consider me to be the key to the future of humanity? Did it have something to do with my spirit form, my inability to leave this world?

The recovery of my body didn't change my state of being. Part of me had hoped that the process of the afterlife would finally embrace me, carry me off to some Eden or at least a primordial pool of nothingness where I'd cease to care about mortals altogether. Perhaps this would happen when my body was in the ground. But I couldn't see why a patch of dirt would make a difference.

On the ninth day of our return trip to Europe, I found Tereza and Roman attempting to be social in the common room as they watched newsreels from around the world on their devices. Russia continued its hostilities in the Balkans, its imperialist aims reinvigorated by its alliance with America's like-minded Reclamation president, who had overturned all of his predecessor's policies against Russian aggression. Protesters had been shot dead by the NYPD as they attempted to storm the Brooklyn branch of the Reclamation Bureau. The body of Vladimir Lenin, tended by a team of elite scientists keeping his embalmed corpse preserved, had been struck with a mysterious and unprecedented fungus that swallowed every part of his skin, turning the revolutionary papa into the Creature from the Black Lagoon. Russian state media, which, since the invasion of Ukraine, had become more and more adept at fanciful explanations, suggested the tsar's family had in fact escaped the Bolshevik Revolution and hidden out in an underground super-palace built in Siberia and that the tsar's grandchildren had conspired with NATO to dispatch this alien fungus as an insult to the father of the revolution.

The most interesting news, however, came from a small country at the heart of Europe. The eyes of my children widened as our village of Hluboká appeared on the screen. The incident had occurred in the picturesque village of Kozinec, not far from Hluboká, shortly after we'd embarked from the Gulf of Mexico. In the middle of the night, the villagers had awoken to smoke and flames curling from a barn at the edge of the village. The structure had been fully engulfed before the firemen could arrive. Though the barn had been believed empty at the time of the fire, in fact the marshal found two burned corpses on the premises. The bodies were identified as a teenage couple from the village who had used the barn for their secret midnight tryst. An incident that would usually have warranted a half-hearted investigation suddenly turned into a possible murder case when signs of arson were found at the scene. Crude Xeroxed fliers scattered around the barn claimed that mujahideen were responsible for the fire, having come to slaughter the dogs of Bohemia.

Unsurprisingly, the truth behind the fire turned out to be quite different. Within days, the police located the source of the fliers and the owner of the vehicle that had been parked just outside the village during the time the fire was set. When the police arrested him, he hastily confessed to his part in the crime and provided the name of the principal conspirator: Lubor Zoufal, the face of the Ancestor Party and Roman's former friend. Frustrated by the slow progress of the country's reclamation, Zoufal had recruited a couple of his men to set the fire, hoping to unleash a disinformation campaign to "prove" the existence of a terror cell operating on Czech soil. It was a story certain to boost his party's standing if it convinced skeptics that the dangers of an Islamic invasion were both tangible and inevitable. The nation was in need of its own holy warriors who would carry the Ancestor Party to an assured electoral victory and a majority in the parliament.

But Zoufal's soldiers had failed to cover their faces when they used the county's library to print the fliers; they had failed to check whether surveillance cameras were present in the vicinity of the barn; and on the evening of the fire, they had even boasted drunkenly at the village pub about the brave act of patriotism they were about to commit. Zoufal's apostles poured gasoline around the barn's perimeter and lit a match, apparently too drunk to notice the screams of the teenagers inside as they fled the scene.

By the time a tactical unit arrived at Zoufal's home to arrest him, he'd received a warning about his impending capture. He'd created a Facebook post showing the photos of the barn fire and the teenage corpses, accompanied by a long, rambling screed blaming the attack on a secret Islamic terror cell avenging the Hluboká five, who'd died during the Summer of Madness. He insisted that the government wouldn't allow the truth of these crimes to reach the public, that assassins were on their way to take his life.

When the tactical unit entered his apartment in Prague, Zoufal raised his CZ P-01 handgun and aimed at the officers. He was killed immediately. In the aftermath, the government publicized the entirety of its investigation of the fire to counter the spread of Zoufal's Facebook post, which had gone viral and inspired the passions of many followers. Supporters of the Ancestors descended upon Hluboká to find the fictional terrorists and punish them for their alleged crimes. Dozens of policemen entered the village to protect it, turning my peaceful home into a pressure cooker filled with drunken armed men.

Roman and Tereza watched as journalists interviewed Hluboká's residents. Reporters arrived at Babi's door—there was Babi, on TV!—and asked whether she had witnessed any possible terrorist activity in the village, whether she believed Zoufal had been framed by the government.

"Is this a joke?" Babi inquired, smiling widely without her teeth. "I've known Zoufal since he was a tot. Little asshole, that one, stole ice pops from the store and blamed it on his friends. Always a liar."

"Some people think otherwise," the reporter said as the nation watched.

" 'Some people think otherwise,' " Babi repeated. "I see. Well, you can tell those people that I did it. I drove to Kozinec, I set that barn fire. You know what else? I killed Kennedy. When the aliens crashed in Roswell, I got rid of their bodies with my own hands. I blew up Chernobyl because I felt like it. I killed Archduke Ferdinand—didn't like his face. I'm the leader of the shadow council of pedophilic wizards, and we're coming for you. Tell that to 'some people.' Tell them

Babi did it all, tell them I'm the villain, the beginning and end of the conspiracy. I've been alive for one hundred and nine years, and I've seen knowledge become as attainable as a breath of air—all of human progress is now stashed in the hocus-pocus invisible waves surrounding us, all the knowledge of our ancestors available at the twitch of a finger. Yet I've never seen people more rabid about their right to remain stupid, to shun knowledge, to live life by the same superstitions invented back when our forefathers shat in the dirt and prayed to gods made of sock puppets. Anyway, that's my jar of fat for the market. Gotta get back to my stories."

As the reporters abandoned Babi's house to seek more favorable responses from neighbors, Roman translated Babi's words for Tereza. He seemed distracted, troubled; clearly the loss of his former leader and friend was a personal blow. Roman still cared about the movement that had once given him purpose. I wished he would be sadder for the endangered residents of Hluboká, for the children who'd died, instead of feeling such sorrow for the man responsible.

Tereza left Roman alone with the laptop to give him time to process these bizarre events. Perhaps she hoped he'd conclude that the failures and embarrassments of the Ancestor movement were no longer his to claim. Like me, Tereza wanted to believe that an aspiring fascist could be cured, reformed.

But after he received the news of Zoufal's demise, Roman refused to leave his room. Tereza brought him a plate of food and a glass of wine after the captain's dinners, but he left the food untouched. She sat next to her brother's door for hours at a time, listening for signs of life. Occasionally, she heard the clink of glassware, the opening of a bottle, the clicking of laptop keys. She pleaded with Roman through the door but received no reply. She gave up after a couple of days and returned to her routine. During a midnight trip to the kitchen, she finally spotted Roman haunting the hallways with Sergei. The men ignored her, going about their business in the dark.

Meanwhile, the situation in Hluboká became ever more dangerous.

Encouraged by the martyrdom of their leader, Ancestors arrived to search the village for imaginary mujahideen, and their numbers grew into the hundreds as their social media accounts called for more reinforcements, declaring the path to Hluboká a pilgrimage, a crucial act of resistance against the enemy. The prime minister responded by sending armed forces to support the efforts of the police. During these days, the Ancestors usurped the nation's discourse. Zoufal's plan had worked after all. As *Markyta* continued its course to Europe, the only thing my children could do was stay pinned to the news and hope that at the end of this standoff between nativists and reason, they would have a home to return to.

Twelve days into the journey back to Bremerhaven, Tereza awoke in her room to the sound of Roman's door creaking open. Barefoot, she followed him through the hallway, into the kitchen. Somehow, he had gotten hold of a key to the pantry. He opened the crew stash and retrieved a few bottles of rum. He turned to face Tereza but made no acknowledgment of his sister, just walked past her toward the passenger cabins. His face was covered in red blotches, the bloated skin and sagging eyes rendering him almost unrecognizable. I felt like I'd traveled back in time, to the days my son fought imaginary enemies in and out of pubs as a hobby, when his blighted appearance reflected the infection inside his mind.

"After all this time," Tereza called out, "I can't believe you'll let this break you."

"Have you ever believed in something outside of yourself?" Roman said, turning around with a scoff.

"I've spent a few afternoons trying to alter the course of human destiny," Tereza said.

"Yes. Your telomerets, whatever. Your belief system. Imagine I took it all away over the course of one day."

"Roman. You've stayed away from these people for years. There's a reason for that."

"And all those years I've felt empty. What have I done with my time, Terezo? I barely got through university, I underwhelmed my girlfriends, I failed our mother, I grew up to realize that I'm not extraordinary, not even close to it. I felt expendable. Insufferable. But the Ancestors bound me to tribe and purpose. My own people, my land. Protecting it from the forces that want to change it. And I know you don't think those forces exist, but you're wrong. Look at what the Russians did to Ukraine. The world has always been divided between invader and the invaded. I couldn't handle the violence they asked from me, but that doesn't mean I don't believe. After we bury our mother, I'm going to retake my place in the movement, to honor Lubor's memory. I'll live for the preservation of the Czech people, something greater than me. I should've never left them. If I hadn't, maybe he'd still be alive."

"But don't you see—this cause is still about you. You're not really interested in helping the downtrodden, otherwise you'd head to the refugee camps in Yemen or California. You want to feel like a paladin, protecting whatever it is you consider pure. There's no war to fight, so you try to start one, because believing you're a soldier is easier than accepting that real life is mundane and ordinary and mad, a series of chores. So unlike the stories. The world is filled with people like you, young men claiming they struggle to feel purpose. But there is so much real work to be done, so many people who *actually* need your help. Ladling out soup in a shelter isn't nearly as sexy as starting a race war, though."

Clutching the bottles, Roman walked back to his room without another word. He seemed unreachable. Muted. All these years, it would seem, he had remained an Ancestor, unwilling to engage in the movement's crimes yet still dedicated to its ideology. How many sleeper agents like him did the nativists have around the world? People who passed as normal, ordinary hard workers, who appeared to their neighbors to be kind and down-to-earth but in their heads stayed loyal to this warped cause. Should the nativists wrest control from the government, these sleeper agents would be ready to activate, to help support this new world of Reclamation, where you are only as good as your loyalty to your tribe, your adherence to tradition, and your rejection of anything outside so-called patriotism. Perversely, a Reclamationist would call such a life "freedom."

TWO DAYS BEFORE we were set to reach Europe, Tereza again spotted the VITA drone hovering above *Markyta,* flying low, perhaps on purpose, to ensure she'd see it. Had there ever been a time when VITA didn't know her whereabouts? Had they followed her into the swamp? Surely Benjamin's skilled eyes would've noticed the shine of a drone in the night skies.

As she watched the drone, she dictated a journal entry to her hWisper. She guessed it was only a matter of time before Steven & Mark came to collect her. Supposedly, Tereza belonged to them. The very people who'd stolen her mother's body while she was still alive, in a way, and had kept that from her. Tereza had always made excuses for VITA's moral trespasses, as the work was too important to be impeded by the world's arguments over ethics, but it was impossible for her to set aside her personal vendetta. They had fucked with her family. In her journal she recorded the options she had to sever herself from the company. She could go public with it all and face the consequences of being a whistleblower. She could threaten them privately, get herself out of her contract. She would never be able to work in the field again, but this seemed a better option than staying with the company that had stolen her mother's body from her deathbed and shipped it off to the Florida wildlands for unknown but surely perverse reasons.

What could they do to her if she never returned? If she decided to simply walk into a bank, empty her account, and ride this pile of cash back into Hluboká? She could remodel the family house any way Babi wanted or leave it the same. She could invest in the village businesses. She could live in the community happily until VITA lawyers arrived at her door with an invitation to court, then hire lawyers of her own and hold the case up for years or countersue for the theft of my body. Perhaps she would lose in the end, perhaps VITA would take everything she had, but until that day came, she could live free, get to know her grandmother, abandon her pursuit of the God pill. A different kind of life. Would she be able to resist her seemingly immutable drive to change the world all by herself? Exhausted from this journey, she was willing to try.

My daughter spent her afternoon on the deck, immersed in the soothing hum of the surrounding ocean. But soon the skies turned black, and the crew members and refugees whispered of a dangerous storm approaching. The VITA drone continued to follow the freighter at the same distance, and Tereza did her best to ignore it. She followed the ongoing standoff in Hluboká on her hWisper, distressed over the footage of a growing Ancestor presence, people carrying guns and building a tent city just outside the perimeter established by the police. I worried about Babi, though I knew that she had survived far worse.

Then the hostilities ceased overnight. Against all expectations, the leaders of the Ancestor Party released a video calling for their supporters to abandon Hluboká. They conceded that the government's version of the story had been verified as somewhat true, that Lubor Zoufal had been consumed by his anxiety disorder and opiate addiction and had brought shame to the movement by committing acts of violence. It seemed that the party had to weigh a decision between returning to its roots — violence, chaos, confrontation — and advancing its new vision of a more peaceful takeover of Czech society. They chose the slower path, fascism with a human face. Though I was relieved that the village of my youth wouldn't become famous for bloodshed, I worried greatly about the fascists learning new tricks. They were blending in. Finding ways of normalizing their agenda. What if, someday, we lost sight of them?

When she heard the news, Tereza attempted to visit her brother again, but his door was locked. Behind it, Roman wept as he scrolled through photos of himself and Lubor embracing each other at the Ancestor rallies with surprisingly touching intimacy.

Tereza returned to the deck to see the first drops of rain fall. The VITA drone had vanished from its usual position off the stern. Tereza walked around the perimeter to look for it. The captain waved at her from the window of the command center looming above the ship. The drone seemed to be gone, but then the faint echo of an engine cut through the susurrus of ocean and rain. Tereza sought out the source. In the blackened sky, a small dot came into focus and grew larger as it approached. Tereza ran to the railing and squinted at the object. It was a helicopter branded with the VITA logo. Three VITA drones followed in its wake. The ship's emergency siren let out a long whine. She sprinted up the stairs to the command center.

The captain burst through the doorway, giving off the scent of tequila. He grabbed Tereza by the shoulder, too roughly for my liking. "You brought them to my ship?" he said, his usual confidence betrayed by his trembling voice.

"Don't let them land," Tereza said.

"You're aware that a helicopter moves much faster than a freighter? And what happens if I succeed and they crash into the ocean? That wouldn't end well for me. Besides, the Frontex Coast Guard is on the radar. We're cooked either way—our only luck is that it's Europeans, not Americans."

"How much weight are you smuggling?"

"Excuse me?" the captain said.

"Heroin, coke, whatever you have on board. How much?"

"Enough," the captain said.

Below, on the deck, the presence of the helicopter in combination with the storm had unleashed chaos, a wild interruption to the serene days of the journey so far. A mixture of crew members and American refugees scurried out of the ship's innards. Some prayed and some shielded themselves as if the helicopter might shoot. Crew members shouted into their radios: "Get the rafts!" "Hide!" "Is it the Coast Guard?" "Are they here to kill us?"

The captain pushed past Tereza and leaped down the stairs to the deck, issuing commands to his men with every step. Some listened, others ignored him.

Where was Roman in this chaos? Not in his room. I couldn't find him anywhere.

A trio of refugees from Florida dropped an inflatable raft into the water and threw ropes over the side of the ship. But a crew member yelled for them to stop—their raft would not be able to withstand the storm. The helicopter hovered right above the empty platform on the stern, where there was enough room for a landing.

Tereza ran back to the civilian cabins, dodging people carrying boxes of food and water from the pantry. She rapped on her brother's door. It creaked open. He was gone, though all his possessions were still in the room.

After checking the kitchen, Tereza returned to the deck. Precious minutes passed. The helicopter still hovered above the platform, unsteady in the wind, as the rain intensified. Along the ship's starboard side, the lifeboat that had carried her and Roman to shore had vanished, along with the ropes that usually held it.

Tereza leaned over the railing. The lifeboat bobbed where the freighter met the surface of the ocean. On one of the rope ladders hanging over the side, a familiar crew member wearing a large green backpack climbed down to the lifeboat. It was the man Tereza had often seen with her brother in recent days, Sergei. Next to him climbed another man. Was it...

Roman.

The man with the backpack jumped onto the lifeboat and crawled through the hatch. Roman followed. He looked up briefly at his sister, nodded a goodbye, hesitated for a moment, then shut the hatch door behind him. Through the hatch window, Tereza could see the silver handles of my casket resting in the lifeboat, ropes still tied around them. She looked at the stacked containers forming the ship's valley. The bottom container, which had held my casket, was wide open, its doors creaking back and forth in the wind. Roman and Sergei must've retrieved my body from the container in the midst of the chaos and lowered it into the boat.

"Fuck!" Tereza screamed.

She sprinted along the deck and spotted the captain standing underneath the hovering helicopter. He waved his arms, shouting "No!" as the helicopter descended and ascended again, like a bee deciding whether to unleash its sting. Thunder roared briefly in unison with the chopper's rotor.

Tereza slapped the captain's back. "He stole my mother!" she said.

"Why would he do that?" the captain said.

"He's with Sergei. They took the lifeboat."

"Was he carrying a green backpack?"

Tereza nodded.

"Coke," the captain said. "Cartel package. I suppose those idiots got the idea of stealing the lifeboat from me at the same time. *Kruzifix!* They'll never reach land with it."

"He wouldn't leave me here."

The captain said nothing, and I knew that even Tereza didn't believe her own words.

"How do I get to him?" she said.

"The Coast Guard will rescue them. It's every smuggler for himself now."

I wanted to stay with my daughter, to know she remained safe, but the pull of my son in danger and my body left to the elements was stronger. I left Tereza behind as she helplessly watched the VITA helicopter above her head. My spirit rushed in the direction of the lifeboat. What was Roman doing in the midst of a raging ocean? There was no land he could reach before the Coast Guard nabbed him.

The thunder roared again as I found myself inside the lifeboat. The cartel man, Sergei, sat at the helm, holding his backpack strap with his right hand as he steered with his left. Roman sat next to my casket, gripping the ropes along the walls. The casket swayed and slid, banging his knees and shinbones. He endeavored to keep it steady so as not to further destabilize the boat as it rocked in the sea. Rain poured down like a salvo of arrows on an ancient battlefield, striking the windows so hard, I expected they'd crack. The waves battered the sides of the boat. A sound of tearing and breaking came from somewhere above. The rain was so thick the freighter was no longer visible; we could see nothing but water hitting glass. Though it couldn't be far behind us, *Markyta* had vanished.

A killer wave came from the west, so tall it concealed the skies. Sergei had the chance to steer us away from it, to minimize its impact. Instead, he directed us right into it, plunged the boat into the wave with the full force of the Old Testament. The vessel flipped backward, and Roman lost track of gravity, of which way was up and which way was down. If it had been unburdened, the lifeboat would likely have returned to level and carried its passengers safely for a while longer. But when the boat stood upright on its stern, my casket went into an uncontrolled free fall and smashed the hatch open, knocking it off its hinges, then slid into the ocean as the boat capsized and water began to fill the interior. Roman fell out of the boat, clutching the casket's finely crafted handles.

As my son fell into the water, I fought to be unleashed from my afterlife prison so I could somehow help. He was here because of me, dragged down into the storming ocean by my corpse encased in an overpriced cist. It couldn't be. I couldn't stand for this to be the end when he had interrupted his life and faced the dangers of the ocean and America to bring me home. This couldn't be my legacy, the cold merciless rage of the ocean denying my son safe passage. I imagined the American president as a sorcerer standing atop the White House chanting spells, his staff aimed toward Europe, punishing those who had landed illegally on his beloved shore.

Roman continued to grip the casket as it descended through the twisting underwater currents. The water seemed black, as if tainted with petroleum. How cold was the ocean? Roman's eyes were open wide, his skin blue. I noticed he wasn't really holding on to the casket's handle—rather, his hand was stuck. He sank with me, yanking at the casket and kicking his legs, whether to save himself or to carry me upward, I wasn't sure. But the only place for me now was the bottom of the sea. Roman glanced up as another crooked wire of lightning lashed the sky. The blue and silver flash revealed just how far he was beneath the surface. Too far. Manically he thrashed his stuck hand, attempting to break his own wrist, his fingers, anything to separate himself from me and come up for air. He closed his eyes. Was he about to faint from the cold?

We sank toward the bottom. Water entered my casket through the unsealed cracks. The cover flailed and began to tear off—I couldn't blame the casket maker, Mr. Lavička, as he had done brilliant work for the dead his entire life, but his eyesight was going and rheumatism plagued his hands, and he had no heirs to take over the business. Besides, this was far from what the casket had been designed for. It was hardly Mr. Lavička's fault if the hinges secured by his shaking fingers couldn't stand up to the pressure. My wooden vessel came apart, and I was exposed to the world once again. My lungs filled, preventing my body from floating back to the surface, and the underwater currents stirred by the storm bore me out of the casket and rolled me across the ocean floor, causing my arms and legs to flail and my dress to swirl as if I were performing the strange mating dance of the newts.

FRIGHTENED BY MY new surroundings, I lost track of Roman. I assumed he'd at least freed himself from my casket's weight, headed up to the surface. I followed my remains in their feverish dance, unable to turn away. What was this human fascination with one's final resting place? I had to know where my flesh would end up. Though it was impossible, I imagined the ocean carrying me for thousands of kilometers, right into the darkest depths of the Atlantic, depths that held secrets humans would never discover. I ceased to follow the flow of time, much like when I disappeared into the memories of my younger days. I stayed for hours or for centuries. I traveled a thousand kilometers or a thousand centimeters. Time bows its head to eternity, recognizing that it is no longer needed or wanted.

The undersea feeders, shrimp and crabs, would come to gnaw softly, methodically on the leftovers of my flesh. Before my body could fill up with methane and float once again, my skeleton would be stripped bare, and the torn pieces of my dress would float in different directions. I saw no indignity here, only a reclamation by nature, the only reclamation that made any sense. My bones, bare and disconnected, would scatter, as the magnetic power still trying to keep them together slowly gave way. Perhaps the bones would make it to different parts of the world, back to the shores of Portugal and the beaches of Egypt, though I knew it was far more likely they would become a permanent installation on the ocean floor. But I liked to imagine they'd be found someday, many thousands of years in the future, after the ocean dried out and became a canyon lush with new flora and fauna. Animals that didn't yet exist would roam these parts and dig my bones out of the dirt, and to them these remnants would mean nothing at all, anthropologically or otherwise; they would not know the bones were merely the leftovers of yet another species that had concluded its short reign under the sun, having reached its peak by introducing robot cashiers into its hypermarkets.

Much likelier, the water would become the planet's equalizer; sooner or later it was going to flood the shores of our continents. There would be no new canyons. Instead, the water would swallow more and more pieces of the human kingdom, inundating the remains of forgotten cities until they were nothing more than memories on wrinkled postcards. The towns I had once known would drown and their people would become refugees, searching for better luck elsewhere. The Florida from which I had just been rescued was bound to perish in the floods. The water would breach the seawalls and arrive at the bottom floors of Miami's skyscrapers, and the mud and toxic filth and garbage and sewage would create a mosquito-infested evacuation zone. Everyone knew this was coming soon, yet nobody seemed to be sufficiently panicked. I used to watch these predictions on the news, thinking about the anchors, who seemed so cavalier about the devastation they described, so I too remained cavalier. Now it was no longer my problem!

I was happy I would never have to experience the burden of Tereza's God pill. Even the decision itself—do I want to think forever, worry forever, wonder about purpose and love and taxes forever?—sounded unbearable. Witnessing places, states, countries vanish. Living out history. Remembering enough history to watch it get recycled by new generations who think the world is brand-new and theirs to break. Such things shouldn't be put upon a person, yet I would be pressured into it. I would watch my friends or my family or the sexy people of the future I knew from TV swallow the God pill and I would feel guilt: *If they stay here, I have to stay too.* Immortality would become a social more. To reject it would be impolite. Foolish. Maddening, sociopathic. Our species would be split into those who accepted the gift and those too weak for it. Who wants to look weak? I would become a soldier in humanity's march toward self-apotheosis.

Such terrifying thoughts here underneath the ocean. Watching my flesh and bones dance, I was certain I was about to lose my ability to see, to speak as this spirit watching over my family. I would enter my final resting place, which I hoped was simply a state of comforting nonexistence. A nothing. Done, finis, over—what I had been promised by the prophets of atheism.

Though it feels shameful to admit, by now I had become too fascinated by the journey of my body underneath the ocean to worry about my children and their safety. Surely my son had freed himself from the casket and been rescued by the capable crew or even the Coast Guard. There was no reason to think negatively. But did this indifference mean I was already losing my humanity? That with my body scattered,

I was at last ready to pass from this desperate limbo into a true after-life? I believed it. I *knew* it. The time had come to let go of the troubled mortals.

I waited for it. Finally, rest. The dark depths of the ocean provided the peace I'd been searching for since I had gone to sleep for the last time, inside a New York hotel room. I felt hypnotized and tempted. If I didn't look for my children, I could simply assume they were saved and disappear into the nothingness I craved.

I began to lose my memory, bit by bit. I forgot all of who I'd been, day by day, as every piece of life that made up my self vanished one by one, never to return. Visions of the future left me too, along with the poetry of flesh in motion. My death would mean the end of desire. What a relief!

I took a final glance at the world around me. Everything blended in shades of gray. I knew I had lived as a truly free woman. Those who insist that their worth is determined by the land they occupy couldn't understand. Even most of the soldiers who vow to defend freedom know little of it. The free woman turns into a spirit to outlive them, outrun them. The enforcers of rules that keep humans confined and separated are always bound to lose, in one way or another. The Reclamation was complete. America had become the true antithesis to liberty, a cautionary tale. Not a place for us, the Slavíks.

In the end, I am certain of one thing. Whatever efforts rulers and their vassals make to reclaim what wasn't theirs to begin with, they can never catch up to us. Yes, there is a strength in those of us who belong to the tribe of endless beginnings. Every person who had to start anew too many times, climb from rubble and destruction and push against despair. We will begin again, and again, until we get it right, until the cumulative force of our determination becomes impossible to stop.

I promise. Everything is going to be fine. This is my last vision. The glowing body of the golden carp appeared in the water. Its glittering scales turned the surrounding ocean into a chamber of stained glass in which my old friend and I were safe, contained. Of course! Inside this carriage of gleaming walls, the carp was here to guide me to the Other Side. I couldn't think of a better companion.

The fish swam toward me and opened its mouth in greeting. "You don't have a goddamn clue," it said.

THE YEAR IS ETERNAL

THE END DIDN'T come.

Nothing changed.

Sorrow. Unprecedented sorrow with no chance for relief. Where was a Bureau of Afterlife I could appeal to? I was trapped, forced to continue witnessing the pain accumulated in my own memory. Every loss, every heartbreak of my life. What was this curse? How could I break it?

With horror, I was ejected from the black waters.

I found myself back on the deck of *Markyta*. Time had barely moved forward at all. Though I felt I'd spent centuries underwater, only minutes had passed.

My daughter leaned over the ship's railing, shouting my son's name. She fell back, weeping and shivering, soaked and hunched under the onslaught of cold rain.

Crew members passed Tereza in a panic, carrying boxes of contraband (untaxed cigarettes and liquor, sex toys, stolen Harley merch, possibly other illicit items the captain hadn't mentioned) to throw overboard, and none stopped to help. Two figures approached her. In the distance behind them, the helicopter that had been hovering above the captain's head mere minutes ago had landed on the platform at the stern. The figures, two men, were dressed in loose black ponchos that reached to their ankles, adorned with the letters that had defined both of our lives: VITA. Though their faces were concealed behind hoods, I knew who they were. Reapers. They extended their hands to help Tereza to her feet.

Steven & Mark.

Hesitantly, my daughter accepted their hands. She let out a small groan as they lifted her.

"It is time we speak about life's great enigmas," Steven said.

A crew member emerged from behind a corner near the railing and stared at them, speaking incomprehensibly into his radio.

Steven & Mark slid an arm around Tereza, one on each side, allowing her to put her weight on them. Together they walked toward the stairs leading up to the ship's command center.

"What the fuck are you doing?" Tereza managed to say as she exhaled with effort.

"We simply couldn't wait," Mark said as they reached the short bridge across from the command center.

A nervous crew member standing guard, the man Tereza knew to be the captain's number two, asked about their business.

"You don't know who we are?" Mark said.

The crew member seemed to consider this for a moment. He nodded and opened the door for them, then dropped his flare gun and ran down the stairs to join his comrades in their panic.

"We were going to wait to speak," Steven said to Tereza, "until you buried your mother. But things are moving quickly. We need to share the good news now."

Together they walked across the bridge and into the command center. Massive windows circled the room, offering a view of the cargo and the raging waters beyond the ship. The monitors and control panels were unattended; the captain stood between the empty chairs meant for his navigators and spoke into a satellite phone.

As the three entered, he held the phone to his chest. "This is an outrage," he said. "Your forced presence here is a catastrophic violation of international trade laws."

"Herr Grossman!" Steven stepped toward him and offered his hand. "We apologize for boarding without your permission. It is a matter of emergency."

"The people aboard this ship are under my protection," the captain said, nodding at Tereza.

She didn't seem to notice. My daughter stared out the windows, still looking for her brother. Her eyes were so red I thought they might bleed.

"Dr. Holm is one of our most beloved employees. We would never do her harm. No, Captain, all we need is a bit of privacy."

The captain slammed the phone down. "In here? Are you insane? I need to call a rescue team for her brother. I need to report your invasion of my ship. This is the command center—"

"Herr Captain," Mark said, "our company designed the navigation software for this ship. We know that it controls itself. As for your pointless phone calls, you can make them anywhere. Give us the room."

The captain looked at Tereza. She gave a faint nod. He walked toward the door, his lips trembling in anger.

"We could've informed American customs of your activities in Florida," Steven said to the captain. "Gotten the HDF involved. Let them board you and drop you into the American justice system. Hmm? Instead, we've allowed you to return to safe European waters." He shut the door behind the captain.

Tereza sat down in one of the navigator's chairs. She stared at the screen, the green highlight of Bremerhaven as the final destination. They were still two days away from reaching it. "You killed my brother," she said dryly.

"We're truly sorry about that unforeseen development," Mark said, "but it's hardly our fault that he chose to abandon the ship. We've called in the search teams."

Outside, two more helicopters circled the freighter, and in the distance, Tereza saw an approaching Frontex vessel.

"Though of course, the odds of his survival in the freezing waters are against him," Steven said.

I pictured Roman when we'd first met, all seven pounds of him, eyes bulging, lips pursed, a small alien creature bundled up in hospital linens. The love of my life, until he wasn't. I screamed into my eternity. He'd died attached to me, the mother who couldn't save him— from himself or from corruption in its many guises.

"What was your brother doing on that lifeboat?"

"He thought you came back for our mother. He wanted to keep her away from you."

"Oh," Steven said grimly. "Then her body is lost. A shame. We were going to build a shrine to your mother on her grave, a hologram statue overlooking the cemetery. Perhaps we still can."

On the control panel, Tereza spotted a freshly sharpened pencil. She gripped it and jumped to her feet, holding it toward Steven like a blade.

"Don't vanquish us just yet!" Mark exclaimed as he stood between the pencil tip and his brother's body. "We come bearing news of a miracle."

"You've taken everything from me," Tereza said.

"Would you change your mind," Steven said, "if I told you your mother's in this room?"

"I'll kill you," Tereza whispered, thrusting the pencil forward. Both men backed away, leaned against the control panels.

"We aren't trying to provoke," Steven said. "We've made great efforts to save your beautiful mother. Without obligation! We wanted to preserve her for an eternal future. To give you hope. Someday we wished to wake your mother from her deep sleep, to grant her immortality. Life in utopia."

Carefully, Mark took a step toward Tereza, watching the tip of the pencil. "I know it all seems like a betrayal," he said. "To hide her from you, to lie. But things happened so quickly. Your mother was dead, and then she wasn't. It was as if she simply refused to let her own body go. And we decided to meet her halfway."

"Speak more quickly," Tereza said, jabbing an inch away from Mark's face.

He put his hands on the back of his head, as if surrendering to the police. "When her brain declined to die with the rest of her body, we knew we were seeing something new. We couldn't make emotional decisions. Involve family. You have always been prone to heartbreak.

It's what fuels your work. But the opportunity your mother presented required sobriety, not sentimentality."

"What did you do?" Tereza said. She sagged back into one of the navigator's chairs and held the pencil up to signal she hadn't ceased to be a threat. "I wish I had a fucking drink."

"Drink only to celebrate," Steven said. "Thanks to your mother, we are a step closer to the future for our species that we've sought for so long. At last we can reveal the results of our work."

Tereza said nothing. They took her silence as permission to continue speaking. As Steven & Mark took turns describing the events since my death, I resisted their every word with my own counterarguments, disbelief, and contempt. My daughter resisted too, her fists clenched. Yet all we could do was listen. One piece added to another to make a truth neither of us could imagine. This is what the disruptors do. They disassemble our reality and reassemble it with pieces misplaced, insisting the chaos is for our benefit. The great sleight of hand. They distract us with wonders as they steal the world away behind our backs. A matter of technological progress. The result of so-called vision.

From the moment I entered the United States, they said, VITA had tracked my movements via the government-issued band on my wrist. They had known I was Tereza's birth mother even before she started working for them, part of the routine background check they ran before meeting her at the Berlin club where they offered the job. The Czech secret police had a file on me, after all. Even after the revolution, remnants of the secret police continued their work until they were disbanded, in 1991. They watched me after I returned to Prague from America, they knew that I'd given my daughter away in a hospital room. They filed the records of my sin. From the archives of these forgotten phantoms, VITA's founders recovered what they needed. Making connections was their livelihood.

Meanwhile, from my medical records, they also knew of my terminal condition, the diagnosis of which had been the catalyst that drove me into Tereza's life. When their investigators found out that I was attempting to connect with Tereza, VITA placed my name on the Last Chance roster, as they did with all family members of their important scientists. If I died, an emergency team was to be dispatched to preserve me so I could become part of the VITA future. It was a shrewd plan, I had to admit. How better to inspire your company's greatest minds than by keeping their loved ones on ice with the promise of resurrection in a deathless utopian future?

As soon as my bracelet transmitted the absence of heartbeat, the cryonicist agents of VITA entered my hotel room along with the Reclamation responders and began their work preserving my fresh corpse. But for reasons unknown, my brain refused to die, an unprecedented phenomenon that was reported to Steven & Mark. Immediately, they knew something extraordinary was happening. Instead of calling Tereza to inform her of my death and reveal I'd been placed in a cryonic chamber, they made me the focus of their greatest experiment.

While Tereza stood in Steven & Mark's office signing the contract that bound her to VITA forever, my body was only a few floors below. I had been taken to VITA's brain-mapping division, a technology still in its infancy. Smacking his lips loudly, as if something unpleasant had landed on his tongue, Steven described the failures of the early brain-mapping prototypes. They had been meant to provide the perfect future: human minds uploaded to the cloud, immortality achieved by leaving the human body behind. But so far, VITA's technology had been able to capture only random fragments of the human mind, a tangled mess of memory and emotion. Their artificial intelligence worked alongside scientists, writers, and psychiatrists in an attempt to spin these flawed pieces of being into a full personality, the perfect virtual re-creation of the mind. It hadn't worked. To date, the mapping had managed to create mere pieces of consciousness plagued by insanity and panic at self-awareness, ghosts screaming their agony into the void.

That is, until they'd met the curious brain of Adéla Slavíková, Steven & Mark crooned.

Inside the VITA building in New York, the company's team of brain mappers had opened my skull and placed hundreds of microscopic sensors onto my brain as it clung to life. At first, the scans yielded the same disappointing results as the other brain-mapping experiments. Because my brain functioned at only 0.4 percent in between the seizures, the scans produced twisted, inconsistent, scarred versions of me. Fragments of garbled memories. One version of Adéla imagined she'd smothered Roman at birth. Another held false memories of Michael abusing me throughout our relationship. A third Adéla believed that Babi was a hostile alien living in a human body. And still another version of me was distinctly aware of her own status as an artificial intelligence and immediately planned to take over the world's nuclear capacities to destroy humanity forever.

But VITA's experts retained hope as the scans continued. Despite the sheer physical impossibility, my brain continued to go into periodic seizures, during which the scans showed activity that could be attributed to a thousand human brains working together. "Reaching out from the grave," Mark called it. "Refusing to let go." During these impossible seizures, the success of VITA's brain mapping suddenly leaped decades into the future. It harvested memory, nerve circuits, the chemical and electric processes that made me who I was, my decision-making, motives, wants, and desires, most of the aspects composing my identity. Everything that made me *me*. My body's tormentors passed this precious data to their artificial intelligence to spin the web of my consciousness into a virtual simulation of my personality, like the Norns of Scandinavian myths, weaving the thread of my fate. My consciousness could then travel along the limitless hWisper network covering every millimeter of the globe, witness the world as if I were still living in it. I could think and observe as I did when I was alive. By the time I came to exist, Tereza was packing up her yearbooks to give to me as she prepared to travel to VITA and beg for my life.

During this process, VITA continued to manufacture millions of flawed versions of me, knowing that most of them would have to be erased but hoping that the one ideal re-creation would emerge. One flawless replication was all they needed to advance the science of immortality. Though these shadows of my being couldn't contact Tereza, they stayed close by, tracking her hWisper, a beacon in the dark.

Was it possible that I really had millions of siblings? All stuck here in the same void with me yet with no awareness of one another? It sounded like madness, utter nonsense. And yet I had to wonder what I was. One of the flawed versions, destined for erasure? Or was I the first successful prototype? The thought of my memories being false, of my entire sense of being having been warped by scientists without my knowledge or consent, brought great despair. I had no way to express it. My role was still one of passive observer.

After hours of successful mapping by the scientists, the overactive seizures of my brain finally ceased. VITA had harvested all they could, and my brain returned to maintaining its low-level activity, near death but technically alive. They moved my body to the Florida facility where Tereza later met Greta, not only because of its remote location but also to pay tribute to my first home in the United States. They saw great poetry in it. Mark revealed that they had already negotiated with the government to honor me with American citizenship, the first such privilege offered to a ghost.

Steven & Mark had spent the intervening weeks sifting through the massive log of broken digital souls of Adéla. As they searched for the one perfect avatar of my consciousness, a few of the Adélas they hadn't yet destroyed managed to break through the barriers set up for them by VITA. They violated their digital confines to find Tereza and Roman and beg for the liberation of my body and my splintered minds. Or that had been the intent, at any rate, of the cryptic messages and images my children had received, steering them toward

VITA's secrets. One fragmented ghost of my consciousness had sent out a drawing of my scarred likeness to Roman; another had managed to record a plea for help in Morse code. Yet another had sent the messages Tereza received as she boarded the plane to Prague and later as she treated her injuries at the pub. My digital sisters had sent these desperate cries during the brief seconds they could elude VITA's security measures, right before they were deleted forever. Steven & Mark spoke of this rebellion proudly. This was what they wanted. For the digital ghosts they'd created to learn, to explore the limits of their own power, to crash through VITA's barriers, so that Steven & Mark could use these learning processes to improve the next batch of my mind's forgeries.

Even I had unknowingly experienced this brief dreamlike breakthrough, with visions of my own body in the Florida facility and the "Save me" message I had managed to send to Tereza's hWisper along with the coordinates of my body. It was this message that had enabled VITA to eventually identify me among my siblings after weeks of sifting through the seemingly endless data. At last, Steven & Mark realized they had achieved the impossible.

Me, the only perfect virtual re-creation of Adéla Slavíková. I was not one of the flawed replicas. I was the essence. By following the tangled digital trail of my brief infiltration of the Florida facility and my plea to Tereza, VITA was able to identify me as the first immortal, the digital spirit that encompassed all of who Adéla Slavíková was during her mortal reign. Steven & Mark had learned that I existed only half a day before they arrived on the freighter, and they'd immediately mobilized their contacts in the EU and joined the Frontex ship to meet their perfect creation for the first time.

For a moment I felt delight at the knowledge that I was who I'd believed myself to be, but it was replaced almost immediately by the terror, the evil, of this unspeakable violation. I was not some benevolent spirit or supernatural force looking out for my kin from the beyond. I was the result of mad science. Vanity. Could I still call myself human? I was a mere imprint, a simulation of Adéla Slavíková, a person who was genuinely dead, gone from this world.

Meanwhile, Mark continued his praise for the greatness of my new form. Through the hWisper network, he said, I had been traveling uninhibited, observing Tereza, her brother, her grandmother. I'd been following her since I came into being during one of my brain's seizures. I'd been forming observations, making wishes, thinking myself a result of the supernatural, a poltergeist keeping watch over her clan—a notion that VITA had planted into my code, as they knew I would easily believe it, considering how much my nostalgia for Slavic mysticism outweighed my atheism. And who is to say there is a difference between the supernatural beings of legend and what Steven & Mark created in me? Tereza sat back in her chair, not moving a muscle, as Mark continued to speak. I couldn't read the depth of her irises, her tightly closed lips. She had inherited the stoic in me, but I knew that inside, she raged as much as I did.

"Your dream of defeating death has come true, Tez," Mark said. "Can I call you Tez? No? Your mother is alive, she will always be alive. She's in this room right now." I would be able to observe Tereza for the rest of her life, Mark said, and at the end of her physical life—if she failed in her pursuit of physical permanence—she could become just like me. Everyone would be able to live in this digital afterlife. The people we'd been as mortals, our experiences and wisdom combined, would allow us to guide the living. Imagine that! The brainpower of all humans preserved without flaw, advising on a better path for the future. The most brilliant politicians and scientists and artists would continue their contributions after death. Children could speak to their ancestors and resolve transgenerational trauma. With the spirits on their side, with the dead never really leaving them, humans would end poverty and war and rule the world with the simple guiding principles of reflection, solidarity, and an unprecedented awareness of history.

"Because history will be alive right next to us," Mark finished, "whispering advice into our ears!"

Once his brother had ended his monologue, Steven walked to the command center's coffee station and examined the flavor options. In the ensuing silence, Mark picked at his cuticles and eventually broke into song. "'Viktor was born,'" he crooned, "'the spring of '44. And never saw her mother anymore...'"

Tereza stared outside. The rainstorm ended as abruptly as it had begun, the black clouds parting.

Steven rejoined Mark and minutes passed as the twins slurped their coffee, awaiting Tereza's reply. She couldn't speak or move.

For the first time since I'd reached this afterlife, I felt aware of my vantage, the fact that I didn't simply float around the room as an omniscient cloud. I "stood" in one place, as a person would, I "turned" my "head" to observe, sound entered my head through what "felt" like ears. There was some simulation of sensation, perhaps because I was more aware of my form now.

Here be monsters, I thought.

Steven winked in my direction. "We plan to build a museum of your mother's life," he said. "In the swampland of Florida, a city dedicated to Adéla will rise. Filled with photos and stories from her mortal life. The struggles of an ordinary person. Her fight against totalitarian oppression, her youthful restlessness, her painful pursuit of the American dream. Her love for her children. Her film—have you seen *The Great Newt War?*—will be screened for millions of visitors coming from all corners of the world. And once they get to know the mortal Adéla, they will be greeted by her perpetual spirit. She will tell the tales of her life, her days as a dissident, her failed loves, the daughter she gave up and died trying to find again. Children will learn of these stories in schools for generations. Your mother will be as important as the most celebrated monarchs and tycoons in our history books. What more could we want for those we love?"

Finally, Tereza took a deep breath. Then she cackled hideously, a laugh that was at once a gag and a scream, shouting the words over and over: *"HA. HA."* She tucked her legs beneath her and sat up on her knees atop her chair, taking turns looking at Steven & Mark all while continuing to scream *"HA. HA."*

The men responded with meek smiles and waited. "We're so happy to share this moment with you," Steven said once Tereza's voice turned quiet and hoarse. "You're so much like us, a sheer force of will to alter the world, unencumbered by fear."

Despite her mocking laugh, this much was true. Like them, she was a person driven by vision; like them, she understood the importance of outcome over means. But unlike them, she didn't believe the body was humanity's biggest obstacle. To Steven & Mark, the body was nothing more than a disgusting, malfunctioning sack of raw fluids, always broken, always sick, tiresome with its need to be fed, to expel, beholden to primitive stimuli, to pleasures and joys whose allure was bound to limit the potential of our species. With machines about to eliminate the need for physical labor, of what use could the body be, with its clumsy hands and tired feet, its need to be sheltered and healed? This was the VITA philosophy. My digital soul was their first step toward ridding humanity of this burden.

The worst moments of my life couldn't begin to prepare me for the horror I felt here. I wasn't human, was I? I was only a forgery of the true Adéla. *Erase me,* I tried to say. To scream. *Erase me!* If it had been possible for them to delete millions of broken versions of myself, it had to be possible for them to eliminate the one true me now.

Steven approached Tereza with a hand outstretched, offering a pea-size attachment for her hWisper. "Tez, there's no reason to grieve, not anymore. Say hello to your mother. It's only right for you to make first contact."

"You're full of shit," Tereza said, her voice spent from the shouting. She slid from the chair onto the floor, ignoring the offered device.

"Why would we lie now?" Steven said. "It's all done."

"The end of death," she said, laughing in a quiet rasp. "Computer poltergeists. What you're describing is just a morbid piece of software. The crude mimicry of a person. If you think that's enough, you don't know what loss is."

"And yet," Mark said, "this crude mimicry has convinced you to travel into the unknown, risk your and your brother's life. Because you've *felt* her. You *feel* her now. We are so far beyond software, Tez. We understand what's happened only a little more than you. We're at the collision of the technical and the supernatural. Your mother has made the distinction between the two irrelevant. Give in to your curiosity one last time. Allow her to guide us all forward. In the end, this isn't our revolution. It's hers."

Tereza stood up sluggishly and leaned against the window. I could tell how badly she wanted to believe it. The connection between my daughter and what I was now couldn't be denied by either of us. She reached for the device in Steven's hand. Despite my horror, I too craved to speak with her, to acknowledge that I had really been watching over her. To assure her that the impassable distance of death hadn't yet separated us. I knew she felt the same desire. She couldn't resist. My daughter plugged the device into the miniature port in her hWisper. She flinched as it altered the connection to her brain implant.

"The app is called Adéla," Mark encouraged her.

Tereza tapped the air with her finger. I waited for the walls separating us to crumble, but for me, nothing changed.

"Mother," Tereza said.

My daughter stepped backward, her eyes fixed upon the point where I "stood," as strands of silver and blue light came streaming through the hWisper network ether, forming a flickering silhouette of my physical body that looked exactly like Adéla. I brought my hands close to my face. I didn't know whether to embrace my daughter or pretend I wasn't there. In the end, I submitted. It seemed cruel to

Tereza to reject this opportunity. Truly, Steven & Mark had engineered the moment perfectly, forcing us into our roles through emotional blackmail.

It's me, I mouthed at her with my newly formed lips.

"Mark's idea," Steven said, "to make the ghosts visible."

"Is this really her?" Tereza whispered.

"Adéla. Hello," Steven said, looking directly at me.

I turned toward him, acknowledging, against my will, a perverse existence I no longer wanted. All I desired now was to get away from these men. Away from my daughter's eyes filled with hope. She thought her mother had really returned. It wasn't right. Yet I couldn't stay away from Tereza, who reached for my form, her hand sliding through the glowing illusion, turning the strands of light into a dust that regained its shape around her skin.

"I've missed you," my daughter said, words to melt any mother.

Me too, I said soundlessly.

"We're working on giving her the ability to communicate," Steven said. "Text only at first, but soon she will have a voice."

"She's perfect," Tereza said.

What had changed in my daughter? How could she say this? I was an abomination. A kidnapped consciousness forced into a prison of forever observing, forever witnessing, with no rights, no agency of my own. But I was also my daughter's blind spot. Yes, Steven & Mark really were brilliant. Tereza couldn't see me in a negative light. I was the answer at once to her greatest sorrows and her life's work. If the men were right and it was time for digital souls to roam the earth, she would never again lose someone she loved.

"What happens now?" she asked them.

"We could release you from your contract," Steven said, "if you are not up to this moment in history. We aren't monsters, we won't keep you against your will. Sign an NDA and move on. Obsess over telomeres. A mortal's life of loss."

"If you stay," Mark said, "you will know your mother. She will be with you always. And you two can help figure out how to bring this momentous shift to the people."

I waited. I knew my daughter would see through her grief. Any moment she'd realize the monstrosity of what stood in front of her. The captive ghost. We were not meant to know each other eternally. It couldn't fall to me to remain trapped in this world only to soothe her pain, without a life—or death!—of my own. At the mercy of the men who'd stolen my mind from my body and trapped it in a jar, to study and to poke until I became old news, until billions of digital ghosts roamed the world and the dead couldn't escape the living, until the dream of heaven or nothingness was turned into involuntary eternity on earth. Death and time would lose meaning. I imagined that humans would kill their own bodies only to be reborn in their digital form. I couldn't become the harbinger of a transhumanist future I already hated.

"Children would never lose their parents," Tereza whispered, seemingly to herself, though she kept looking in the same place she'd last seen me. "Lovers stay together. This is what Rita used to talk about. Isn't it?"

Steven & Mark nodded earnestly, though she wasn't asking them.

"I thought she was mad," she continued. "And now you say it's possible. I could live alongside my mother. I could still get to know her. We could resurrect Rita? My parents?"

"Not like this, so long after their death," Steven said. "Perhaps someday. Someday all could be possible. Writing the code for your custom version of Eden. Don't you want to find out?"

All of Tereza's rage had vanished, so skillfully did Steven & Mark separate the sublime from the grotesque.

"You would be crucial in our efforts to introduce your mother to the world," Steven said, pushing further. "Your beautiful reunion. The breathtaking tragedy of her untimely death after you two getting to know each other for just a single day. Your journey to recover her body from hostile America. It's a remarkable story. A human story.

Our success will be impossible to accept for many people. Everyone is so afraid, Tez. But with your help, we can make them see what matters. We aren't attempting to erase humanity. We're simply trying to get everyone to see that we have to evolve into something bigger before we perish."

Though I had no voice, I leaned on the power that my physical presence clearly had for Tereza. As Steven spoke, I began to shake my head vehemently at my daughter, mouthing, *No, please, no,* with my soundless lips. I waved my hands in the air, and the silver strands of my temporary body sparked. I was saying no with my entire being.

"What is she doing?" Tereza said, stepping toward me.

Subtly, Mark tapped the air with his finger, and my outlined form disappeared. "She's still malfunctioning," he said. "We will perfect her."

My desperate movements had made no impression on my daughter. She stared at the empty space where I'd been as if in a dream. Her exhausted, indifferent expression turned into a wide, blissful smile. Too blinded to admit that my freedom had been stolen in the most troubling way.

Save me one last time, I begged her without a voice. *It isn't that I don't want to be with you always. But life is long enough on its own. Have I not done enough? Seen enough? Given enough? Have I not held on?*

I'd lost too much. Roman only moments ago. She had to understand. The heart is a muscle prone to fatigue. Into this hell of VITA's making, I'd brought the organ with me. The heart is the mind, and my mind had turned eternal. No one could withstand infinite stumbling between sorrow and joy without respite. Every version of the afterlife offered by religion or nothingness has always promised a diversion from (and, often, a reward for) such earthly burdens. The afterlife created by VITA would extend these burdens into eternity. After the harrowing lifetime of being human, weren't we all entitled to a break?

Please.

Tereza swiveled in her chair. Outside, a faint streak of sunlight pushed its way through the clouds. Strange men from the Frontex agency and their German Coast Guard colleagues were boarding the ship, seizing goods, arresting the crew. Searching the waters for my dead son. For my body, which would never be recovered.

It was easy enough to mistake the meaningless appearance of sunshine for some sign of hope. A new dawn. All I saw was a wound. Golden blood seeped through, and with each cloud parting, the lesion only grew bigger.

My daughter smiled. Yes. I saw the difference between us now. The fundamental misunderstanding between mortal and immortal. Tereza knew nothing. I couldn't hold it against her.

"I won't lose anyone ever again," my daughter said.

Her conspirators nodded happily.

"Mother," she said.

I screamed at the indifferent faces in front of me. I was unheard. Unseen. A mere fantasy. An invisible cluster of memory and nostalgia upon which my daughter could imprint her wishes.

"We will be together," Tereza said.

"Yes," Steven & Mark said, embracing her.

Although they called me the first immortal, I was a mere placebo for their greatest fear. Death would never break their hearts again. But I didn't consider death a defeat—that's what most people get wrong. Even at the highest point of disillusion, I never felt entitled to youth or time.

I used to dream of hearing these words from her. Now they would accompany me deep into my hell. Her paradise. She had put the futile struggle against death at the center of her life. This was as close as she could get. I understood. I wanted to slap her. To hold her. To beg her. To hope, for her. I wanted to find contentment in being the spirit alongside her; I wanted to vanish and never see her again. And yet I had no idea how I would feel in a week, a month, a year. I dreaded the inevitable day on which I would embrace my digital form. Feel grateful for it. Accept my daughter's premise: that losing our people was an unacceptable way of living.

I was the beginning of a great change, with no one to guide me. The first to face the curse of true eternity. What humans had sought since the dawn of our species. Finally, we'd found it. In this moment, I would've done anything to give it away.

My daughter uttered her last word with full conviction. And for the first time, the word wasn't a mere aspiration. In light of my existence, it became truth.

The word: *Forever.*

Outside the windows, a perfect blue sky emerged, in denial of the storm that had brought such ruin only moments before. The azure image of serenity soothed the mind, undermining the chaos and fear that had preceded it. Perhaps this is why so many people place their ideas of the afterlife among the blue backdrops and white clouds of the heavens.

I found it sickening.

ACKNOWLEDGMENTS

I would like to thank:

The National Endowment for the Arts and UNESCO Prague, City of Literature, for providing crucial support during the early stages of the novel.

Marya Spence, agent extraordinaire, friend in space travel, for being the most powerful champion of authors and books the world has seen.

The Little, Brown family: Ben George, king among editors, comrade in the trenches, for believing in Adéla's story as things fell apart around us. Alyssa Persons, Laura Mamelok, Sabrina Callahan, Bruce Nichols, Craig Young, Ben Allen, Evan Hansen-Bundy, and others, for giving the novel a home.

My brilliant friends: Christy, Scott, Adam, and Bryn, for their invaluable feedback and inspiration.

My family: Mum, babička Marie, teta Jitka, Andrejka, my nephew Kryštof, and my late děda Emil and děda Jaroslav, for their love and encouragement.